CLODAGH MURPHY

GIRL IN A SPIN

HACHETTE
BOOKS
IRELAND

A CIP catalogue record for this title is available from the British Library.

ISBN 978 0 340 97735 4

Typeset in Sabon and Garamond by Hachette Books Ireland
Printed and bound in Great Britain by Mackays, Chatham ME5 8TD

Hachette Books Ireland policy is to use papers that are natural, renewable and
recyclable products and made from wood grown in sustainable forests. The
logging and manufacturing processes are expected to conform to the
environmental regulations of the country of origin.

Hachette Books Ireland
8 Castlecourt Centre
Castleknock
Dublin 15, Ireland

www.hachette.ie

A division of Hachette UK
338 Euston Road
London NW1 3BH

To my godmother Eithne Murphy,
with much love

Chapter 1

Jenny Hannigan stood slightly apart from chattering groups in the little country churchyard, mentally cursing the stubborn impulse that had made her come here today. She hated going to parties alone, and weddings were the worst. The trouble was, when she had accepted the invitation, she hadn't expected to be coming on her own. When the thick embossed card had plopped fatly through her letterbox, positively dripping smugness, she had felt a little frisson of spiteful glee at the thought of turning up with Richard and stealing some of Fiona's thunder on her wedding day. So it probably served her right that she was stuck here now on her own, feeling like a fifth wheel.

What the hell had possessed her? When she had found out Richard wouldn't be coming with her, she should have cancelled. She could have had a nice lie-in and spent the rest of the day nursing her hangover. Instead she had got up only a couple of hours after she had gone to bed and spent a small fortune on a series of Tubes, trains and taxis to get here, not to mention what she had forked out for a new dress, shoes and a present she couldn't afford. All this, just because she wasn't willing to let a girl she didn't even know any more, much less care about, think she'd got the better of her.

'Such a lovely couple, aren't they?' A tall woman had materialised at her side, her eyes trained on the church door: guests were still filing into the glorious August sunshine past the bride and groom in a flurry of air kisses.

Jenny smiled politely, following the other woman's gaze, but said nothing.

Spotting some friends in the crowd, the woman drifted off, but she was soon replaced by a gaggle of middle-aged women who surrounded Jenny like a flock of exotic jabbering birds.

'Doesn't Fiona look *gorgeous*?' The lime-green one beamed down at her without introduction, revealing long, horsy teeth.

'Mmm.' Jenny nodded.

'It was a lovely ceremony, wasn't it?' the lemon-yellow one gushed, at no one in particular.

Pink and Lilac exchanged simpering smiles.

'They're *such* a lovely couple, Fiona and Tim.'

Oh, fuck, I've strayed into a wedding in Stepford, Jenny thought. It *was* all rather Stepford-like. The quaint village church, deep in the East Sussex countryside, with its manicured lawn and clipped hedges, was too idyllic to be true. The sun shone in a cloudless blue sky; the gentle buzz of conversation mingled with the hum of bees in the neatly trimmed borders; women in floral dresses smiled from beneath big, floppy hats; and in the church doorway stood the perfect couple – Fiona, petite and doll-like with her bouncing blonde curls, and Tim, tall and handsome, bursting with pride – while all around were their adoring worshippers. All it needed was some woodland creatures to appear out of the hedgerows to join in the adulation, like in a Disney cartoon.

'Are you on your own, dear?' Pink asked.

'Yes, I am,' Jenny answered brightly.

'Oh dear.' All four tilted their heads to the side and regarded her with pitying smiles.

Jenny wondered if she should sneak away now – just admit she had made a mistake, cut her losses and make a break for freedom. She felt in serious danger of these women taking her under their colourful wings if she stayed. But the pride that had forced her to come wouldn't allow her to leave. Fiona knew she was here, and Jenny wouldn't give her the satisfaction of thinking she had bottled it. She would just have to tough it out.

To her relief, the posse drifted off. Her face was aching from trying to match their doting smiles, and they made her feel gruff and oafish. It didn't help that she was in dire need of a hangover feed or that she hadn't quite managed to scrub the dirty black tattoo of last night's club stamp off the back of her hand. These people didn't look as if they ever got hung-over or stayed out too late clubbing. They were like the cast of one of the cosy Sunday-evening TV shows that she, Liam and Ollie sometimes flopped in front of, comatose after one of Liam's huge roast dinners – *Midsomer Murders* or an Agatha Christie mystery. Any minute now, Miss Marple would pop out from behind a hedge. She wished Miss Marple *would* show up – at least then there would be a murder. It was all so genteel, so refined, so ... *English*.

Not that she had anything against English people, of course – after all, her favourite person in the world was English. They didn't come much more English than Richard, she thought, smiling fondly to herself. He was the very epitome of Englishness. Blond and blue-eyed, his pink-cheeked face shone as if it had been scrubbed by Mary Poppins herself, while his strong forearms and slightly soft body were redolent of afternoons spent tossing balls on village greens and scoffing cricket teas. She loved English people, she really did – it was just that when they were *swarming* like this, they could be a bit unnerving. But even the most innocuous creatures could be intimidating when they swarmed.

If only Richard was here, she thought, rubbing at the stamp on her hand self-consciously, he'd be in his element, schmoozing the old dears, flirting with the young women and all back-slapping, shoulder-punching camaraderie with the men. And with the nation's golden boy at her side, no one would notice the smudge on her hand or her incongruous nail varnish, which she hadn't had time to redo this morning. The purple and silver stripes didn't go at all with her floaty green dress. Still, he wasn't here, so she would just have to make the best of it.

Shaking her kitten heels loose from the gravel, she moved towards the cluster of people nearest to her. She wove through the crowd, introducing herself and making small talk. Everyone said the same things – lovely couple … lovely ceremony … didn't Fiona look stunning … such a happy day … such a lovely couple …

Oh, hell, if you can't beat them, join them, she thought. Plastering a suitably Stepford smile to her face, she turned to the person nearest to her. 'They're a lovely couple, aren't they?' she said. She found herself talking to a sleeve. She looked up – and up – to find a very attractive but rather cross-looking man peering down his long, thin nose at her.

'You must be on the bride's side,' he said in a bored voice, barely glancing at the top of her head before he turned away again.

Taken aback, Jenny's Stepford smile slipped – to be replaced by a genuine grin. She knew she should have felt rebuked, but she couldn't help finding his rudeness cheering. 'I am, actually. How did you know?' she asked. He must be more than a foot taller than her.

'Because *he*'s a complete shit,' he said, his eyes narrowed on the groom.

'Oh!' Wow, not only had he not been cloned by androids, but he wasn't afraid to use the S-word – right here in Stepford! 'I don't know *him*,' she said, 'but *she*'s a total wagon.'

His head swivelled in her direction, and he looked at her properly for the first time. Jenny saw his features soften and the beginnings of a smile play across his lips. 'Sorry? A *what*?' His eyes twinkled with amusement.

She had forgotten that English people didn't use the term. 'A wagon. It means a bitch, a cow,' she elaborated.

'Ah, I see. They're well matched then. So why did you say they were a lovely couple?'

Jenny shrugged. 'It's all anyone's said to me so far. I thought I'd go with the flow, get in the swing of things. How do you know the shit?'

'We went to college together. We used to be friends.'

'What happened?'

'He screwed me over in business. What happened with you and the – er – wagon?'

'She stole my boyfriend.'

They looked at each other for a moment, then burst out laughing.

'Good God!' He frowned, sobering up. 'Not *him*?' He nodded to the groom.

'*Tim*? Christ, no! It was someone else.'

'He must have been mad.' He was smiling at her again. He had a warm, slightly husky voice, and a lovely soft northern English accent that Jenny couldn't quite place.

'I like to think so. He came back – but she'd sort of written him off.'

'I can see how that would happen.'

'You can?'

'Yes, of course.'

'How about your business? Was that a write-off?'

'Oh, the whole thing backfired on him pretty spectacularly.'

'That was lucky!'

'Not really – I made sure it did.'

'So you got your revenge?' Jenny grinned. 'Was it sweet?'

'I hardly remember. It was a long time ago.' He shrugged.

'But you're still holding on to it? Good for you! I like a man who bears a grudge.'

'Really?'

'Oh, absolutely! It shows commitment.'

'I suppose that's one way of looking at it.' He laughed.

'How tall are you?' she asked, shielding her eyes from the sun to squint up at him. She was starting to get a crick in her neck.

'Six foot four, last time I looked. But I'm told I've stopped growing. How short are you?'

'Five foot. But I've stopped growing too.' Jenny smiled ruefully. 'Still, you'd be amazed what I can get up to.'

'I bet.' He chuckled. 'That's an amazing dress,' he said. It was clear from the way he was looking at her that it wasn't just her dress he liked.

'Thanks. I bought it specially. It's vintage.' She swayed from side to side so that the skirt swished softly on its netting. 'I like your suit.'

'Oh, this old thing – I've had it for yonks.'

Jenny giggled. 'I'm Jenny, by the way,' she said, holding out a hand.

'Dev.' He took it, holding it slightly too long.

'Dev,' she repeated. 'That's a nice name.'

'It's short for Devlin. My mother named me after a character in a Cary Grant film. She had a thing for Cary Grant.'

'Very understandable.'

'What made you come today – if the bride isn't a friend?'

'She's a frienemy, and you know what they say – keep your friends close and your frienemies closer.'

'Is that the saying?' He was clearly amused by this.

'How about you? Why did you come?'

'Similar reason, I suppose,' he said. 'Anyway, I'm very glad I did.'

'I'm very glad you did too.' The day was looking up now that there was someone really attractive to flirt with. And it would make Fiona sick to see she had hooked up with the best-looking man at the wedding.

'Are you here on your own?' Dev asked.

'Not any more ...'

The guests walked the short distance from the church to the hotel. When everyone was having drinks in the bar, Dev excused himself and disappeared. Jenny thought she had seen the last of him, so she was surprised when they took their seats for dinner to find that she was beside him.

'Oh, hello again!' she said as he sat down beside her. 'This is a lucky coincidence, isn't it?'

'I believe in making your own luck,' he told her. 'I swapped the place cards.'

'Oh!' she gasped. 'You're going to be in trouble with Fiona for that. You're supposed to sit where you're told.'

'The bride's not the boss of us, is she?'

'Oh, but she is,' Jenny said. 'The bride's the boss of everyone. Have you never been to a wedding before?'

Dev laughed. 'I can swap them back if you like. You're supposed to be over there.' He pointed to a table in front of theirs.

'Oh, no, thanks – I'm fine where I am.' Ha! Jenny thought. That would show Fiona. This table was full of glamorous people. They all seemed to be in couples apart from Dev, and they had the glow of money and success about them. Glancing across to where she should have been sitting, she could tell it was the 'other' singles table, the ones you wouldn't dream of fixing up with any of your real single friends. It was full of oddly assorted misfits – except for one tall, glossy redhead who looked as out of place as an orchid in a field of dandelions. She was seated next to a bespectacled geek, dressed in cords and a plaid shirt, whose eyes were permanently trained on her impressive cleavage as he droned on – probably about the finer points of train spotting, Jenny decided. The redhead was obviously intended for Dev – and the geek for her.

Dev seemed to know everyone else – Oliver and Emma, Mark and Liz, Lawrence and Caroline – and they were introducing themselves to Jenny when Fiona swooped down on the table.

'Dev! How lovely to see you.' She kissed him on both cheeks. 'And Jenny.' Her smile didn't slip but it lost all of its warmth. 'It's great to see you here. You're so brave to come on your own!'

Jenny smiled back with equal insincerity.

'Anyway, I'm afraid there's been a teensy bit of a mix-up.' Fiona grimaced apologetically. 'You should have been sitting over there.' She pointed to the redhead, who was now sandwiched between the geek and Fiona's cousin Reggie, who Jenny knew suffered from halitosis. The redhead was leaning so far away from him, she almost had her head in the geek's lap. 'I can't think how this happened,' Fiona continued. 'It's so embarrassing, but would you mind awfully—'

'I'm afraid I'm the culprit,' Dev interrupted. 'I switched the place cards so Jenny could sit beside me.'

'Oh!' Fiona valiantly tried to maintain her smile, but she looked sick. 'Haven't lost your touch with the men I see, Jenny. I can't believe I'm getting married first. I always thought you'd be the first to go, you were always so ... *popular*. So *many* boyfriends – and still no ring?'

'No man's managed to tie me down yet. I'm having way too much fun playing the field.'

'Well, would you mind terribly moving?' Fiona said sweetly, but her eyes were cold. 'We went to a lot of trouble with the seating plan, and I know you'll be happier over there – there are loads of single men for you to meet. This is a couples table.'

'I'm single,' Dev said to Fiona. 'She can stay here and meet me.'

'Yes, but—'

'I think we're all happy where we are. I know I am. Jenny?' he consulted her.

Fiona glanced nervously at the redhead, who clearly wasn't at all happy.

'Oh, yes, happy as Larry!' Jenny took a large swig of her drink. God, this was fun – Fiona's face was a picture! 'It's really sweet of you to think of fixing me up, Fiona, but I'm doing fine on my own.'

'You don't mind, do you, Fiona?' Dev asked. Fiona's smile faded momentarily as Dev eyeballed her. She looked as if she was being hypnotised by a snake.

'Of course not! I'm not going to come over all Bridezilla!' she giggled with only the hint of an edge. 'No, you stay where you are. I hope you both enjoy the day.' She looked confused, as if she couldn't quite believe what was coming out of her mouth. 'But you'd better watch your step with Jenny,' she said jovially to Dev. 'She's a bit of a man-eater, our Jen.'

'I'll take my chances.'

She melted away. Jenny was half expecting a puff of smoke.

'Wagon!' Dev mumbled, watching her go.

'My God, that was amazing!' Jenny gasped. 'How did you do that? You're like Obi Wan Kenobi.'

'That's kind of Dev's job,' Mark, on her other side, put in.

'Really?' She turned back to Dev, wide-eyed. 'You're a Jedi knight?'

'The force is strong in this one,' Mark intoned, laughing.

'No, I'm not a Jedi knight,' Dev drawled, throwing Mark a scathing look.

'But he is in the mind-control game.'

'So what are you, then? A hypnotist? A magician?' Somehow she couldn't quite see him in a cape pulling rabbits out of a hat and sawing women in half. Still, he might be one of those posh illusionists, who did mind-reading and made whole buildings disappear.

'You really don't know what Dev does?' Mark asked her. 'He's pretty famous, you know.'

'Oh?' Jenny turned to Dev. 'What are you famous for?'

'I'm a publicist,' he said.

'He's being modest,' Mark's girlfriend Liz told Jenny. 'Dev is *the* publicist. He's always getting the rich and famous out of trouble and into the papers.'

'Or out of the papers, if that's what they want,' Mark added.

'I manipulate public opinion that's all.' Dev demurred.

'Well, you're obviously very good at it.'

'He is,' Mark said. 'For instance, what do you think of Kim Wilton?'

Kim Wilton was a D-list celeb who had followed the well-worn career trajectory from girl band through marriage to a footballer to reality show, punctuated by weight gain, weight loss, babies, drugs, divorce and rehab.

'Well, I used to think she was an awful slapper, but I really admire the way she's turned her life around since the break-up with Richie, and she seems to be a terrific mum.'

'Exactly,' Mark agreed. 'Mission accomplished. She's one of yours, isn't she, Dev?'

'Mark,' Dev said warningly, 'you know I don't discuss my clients.'

'She is, though,' Mark whispered to Jenny as the waitresses placed the first course on the table. 'Whatever Dev wants people to think about someone – that's what they think.'

'So, why does Bridezilla have it in for you?' Dev asked her. 'What on earth did you do to her – apart from letting her steal your boyfriend?'

'Well, like I said, he didn't stay away for long.'

Jenny had later discovered that it was only after a long campaign that Fiona had managed to lure Alan into her bed, if only momentarily. They used to be friends, she thought sadly – or at least she had thought they were friends. They had shared a flat and gone out on the pull together. But Jenny had always been more successful with men, and Fiona had got fed up with always being the 'other one'. She began to resent Jenny's effortless appeal to the opposite sex, and that resentment had turned to bitter, poisonous jealousy when Jenny had started going out with Alan. Fiona had known him first and had fancied him for ages, and she couldn't forgive Jenny for succeeding where she had failed. When she finally managed to entice Alan away, it was a hollow victory. After a one-night stand, which he had dismissed as a drunken mistake, he had come crawling back to Jenny, begging her to forgive him and swearing that Fiona meant nothing to him.

As details of Fiona's betrayal seeped out, Jenny discovered the extent of her resentment and realised that Fiona hadn't been her friend for a long time. She found out that she had been bitching about her behind her back and spreading rumours about her on the internet. Loathing confrontation, Jenny had simply moved out and they had drifted apart without ever acknowledging that their friendship was over.

'Where are you from?' Dev was asking her now.

'Dublin, but I've lived in London for a long time.'

'Really? You don't look old enough to have lived anywhere for a long time.'

'I started young.'

'Whereabouts do you live?'

'Camden.'

'Oh, we're practically neighbours then. I live in Primrose Hill – just up the road from you.'

Just up the road and half a world away, Jenny thought. 'Maybe we'll bump into each other some time,' she said.

'Let's make sure we do.'

'Sorry?'

'I'd really like to see you again,' he said. 'Can I take you to dinner?'

'Oh, um ...' Jenny bit her lip awkwardly. She took another swig of champagne to stall for time. 'Thanks, but I can't.'

'Oh!' Dev's smile faded.

She probably *had* been giving him the wrong impression, damn it! Flirtatious was simply her default mode – but, of course, he wasn't to know that. 'I'd really like to if ... I'm sorry, it's just that ... I have a boyfriend.'

'Right, of course.'

'I should have said. I didn't think ...' She trailed off miserably.

'So, where is he today, this boyfriend of yours?' Dev asked.

Oh, God, he doesn't believe me, Jenny thought. He thinks I'm inventing a boyfriend to give him the brush-off. 'He ... couldn't make it,' she said. 'He couldn't get away.'

'Wife wouldn't let him?' Dev drawled.

'No!' Jenny said indignantly. Bloody cheek! Why did men turn so nasty the second you turned them down? 'He's not married – except to his job.' She sighed. She knew she would always come second to the Job. 'He couldn't get away from work.'

'On a Saturday?'

'Yes, well, his work is very full-on.' She knew it didn't sound very convincing. But how did you explain that your boyfriend simply refused to be seen in public with you? 'It's very important to him.'

'More important than you?'

Bastard! 'Yes,' Jenny said defiantly, refusing to let him get to her. 'Probably.'

'Sounds like a tosser.'

'You don't know the first thing about him.'

'Sorry.' Dev smiled ruefully. 'I just don't handle rejection very well.'

'I don't suppose you've had much experience of it.' Shit! There I go again, she thought – straight back to flirting. No wonder the poor guy thought I was interested.

'Ahem, yes.' Dev looked slightly confused. 'Well, if you ever decide to pack in the tosser, why don't you give me a call?' He took a card from his pocket and handed it to her.

'Thanks, I will.' Jenny studied it thoughtfully. 'Actually, maybe you could help me,' she said, turning it over in her fingers.

'Help you? How?'

'Well, you said you can make people think whatever you want them to think about a person.'

'Actually, Mark said that.'

'Well, anyway, maybe you could do that for me. You know, like you did for Kim Wilton – make everyone think I'm the dog's *cojones*.'

'Act as your publicist, you mean? But you're not famous, are you?'

'No.'

'So why would you need a publicist? What do you do?'

'I'm a nanny.'

'Ah. Is this something to do with your boyfriend – the one who isn't here?'

'Yes, it is. How did you guess?'

'Well,' he said, 'I get that a lot in my line of work.'

'The thing is, no one really knows about us yet – that we're together. It's sort of a secret.'

'Right, I see. So who is he?'

'Oh, I can't say. He's very well known,' Jenny told him, leaning towards him confidentially.

'I gathered that. Otherwise you wouldn't need me.'

'I suppose so.'

'Actually, I'm on a sort of sabbatical at the moment. I've taken some time out to work on a ... special project. But I could put you in touch with one of my colleagues.'

'Oh, well,' she sighed, 'I doubt I could afford you anyway. I bet you're very expensive.'

'Well, you wouldn't have to worry about that. We'd get you a very nice deal for your story and you could pay us out of that.'

'What story?'

'You know – "my nights of passion with ... whoever",' Dev said wearily. 'The nanny who's shagging her famous boss isn't exactly new, but it always goes down well. The old stories are the best. What is he? Footballer? Actor? What we can get you will depend on how well-known he is, but—'

'I don't want to sell a story.' Jenny frowned at him. 'I don't kiss and tell. And I am not shagging my boss,' she added indignantly.

'What do you want a publicist for, then?'

'I don't know.' She was feeling foolish now. 'It was a stupid idea. I just thought maybe if it came out that I'm with this person you could make it seem like a good thing. Make *me* seem like a good thing.'

Dev looked at her strangely. 'And are you?' he asked.

'Am I what?'

'A good thing?'

'Oh, yes. I'm a *very* good thing. I'm the best thing since sliced bread.'

'Dev!' Jenny jumped, and looked round to find Fiona baring her teeth at him in a mockery of a smile. 'I know you wanted to monopolise Jenny for the day, but there's someone you absolutely *must* meet. I'm dying to get the two of you together.'

Fiona had the advantage of surprise and grabbed Dev's hand before he had a chance to argue, bearing him off in the direction of the lanky redhead. He threw an apologetic look at Jenny, and then Fiona was introducing him to the other girl. As Jenny watched, Fiona bent and whispered something in the geek's ear. The next minute, she was heading back towards Jenny with him in tow.

Oh, no, you don't, she thought. She stood, picking her bag up from the floor, and pulled her wrap over her shoulders. She had had enough of this wedding – and it was clearly about to get a lot worse. She was going home now, while she could still salvage some of the evening.

'Jenny, you must meet David,' Fiona was saying as she reached the table.

'Oh, I'd love to,' Jenny smiled, 'but I've got to be off.'

'Oh!' Fiona stopped in her tracks, stunned into silence. 'But the party's only just getting started.' She put her head on one side pettishly.

'Sorry, but I have to get back to London.'

'Oh dear, will your dress turn back into rags on the stroke of midnight?' Fiona laughed raucously at her own joke, turning to David, who joined in politely.

'I've got another party to go to.' Jenny smiled sweetly, hoping Fiona would pick up on the implied 'and a much more exciting one than this'.

'Oh, shame.' Fiona mock-pouted. 'A single gal's work is never done, eh? God, I'm so glad I'm not single any more. It's exhausting, isn't it?'

'Lucky for me I have such stamina,' Jenny said. 'Well, congratulations again.' She gave Fiona a brief kiss on the cheek before fleeing downstairs to Reception, where she asked them to call her a taxi.

Chapter 2

Jenny arrived back in London just before seven o'clock, and dashed through the crowded concourse of Victoria station, searching for a payphone so she could ring Richard. Now that she had the evening free, she was hoping she could spend it with him. Both her flatmates were away, and she really didn't fancy the prospect of an evening at home alone. She wished she could surprise him, just jump on the Tube, show up at his door and watch his face light up at seeing her. But he wasn't ready for people to know about them yet, so she had to make sure he was alone and it was safe for her to go to his flat – and she had to do it from a landline. He was paranoid about his phone being hacked, and she was banned from ringing him on her mobile.

At least he was pleasantly surprised by her call – she could hear the smile in his voice.

'You're back very early.'

'Yeah. I can come over, if that's okay?'

'Yes, great. Where are you now?'

'Victoria. I'll see you shortly.'

It was only a couple of stops to Bond Street, the nearest station to Richard's Mayfair flat, and she was soon strolling along the tree-lined square in the warm night air. She loved these old London squares. There was something so reassuring about the solid grandeur of the period buildings. Richard had given her a key to his flat so she could come and go like a resident. She nodded to the policeman stationed at the door as she let herself into the red-brick mansion block. Once inside, she rode in the lift to the third floor, taking the stairs for the final flight as an added precaution.

'Hello.' Richard looked up as she let herself into the flat, dropping the sheaf of papers he had in his hand onto the coffee table in front of him. He was sitting on the black leather sofa by the window. The balcony doors were open, and a light breeze ruffled the curtains.

A feeling of pure contentment washed over Jenny. She loved coming home to him.

'Did you have a nice time at the wedding?' he asked.

'It was okay,' she said, removing her wrap and kicking off her shoes.

'You look gorgeous,' he said and held out his arms as she walked towards him.

'I missed you,' she said, sinking into his lap and winding her arms around his neck, the skirt of her dress rustling softly as it settled around her. 'I wished you were there.' She rubbed her cheek against the stubble on his chin.

'I know – me too. I hate the thought of you going out without me. Were all the men hitting on you?'

'No – well, just one.'

'Bastard!' Richard mumbled, leaning in to kiss her.

'Actually, he was very nice,' Jenny said as his lips moved down to her neck.

'Double bastard then.' Richard eased off one of the straps of her dress, kissing her bare shoulder, his hands moving over the fitted bodice. Jenny wriggled excitedly.

'This is a beautiful dress,' he said, lifting his head, his eyes dark with desire. 'Let's take it off, shall we?' He was already tugging at the zip.

When she woke the next morning, Jenny rolled over, instinctively reaching out for Richard. Finding his side of the bed empty, she opened her eyes and sat up, blinking in the sunlight that was streaming through the curtains. Richard was standing by the wardrobe, getting dressed.

'What time is it?' she asked, hugging her knees to her chest.

'Twenty past eight,' he said, glancing at his watch. 'Sorry, did I wake you?'

She laid her head on her knees and watched him zip up his jeans. 'Why don't you come back to bed?' she asked.

He crossed to the bed and sat down, pulling her into his arms. 'Can't,' he said between kisses. 'I'm taking James to his tennis match. I have to go.'

'Oh, okay,' she said, snuggling into the warmth of his bare chest. 'It's going to be a beautiful day,' she said, looking out of the window. 'We could do something later.'

'Like what?'

'Have a picnic in the park, go for a drive in the country ... you know, stuff people do on Sundays.'

'Come on, Jenny, you know we can't do that,' he said, standing again. He took a T-shirt from a drawer and pulled it on.

She hated it when he spoke to her in that tone – as if she was an unreasonable child, asking for more sweets. 'I know.' She sighed. 'But I don't see why we still have to sneak around now. It's not as if we're doing anything wrong. I mean, you're not married – not any more. We have nothing to hide.'

'No, I'm not married, but I'm not divorced yet either, and my separation is very recent. We just have to be careful about the timing of this. If it comes out too soon that we're seeing each other, the papers will have a field day. They could really go for you, Jen – implying that you were on the scene before Julia and I separated.'

'Well ... you *were* still living with her—'

'No!' he said sharply. 'I've told you, you had nothing to do with my marriage breaking down. It was over in all but name when I met you.'

'But if that's true, why do we have to sneak around like this? Like we have something to be ashamed of?'

He sat down on the bed again. 'You know what the papers are like, darling,' he said, stroking her bare arm soothingly. 'There's likely to be an election soon, and my enemies are working overtime trying to dig up any dirt on me, anything they can use to discredit me.'

'And you think it'll discredit you if they find out about me?'

'No, of course not. But you know how they twist things. We just have to leave a decent interval before we go public. It's only been three months since the announcement of my separation.'

'You're just worried I'll lose you votes, aren't you?'

'Don't be silly.' He frowned impatiently.

'I know I'm not an asset to you, like Julia was.'

'Stop talking rubbish. I'm not with Julia, I'm with you.'

'I bet the Party wish you were with Julia. She's the perfect wife for the leader of the Moderate Party, isn't she? She's got the right clothes, the right hairstyle, the right accent ... the right background,' she added faintly.

'I don't give a toss about all that.'

'She couldn't be more perfect for the job if she'd been built to specification,' Jenny continued. She was convinced that Julia had been born not only with a silver spoon in her mouth, but with a Chanel suit on her back and 'PM's wife' stamped through her, like a stick of rock. 'And I'm the complete opposite of her in every way. I'm the anti-Julia.'

'You're not!' Richard laughed.

'But I am! Think about it – she's Harvey Nicks, I'm Camden Market. She's English, I'm Irish. She can trace her ancestry back to — to the guys who built Stonehenge. I can't even trace my own mother.'

'Shut up.' Richard stopped her saying any more by kissing her. 'I can think of one thing you have that Julia doesn't,' he said, pulling away. 'Something much more important to the Party than any of that stuff.'

'What?'

'Me.'

She grinned back at him. 'Hmm, that's true,' she said, putting her arms around him and burying her face in his neck, breathing in the smell of him. 'So why don't we just stay here? When you come back, I mean.'

'Sorry, I promised to spend the day with the boys.'

'Oh, okay.' She unwound her arms from his neck, giving him a carefree smile. She mustn't cling – clinginess was so unattractive. 'What are you going to do with them?' she asked.

'I don't know – maybe have a picnic on the Heath, go to the park … you know, stuff people do on Sundays.'

'Sounds nice.'

Richard stood up and shrugged on a light jacket. Jenny smiled to herself, watching him. She always thought he looked a little odd in casual clothes, unnatural somehow – like a monkey dressed up as a human being.

'So I stay your dirty little secret until after the election, is that it?' she asked. 'And then you spring me on the country when they've already elected you and it's too late for them to back down?'

'We may not win, you know.'

'You'll win.'

'Look,' he said, 'it won't be much longer, I promise. I certainly don't intend to wait until after the election. An old friend of mine has just come to work for me as my director of communications.'

'Is that like a spin doctor?'

'Yes. He'll know the best way of rolling "us" out.'

'You make us sound like a new tax policy or something.'

'Oh, we'll be *much* more controversial than that,' he said. 'I'll take you to meet Dev next week, and we'll discuss how to handle the whole thing.'

'Who?'

'The spin doctor I was telling you about – Dev Tennant. He's the best in the business.'

'Oh!' Shit! What were the chances? She hoped that wasn't going to be awkward.

'Can you come into the office some day during the week?'

'Yes – I'll say I have a dental appointment or something.'

'Good. I'll let you know what day suits best. Why don't you go back to sleep?' he said, bending to give her a swift kiss on the lips. 'Stay as long as you like.'

And then he was gone.

Jenny sank back against the pillows, deflated. When they were together, she felt so confident, so sure of herself, so certain that their rosy future together was out there just waiting for them to step into it. But the moment Richard left he took all of that with him, and her happiness and optimism evaporated. She felt edgy and insecure, her world wobbling nauseatingly on its axis.

There were some memories that she wished she could bottle, so she could take them out and live them all over again when she was feeling low to remind herself that life could be wonderful – sometimes even magical, transcendent in a way that took you totally by surprise. The day she'd met Richard had been like that.

She had been in her present job a few months, looking after Oscar, the five-year-old son of Alice and Michael Young. Alice was an academic and Michael a high-flying solicitor. They had gone to Paris to celebrate their wedding anniversary and Jenny had moved into their enormous house in Hampstead for the weekend to babysit. On the Saturday, Oscar was going to a friend's birthday party, and Alice asked Jenny if she would collect another little boy from the party and bring him home.

'His mum's away, and the nanny has to take his brother to a different party, but she should be back by the time you get home. If she isn't, just bring James here to play with Oscar for a while. He's Richard Allam's son,' Alice told her. 'I'll write you out the address. It's only a short walk from here.'

'Richard Allam!' Jenny's eyes had lit up.

'Yes.' Alice smiled. 'Don't get any ideas, will you, Jenny? We are not *Jane Eyre*.' This was said with a conspiratorial wink that rendered it inoffensive.

'A cat can look at a king.' Jenny sniffed, with mock hauteur.

'She can indeed, Jenny,' Alice said, waving the card she had written the address on to dry the ink. 'However, she can't shag him and try to pass her kittens off as heirs to the throne.'

Jenny laughed to herself, remembering. She was very fond of Alice and she would miss her. The family were moving to Edinburgh in a few weeks' time – Michael was being relocated there for work.

'He's very good-looking, though, isn't he – Richard Allam?' she had continued.

'Hmm. "Handsome is as handsome does", as my mum used to say.'

'Oh, come on – he's gorgeous. He'd almost make you want to vote!'

Alice looked at Jenny over the top of her glasses. 'I do hope you mean he'd almost make you want to vote *Moderate*,' she said. 'Unless you want a twenty-minute lecture on the suffragettes.'

'Absolutely that's what I meant. You can save your lectures for your students.'

She had been aware of Richard before, of course. His children attended the same exclusive private school as Oscar, and he was occasionally to be seen there on gala days, at school plays and carol services. Sometimes he even dropped them off in the morning, prompting mutterings from the more cynical mothers that he was only doing it to show off, and he wouldn't be seen dead doing the school run if he wasn't gunning for high office. There was a discernible flurry of excitement whenever he made an appearance outside the school, partly because he was such a star, but mostly, Jenny suspected, because he was an alpha male in a usually all-female gathering of mums and nannies. She had occasionally spotted him in the distance, always nobbled by some pushy mother who wanted to be his best friend or to harangue him about some issue. She felt a little sorry for him, always having to be *über*-polite and friendly to the playground's most crashing bores.

That day, she had collected Oscar and James from the party and the three of them had arrived at Richard's house to be met by the nanny – who was clearly about to do a runner. She was a dramatically attractive Spanish girl, with a rope of thick dark hair and flashing eyes. Bags and suitcases littered the hallway, and James's younger brother, Felix, was busying himself with emptying one while a stunningly beautiful boy hovered in the background with his hands in his pockets.

'Thank God you have come,' she said, pulling Jenny into the hallway. She explained breathlessly that there had been a death in her family and she had to return to Spain immediately. 'You will look after the boys until Richard comes home, yes? You will stay?' She had taken Jenny by the arms, smiling pleadingly at her, but with a determined set to her face that said she wasn't going to take no for an answer.

'No! I can't, I—'

'He will not be long, I promise. You tell him I had to go and I am so sorry.'

'But – can't you wait and tell him yourself? I mean, if he's not going to be long ...'

'No.' The girl shook her head firmly. 'If I stay any longer I will miss my plane.'

She looked far too happy about the alleged bereavement, her eyes glowing with excitement, and Jenny suspected her sudden departure had a lot to do with the beautiful boy. She crushed Jenny in a hug and kissed her on both cheeks. Then, after a brief goodbye to the children, she gathered up her bags, grabbed the boy's hand and was gone.

The sudden departure of his nanny had upset Felix, and it had taken Jenny quite some time, and two packets of chocolate buttons, to calm him down. But by the time Richard got home, they were all sprawled on the floor, happily playing Junior Pictionary. Jenny heard his voice before she saw him.

'Hello,' he called from the hall. 'Sorry I'm late. I got caught up with – oh!'

Jenny looked up to find him standing in the doorway, bemused.

'Hello. Who are you? Where's Dolores?' His eyes darted around the kitchen.

'She's called Jenny.' Felix glanced up at his father before bending to his drawing again.

'She's Oscar's nanny,' James explained.

Jenny gave Richard what she hoped was a reassuring smile.

'Oh, Oscar, I didn't see you there.' He smiled, visibly relaxing. He came over and got down on his hunkers beside Oscar. 'Hello,' he said. He ruffled James's blond hair affectionately. 'Did you guys have fun at your parties?' he asked the boys, who all nodded enthusiastically.

'Sam threw up!'

'There was a clown!'

'I got a dinosaur balloon. The clown maked it.'

'Hello, I'm Richard,' he said, standing and extending a hand.

She got to her feet and took it. 'Jenny.' She was struck by how attractive he was up close – the pictures really didn't do him justice. He was wearing a dazzling white shirt, the sleeves rolled up to reveal strong, tanned forearms. He looked so healthy and wholesome, and exuded an aura of power and confidence.

'So where's Dolores?'

'Um, Dolores has left. I said I'd wait with the boys until you got home.'

'Left?' He seemed confused and a bit annoyed. 'Where's she gone? When will she be back?'

'She's gone to Spain.'

'*What*? Bloody hell!'

'She, um … said something about a death in the family,' Jenny mumbled, eyes on her shoes, embarrassed by the lie, even though it wasn't hers.

'Really?' Richard seemed a little chastened, though not entirely convinced.

'Actually, she wasn't very upset,' she told him.

'José was here,' James informed his father, impressively guttural on the 'J'. 'She went off with him.'

'Her boyfriend,' Richard explained to Jenny. 'They had a big bust-up just before she came over here, but she spent hours screaming her head off on the phone to him and she was always talking about him. Then he turned up last week.'

Jenny smiled sympathetically.

'Christ! Wretched girl!' Richard fumed. 'I can't believe she did that. You'd think at least she'd have had the decency to—' He broke off, casting an apologetic look at Jenny. 'Sorry, I'm forgetting my manners. Look, thanks for staying. I'm so sorry you got dragged into this.'

'It's fine. I don't mind.'

'I hope they weren't too much trouble.' He waved at the children.

'No trouble at all. Will you be okay? Without your nanny, I mean?'

'Oh, I'll be fine. The office will arrange a replacement. Julia will be back tomorrow anyway. Have they eaten?'

'At the party. Lasagne and chips, apparently. And cake ... and tons of sweets. I don't think they're hungry.'

'What about you? Have you eaten?'

'No, not yet.'

'Well, let me buy you dinner. It's the least I can do. Stay and we'll get a takeaway.'

'Thanks,' she smiled regretfully, 'but I'd better get Oscar home to bed.'

'Right. Well, thanks again. I hope it hasn't mucked up any plans you had for tonight?'

'No, I'm babysitting. Alice and Michael are away at the moment.'

'Oh, yes, of course – I'd forgotten.'

They looked at each other for a moment in silence.

'Well, we'd better go,' she finally said. 'Come on, Oscar.'

'Are you doing anything tomorrow?' Richard said quickly as Oscar got up and took Jenny's hand. 'I was going to take the boys for a picnic on the Heath. Why don't you and Oscar come with us?'

Oscar's eyes lit up. 'Yes! Can we?' he asked Jenny.

'That would be lovely,' she said to Richard.

The next afternoon was glorious, and the children had played happily together while she and Richard sat on the grass talking. She remembered the sensations of the day so clearly – the warmth of the sun on her shoulders, the taste of cherries in the open air, the distant squeals of the children, the fluttering of butterfly wings in her stomach when Richard's eyes met and held hers. She felt the spark between them and knew as sure as anything that he did too. It was just *there*, undeniable, a physical thing, as real as the grass tickling her legs.

'I'd like to see you again,' he had said as they sat side by side, watching the children playing ball. 'Why don't you come to dinner during the week, when Michael and Alice are back?'

She looked at him speculatively. 'Would your wife be there?' she asked.

He shook his head. 'Julia's taking the children to Cornwall tomorrow to stay with her parents.'

'I don't think that would be a good idea.'

He grinned. 'What makes you think my intentions aren't entirely honourable?'

'You're not the first man I've ever met.' She laughed. 'Besides, what makes *you* think I'd want them to be?'

'Come on, come to dinner. I still owe you for yesterday. And I like talking to you. We'll just talk.'

She had allowed him to persuade her. Later that week she had gone to meet him at his flat in Mayfair, telling herself they would just talk and that there was no significance in the fact that he didn't want her to come to his family home. He had cooked for her, and at first they *had* just talked. But later, as they sat side by side on the sofa, Richard had leaned in and kissed her. When she had felt his mouth and hands on her, lust had taken over and Jenny's resolve had melted away. They didn't even make it to the bedroom that first time, tearing each other's clothes off before tumbling to the floor in a knot of limbs.

Guilt and regret had set in the next morning as the reality of what she had done hit her. Richard was a married man, a family man. She had been in his home; she had played with his children. She felt the betrayal of his children more keenly than that of his wife. But she consoled herself with the thought that it was a once-off thing. It would never happen again, no one would ever find out and there would be no lasting consequences. It was just one lovely night of madness. When she said this to Richard, however, he told her the truth about his marriage – that it had been over for a long time and he and Julia were just keeping up the charade for the sake of his political career. There was no reason why they couldn't go on seeing each other – as long as no one found out.

She hated that they couldn't be open about their relationship, and she resented having to behave like a mistress, meeting him in secret, not being introduced to his friends, unable to talk about him to her own. Even her best friends and flatmates, Ollie and Liam, didn't know who her secret boyfriend was. But as long as he kept up the pretence of his marriage that was the way it had to be.

It had been tricky having an affair with such a high-profile man, but somehow they had managed it. Jenny's fence-climbing skills were honed to perfection, and she had become a master of disguise. She could probably have counted the hours they had spent together in the first few months, but they made up for it in intensity when they were together. It became all-consuming. It was a full-time job planning the logistics of being with Richard and covering her tracks afterwards.

It wasn't long before doubt crept in. Maybe she had been too quick to believe Richard when he had told her his marriage was over. He claimed he and Julia were just waiting for the right moment to announce their separation publicly, but the right moment never seemed to come. First he wanted to wait until after the leadership election. Then it was the Party conference, Christmas, holidays with the children – one thing after another until Jenny began to suspect he was stringing her along and his marriage was very much a going concern. They would have fought about it if Jenny 'did' fighting, but she didn't.

'Your marriage isn't really over at all, is it?' she would accuse him gently, not wanting a fight, but craving reassurance.

'Of course it is,' he would say. 'How many times do I have to tell you?'

But no matter how many times he told her, it got harder and harder to believe him. And then suddenly, one day in the spring, he had turned up unexpectedly and told her the pretence was over. He and Julia were ready to separate officially. She still hadn't quite believed it until she saw it in print the next day. It was all over the media. She bought every paper, devoured every news bulletin and danced around the flat, celebrating her imminent emergence from the shadows. She had done her time hiding in rain-sodden bushes, crouching in cars and grazing her knees jumping off walls. She could finally take her place at Richard's side.

But her celebrations had proved premature. Richard insisted they had to leave a decent interval before going public about their relationship. He didn't want the scandalmongers suggesting they had been having an affair while he and Julia were still together. So Jenny had to stay out of sight a while longer. She had told Ollie and Liam, swearing them to secrecy, but apart from that, nothing had changed. It had been more than a year now since she had first met Richard. She was so proud of him, and so proud that he had chosen her. She wished the rest of the world could see her through his eyes. She wanted to shout it from the rooftops that Richard Allam loved her. She hated to whine or make demands, but she had done everything he had asked: she had stayed in the background and hadn't complained; she had refrained from boasting to random strangers in the street that he loved her. Surely she had earned her reward.

Chapter 3

With Richard gone, staying in bed lost its charm. Jenny got up, pulled on a dressing gown and padded into the living room, sighing with dissatisfaction as she looked around the large, open-plan space. She wished Richard would let her give it a makeover, but he seemed to like all the hard, shiny surfaces, the high gloss and chrome of the gadget-ridden kitchen, the leather sofas and glass tables. Maybe all men would live like this, given the choice. Or maybe it was just what you ended up with if you didn't care about your surroundings – default décor. Ollie and Liam never complained about her sequined cushions and mirrored throws, the sari lengths in vibrant shades of purple, red and orange that she draped over poles in lieu of curtains, her coloured glass and scented candles or the fairy-lights she strung along shelves and trailed down walls. Ollie had once described her interior style as Cath Kidston meets Bangkok brothel, which she had taken as a compliment. But they probably wouldn't miss all that stuff if it was gone.

She decided she would go home for breakfast. She had yet to wring a cup of coffee from the high-tech built-in coffee machine, and would much rather have low-tech tea from her kitsch flowery china, curled up in a squashy armchair. Besides, it was going to be a beautiful day and she didn't want to be cooped up in here all morning.

She couldn't even go out on the balcony in case someone spotted her. She'd go home, have breakfast, then ring round her friends and scare up some company for the day.

Emerging from Camden Town Tube station, she joined the tide of people heading to the market, feeling out of place in the gauzy chiffon dress she had worn to the wedding. She would have to start leaving some clothes at Richard's flat. Because their meetings were usually arranged with military precision, she had never been caught unprepared there before. It was nothing new to her, crashing in other people's houses after parties, going home the morning after in the clothes from the night before, but she was ready to leave that phase of her life behind. She wanted to have all her things in one place, go to sleep in the bed she'd woken up in. She'd had enough of borrowing toothbrushes and T-shirts for impromptu sleepovers.

Leaving the crowds, she turned into a side-road by the canal, the clamour of the main street receding further the closer she got to home. Her heart gave a little skip as she reached the gate and saw that the living room window was open. She hadn't expected anyone to be home. Liam had gone to Dublin for the weekend to attend (of all things) a school reunion, and Ollie was at a stag weekend in Barcelona. She ran up the stairs to her first-floor flat, smiling to herself as she turned the key in the lock.

She found Liam in the living room, sprawled on the sofa. 'You're home!' She threw herself down beside him. 'I wasn't expecting you back until tonight.'

'I'd had all the family fun I could hack for one weekend,' he said, pushing his dishevelled curls out of his eyes. 'My ma sends her love, by the way.'

'Of course she does,' Jenny said drily. She knew Mrs Mulligan was no fan of hers. 'God, you look rough.'

'Thanks. I feel it.'

'Is that a black eye?'

'Yeah. Long story. You look nice. Where have you been, you dirty stop-out?'

'I was at Richard's.'

'Really? He let you stay a whole night? That was big of him.'

'Shut up!'

'You should get him to stay over here some time. Then we could have one of those plaques on the wall – "Bollocky Bill slept here". I could do guided tours.'

Jenny laughed. 'You can forget that. We won't be getting a plaque any time soon.'

'So where's lover boy today?'

'With his kids.'

Liam rolled his eyes.

'What? It's nice. I like that he's a good dad.'

'He's a prick.'

'He's not. He's going to be prime minister.'

'I rest my case.'

Jenny sighed. 'I'm not going to sit here and listen to you bad-mouthing the man I love,' she said, standing up. 'I'm going to get changed into something less ridiculous, and then we're going out. We'll get you a smoothie – one with lots of beetroot that's good for your liver. We can detox! We'll eat leaves and drink vegetables, and get all healthy. It'll be brilliant – and I want to hear all about that black eye.'

She went to her bedroom, changed into a sundress and sandals, then returned to the living room. 'Right, let's go,' she said, holding out a hand to Liam.

'Okay.' He got up. 'I've got wedge,' he said, digging in his pocket with his free hand and producing a thick wad of notes.

'Wow! Where did you get all that?'

'Ask me no questions and I'll tell you no shite. Come on, let's go to the market. If you're very good, I'll buy you a hat.'

The market was bustling, delicious cooking smells mingling with incense as they wandered slowly around the stalls hand in hand, stopping occasionally to admire jewellery or browse through quirky knick-knacks.

'I still can't believe you went to a school reunion,' Jenny said later, as they sat eating lunch at an outdoor café overlooking Regent's Canal.

'I was being ironic.'

'What was it like?'

'It was like being back at school.'

'Sounds great.'

'Everyone was asking about you when I told them we were living together.'

'What did you say?'

'That you were as gorgeous as ever, breaking hearts all over London.'

'You know they all thought we were doing it back then.'

'I know,' he grinned, pushing away his plate and lighting a cigarette. 'Why weren't we?' He frowned, perplexed.

Jenny shrugged. 'I don't know. To spite them, maybe?'

'I think it was because I liked you too much. I saw the way you chewed boys up and spat them out. I didn't want to be cannon fodder.'

'That sounds horrible!' she protested. 'You make me sound like a right bitch.'

'No,' he smiled, 'but you weren't good at staying friends.'

'True. Moving on was my forte – still is. *We* stayed friends, though – even after that one time ...'

'Ah, well, there's no getting rid of me.' He took a long drag on his cigarette, tilting his head back to exhale slowly. 'I'm a keeper.'

'So, tell me about the black eye.'

'You remember Freckles from our class?'

'Freckles Quinn?'

'Was there more than one Freckles?'

'I suppose not. Yeah, I remember her – quiet, geeky girl. Buck teeth.'

'Not any more. Anyway, I bumped into her at the reunion—'

'When you say you "bumped into" her ...'

'I mean I showed her the time of her life behind the bike sheds.'

'Holy shit! It really was like being back at school, then.'

'It was unfinished business. She was the only girl in the sixth form that I didn't *at least* feel up.'

'Hello?' Jenny waved her hand.

'Okay, apart from you. Anyway, I felt sort of bad for her, so I decided to put it right. Give her closure.'

'That was nice of you.'

'Wouldn't want her to feel left out – like she'd missed out on the best part of school or something.'

'So you showed her heaven behind the bike sheds.'

'It's what a reunion's all about, isn't it? Bit of nostalgia, a trip down Memory Lane?'

'And she punched you? Is that part of her, um ... celebration?'

'No, Freckles didn't punch me. You remember Philip Wilson?'

'Yeah.'

'Well, it turns out they're married now – him and Freckles.'

'And he was at the reunion too?'

'Yeah.'

Jenny gave him a meaningful look.

'Well, how the fuck was I supposed to know? Freckles kept very quiet about it.'

'Afraid she wouldn't get her moment behind the bike sheds with you. So what happened then? You and Philip went at it and everyone formed a circle around you, chanting, "Fight"?'

'Pretty much. Told you it was like being back at school.'

'At least your mum couldn't blame it on me this time,' Jenny said.

'Don't be so sure. She still thinks you're a bad influence.' He grinned. 'You're leading me astray again, like you used to at school.'

'Huh!' Liam's mother was too doting to admit that her precious son was perfectly capable of going astray all on his own.

'She kept mentioning people I used to knock around with who'd moved to London and might be looking for someone to flat-share, suggesting I should look them up.'

'Subtle!'

'Yeah, it was really starting to piss me off, so I changed my flight and came back early.'

Jenny took a sip of her sludge-coloured smoothie through a straw and made a face. 'How's your smoothie?' she asked Liam, nodding to the clear plastic cup in front of him, still almost full of livid red juice.

'It's beetroot, Jenny. It's a beetroot drink. How's yours?'

She took another tiny sip, rolling it around her mouth thoughtfully. 'It's like regurgitated mulch.'

'This detoxing isn't all it's cracked up to be, is it?'

'Well, at least we gave it a go. No one can say we didn't try. It's just not for us,' she said, plonking her cup back on the table. 'Hair of the dog?' she asked, smiling up at him mischievously from beneath her lashes.

'My mother was right about you. You're trouble.'

'That's what you love about me,' she said, getting up.

'Did you do anything nice at the weekend?' Alice asked the next morning as they sat among the breakfast mess in her big rustic kitchen.

Jenny always had breakfast at Alice and Michael's house on weekdays because they left for work early. Alice had already resigned from her position at Birkbeck College, but this morning she was travelling to Edinburgh for an interview. 'Fantastic weather, wasn't it?'

'Yes, it was. On Saturday we went to that wedding I told you about,' she said, painfully aware that the 'we' was a lie. She hated lying to Alice.

'How was it?'

'It was a wedding – the bride looked beautiful, blah, blah, blah.'

Alice laughed. 'You old cynic.'

'Yesterday I went to the market with Liam. He bought me this – look.' She fished in her bag and pulled out a floppy red hat covered with embroidered flowers. 'Isn't it cute?' She placed it on her head.

'It's lovely. But didn't he buy you a hat the last time you went to the market with him?'

Jenny grinned. 'Yeah. I think he fancies Birgitte, the girl who makes them. He's trying to butter her up.'

'I thought your friend Liam was irresistible to all womankind,' Alice said, smiling. Alice was fiercely feminist and Jenny knew she didn't really approve of boys like Liam, but she always loved hearing about him and Jenny suspected she had a sort of long-distance soft spot for him.

'He usually is, but the hatter has a good head on her shoulders. She's managed to hold out on him so far. Which is nice for me, because it means I get lots of hats.'

Just then Michael came into the kitchen, dressed for work in a very expensive-looking suit. 'I'm off,' he said, crossing the kitchen to his wife. 'Hello, Jenny. Nice hat.'

'Thanks.' She pulled it off as Michael bent to kiss Alice goodbye, both of them murmuring arrangements about home times and dinner.

Shortly after he had left, Oscar came into the kitchen, sleepy-eyed, still in his pyjamas. 'Hi, Jenny.' He came to stand beside her chair. 'I drawed a picture for you,' he said, placing a sheet of paper in front of her.

'Oh, that's *beautiful*, Oscar. Thank you.' She kissed the top of his head. 'Is that me?' she asked, pointing to one of the stick figures.

'Yes, and that's Mum, that's Dad and that's Granny,' he said, pointing to the others.

'Did you do anything nice at the weekend?' she asked him.

'We drove down to Hastings to visit Granny, didn't we, Oscar?' Alice said.

'Yes.' Oscar nodded. 'Granny gived me a gun!'

'Did she?' Jenny snuck a glance at Alice.

'Yes, she bloody did,' Alice said quietly, burying her head in her hands. 'I swear she does it to wind me up.'

Jenny laughed sympathetically.

'Mothers! Who'd have 'em?' Alice said, and winced. 'Sorry, Jenny – that was a stupid thing to say.'

'No, it's fine. You're right – I don't know how lucky I am.'

'Are you still looking?'

'Kind of.'

'Well, if there's anything I can do to help, just let me know.'

'Thanks. Oh, by the way, I need to go to the dentist some day this week – any day that suits you. I haven't made an appointment yet.' She was shocked at how easily the lies tripped off her tongue these days.

'That's fine, Jenny – I've nothing on for the rest of the week anyway. I'll be home doing packing. You can go tomorrow if you like – if you can get an appointment.'

'Okay. I won't be long – it'll just be an hour or so in the morning.'

'Don't forget Oscar has a play date with Joshua this afternoon. I said you'd drop him off around two.'

'Is there anything you want me to do while he's gone? Ironing, maybe?'

'Jenny,' Alice said sternly, 'you know I don't expect you to do any housework. That's not your job.'

'I don't mind doing it. I'm happy to help. And I have plenty of time to do other things when Oscar's out.' It was a discussion they had had many times before, especially during term time. Jenny felt guilty lounging around the house while Oscar was at school.

'I'd be much happier if you studied something in your downtime. Did you look at those college prospectuses I gave you?'

'Um ...' Jenny smiled sheepishly.

Alice sighed. 'Sometimes I despair! My generation has spent decades battling to further the cause of women, and a young girl like you wants nothing more than to be a nineteen-fifties housewife!' She shook her head.

'I know.' Jenny giggled. 'I'm a lost cause.'

'And I'm a bossy old cow,' Alice said with a conciliatory smile. 'I'll mind my own business.' She drained her coffee and got up. 'Right, I'd better be off,' she said. 'Wish me luck.'

'Good luck! Not that you'll need it. They'd be mad not to snap you up.'

Alice bent to kiss Oscar. 'Have fun, you two! See you tomorrow, Jenny – whenever.'

When Alice had gone, Jenny looked around the kitchen. She loved the domestic chaos of mornings here. She knew Alice didn't approve of her ambition – or lack of it, in Alice's view – to be a wife and stay-at-home mother, but it was easy for Alice to scoff when she had all that. Okay, she didn't stay at home with Oscar, but that was her choice. She had a lovely husband, a gorgeous son, a beautiful big house in Hampstead. She had family breakfasts and Sunday outings and birthday parties with cake and candles. She had visits to Granny and school carol concerts and Mother's Day presents and jaunty holidays to France.

People said you didn't miss what you never had, but she knew it wasn't true. She had never had this, but she craved it so much it hurt. She looked at Oscar, his head bent over his Nintendo. He was six, the same age she had been when she had last seen her mother. If Alice left now, she wondered what memories Oscar would have of her. Jenny's memories were really just an assortment of vague impressions – a moment's warmth and a waft of perfume when her mother bent to give her a lipsticky kiss before going out for the night; a dressing table covered with mysterious powders and lotions; lying snuggled up to the soft warmth of her body on Sunday mornings when she complained of a headache; the scatter of pills and bottles of water on the bedside table.

She had photographs, of course – a beautiful smiling woman in pretty dresses. She remembered being pleased when her father said she was turning out like her mother, until she was old enough to recognise the snarl in his voice when he said it. As she grew older, she realised he only said it when he was drunk and that it was meant as a slur. He didn't mean that she was becoming a beautiful girl but that she was turning into someone flighty, vain, untrustworthy.

Well, the past was the past – there was nothing you could do about it. The future was another matter, and she was determined she was not going to turn out like her mother *or* her father. She was her own invention, and she was going to have the blissful family life as an adult that she had never had as a child. Tomorrow she would go with Richard to see Dev Tennant, and she would take the first step towards getting the life she wanted.

Chapter 4

Dev Tennant was sitting behind his desk at Moderate Party Headquarters, trying to concentrate on the speech he was rewriting for the umpteenth time, but his eye kept drifting to the morning papers. A story about famous Wag Tracey Turner being beaten up by her husband dominated the tabloids. Tracey was a client who had become a friend, and he was very fond of her in an avuncular way. He sighed as he gazed at the graphic images of her brutalised face.

The story wasn't news to him. He had been working on this speech last night at home, hoping to get it finished before bed, when Tracey had turned up at his door, screaming and hysterical, her face a mess of blood and mucus. She could barely speak when he'd brought her in, unable to control her sobs and choking on the drink he gave her. He just held her until she stopped shaking, trying to reassure her that she was safe. It had taken the best part of an hour for him to calm her down enough to talk – not that he needed her to explain what had happened. Until today he had probably been one of the few people in the world who knew that her husband beat her. Still, it was hard to reconcile the pictures in today's papers with the open, bubbly young girl whose twenty-first birthday party he had attended only months ago.

When she had started talking, it was the usual story. Damien had got drunk and laid into her, only it had been worse this time. She had never seen him so violent, and for the first time she had actually feared for her life. Somehow she had managed to get away from him, running out of the house and jumping into her car.

'This was the first place I thought of coming,' she said.

'I'm glad you did.' The state she was in, it was a miracle she had managed to drive.

'Can I stay? I'm afraid to go home, and I've got nowhere else to go.'

He knew she had hidden her husband's violence from her family, so she wouldn't turn to them. 'Yes, of course you can stay, if you want to,' he said, taking the empty tumbler from her and placing it on the coffee table. 'After,' he continued, standing up and holding out his hand to her.

'After?' She looked up at him in confusion.

'After we've been to the police.' He knew he was taking a chance, and he held his breath, waiting for her to respond. He had begged her so many times to press charges, to go public about Damien's abuse, but she'd always refused, protesting that he loved her and had promised it would never happen again. But of course it always did.

Tears filled her eyes, but she nodded and stood up. He breathed a sigh of relief.

'Maybe then you should call your mother,' he said, putting his arm around her to support her as they walked to the car.

She had done that, and he stayed at the police station until her mother showed up and Tracey walked sobbing into her arms.

He yawned, rubbing his eyes wearily with the heel of his hands. He hadn't got much sleep last night. But he felt a small glimmer of satisfaction that this morning the world would wake up to the truth about Damien Turner – superstar footballer, wife-beater and class-A scumbag.

In a weird way he had been grateful for the intrusion last night – not for the cause, of course – because it had taken him out of himself for a few hours. It had felt good to be doing something active, to feel he was being useful to another person. He needed that. This job for Richard had come along at just the right time.

He hunched over the computer screen once more, trying to pick up his train of thought. He'd better get on with this: Richard would be here shortly with his new girlfriend. He was surprised when Richard had told him he was seeing someone – even a little shocked, if he was honest, that he'd moved on so fast. Maybe he should ask him what the secret was. Everyone was telling him *he* should move on, but so far, he hadn't been able to. He knew people meant well, and he had allowed himself to be talked into a couple of blind dates recently, thinking going out might help and would at least be preferable to his cold, empty house – but he found meeting new people unbearable at the moment and had just wanted to get away. He couldn't stand the asking and answering of questions, the whole rigmarole of getting to know someone. He sighed, his eyes drifting to the framed photograph of Sally beside his laptop.

He was glad now that that girl he had asked out at the wedding last week had turned him down. He had regretted it almost immediately and was relieved later when she disappeared. He was too old for her – too jaded and battle-scarred – and besides, he wasn't ready to start a relationship with anyone at the moment. He was lousy company these days, and it wouldn't take him long to screw it up anyway. He felt trapped, numb, frozen in a moment in time and clueless as to how he could get unstuck. He'd be better off just throwing himself completely into his work. Fortunately, this job promised to be all-consuming, so he would have no time for a social life in any case.

His thoughts were interrupted by a light tap on the door. 'Come in,' he called.

As the door was pushed open, he was surprised to see the very person he had just been thinking about standing there – the petite platinum blonde from the wedding. That was weird.

'Hello.'

'Hi,' she said as she moved into the room, glancing back anxiously at the door.

Dev sat back in his chair. What on earth was she doing here? Then he remembered giving her his card, telling her to look him up. 'I can't believe you came to see me,' he said as she advanced towards his desk.

'Oh, I didn't!'

Dev looked at her quizzically, motioning her to a seat. 'You didn't?'

'No – at least, not in the way you mean.' She perched on the edge of the chair, biting her lip. She glanced at the door again.

'Look, I'd love to take you to lunch or something, but I've got a meeting in a minute. Could you—'

'Ah, Dev.' He was cut off by Richard bursting into the room. 'I see you've met Jenny,' he said, striding up to the desk. He sat in the chair beside her and took her hand while Dev looked on in bewilderment. 'Sorry, darling,' he said to Jenny. 'I got waylaid by some people out there. So – you two have met.'

'Yes, sort of …' Jenny trailed off.

Dev looked from one to the other. 'So this is …'

'Jenny. The girl I told you about.' Richard smiled proudly at her.

'We've met before,' Jenny said to Richard quietly.

'Oh, really? Where?'

'At that wedding I went to last week.'

'Oh! That's a coincidence.' A slow smile spread across Richard's face. 'Oh, my God, I hope you weren't the bloke who was trying to chat her up,' he said to Dev.

Dev scowled at Jenny, who squirmed in her seat. 'I apologise if I made a nuisance of myself,' he said to her coldly.

'I never said that.' Jenny blushed.

'I didn't realise at the time she was spoken for,' he added to Richard.

'She didn't say you were making a nuisance of yourself,' Richard said. 'Actually, she said you were very nice. Anyway,' he continued breezily, 'Jenny can't stay, she has to get to work. I just thought I'd bring her in to introduce you – not necessary, as it turns out. But why don't you come over for dinner at my place some evening and we can discuss how we're going to handle us going public?'

'Right. So you're ready for that? You don't want to keep it a secret any longer?'

'No, I think it's time. We're probably not going to get away with it much longer anyway, are we? We're bound to get found out sooner or later, and it's better if it's on our terms, don't you think?'

'Absolutely. We want to be leading this story, not following it.'

'Besides, we were hoping to go on holiday together, so it would be great if any media fuss could have died down by then. Jenny'd like to go to America.'

'Really?' Dev looked at her.

'Yeah, I've always wanted to go to Disneyland.'

'Fond of rollercoasters, are you?'

'I'm not big on them, but they have these giant teacups that spin around – they look fantastic. And you can meet Mickey Mouse, and there's Cinderella's castle. Everyone says it's amazing.'

'I don't think that's a good idea,' Dev said flatly to Richard.

'Disneyland? Or America in general?'

'Any of it – but especially Disneyland.'

'What have you got against Disneyland?' Jenny asked. 'I bet it's brilliant!'

'Yes, what *have* you got against it?' Richard asked.

'Richard, do I need to remind you the country's in the shit? The economy's going down the toilet, fast. People are worried about the environment. The last thing we need is you flying halfway around the world to meet Mickey Mouse and go for a ride in a giant teacup!'

'Oh.' Richard sighed. 'I suppose you have a point.'

'Besides, I don't think the first thing the public should see of Jenny is her taking you off on flash holidays like you've never gone on before. It sends out the wrong signal – about her as well as you.'

'So where do you suggest we go? Blackpool?' Richard said sarcastically.

'Why not? Holidaying in Britain would send a very positive message. And it would show your new relationship in a good light. You always used to go to France with Julia, but now you're with Jenny you go on a traditional British seaside holiday.'

'I don't mind,' Jenny said. 'I've never been to Blackpool.'

'Well, we'll see.' Richard threw Dev a huffy look. 'I think we should go somewhere more low-key.'

'I don't care where we go, as long as you're there.' Jenny beamed at him and he smiled back.

He glanced at his watch. 'Well, you'd better be off, hadn't you, darling?' he said.

'Nice to meet you again, Jenny.' Dev stood as she got up to go and shook her hand.

'You too. Bye.'

Richard followed her to the door and Dev heard them speaking in hushed tones for a few minutes. Then he gave her a brief kiss and she was gone.

'Jesus, Richard, are you kidding me?' Dev waved at the door that had just closed behind her.

'What?' Richard looked bewildered as he walked back across the room and stood in front of Dev's desk, his hands on his hips.

'You can't be serious.'

'About what?'

'About … this girl!'

'*Jenny?*'

'Yes, Jenny. I notice you waited to spring this on me until after I'd agreed to take the job.'

'But,' Richard spluttered, 'I didn't. I told you I was seeing someone.'

'Yes, but you didn't tell me who. You waited until I was committed before you introduced me to her.'

'What's the problem?' Richard asked.

Dev couldn't decide if he was being disingenuous. Surely he couldn't be that naïve. 'Where would you like me to start?'

'Blimey!' Richard sank into a chair. 'Tell me what you really think.'

'Believe me, you don't want to hear what I *really* think.'

'But *why*? I don't understand. What's so terrible about Jenny? You don't even know her.'

'Well, how the fuck old is she for starters?'

'She's twenty-four.'

Dev raised his eyebrows meaningfully.

'Twenty-four and a half,' Richard amended.

'If you think that makes it sound better, you're sadly mistaken.'

'She'll be twenty-five in May,' Richard persisted.

'Are you going to get her a clown?'

'Oh, shut up! She's very mature for her age. We don't even notice the age gap – and if it doesn't matter to us, I don't see how it can possibly matter to anyone else.'

'Don't you really?'

Richard stirred uncomfortably. 'Look, you don't have to worry about Jenny. She's a very sweet girl.'

'I'm sure she's great. Just not for you – not now.'

'Why the hell not?'

'Let me think. Maybe because you want to sell yourself as the next leader of the country? I mean, how do you think it's going to look? You're constantly banging on about the breakdown of the family, absent fathers, how important it is to support the traditional family. It's bad enough that you've left your wife and kids but now you've gone and shacked up with a – a child!' Dev remonstrated.

'Oh, come on, she's hardly a child. She's over twenty-one – old enough to vote,' Richard pointed out.

'Yes, and so is her father – and the fathers of other young girls her age. How do you think it will look to *them*?'

'Well, how it looks is up to you, isn't it?' Richard smiled coolly.

'You certainly don't believe in making my job easy, do you?'

'That's why I pay you the big bucks.'

Dev gave a bitter laugh. 'You do know I'm taking a massive pay cut to come and work for you?'

'Yes,' Richard said. 'You never cease reminding me of that fact.'

Dev stood and began pacing around the room.

'I don't see why you're getting so worked up about it,' Richard said reasonably. 'Plenty of men go out with much younger women. You're carrying on like I'm a paedophile! Jenny's twenty-four.'

'And you're thirty-six.'

'So are you!' Richard countered defensively.

'Actually, I'm only thirty-five.'

'Oh, yes, I forgot you're younger than me.' Richard thought for a moment. 'You're thirty-five and a half.'

'How old I am is beside the point,' Dev said. '*I'm* not shagging a twenty-four-year-old.'

'You're not shagging anyone,' Richard mumbled. 'That's your problem.'

'Neither am I putting myself forward as the next prime minister of this country,' Dev continued, ignoring him. 'Fantastic timing on the mid-life crisis, by the way – though isn't it a bit early for that?'

'For God's sake, Dev!'

But Dev was in his stride now and there was no stopping him. 'No, really, you couldn't have picked a better time to ditch the wife and kids and take up with an unsuitable girlfriend half your age. It's brilliant – a stroke of genius! Congratulations! What's next – a sports car?'

'I really don't see that it's such a big deal! Marriages break down all the time. There's nothing particularly shocking about that. If anything, it will help people to relate to me.'

'Not those people you've already sold yourself to as the champion of the traditional nuclear family. It doesn't exactly convey an image of stability, does it? You represent old-fashioned family values, tradition, continuity – that's what people like about you. It's like Father Christmas deciding he's not going to give any presents this year.'

'It's nothing like that!' Richard flopped against the back of his chair. 'You didn't seem to think any of this was a problem before,' he said eventually. 'You knew I was separated, you knew I was seeing someone new, but you didn't bat an eyelid. Then I bring Jenny to meet you and you go ballistic. What have you got against her – apart from her age? Because I don't believe for a minute it's just that.'

'Well, she's not—'

'What? *Our sort?*' Richard snarled, interrupting.

'No! Of course not! Jesus, don't be ridiculous! For one thing, you and I aren't even the same *sort*.'

They had been friends at Cambridge, but Richard had arrived from Harrow while Dev had come from a state school. Dev's background was solid middle class – not poor, but still light years away from Richard's privileged upbringing.

'What, then?'

'Well, she's not exactly Miss Moderate Party, is she?'

'I know what you think. You think she's just a flighty, frivolous girl without a serious thought in her head.'

'Well, if the cap fits …'

'Didn't stop you chatting her up, though, did it?'

Dev stopped pacing and sat down at his desk with a sigh.

'Sorry,' Richard said. He was silent for a moment, looking at Dev thoughtfully. 'You're not, are you – shagging anyone?'

Dev's jaw set. 'Not that it's any of your business, but … no, as it happens.'

'As it happens?' Richard looked at him probingly. 'That sounds promising. Have you been seeing anyone?'

'Not really. I'm just not interested. Not at the moment.'

'Not *interested*?'

'Jesus, will you stop repeating everything I say? Yes, not interested, okay? I've been out a few times, but I can't …' He ran a hand through his hair. 'I just *can't*,' he said finally. 'I can't, you know, get—'

'Oh! Right.' Richard seemed embarrassed. 'Well, um, maybe you should … get some help,' he said.

'Help?'

'Yes, you know … see a doctor.' Richard's eyes flitted around the room as he spoke.

'You think I need a *psychiatrist*?'

'Oh! No – that hadn't occurred to me, actually,' Richard said, surprised into looking at Dev. 'But I suppose it could be psychological, couldn't it?'

'What could?'

'You know, if you can't—' Richard broke off to clear his throat unnecessarily. 'If you can't get … *hard*.' The last word was barely audible.

Dev was aghast. 'I'm not *impotent*,' he snapped.

Richard's relief was almost palpable, his body relaxing. 'Oh, sorry

– I thought that was what you were trying to say. What is it, then?'

'I just can't get … interested. I feel numb. It's like I'm just going through the motions. I go out with a woman and I just want it to be over. I don't *care*, and I can't be arsed pretending I do – I don't *care* what she works at or what her hobbies are or where she's been on holiday or what music she likes or any of that crap. I can't enjoy myself – which means they don't enjoy themselves either.'

'Wow! I bet they're gutted when you don't call them for a second date,' Richard said, a tentative smile playing around his lips.

Dev laughed. 'I know. I'm a miserable git.'

'Well, it's early days,' Richard said, his smile fading as he glanced at the photo of Sally. 'It will pass.'

'I suppose so.' Dev sighed.

'You should come to Felix's birthday party next week,' Richard said. 'I'm sure Julia would love to see you.'

'I'd love to see her. Just make sure she doesn't try to set me up with anyone.'

'Are you sure? There are some very nice single mums in Felix's class.'

Dev smiled. 'They start young, these days, don't they? However, unlike you, I aim a little higher than kindergarten.'

'You know what I mean.'

'Yes, I do.' Dev sighed. 'About this thing with Jenny – are you sure you want to go public? Why not just keep seeing each other in secret for a bit longer?'

'No! Why would we want to do that? It's been a real nightmare keeping it quiet.'

'I just don't see the point in putting her through all that. And it's not going to look good when—'

'When what?' Richard looked closely at Dev. 'Oh. You don't think this is going to last, do you?'

'No, I don't.'

'You think it's just a fling. Well, you're wrong. I'm serious about Jenny. We're serious about each other.'

'Okay, I stand corrected,' Dev said, holding up his hands defensively. 'So, tell me about Jenny,' he said briskly. 'What do we know about her?'

'Well, she's been vetted.'

'Right. So we can be pretty sure she's not a terrorist. Anything else?'

'Look, just come over for dinner some evening. Then you can ask her anything you want to know.'

'I can hardly give her the third degree over dinner.'

'You want to give her the third degree? What do you want to know?'

'Everything.'

'Okay,' Richard said, standing to go. 'Well, why don't you call round to her flat?' He grabbed a piece of paper and a pen from Dev's desk and scribbled on it. 'That's her address,' he said. 'I'll tell her to expect you.'

That evening Dev felt a familiar tightening in his stomach as he pushed open the door of his house. Once it had been a refuge, but all his home represented now was a catalogue of what was missing. Instead of Sally's voice calling from the kitchen, there was silence. The enticing aromas of her cooking that had greeted him at the door had been replaced by the sterile smells of bleach and furniture polish, evidence that the cleaner had been.

He went into the kitchen and opened the fridge, gazing absently at the almost empty shelves. It had been stuffed when Sally lived here. She would spend evenings curled up on the sofa perusing cookery books, making epic grocery lists and planning elaborate meals to cook for him – meals that she rarely shared. Most days she would sit and chat to him as he ate, claiming she had already eaten. She was an excellent cook, but no matter how delicious the food was, he couldn't enjoy it because it was just a symptom of her illness. He sighed, taking a beer from the fridge and closing the door. He would have to go shopping, he thought as he opened the freezer and took out a pizza. He would buy some healthy stuff, start eating properly again. He turned on the oven and slid the pizza onto the shelf, then opened his beer and took it into the living room.

He threw himself onto the sofa, switched on the TV and put his feet up on the coffee table, flicking through the channels until he came to Sky News. The headlines were full of Tracey, bumping the latest government blunder into second place, with images of her battered face and the report of Damien's arrest. From Richard's point of view, it was a pity that the story gave the government a perfect opportunity to bury bad news, but he felt a grim satisfaction that Tracey's scumbag of a husband had nowhere to hide from the beam of publicity.

He flicked the TV off. He was glad it was out in the open and Tracey was safe, but he found the almost pornographic coverage of the story sickening. He sighed, sipping beer from the bottle, longing for Sally to talk to. He still found himself thinking of her when something happened during the day, storing it away to tell her later, and it still came like a punch to the gut every time he remembered that he couldn't. He hadn't realised until she was gone how much his life had revolved around her over the last couple of years.

She had been so excited about him taking this job, and he would have loved sharing it all with her. If she was here now, he would be telling her about Richard's new girlfriend, and they would laugh at Richard for succumbing to a premature mid-life crisis and agree it would never last, that Julia and he would end up back together. Dev couldn't see him staying with Jenny in the long term. He had been amazed when Richard had told him he and Julia were separating. They had always seemed perfectly matched, and in many ways, she had been the making of him. Jenny seemed like a sweet girl and he had nothing against her personally, but she just didn't seem Richard's type at all.

Then again, she wasn't Dev's type, and he had asked her out – and he had been about to do so again today. It was ridiculous. He had just been congratulating himself on his lucky escape when she had appeared in his office and the next thing he knew he was offering to take her to lunch. It was as though the rational part of his brain had switched off the minute she stepped into the room.

What had he been thinking? If Jenny was wrong for Richard, she was doubly wrong for him. He liked tall, dark-haired women with strong views on social justice – not platinum-haired dolls who wanted to visit Cinderella's castle. Then again, he mused, Jenny might be a brunette if she stopped dyeing her hair that improbable colour ...

His musings were interrupted by the shriek of the smoke alarm. Shit, the pizza. He jumped up and headed for the kitchen to see what he could salvage of his dinner.

Chapter 5

The following Saturday Jenny woke with a jolt to the high-pitched shriek of the door buzzer.

'Okay, okay,' she mumbled blearily to herself, trying to peel her eyes open as it sounded again, echoing the sickening pounding in her head. She staggered out of bed and into the hall, lunging for the intercom. 'Hello,' she croaked into the handset, leaning back against the wall for support and allowing her eyes to droop shut.

'Hello. It's Dev Tennant,' came the crisp reply.

Oh, bugger! She slid down the wall, resting her forehead wearily on her hand. She was in no shape to deal with *him* right now. What the hell was he thinking coming here at this hour? Bloody cheek!

'Come up,' she said, standing again and trying to sound bright and wide awake. 'It's on the first floor.' She buzzed him in. While she waited for him to come up the stairs, she took the opportunity to spend a few minutes rubbing her eyes and slapping her face in an effort to wake herself up.

It was only when she opened the door that she realised she had forgotten to put anything on and was standing in front of him in her favourite baby-doll pyjamas – very fifties Hollywood glamour and *very* flimsy. Jenny was a firm believer in wearing proper outfits, even to bed.

'Hi.' She smiled up at him, maintaining eye contact so that he couldn't drop his gaze to her chest. 'Come in.'

Dev hesitated. 'Sorry – did I get you out of bed? Are you ill?'

God, she must look dog rough. 'No, I'm fine, thanks. I just wasn't expecting you so early.' *Or at all.* 'What time is it?' she said accusingly.

Dev glanced at his watch. 'Ten past two.'

'Oh! Anyway, come in.' She turned around to lead him through to the kitchen.

'Christ! What happened?' Dev exclaimed.

'We had a party last night,' she mumbled, assuming he was referring to the state of the living room, which was a complete write-off. Hopefully the kitchen would be in better shape.

'I meant what happened to *you?*'

Christ, hadn't he ever seen anyone with a hangover before, she thought. Okay, so she probably *did* look like Keith Richards' evil twin, but it wasn't very nice of him to keep banging on about it. To her astonishment, she felt a warm hand on her back, burning through the flimsy material of her pyjama top.

'Hey!' she protested indignantly, wriggling away and turning to glare at him. Obviously she had given him the wrong impression by answering the door half naked, but if he thought it gave him permission to paw her, she'd knock that on the head right now.

'Sorry. Does it hurt?'

'No, it doesn't *hurt*, but it's bloody rude.'

'Are you sure?' His fingers touched the small of her back again gently.

'Yes, I'm sure – it's definitely rude. Now, would you please knock it off?'

'I meant are you sure it doesn't hurt?'

'*What* doesn't hurt?' She frowned at him over her shoulder.

'That.' He pointed to the small of her back, looking rather alarmed.

Jenny craned her neck around but she couldn't see what he was pointing at. Sighing impatiently, she went back to the full-length mirror by the door and peered over her shoulder at her reflection.

'Oh! Golly!' In the middle of her pyjama top was the print of a large boot. 'I wonder how that got there.'

'You mean you don't *know*?' Dev had followed her back down the hall and was scowling at the reflection of her back.

'No, no idea.' She examined the boot print speculatively. It was at least a man's size thirteen, she reckoned. 'Maybe I could do a search for the owner, like in *Cinderella*.' She giggled. 'Whoever fits the boot print …'

Dev did not look amused. 'Just don't expect to find Prince Charming at the end of the trail.'

'Anyway, no harm done,' Jenny said cheerily. 'Come on in.' She led him back through the living room to the kitchen. 'I'm afraid the place is a bit of a mess,' she said – completely unnecessarily, since every surface was covered with beer cans, trays of congealing dips, wine-stained glasses, bottles and pizza boxes. Cereal packets spewed their contents onto the worktop and tortilla chips crunched underfoot. Jenny hoped Dev didn't spot the bra that was hanging out of the cutlery drawer.

'It's not usually like this. We had a party last night.'

'You said.'

She was horribly aware of him towering over her, glowering disapprovingly.

'Um … why don't you sit down?' She waved vaguely in the direction of the table.

'Because there's nowhere to sit,' he said flatly.

'Oh, right. Hang on.' Bloody princess and the pea, she thought huffily, scooping up armfuls of bottles and overflowing ashtrays from the table. Still, she really wanted to get him sitting down. The flat was poky enough without him looming around the place, making it feel like something even a Polly Pocket estate agent would describe as 'bijou'. As she transferred dirty plates and glasses from the table to the worktop, she took the opportunity to stuff the bra into the cutlery drawer and slam it shut. She swept a pile of pizza boxes off a chair onto the floor.

'There you go,' she said, patting the seat and smiling up at him encouragingly, as if he was a recalcitrant puppy she was trying to train. After he had examined it fastidiously, Dev sat down and pushed back from the table to stretch his long legs in front of him.

'Okay, I'm all yours,' Jenny said, sitting opposite and folding her arms on the table. 'Ask me anything.'

'Don't you think you should, um …' Dev's eyes flitted around the room as he spoke, finally fixing on the ceiling.

'What?' Jenny tried to catch his eye, but he seemed to be deliberately avoiding hers. 'Come on, spit it out – don't be shy.'

'You know, um …' He nodded in her direction, but was still addressing his remarks to somewhere over her left shoulder. 'Put something on?' he said finally, looking distinctly uncomfortable.

'Oh, God!' Jenny shrieked, crossing her arms over her chest instinctively. She felt herself blushing. He'd got her so flustered she had completely forgotten she was still in her see-through baby-doll pyjamas, sitting here chatting to him with everything on show, like a member of staff at the best little whorehouse in north London.

'I'll be back in a sec.' She ran to her bedroom, grabbed her dressing gown from behind the door and pulled it on.

Ugh, no, she thought, pulling it off again. She felt at enough of a disadvantage already without having to talk to Dev in her dressing gown like some slobby housewife. Flinging off her pyjamas, she scrabbled in the wardrobe and grabbed the first things that came to hand. Hastily, she dragged on a pair of jeans and a fluffy pink cropped cardigan. Her fingers fumbled with the little pearl buttons and the angora was hot and itchy against her skin, but it would have to do. She didn't want to leave Dev alone for too long – God only knew what he might find! She checked her reflection in the mirror, running a hand through her hair and pinching her cheeks. Then she raced back to the kitchen.

'Sorry about that,' she said. 'Would you like some tea or coffee?'

'Coffee would be great, thanks.'

'Instant okay?' she asked, flicking the switch on the kettle.

'Fine.'

She took mugs and a jar of coffee from a cupboard and opened the fridge. 'Or a cocktail?'

'Sorry?'

'Would you like a cocktail instead?' She turned to him, still holding the fridge door open. 'There's some margarita mix from last night.'

'No, thanks. Just the coffee is fine.'

She rooted around in the fridge again. 'How about a Cosmopolitan?' she asked, brandishing a painted ceramic jug. 'It's got cranberry juice in it. It's very healthy – one of your five a day.'

'It's a bit early for cocktails, isn't it?'

Jenny looked at her watch. 'Not really. That's the great thing about sleeping late – it's already cocktail hour when you wake up.'

'Really, I'll just have coffee, thanks.'

'The thing is,' she bit her lip, 'I don't have any milk.'

'That's okay. I take it black.'

'You do? Great!' She closed the fridge door and went back to making the coffee.

'There you go,' she said, placing two steaming mugs on the table and sitting down opposite Dev again. To her annoyance, his eyes were still fixed on the ceiling.

'I'm down here.' She waved a hand in front of his eyes, trying to get his attention. 'It's okay, I'm decent. I'm not going to flash you again.'

'There's a fish finger on your ceiling,' he said, still gazing over her head.

'What?'

'Up there.' He pointed to a spot behind her. 'There's a fish finger.'

Jenny turned and looked up. 'So there is. Like I said, we had a party last night,' she said patiently. *Jesus, how many times?*

'Right.' Dev nodded, bemused.

She could see she was going to have to spell it out for him. 'Food fight.'

'Ah! Fish fingers are your weapon of choice?'

'*Sardines!*' Jenny exclaimed, slapping the table.

'Where?' Dev looked around, expecting to see sardines decorating the walls.

'No, I mean we *played* sardines,' Jenny said with a bright smile. 'That explains it, doesn't it?'

Dev looked at her blankly.

'The boot print,' she elucidated.

'Oh, right. The boot print.' Dev was bewildered. Why on earth, he wondered, was she at her party dressed like that? And what the hell was Richard doing with a girl who had parties that featured food fights and games of sardines? A girl who was still in bed at two o'clock in the afternoon and swanned about looking like a scale model Marilyn Monroe.

'So?' She was looking at him expectantly.

'Right.' He shook himself, finally focusing on her face – though his eyes still kept darting warily to the fish finger, as though he expected it to spring into life and attack him.

'Just ignore it,' she said. 'It'll come down when it's ready.'

'Okay.' He took an A4 pad from his briefcase and placed it on the table in front of him, then a pen from the inside pocket of his jacket.

'What do you want to know?' Jenny asked.

'You tell me.'

'Sorry?'

'What do I want to know? What do I *need* to know? What can they dig up on you to hit us with?'

'Nothing,' she said. 'Gosh, if that's all, you could have saved yourself the trip.'

Dev sighed. 'Look, I need you to be completely honest with me. Once the papers are on to you, they'll start digging around in your past for anything they can use to damage Richard. The other lot will be on to it too – not to mention Richard's enemies inside the Party.'

'He has enemies inside the Party?' She gasped.

Dev looked at her scathingly. 'Did you think it was all one big happy family?'

'No, of course not,' she said, feeling very naïve. That was exactly what she had thought. She knew politics was a cut-throat business, but she'd believed that inside the Party at least they were all on the same side, pulling together for Richard.

'When you're in Richard's position, you have enemies everywhere. That's why it's important you tell me everything. If I know what we're dealing with, it can be handled. What we don't want is for the other lot to spring any nasty surprises on us down the line and catch us on the hop. I don't need to end up fighting fires.'

'Okay.' Jenny tried to look more confident than she felt. Her mouth had suddenly gone dry.

'So, think,' Dev said. 'Is there anything in your past that could come back to haunt us?'

'Umm ...' Jenny screwed her eyes up to the right as if she was mentally raking through her past. Then she remembered reading somewhere that if you did this on one particular side, it was an indication that you were lying. Only trouble was, she couldn't remember which side. Dev was watching her intently, so she repeated the pantomime to the left and centre as well, just to be on the safe side. It was the sort of thing he would know and pounce on.

'No, nothing,' she said finally, with all the innocence she could muster.

Dev stared hard at her. 'Are you sure about that?'

'Positive.'

'Because if there is anything, they *will* dig it up. So it's better you tell me now.'

'There's nothing,' she said, a little shakily.

'No shady characters in your family?'

'No. No family, really.' For the first time in her life that seemed like a plus.

'No dodgy ex-boyfriends?'

'No. Although …' She hesitated, reconsidering.

'Yes?'

'No.' She shook her head. 'Nothing important.'

'I'll be the judge of that.'

'Well … a few of them did turn into stalkers,' she said.

'Stalkers?'

'Some guys just have a hard time letting go.'

'Hmm. I can imagine.'

'But it's nothing scary or threatening,' she added.

'Have you always worked as a nanny?'

'Yes, mostly.'

'Have you ever been involved with anyone you worked for?'

'You mean—'

'I mean sexually.'

'No! Absolutely not!'

'Ever done any nude modelling, topless stuff?'

'No!'

'I have to ask,' Dev said unapologetically. 'Look, nothing you tell me goes beyond this room.'

Like a priest, Jenny thought, eyeing him warily. He was a very unlikely confessor, but something in his manner inspired trust. She almost felt tempted to confide in him. *Almost.*

'There's just nothing to tell.'

'No pornography?'

'No.'

'Homemade sex tapes?'

'*No!*'

'What about with Richard?'

'What about— You mean have we made sex tapes?' she shrieked, outraged. 'Why don't you ask him?'

'I'm asking you.'

'I'm sure he doesn't want you to pry into his sex life.'

'Anything else kinky?' he continued, ignoring her. 'Threesomes, orgies ...'

'No!'

'Bondage, S and M?'

'No,' she snapped. 'It's all perfectly ordinary. Look, I really don't think Richard would want you to ...' But Dev wasn't listening. He was preoccupied with jotting something in his notepad, smirking to himself.

Jenny leaned over to peer at what he'd written. 'Oh, that's not true! Cross that out,' she demanded, jabbing her finger angrily on the pad where he'd scrawled, 'Sex life – DULL!' in his large, loopy hand-writing. 'I never said that!'

Bugger him! His rapid-fire interrogation had caught her off

guard. She should have just told him to fuck off and mind his own business. Why did he have to come here today, when she was hungover and not firing on all cylinders?

Dev smiled at her discomfiture. 'You said it was ordinary,' he said. 'Not exactly a ringing endorsement.'

'You know that's not what I meant,' she fumed. 'I meant no – no ligatures, no third parties, no golden showers, no orgies, no plastic bags, no oranges stuffed in mouths, no one taking a dump on anyone.'

'Spare me the detail,' Dev drawled.

'Well, you asked!'

Yes, you *did* ask, Dev chided himself.

'Were you with Richard before he separated from Julia?' he asked, resuming his bad cop-bad cop routine.

Jenny hesitated. 'What did *he* tell you?'

'He says not.'

'Well, that's right. I wasn't.'

Dev looked at her sharply. 'Is that what he told you? Or do you know it for a fact?'

'It's what he told me. And I believe him,' she added staunchly.

'Good for you.' He shot her an almost pitying look.

Jenny longed to ask him if he knew any different, but she daren't risk it. If only she felt he was more on her side.

'Have you ever been arrested or in any trouble with the law?'

'No, of course not.'

'What about your politics?'

'My what?'

'Your politics. Have you ever been involved in any anti-government protests, any dodgy political organisations?'

'No, absolutely not.' Phew! At least she was on safe ground there.

'Ever voted for the other lot?'

'Oh, no, I never vote,' she told him with a reassuring smile.

'You *what*?' he said witheringly.

'I – I never vote,' she faltered, her smile fading. Shit! That had been meant to put his mind at rest but he looked ... shocked almost.

She was saved by Ollie lurching in from the living room, a cigarette hanging on his bottom lip. 'Morning, darling.' He burped gently, weaving up to Jenny and squinting at her through the smoke, ignoring Dev. He appeared to be still drunk and he was so tall and gangly that Jenny was afraid he'd topple over and set her hair on fire. She cringed a little as he swayed in front of her. He looked incredibly louche, not helped by the fact that he was dressed in a school uniform, tie askew.

'I didn't know you were home. Where were you?'

'I'm not sure.' He frowned. 'I think I was under the coats in Liam's room.'

'Why were you in Liam's room?'

'I seem to remember there were some people in my bed when I got home this morning – and Liam wasn't around, so ...' He shrugged.

'People? What sort of people?'

'A mixture, I'd say, judging by the shape of the many-backed beast they were making. I didn't hang around to find out.'

'So what happened to you last night?' Jenny smiled up at him.

'I got led astray by *the* most divine little stagehand. You should have seen him, Jen.' He sighed dreamily. 'He's got it all – six-pack, arms, the lot.'

'Arms! You don't see those every day.'

'I know! Total chav, of course – needs a lot of work. But he's a nice little fixer-upper for me. How was the party? Sorry I missed it.'

'It was fun.'

Ollie threw a suspicious glance in Dev's direction, but still didn't acknowledge his presence. 'Having leftovers for breakfast, I see,' he said without lowering his voice, nodding to Dev and winking at Jenny. 'Always a good sign.'

'Oh, no, this is Dev. He's Richard's spin doctor. He wasn't at the party. Dev, this is Ollie.'

'Hello.' They nodded at each other.

'You've done your cardie up all wrong, sweetie.' Ollie smiled affectionately, dropping to his knees in front of Jenny and undoing the buttons with clumsy fingers, the cigarette dangling precariously from his lip. He did them up again properly, but not before he'd treated Dev to a flash of Jenny's bra.

'There you go, poppet.' He gave Jenny's chest an affectionate pat. The cigarette bobbed dangerously as he spoke, but he caught it just in time.

'Thanks.' Jenny blushed slightly. 'What's this?' she asked, fingering the school tie.

'Oh, I left the theatre in a bit of a hurry last night.' Ollie rolled his eyes. 'Had to strike while the stagehand was hot. I ended up going clubbing in this little number. Actually, you wouldn't believe its pulling power! And I slept in it last night – can you tell?' He spread his arms wide for Jenny to inspect the costume.

'Mmm, a bit,' she said, soft-pedalling. He looked as if he'd just got out of a skip. Jenny began reknotting the tie.

'Shit! I'm going to be in the doghouse with bloody Wardrobe – that woman already hates me. We're not supposed to leave the theatre in costume. She'll probably try to get me the sack. The makeup artist loves me, though.'

'Well, her work is done,' Jenny said, giving his chiselled jaw a pat.

Dev took a sip of coffee and put his mug on the table with a bang.

Ollie stared at him through glassy eyes.

'What's your relationship with Jenny?' Dev asked him, picking up his pen and gazing studiously at his pad.

'Ah. Well.' Ollie grinned. 'That's rather complicated.'

'No, it isn't,' Jenny shot him a warning look. 'Ollie is one of my flatmates,' she said to Dev.

'One? You have more?'

'Yes – Liam. I don't know where he is.'

'He must have got lucky last night,' Ollie said to Jenny. 'Probably went to stay at her place.'

That seemed likely, Jenny thought, given the bra in the cutlery drawer. Besides, Liam always got lucky – though he would claim that luck had nothing to do with it.

'I'll give your uniform a zizz with the iron later, if you like?' she said to Ollie.

'Oh, would you? Thanks!' Ollie lurched down to give her a sloppy kiss on the cheek. 'Jenny's a whizz with an iron,' he said to Dev. 'She's a bit of an all-round domestic goddess, in fact.' He put his arm around her shoulders.

'Really?'

Jenny could understand Dev's scepticism, given the state of the place.

'Well, kids, I can't stay,' Ollie said cheerfully. 'Is that coffee?' He grabbed Dev's mug and took several large slugs before putting it back in front of him. 'Thanks. Got to go – I'll be late for rehearsal. Bye, darling.' He bent to kiss Jenny on the cheek and then he was gone.

'So,' she said, turning to Dev, 'where were we?'

'I was asking you about your politics.'

'Oh! Yes.' Damn, she was hoping he'd have lost his place.

'You were telling me you never vote.'

'Ah, well, that's not strictly true, actually. I did vote on *The X Factor* final last year.'

'Really?' Dev said drily.

Jenny squirmed uncomfortably under his steady gaze. 'The thing is, I never got signed up to vote when I came here. To vote on *The X Factor*, you just send a text. They should have that in general elections – I bet loads more people would vote.'

'Right, we'll have to get you registered,' he said, making a note. 'Now, what about work? Who are you working for at the moment?'

'Alice and Michael Young. I'm nanny to their little boy Oscar. He's six. But they're moving away next week.'

'So you'll be looking for another job?'

'Yes, but I'm going to take a few weeks off first. I was owed some holiday pay.' She had decided to take a break before looking for another job because she wanted to be free to go to Brighton with Richard for the Moderate Party Conference at the beginning of October. She didn't know much about politics, but she wanted to learn so she could be a real part of his life, and she knew the Party Conference would be the best place to immerse herself in his world and find out more about the things that were most important to him.

'Okay, about these ex-boyfriends—'

She was rescued by the intercom. 'Oh, who could that be?' She leaped up to answer it, grateful for the reprieve.

'Hello, Jenny, it's Alan Hodge,' a familiar voice said.

'Oh!' Jenny gasped. 'Um … okay, come in.' She buzzed the door open, her eyes darting in panic to Dev.

'Everything okay?' he asked.

She realised she was standing dumbly with the entryphone still in her hand. 'It's Mr Hodge,' she said vaguely. 'I'd forgotten it was his day,' she said, more to herself than to Dev.

'Who's Mr Hodge?'

'He's … he's, um … he's the plumber!'

'Oh, right.' Dev drank some coffee. Then he did a double-take. 'Your plumber has a *day*?' he exclaimed.

'Oh, well … the loo is a bit tricky.' Jenny laughed nervously. 'Very high maintenance.'

'So how often does he come, the plumber?'

'Oh, I've never asked him – that's a bit personal.' She giggled shrilly. God, she was losing it! She had to get Dev out of here. 'Sorry, stupid joke,' she said, sobering up. 'Once a month. Look, do you think we could finish this another day?'

'Well, there's a bit more I want to go through with you, and I'd rather get it done now, if that's all right with you.'

'It's just – Mr Hodge …' Jenny trailed off unhappily.

'Just leave him to it. He must know where everything is by now. I'm sure he doesn't need you to hold his hand.'

'Well, he's a bit shy.'

'I won't try to engage him in conversation.'

'And he does like me to … um, hold his tools and stuff.'

'I bet he does!' Dev said.

'And what if you want to use the loo?' Jenny said, brightening. Ha! That would shift him.

'I'll hang on,' Dev said tightly, clearly not about to budge.

'Oh, okay,' she said, deflated. 'I'd better go and let him in.'

Dev waited in the kitchen while Jenny went to the front door. He couldn't understand for the life of him what was going on with her. She seemed jittery as hell over the plumber calling. The front door opened and he could hear her whispering frantically to Mr Hodge. As they passed the kitchen door, he caught a glimpse of a tall middle-aged man with grey hair dressed in a smart suit. He looked more like a stockbroker than a plumber. Even more incongruously, he was carrying a large carpet bag.

'You know where everything is,' Jenny was saying very loudly to Mr Hodge, who was evidently deaf. 'Why don't you get started in the bathroom? I'll be right with you.'

'Was that him?' Dev asked, as Jenny reappeared in the kitchen. 'The plumber?'

'Yes, of course.'

'He doesn't look much like a plumber to me.'

'What did you expect?' she said indignantly. 'A little man in overalls carrying a spanner?'

'Well … yes.' Not unreasonably, he thought.

'He takes pride in his appearance,' Jenny said. 'There's nothing wrong with that.'

'I'm not saying there is. I just think he might ruin his suit getting to grips with your loo.'

'Oh, he brings a change of clothes.'

'And what's with the carpet bag?'

'That's … that's his toolbag. He's a bit old-fashioned. So, where were we?' Jenny said.

'Actually, I'm looking for a plumber myself. Maybe I could ask Mr Hodge—'

'He's not taking on any new clients,' Jenny said hastily. 'He's practically retired. He only works for a few people now – in fact, I think I'm the only one.'

'Still, no harm in asking,' Dev said. He was out of his seat and striding down the hall before Jenny could stop him. He wanted to satisfy his curiosity about Jenny's plumber – he felt there was something not quite right about him. If nothing else, he wanted to see Mr Hodge at work on the loo in his expensive suit.

'Oh, no, wait!' Jenny trotted after him, but she couldn't keep up with his long strides, and besides, the corridor was too narrow for her to get in front of him.

Noises were emerging from the door at the end, so Dev made a beeline for that and pushed it open.

He didn't know what he had expected to see, but he certainly wasn't prepared for the sight of Mr Hodge's hairy thighs and arse bulging out of a frilly French maid's outfit. He was on all fours, washing the bathroom floor.

'I'm scrubbing as hard as I can, Mistress,' he panted, hearing the door open behind him.

Dev took in the situation at a glance. Jenny caught up with him and he turned to her. 'Oh, God!' he groaned. 'You're a prostitute!'

Mr Hodge turned around, cowering in shame when he saw Dev.

'I am not!' Jenny protested indignantly. 'Now look what you've done. You've scared poor Mr Hodge.' She pulled the bathroom door closed. 'I think you'd better leave' she said with dignity, pulling herself up to her full five feet.

'Don't worry,' Dev thundered, 'I'm going.' He strode quickly to the door.

'Wait, it's not what you think!' Jenny called, running after him.

'Really?' He stopped at the door and turned to her. Arms folded, he glared down at her. If she could put an innocent spin on this, he should be taking lessons from her.

'I know it looks a bit … funny. But I'm not a prostitute. It's all perfectly innocent. He's never laid a finger on me. He just cleans the bathroom.'

'In a French maid's uniform?'

'Yes.'

'And he calls you "Mistress"?'

'Yes … well, he does like me to boss him about a bit while he does it. It's just a little game he likes to play.' She giggled nervously.

'Right. And he pays you to … play this game with him?'

'Yes.'

'So you're a dominatrix,' Dev said flatly.

'No!' Jenny protested. 'I mean, it's not as if I do this sort of thing for a living. Mr Hodge is my only—'

'Client?'

'I wouldn't call him that.'

'So it's more of a hobby for you?'

'Look, just stay and I'll explain everything – please?'

Dev sighed. 'All right,' he said eventually. 'But this had better be good.'

'It all started out by accident – it was a complete misunderstanding,' Jenny said when they were both seated at the kitchen table again.

'A misunderstanding?' Dev looked at her disbelievingly.

'Yes. You see, when I first moved into this flat, I used to get a lot of strange phone calls. Eventually I realised that the woman who lived here before me was a call girl. Anyway, one day the doorbell rang and it was Mr Hodge. He said someone had sent him, and he was here to do the bathroom. As it happened, I was waiting for the landlord to send a plumber around, so I let him in. I just showed him to the bathroom and left him to get on with it.'

'And you didn't think there was anything strange about him?'

'No … well, I did think he was a bit smartly dressed for a plumber. But he asked if he could get changed in the bathroom so I presumed he'd brought his overalls with him. He said something about having brought his own costume, and I remember thinking it was a bit odd that he called it a "costume". But it takes all sorts, doesn't it?'

'Evidently.'

'Well, after a while he called that he was ready, so I went to see what he wanted – and, like you today, I found him all togged out in his little French maid's outfit. You can't imagine the shock I got!'

'I don't have to imagine,' Dev interjected.

'He could see how shocked I was, poor old thing.' Jenny smiled fondly. 'He was absolutely mortified. He was so disappointed when I explained about the girl who'd lived here before me and that she'd moved. So anyway, one thing led to another, and … here we are,' she finished.

'Right. And at no point during this charming conversation did it occur to you to tell Mr Hodge that he'd made a mistake and send him on his way?'

'Well, yes, of course it did. I told him that exact thing. I wasn't too hard on him because he was so embarrassed and I didn't want to make him feel worse. But I told him in no uncertain terms that he'd got the wrong person and that I didn't provide those kinds of … um, services. But he was so upset, and I felt really sorry for him. He'd come all this way, and it had taken him ages to screw up the courage. So I said I'd give it a go – just the once, you know, to cheer him up so that his journey hadn't been completely wasted.'

Dev raised his eyes to Heaven, but said nothing.

'He was very clear that there was no sex involved. He just wanted to clean my bathroom, and for me to be a real stickler about it. Well, I didn't have the heart to throw him out without at least giving it a bash.'

'And you discovered you had a natural talent for it?'

'No,' Jenny frowned, 'not at first. I did find it a bit embarrassing bossing Mr Hodge around. He's a lot older than me for one thing, and he's very distinguished too. He's a magistrate, you know. But he told me what sort of things to say and how to act. It was quite good fun once I got the hang of it. I started to enjoy it – especially once I got my own outfit.'

'You – you have an outfit?' Dev croaked.

'Yes. It's very tasteful, not revealing or anything. And it's not rubber, either, in case that's what you're thinking. Really it's more burlesque. I could show you.'

'That won't be necessary.'

'Anyway, that first day he insisted on paying me. When he told me the going rate for this sort of thing, I couldn't believe it!'

'So that was when you decided to continue?'

'Well, I was pretty skint and it was a lot of money. I said I'd give him a discount since I didn't know the ropes or even if I'd be any good at it, but he wouldn't hear of it. So we agreed to give each other a go and see how we got on, and … well, we haven't looked back!' she concluded cheerfully. 'It's just a bit of fun. I mean, there's no law against it, is there?'

Dev looked at her stonily.

'Oh, yes … I suppose there is,' she mumbled. 'But it's not one of those really serious laws that you're not supposed to break,' she continued more boldly. 'Not like murder or something.'

'Didn't it bother you that what you were doing was … wrong?' Dev asked, realising he sounded like a nun.

'Well, I felt very mean not helping Mr Hodge with the cleaning. But he really didn't want me to. It would have sort of spoiled his fun.'

'That's not quite what I meant.'

'There was absolutely no sex involved,' she said. 'He never touched me. It was money for old rope, really. And besides—' She stopped herself.

'Besides?' Dev prompted.

'Well, you should see the job he does on the bathroom!'

Dev rolled his eyes in exasperation.

'He really makes it sparkle,' Jenny said defensively. 'I could never get it that clean myself. He scrubs the grouting with a *toothbrush*!'

'Does Richard know about Mr Hodge?'

'Oh, no. I didn't think he'd understand.'

'Very wise. Look, you're going to have to give him the sack.'

'R-Richard?' Jenny stammered in dismay.

Dev shook his head. 'Mr Hodge.'

'And you're not going to walk out on me?' Jenny smiled hopefully.

'No, but you'll have to be straight with me from now on,' he said sternly. 'Any more surprises like Mr Hodge and I'm out.'

'Oh, my God, Mr Hodge!' Jenny clapped a hand to her mouth. 'He's still in the bathroom.'

'Better let him out.'

Chapter 6

Jenny finally persuaded Mr Hodge out of the bathroom and he scuttled to the door, but Dev was there before him, blocking his exit. 'No, you don't,' he said implacably, his arms folded. 'We need to talk first.'

Despite Jenny's pleas for clemency on Mr Hodge's behalf, Dev forced him to sit down and grilled him mercilessly until he was satisfied that he had been sworn to secrecy and vowed never to return or to tell anyone what had transpired between him and Jenny. Finally he was allowed to go, and Jenny saw him to the door.

'I'm really sorry about all that,' she whispered, glancing back towards Dev. 'And sorry I can't, you know … see you any more.'

'Ah, well, all good things must come to an end, I suppose,' he muttered. 'I will miss coming here. But to be honest, I think my days as a bathroom slave are numbered. Very hard on the knees, you know, when you get to my age. Might be time to retire.'

'Oh, you should have said.' Jenny felt guilty. 'I hope I wasn't too … exacting. But you could have stopped any time, you know.'

'You were perfect. I couldn't have wished for a better mistress. We've had a pretty good innings, I think. It's been a lot of fun.' He smiled at her.

'I've enjoyed it too.' Jenny beamed back.

'Well, take care of yourself, Jenny. You're a wonderful girl. Don't let anyone tell you otherwise,' he said darkly, throwing a filthy look at Dev before he turned to go.

'There was no need to humiliate him like that,' she said crossly to Dev as she came back into the room. 'He'd never have told anyone what he was up to here anyway.'

'You can't be too careful.'

'But you could have gone a bit easier on him. You saw how embarrassed he was about the whole thing.'

'Bloody should be, stupid old goat!' He got up and followed her into the kitchen. 'I think we need to start again from the beginning,' he said. 'What else haven't you told me?'

'Nothing, really. Mr Hodge just … slipped my mind.'

'Right.'

Jenny was standing in the middle of the kitchen. 'Look, I want to get this place sorted out. Do you mind? I really am a bit obsessive compulsive about the cleaning.'

'Okay, go ahead. We can talk at the same time. Can I help?'

Jenny pulled a black bin bag from a cupboard and handed it to him. 'You can fill this up.'

Dev took it. 'Wait – am I going to have to pay you?'

'Only if you do a really good job,' Jenny said. Then she pulled on a pair of yellow rubber gloves and filled the sink with hot, sudsy water. 'So, what else do you want to know?' she asked, swishing the water with her hand.

'You said you have no family,' Dev said. He had removed his suit jacket and rolled up his sleeves and was hurling pizza boxes into the bag.

'That's right.' Jenny plunged a pile of dishes into the sink and started scrubbing, rinsing them under a scalding tap before placing them on the draining board.

'Your parents are both dead?' he probed.

'My father's dead. I don't know about my mother. She left.'

'*Left*?'

She was glad she had her back to him. She heard him stop what he was doing and sensed that he was watching her. 'She just walked out one day – disappeared. No one knew where she went. We never saw her again.'

'Christ! How old were you when this happened?'

'Six.'

'Shit!' he mumbled.

She took a deep breath, deciding she might as well get the whole story out of the way now, especially while she still had her back to him. She hated the sympathy that it inevitably provoked. The pitying looks made her skin crawl, especially if they came from someone she wasn't close to. It enraged her. She didn't feel sorry for herself – what right had anyone else to feel sorry for her? In fact, how dare they?

'She left me with a neighbour, said she was going shopping for the day, and that was it. She never came home.'

'What made them so sure she'd walked out? I mean, that she hadn't been—'

'Murdered?' Jenny gave a short laugh. 'It was pretty obvious, apparently. She'd taken all her stuff, her passport and everything, and she'd withdrawn a pile of money from their bank account. Anyway,' she continued, 'my father kind of lost it after she left. He started drinking, stopped going to work. He couldn't cope. So eventually I got put into foster care.'

Dev went back to work. She heard the bag rustle as he moved around the kitchen scooping stuff into it.

'What was that like?'

'Oh, it was a barrel of laughs.'

'Sorry. Stupid question.'

'Nah, it could have been okay, I suppose. It just wasn't. At first I thought it was going to be brilliant. The first family I went to had two daughters, and I thought it would be great having sisters.'

'It wasn't?'

'God, no. They were a right pair of wagons. They already had each other, they didn't want me, and they did everything they could to get rid of me. They used to do stuff and blame it on me to get me into trouble.'

'Like what?'

'Break things, make a mess, that sort of thing.'

'Didn't their parents ever see what was going on?'

She shrugged. 'If they did, they turned a blind eye. They were their real children. They were the ones they cared about. Besides, I was the foster kid – I was supposed to be trouble.'

'Right, that's that lot,' he said, tying a knot in the top of the bin bag. 'Got a sweeping brush?'

She gesticulated at a corner of the room. 'Over there.'

'So they got you thrown out?'

'Well, it wasn't that easy. As I was the foster kid, allowances were made. They had to move on to bigger things – stealing money, vandalising their stuff. The last straw was when they keyed their dad's car and claimed they'd seen me do it.'

'And they didn't believe you hadn't?'

'Oh, at that stage I didn't even bother denying it. I wanted out of there as much as they wanted to be rid of me. So I was bundled back into care. I didn't really mind the care home – at least all the kids were in the same boat. But Social Services always wanted to get foster families for us.' She laughed bitterly. 'They thought we were better off in a "loving home environment".'

'So you were fostered again?'

'Yeah, a few times. I never really took, though. It wasn't their fault. I was a teenager by then, and living up to the whole trouble-child thing without any help from anyone. I was a bit wild, I suppose. The next family I was sent to had teenage boys – big mistake!'

'What happened?'

'I got kicked out when they caught me messing around with their precious son.' She put the last of the cutlery in the wire rack and pulled out the plug. 'I don't think I even fancied him particularly. I was just acting up because I wanted to go back to the home.'

'And were you sent back there?'

'No.' She watched the water drain out of the sink and ran the tap to clear away the suds. 'I was sent to another family.' She was silent for a while. 'I blotted my copybook there big time,' she said quietly. 'Anyway,' she went on, more brightly, 'then I left school and I was free of the lot of them. The last day of school, I ran home, burned my uniform in the back garden, packed my bags and moved to London.'

'Have you ever … tried to find your mother?' he asked hesitantly.

'Yes, but I didn't get anywhere with it – and I wasn't going to get obsessed.'

The truth was, her attempts to find her mother had been pretty half-hearted. She had done it more out of a feeling that she should than any real desire to, and she had been relieved rather than disappointed when her searches had turned up nothing. Afraid of what she might find, she had stacked the odds against success by searching for her mother with her married name – and what were the chances she was still using it if she'd wanted to disappear? Besides, Jenny knew that if her mother wanted to find her, it would be easy enough for her. She had disappeared because she wanted to, and there was no reason to suppose that had changed.

'What about your father? When did he die?'

She watched Dev sweep the last round of crumbs into the dustpan. 'A couple of years before I moved here. But I hadn't seen him much for a long time before that.' She took a cloth and an antibacterial spray from the cupboard beneath the sink and began wiping down the worktops. Funny, she didn't usually go on about her childhood so much all in one go. It unnerved her a little, but strangely, she didn't feel uncomfortable, as she did when she told boyfriends about it, even if she only fed it to them in dribs and drabs. Maybe it was easier to talk about it to someone who didn't really care about her – someone who perhaps actively disliked her. She wasn't on edge because she knew there was no danger of Dev feeling the need to respond by crushing her to him and telling her he would make everything all right. It seemed that the appropriate antidote to childhood trauma was suffocation. She hated boyfriends making a big deal of it and casting her as a tragic victim, coming over all protective. She really didn't get the protective thing. What the hell did they think they were going to protect her from – the past? How was that supposed to work, unless you were bloody Superman and could turn back time? That was one of the things she loved about Richard – he was too self-absorbed to take it in, which suited her just fine. 'So – not exactly a poster child for family values, am I?' she said, turning to him with a smile.

He had stowed the brush back in its corner and was looking at her carefully. 'I hope you don't think—'

Whatever he was about to say, he was interrupted by Ollie erupting back into the flat.

'Golly, still here?' he said to Dev as he swept into the kitchen sucking a lollipop, still dressed in his school uniform.

'Mmm – it took a bit longer than I'd expected,' Dev said, looking at his watch.

'Thanks for the help.' Jenny smiled at him, waving around the kitchen, which was now sparkling. She would defy Mr Hodge to have done a better job.

'You're welcome.' He smiled back. 'And you didn't once use your whip on me.'

Jenny giggled. 'I hope you're not too disappointed. Tell you what – I won't charge you this time.'

'So what have you two been up to?' Ollie asked, sitting at the table and pulling Dev's A4 pad towards him.

'Oh, Dev's just been asking me a few questions about my past, finding out about me.'

'You want to know about Jenny's exes? "Dodgy ex-boyfriends",' he read. 'You've put "none". Well, that's not right for a start.' He crossed a line through it and turned over a new page. 'You're going to need more room,' he said, handing the pad back to Dev and sticking the lollipop into his mouth.

Ollie waved Dev to the chair opposite him. Dev sat down, picked up his pen and held it poised over the pad, as if he was about to take dictation.

'Okay, there was Colin.' Ollie brandished the lollipop at him. 'He was dodgy.'

'In what way?'

'Well,' Ollie mused, 'he had this terrible novelty facial hair, and he knew way too much about computers.'

'That's not really the sort of thing I'm concerned about.'

'Oh, I'm sure if you looked into it you'd find he was up to all sorts. Why don't you just put a question mark over him for the moment – for further investigation at a later date? Well, suit yourself,' he said when Dev didn't move to write anything. 'Okay, then there was Paul. He was seriously dodgy.'

'He was not!' Jenny protested.

'Oh, come on! He claimed to be metrosexual, but he was an out-and-out friend of Dorothy, if you ask me. He used to go on spa weekends – voluntarily!'

'There's no law against a man having a few facials,' Jenny said.

'Darling, you don't have to tell *me* that. There is, however, a law against kidnapping.'

Dev's eyes shot up. 'Kidnapping?'

'Oh, yes.' Ollie nodded. 'When Jenny broke up with him, Paul took Johnny. He's been holding him hostage ever since.'

'Who's Johnny?'

'He's my baby,' Jenny said.

'He posts pictures of him on the internet, on his Facebook and Bebo pages where he knows Jenny will see them, just to torture her – and to make sure she doesn't delete him from her friends.'

'I don't think he's taking proper care of him either,' Jenny said. 'Johnny's hair goes all crazy if it's not washed and combed properly. He looked awful in that last lot of pictures Paul posted.'

Dev was appalled. 'But – but he can't do that!'

'Well, he did. He says the only way I'll ever see Johnny again is if I go back to him.'

'Have you informed the police?'

'The police? No … I didn't think they'd be able to do anything. Do you think they would?' she asked hopefully.

'*Of course.*' Dev frowned, 'I take it he was the father?'

'Whose father?'

'The father of your baby—'

'I don't have a baby.' Jenny looked perplexed.

'But you said—'

Ollie burst out laughing. 'Oh, that's Paul, all right – half man, half guinea pig.'

'What?' Now Dev was confused.

'Oh, you thought I was talking about a real baby!' Jenny laughed. 'Johnny's not a baby – well, he is, but not that kind of baby. He's – was – my guinea pig.'

'You're talking about a *guinea pig*?'

'Yes. Johnny Scrambod, to give him his full name. So, do you still think the police would be able to get him back?'

'I doubt they'd want to get involved in a custody battle over a guinea pig.'

Jenny sighed despondently.

'So you don't think Paul's kidnapping record is a problem?' Ollie asked.

'Not from my point of view, no.'

'Right. Well, the others were a pretty blameless lot, I suppose, if you're going to take such a broad view of it. Peter ... Mac ... Laurence ...' He seemed to be mulling them over in his mind, giving each due consideration before dismissing them as non-threatening. 'I don't know about the Irish ones, of course – apart from Liam, and he'd never do anything to hurt Jen.'

'Liam was never my boyfriend!' Jenny protested.

Ollie looked up at her queryingly. 'I thought you said you nearly got expelled from school when his ma caught you in bed together.'

Jenny blushed, her eyes darting to Dev to check his reaction. He didn't look pleased. 'It wasn't like that,' she said crossly to Ollie. 'We weren't doing anything. I just went over to his house because I was locked out at home and it was bloody freezing.'

Liam had let her in through his window. She could still remember the relief of feeling warm and safe in the sanctuary of his bedroom as she sat huddled against the radiator in her holey tights and thin denim jacket. Eventually she had crawled into bed with him in all her clothes and spent the night snuggled up to him. Absolutely nothing had happened, but the next morning Mrs Mulligan had found them and gone ballistic. Of course, no matter how much Liam protested that they weren't doing anything wrong, Jenny had got all the blame for leading him astray. She was Trouble, with a capital T – everyone knew that.

'Liam was my best friend,' she said to Dev. 'That's all.' *All* – it seemed wrong to put it like that, as if it didn't count for much. She didn't know how she would have survived school – or her various homes, for that matter – without him.

'You don't have to answer to me for every boyfriend you've ever had,' he said to her, 'but I am a bit worried about the ones you said turned into stalkers. What form did the stalking take?'

'Oh, the usual. Sometimes just hanging around outside here or going to places where they knew I'd be. And they'd cyberstalk me on Facebook and Bebo. One of them spread rumours about me online.'

'You're on Bebo and Facebook? You'll have to shut them down.'

'Why?'

'We don't want your personal stuff splashed all over the internet. And if it allows people to spread rumours about you in a public domain—'

'But it's not exactly public,' Jenny interrupted. 'You decide who has access to your pages. Only people I've accepted as my friends can view them.'

'And how many friends do you have?'

'Well, a few.'

'How many?' he persisted.

'I've got about sixty on Facebook.'

'And on Bebo?'

'Um … about five hundred.'

'You've obviously been very selective. I take it you don't know who all these people are in real life?'

'Well … no, not exactly,' she admitted. 'A lot of them I only know online.' In fact, she had a deliberate policy of taking on as a friend anyone who requested it. Though she was uncertain whether she wanted to find her mother, she had dreamed for years of her mother finding *her*. It was one of the reasons she was so keen to maintain a presence online. She had heard stories of estranged families finding each other through social networking sites, and she wanted to know her mother would be able to find her if she ever went looking.

'Shut them down,' he said firmly.

'Oh, but I love my Bebo page! And there's really nothing bad on there now. I reported the people who were giving me trouble and it all got sorted out. *Please* can I keep it?'

'Well, I'll have to check it out.'

'But you wouldn't be able to see it because you're not one of my friends. See how secure it is?' she appealed to him.

'Okay, add me as a friend and I'll take a look at it.'

'Okay, I'll shut it down.'

He gave her a meaningful look.

'No, I really will – honest.'

'I'm worried about these stalkers, though. Is it still going on?'

'Oh, don't worry about them.'

'I think I will, if it's all the same to you.' A bunch of rejected, embittered young men with axes to grind, and Jenny about to give them a perfect opportunity to cash in on their misery? It was definitely something to worry about.

'I've had hardly any trouble from them since they started the support group.'

Dev's eyes flew up. 'There's a *support group?*'

'Um … yeah.' He didn't seem to find that as reassuring as she'd hoped. 'They have a website. They chat to each other online, try to encourage each other to move on and to leave me alone. It's quite sweet, really. If one of them's having a bad day and thinking about coming around, they can go on there and the others will talk them down.'

'How did they get to know each other?'

'Colin had a blog for a while and some of them hooked up

through that. And I think a couple of them bumped into each other outside here one night when they were doing their stalking, and they got chatting. Colin started up the website – like Ollie said, he's very good with computers.'

'I'll have to check it out. What's it called?'

'Jenanon dot com. Colin's great with computers, but he's not very imaginative.' She smiled wryly.

'Is there anything incriminating on it?' Dev asked, scribbling down the name.

'I don't know,' Jenny said. 'I've never seen it. You won't be able to either. It's members only.'

'Aren't you curious to find out what they're saying about you?'

'Not really. They're the ones who have problems moving on, not me. Anyway, it wouldn't be fair to spy on them when they're trying to get over me.'

'What about this guy – Paul, was it? The one who has your guinea pig?'

'That's the problem. I think the other guys have tried, but they can't get him to join the programme.'

'Programme?' Dev scoffed. 'Do they have twelve steps to recovery?'

'Probably,' Ollie put in. 'Jenny's a girl who takes a lot of getting over. Take it from one who knows.'

Dev looked at him incredulously. Bloody show-off, Jenny thought – that was exactly the reaction he was hoping for.

'But I thought ...' Dev stuttered.

Finally Ollie decided to put him out of his misery. 'I wasn't always so single-mindedly gay, you know. Jenny and I had rather a *grande affaire* when she first came to London.'

'Really?' Dev turned to Jenny for confirmation.

'Yes. Ollie and I used to go out.' That wasn't quite true. When they were together, she and Ollie had rarely gone out. They had found each other in the netherworld of Clubland and had fallen instantly into mutual and exclusive adoration. They had lived in each other's pockets for just over a year, like two peas in a pod, surviving on benefits and the hospitality of others. Interested only in each other and happy in their own little cocoon, they became almost completely divorced from the outside world. They had probably known from the start that it couldn't last, but for that entire blissful year they had maintained the illusion, not admitting it to themselves or each other. Jenny had been content to be the kind of girlfriend who spent all day perched on her lover's lap, kissing for hours on end or feeding him éclairs, and Ollie had wanted exactly the same, never feeling the need to do anything more productive.

Starvation and stagnation beckoned, but neither had had the will or the energy to call it a day. It had taken Liam's arrival to shake them out of their somnambulant state. He had burst into their lives, bringing the cold wind of reality with him. He basically told them they were being ridiculous and to snap out of it, bawling Jenny out for not getting a job and telling Ollie he should pick one way to swing and get on with it. Jenny was sad when it ended, but neither of them was heartbroken. She got a job and started dating again, and Ollie went to auditions and threw himself into the gay scene.

'Jenny was my last hurrah with the female of the species,' Ollie said to Dev.

'That's his way of saying I put him off women for life,' Jenny joked.

'You just ruined me for other women,' Ollie corrected her.

'You ruined yourself,' she said.

'As Nanny always told me I would.'

Just then the door opened. Dev looked up to see a thick-set bruiser of a boy with dark-ringed eyes and a wild mane of unruly curls. He glanced around unsmilingly until his eyes rested on Jenny. A gentle smile softened his features. It disappeared when he looked at Dev.

'Hello,' he said, making it sound like a challenge as he fixed him with a steely-eyed stare.

'Hello,' Dev answered.

'This is Liam,' Jenny told him. 'Liam, this is Dev. He works for Richard.'

Liam nodded slowly, still eyeing Dev. Without another word, he began moving around the kitchen and came to the table armed with a bowl and a box of cereal.

'Oh, there's no milk,' Jenny said apologetically as Liam went to the fridge.

He sat down at the table and munched his way through a heap of dry cornflakes, staring into space and not speaking to anyone. His casual air of superiority reminded Dev of an alpha-male gorilla – so much so that he almost expected to hear David Attenborough's voice giving a hushed commentary on his behaviour. Dev was in no doubt that in such a scenario, he would be cast as the invader in their dysfunctional family group, with Liam wary and ready to defend his territory.

When he had finished eating, Liam lit a cigarette and leaned back in his chair. 'I'll go shopping in the morning,' he said to Jenny. 'Anything else we need besides milk?'

'Vodka. And knickers – I haven't got any washing done this week.' This earned her a scowl from Dev.

Liam took a piece of paper and a pen from his pocket and began making a list. 'Better get knickers for all of us, then.'

'What will you use for money?' Jenny asked.

'That's sorted. I made a fortune in tips last night.'

'What do you do?' Dev asked him.

'I wave my todger at gaggles of girls at hen parties and the like.'

'You're a stripper?'

'I prefer exotic dancer,' Liam said. 'Though in fairness, it's not very exotic.'

'He doesn't do the dance of the seven veils,' Ollie said.

'But it's not folk either.'

'He's not a morris dancer.'

'I get the picture,' Dev said.

'There's not much dancing involved at all, to be honest,' Liam said. 'You just get your kit off, wave your tackle around, let them feel you up a bit if they want. Plus you get to shag at least one of the hens – sometimes even the bride herself.' He took a long drag on his cigarette. 'I'm hung like a horse,' he informed Dev, blowing smoke towards the ceiling. 'Which helps.'

'Right.' Dev wasn't sure what to say to this. Congratulations? Snap? Or perhaps he should challenge him to a who's-got-the-biggest-willy duel – todgers at dawn?

'He's not really a str— exotic dancer,' Jenny said. 'I mean, that's not his career or anything.'

'No,' Liam said. 'It's just a sideline while I'm between jobs.'

'He's really a chef.'

'So, what's for dinner tonight?' Liam asked Jenny.

Jenny turned and took a sheaf of what Dev presumed were takeaway menus from a shelf and began flipping through them. 'Well,' she said, 'there's a new exhibition opening at the Smart Gallery, so we could go there. They'll have smoked salmon on brown bread, and crudités, maybe some chips and dips. And there'll be wine, of course.'

'Anything more substantial on offer?' Liam asked. 'I'm starving.'

Jenny shuffled through the cards and flyers again. 'It's Lady Annabelle Cooper's twenty-first birthday party at the Ritz,' she said, pulling out a thick card. 'That must be one of yours,' she said to Ollie.

'Yeah, you should go to that. She's an awful cow, but the tuck will be good.'

'Okay, then, Lady Annabelle's it is.'

'Give the silly moo my love,' Ollie said, getting up from the table. 'Tell her I'd have liked to come, but fame and fortune beckon.'

'You'd better go and get cleaned up if we're going to the Ritz,' Jenny said to Liam. 'And Ollie, hang your trousers and jacket in the bathroom while Liam has a shower – it'll steam out the creases. If you take the shirt off now, I'll iron it.'

They both shuffled out of the room, Liam giving Dev one last glare as he went.

'Well, if that's all,' Jenny said to Dev, 'I'd better get my party shoes on.'

Dev stood, gathering up his things. 'Don't you ever eat at home?' he asked her, indicating the pile of invitations she had dumped on the table.

'Not if we can help it. Have you seen the cost of food lately? It's outrageous! Especially when they're giving it away for free all over London.'

'Right, well, I'll see you next week, then,' he said, heading for the door.

'Next week?'

'Didn't Richard tell you? We're having dinner at his place one evening to discuss your outing as a couple.'

'Oh, yes!' She had thought this little inquisition would make that unnecessary. 'Of course.' She smiled brightly. 'Looking forward to it.'

Chapter 7

The following day was devoted, as most Sundays were, to recovering from Saturday night. Liam was stretched out on the sofa, reading the papers, while Jenny sat at the table, frowning over a cookbook, making notes. Ollie was slumped opposite her in a hung-over stupor. Liam was making one of his epic Sunday dinners, and the delicious smell of roasting meat wafted from the kitchen.

'What's a ballotine?' Jenny asked, looking up from the book and tapping her pen absently against her teeth.

'You don't want to do that,' Liam said from behind his paper.

'Why not? Is it hard?'

'Is there a picture?' Ollie roused himself to ask.

She bent her head to the book again, flipping a few pages. 'Blimey, this recipe goes on for three pages.' She finally came to a photograph and turned the book to face Ollie.

'Oh,' he said, 'it's like a giant chicken nugget. Except without the crispy coating.'

'The crispy coating is the best bit,' Jenny said, pulling the book back towards her and gazing down at it morosely. 'All this work for a chicken nugget! You seem to have to perform surgery on the bloody chicken first. What's the ball joint?'

'I'll make whatever you want for your dinner party.' Liam peered around his paper at her.

'No. I want to be able to say I did it myself.'

'You *can* say you did it yourself,' Liam murmured idly.

'I want it to be true.'

'Just give them shepherd's pie, then. Toffs love nursery food. Ask Ollie.'

''S true,' Ollie mumbled. 'Reminds us of happy days in the ample bosom of Nanny.'

'I don't think Dev is a toff, though – not like Richard anyway. Or you,' she said to Ollie.

'He's from the north, isn't he?' Ollie drawled. 'Just give him pie and chips and he'll be happy.'

'I don't know why you're going to so much trouble for that tosser anyway,' Liam said.

'Because it's important to Richard. And besides, if I'm going to be the prime minister's wife, I'll need to know how to do these things myself. I bet Julia could make chicken ballotine.'

'You can't be the prime minister's wife,' Ollie scoffed.

'Of course she can. Leave her alone,' Liam said belligerently, glaring at him over the top of his paper. 'She can be whatever she wants to be.'

'Thank you.' Jenny made a so-there face at Ollie.

'But she can't be the prime minister's wife.'

'It's a free country,' Liam said. 'Anyone who wants can be the prime minister's wife. It's not like royalty.'

'Oh! Is that true?' Ollie straightened with a jolt. 'Someone might have told me.'

'Anyone willing to shag the prime minister, of course,' Liam drawled.

'Ugh!' Suddenly Ollie didn't seem so keen.

'Oh, come on,' Jenny protested. 'Richard is gorgeous and you know it. Don't tell me you wouldn't, given half a chance.'

'He's not my type.' Ollie grimaced. 'Too manicured and … antiseptic.'

Jenny rolled her eyes.

'And what will you do when you're the prime minister's wife?' Liam smiled indulgently at Jenny as he folded his paper and sat up.

'I'll … do what the prime minister's wife does.'

'And what is that?'

'Oh, you know,' Jenny shrugged airily, 'duties.'

'Duties?' Ollie grinned mockingly.

'Yes, you know – being patron of things … opening fêtes and judging the Victoria sandwich contest and, um, presenting trophies at cricket games and—'

'Matches,' Liam said.

'Sorry?'

'They're called matches, love – cricket matches.'

'Okay, cricket matches … and handing out the rosettes at horse, um … trials.'

'Shows,' Ollie prompted her in a stage whisper. 'Horse shows.'

'Yes, well – all that kind of stuff. And I'll wear hats!'

'Ooh, yes.' Ollie clapped enthusiastically. 'You can bring back hats! You could be an icon of British fashion.'

Liam laughed. 'I think you'll find there's more to being the prime minister's wife than judging cake contests and wearing hats. That's not what the prime minister's wife does. The job you're thinking of is princess.'

'What does she do, then?' Jenny asked.

'Fucked if I know.'

'Well, maybe she does judge cake contests.'

'Anyway,' Liam said, shaking his head, 'all that stuff goes on in the country. When was the last time you saw a village fête in London?'

'Richard's constituency is in the country,' Jenny pointed out. 'We could live there.'

'Jenny,' Liam said, 'whatever about being the prime minister's wife, you *cannot* live in the country.'

'I don't see why not,' she said primly. 'I've always kind of fancied living in a country village, making jam, getting involved in the village fête and that sort of thing.'

'The village fête happens once a year. What would you do for the other fifty-one weeks?'

'I don't know. There must be something – plenty of people live in the country and they seem perfectly happy.'

'That's because they're morons,' Liam said.

'He's right,' Ollie said. 'It's unutterably tedious. There's absolutely nothing to do. Why do you think sheep-shagging got started?'

'Yeah,' Liam chimed in. 'Imagine how fucking bored out of your tree you'd have to be before sticking your knob into a sheep starts to look like fun.'

'I don't have a knob. Women don't do sheep-shagging. We're too high-minded for that sort of thing.'

'You'll have even fewer outlets, then,' Ollie said.

'You'll end up having *early nights*, just to escape the boredom,' Liam said ominously.

'Well, I've never had an early night – might be nice for a change.'

'Believe me, it's not,' Liam said. 'I had an early night once. I wouldn't recommend it.'

'I'll try anything once,' Jenny said. 'They're meant to be very good for you.'

'But one doesn't work,' Ollie said. 'You have to have a whole string of them. Might as well just shoot yourself now.'

'Well, I could do … country pursuits,' Jenny said. She had no idea what they were, but they sounded quite fun.

'You know what country pursuits are, Jen?' Ollie raised an eyebrow at her.

'Well … no. But I'm sure I could pick it up in no time. What are they?'

'Killing stuff,' Ollie answered.

'No, seriously.' Jenny laughed.

'Seriously – killing stuff. Hunting, shooting, fishing – well, okay, not hunting any more. But the rest.'

'There must be other things. Horse riding – I could take that up.'

Ollie snorted. 'You're terrified of horses.'

'I could go on long country walks – with a dog.'

'You don't have a dog,' Liam said.

'I could get one.'

'But you're scared of dogs.'

'And in the country no one can hear you scream,' Ollie said in a ghoulish voice.

'There are no Tubes or taxis.'

'No theatres or cinemas.'

'No beer gardens.'

'No hotels or restaurants.'

'No shelter, basically. You have to be outside all the time.'

'And wear horrible clothes – sludge-green waxed coats and mud-brown hats.'

'You have to make your own dinner. Every night. From scratch. There's no pizza delivery.'

'No gallery openings.'

'No cool parties to crash.'

'Okay, okay – so I won't move to the country.' God, she sincerely hoped Richard wouldn't want her to go and live in his constituency.

The countryside sounded like a nightmare! 'I'll stay in London and I'll … do charity work.'

'Oh, yes!' Ollie exclaimed, perking up again. 'You can be fabulous with the poor and needy – in hats. The whole country will adore you.'

'I'll go on foreign trips and showcase British fashion in exotic settings. And I'll entertain,' she said, her eyes lighting up. 'I'll hold fabulous dinner parties and make chicken ballotine, and …' she flipped a few pages of the cookbook, '… beef Wellington.'

'Of course,' Ollie agreed. 'And have the prime ministerial children.'

'Gosh, yes, the prime ministerial children.' Jenny giggled happily. 'I'll make their tea and take them to the park and read them bedtime stories. And I'll make them lovely cakes for their birthdays.'

'Victoria sandwiches, I suppose?' Liam smiled at her. 'You'll be an expert on them by then, after all the village fêtes.'

'And I'll do up Number Ten, and make it pretty,' Jenny continued, ignoring him.

'And shag the prime minister, of course,' Ollie said.

'And shag the prime minister,' Jenny sighed dreamily. 'Of course.'

Chapter 8

'I don't get why we still have to have this dinner with Dev,' Jenny said the following Friday as she set the table in Richard's Mayfair flat. 'I already had the bloody inquisition from him last week.'

'I told you,' Richard said, turning from stirring his pots to talk to her. 'He wants to discuss how we're going to manage the story about us coming out, and how to handle your public profile.'

Jenny had had a trying week, and she would have liked to relax with Richard that night. Alice, Michael and Oscar had left for Edinburgh yesterday, and it had been an emotional parting for all of them. They had had a little farewell party with her, and Oscar had been inconsolable when it was finally time for her to go, clinging to her legs and begging her to come to Edinburgh with them, his pitiful sobs tearing at Jenny's heart. She already missed him dreadfully – and she missed Alice just as much.

'That smells good,' she said as she went to the kitchen cupboard to get wine glasses. Richard was stirring a redcurrant sauce, while the scent of roasting lamb emanated from the oven. He held a spoonful of sauce to her mouth for her to taste. She blew on it before she sipped carefully.

'Mmm, lovely,' she murmured, kissing him when she had swallowed. Richard was very proud of his cooking skills. He could be annoyingly show-offy about it, but she had to admit he was really good. He enjoyed letting rip in the kitchen occasionally, and she had been relieved that he had decided to make this dinner for Dev. She had been having nightmares about chicken ballotines for the past week. He was alarmingly neat and methodical about it too, she thought, looking around the shiny kitchen, light bouncing off high-gloss cupboards and stainless steel appliances. He had prepared a three-course meal and barely a pot was out of place.

'Besides,' Richard said, picking up the thread of their conversation, 'Dev is a friend. You two should get to know each other.'

'Hmm, I don't think your friend likes me very much,' Jenny said, opening a cupboard. The glasses were too high for her to reach even on tiptoe. 'Could you get the wine glasses down for me?' she asked Richard.

'I think Dev likes you a lot,' Richard said, handing her three. 'Too much, for my liking.' He grinned at her.

Fancies me maybe, Jenny thought. It's not the same thing. 'I don't think he dislikes me exactly, but he doesn't approve of me as your girlfriend. He thinks I'm not right for you.'

'Well, Dev's not my mother – I don't need his approval.'

'Are these the only ones you've got?' she asked, holding the glasses up for inspection.

'Yep. Something wrong with them?'

'No. I just thought you might have something more ... colourful.'

'Just boring old crystal, I'm afraid.'

Jenny went to put them on the table. They were obviously very good glasses – they weighed a ton. It was just a pity they didn't have a bit more personality – like everything else around here. She sighed with dissatisfaction. She had bought oodles of fresh flowers and dotted them around, splashes of colour lighting up every corner and reflected back from huge mirrors. But somehow the place still seemed bare and cold.

'Let's taste the wine,' Richard said, picking up the bottle that was already breathing on the table and pouring a mouthful into two glasses.

'Steady,' Jenny teased. 'You don't want to get us pissed.'

'It's just to taste.' He smiled, swirling the wine around the glass before burying his nose in it. 'What do you think?' he asked her.

'Very nice,' she said as she knocked hers back, smacking her lips. 'Tastes like more.'

Richard looked disappointed and she realised she probably should have said something better – something interesting and intelligent about its nose or its legs or some other part of its anatomy. Julia no doubt would have had something incredibly clever to say about it.

'Mmm, it's very good,' he murmured almost to himself. 'I brought a case of it back from France last year,' he told her. 'This is the last bottle.'

France, Jenny thought. Julia. Why would he think she'd want to hear about that?

Richard drained his glass and put it on the table.

'Hmm, maybe I'd better have another taste,' Jenny said, walking up to him and winding her arms around his neck. Pulling his head down to hers, she stood on tiptoe to kiss him, sliding her tongue into his mouth and running it along the curve of his lips. 'Mmm,' she smiled, licking her lips, 'delicious.' She pulled away from him, cocking her head to one side consideringly. 'I'd say it's mature, very sexy and perfect for laying down – right now.' She grinned suggestively.

Richard laughed, kissing her again.

'What time is Dev coming?' she mumbled against his lips, starting to unbutton his shirt.

'He should be here any minute,' Richard said between kisses.

Right on cue, the doorbell rang. 'Let's not answer it,' Jenny said, nuzzling into his neck.

Richard just smiled, unwinding her arms from around his neck and pushing her away. He did up his buttons as he went to open the door.

'Doing your Delia impersonation, I see,' Dev mocked Richard as they came back into the room. 'Hello, Jenny.'

'Hi, Dev.'

'Hey, I like to think I'm more Gordon Ramsay.' Richard laughed, pretending to be peeved. 'Why don't you two pour yourselves some wine? I'm almost ready.' He bustled back into the kitchen.

Jenny filled three glasses. She handed Richard his over the breakfast bar and went to join Dev on one of the leather sofas, putting their glasses on the coffee table.

'Thanks,' he said. 'So, what have you been up to?'

'Nothing!' she yelped.

Dev laughed. 'I wasn't accusing you of anything.'

'Oh ... no, of course not. I didn't think you were.' She blushed. She was probably being unfair to him, reacting like that to a perfectly innocent question. After all, he hadn't shopped her to Richard about Mr Hodge.

'Have you finished work yet?'

'Yes,' she said. 'On Wednesday.' Her eyes welled up as she was reminded of Oscar crying and begging her to go with them.

'Sorry,' Dev said. 'You must get very attached.'

'Yes, I'm really going to miss them,' she said, brushing a tear from the corner of her eye.

'I see you've worked your magic on this place.' He picked up his wine glass and gestured with his other hand around the room.

'Um ... yeah. It's just a few flowers.' Her lips pursed in disapproval as she looked around. It was a bit sad if this was his idea of 'magic'.

'Starters are ready,' Richard called from the kitchen. 'What do you think of that wine, Dev?' he asked as they took their places at the table.

'Oh, yeah.' Dev took another sip, as if he was considering it for the first time. 'Very nice,' he said.

Richard rolled his eyes. 'Well, I'm obviously wasting it on you two Philistines.'

'Ooh, yum,' Jenny exclaimed as he placed a crab tartlet in front of her. 'This looks fab!'

'I got the recipe from *Masterchef*,' he said. 'I just added my own little twist.'

Dev looked at him. 'You're not going on *Masterchef*,' he said firmly.

'I *know* I'm not going on *Masterchef*,' Richard said in a weary voice.

Jenny suppressed a giggle. She knew Richard would secretly love to be on *Masterchef*, almost more than he'd love to be prime minister. 'Never mind,' she told him. 'Maybe when you're prime minister, the *Masterchef* finalists will come to Number Ten to cook for you.'

'Yes – it could be one of their challenges,' Richard said, brightening. 'Maybe you could arrange that, Dev?'

'Thankfully, I won't be around at that stage.'

'Oh?' Jenny was surprised.

'Dev is only working for me until the next election,' Richard explained. 'Win or lose – that's the deal.'

Dev didn't waste any time getting down to business. As soon as they started eating, he was discussing strategy for managing the story. The plan was for her and Richard to go out together on a date, the details of which would be leaked to a friendly editor. Pictures would be taken, Dev would give them an exclusive and that would be that – they would be outed as a couple.

'Who'd have thought it would be so controversial,' Jenny marvelled, 'to come out as a pair of heterosexuals?'

'Just let me know where you intend to go and I'll tip off our friends in the press,' Dev added.

'Jenny could come to Jeremy's party next week,' Richard suggested. Jeremy was the shadow chancellor.

'That would be perfect,' Dev said. 'It's nice and low-key, nothing glitzy.'

'It certainly won't be glitzy!' Richard said.

'We don't want any big splashes on this – just for it to trickle out slowly that you're with someone and then for it to fade into the background again. We don't want too much interest in Jenny.'

'Don't you think that's inevitable?' Richard asked.

'Doesn't have to be. She should stay very much in the background.'

'But don't you think there's likely to be a lot of press interest in her?' Richard asked.

Dev looked at Jenny. 'Yes, I do. That's why we should keep her out of the public eye as much as possible.'

'Well, that's not going to be easy in Brighton.'

'Exactly. So she shouldn't come to Brighton.'

'You don't think she should come to Conference at all?'

'Definitely not. There's absolutely no reason for her to be there.'

Jenny flinched from the finality in Dev's voice. He wanted to write her out of Richard's life almost before they'd begun. She was damned if she was having that. There was every reason for her to go to Conference. She knew how important it was to Richard. It was the most important event in the year for the Party, and if it was important to him, it should be important to her too. She knew Julia had always gone with him. Last year she had had to watch the footage of them arriving together, hand in hand. She had had to endure it when Julia joined him on stage after his speech and gave him a kiss, playing the supportive wife. She had watched that kiss with a forensic eye, hunting for clues, telling herself over and over that it was just an act and nothing to get upset about. She was unsure if she was reminding or trying to convince herself. The jealousy she had felt was a physical thing that gnawed at her stomach. She wanted to be the one standing beside him in public, showing the world that she was his – that he, Richard Allam, had chosen *her*. Well, now it was her turn, and she was damned if she was going to let Dev cheat her out of it.

'Oh, but I was really looking forward to Brighton,' she said, putting an arm around Richard and smiling at him seductively. 'The thought of all that sand and sea air is so sexy. And since we didn't get to go to Blackpool—'

'It's not a holiday,' Dev said, shooting her a steely look.

'I know that. I won't get in the way.'

'Richard will be busy the whole time. He won't have a spare minute. He certainly won't be able to pay attention to you twenty-four hours a day.'

'I don't need him to pay attention to me twenty-four hours a day,' Jenny said, stung. He was treating her like a spoiled, demanding child. 'I'm really not that high-maintenance, you know.' She wanted to ask him why Julia was allowed to go to Conference and not her, but she didn't want to bring the woman's name up. 'Look, what's your real problem with me?' she asked. 'Obviously it's not just that you're worried I'll be bored and feeling left out.'

'Yes, what is your problem with Jenny coming?' Richard asked.

Dev sighed. 'I'm afraid she'll become the story. You know what the press are like. They'll take one look at her and that'll be it. It won't matter what the hell you say after that,' he said to Richard, 'because the stories will be about Jenny's hairstyle or shoes or something.'

'Oh, come on, you don't really believe that, do you?' Richard asked.

Jenny smiled to herself. Of course Richard didn't believe for a minute that he could be outshone. His unshakeable self-belief was kind of sweet.

'I know the media, Richard,' Dev said. 'That's why you hired me, remember?'

'But you don't honestly think they're going to be so dazzled by a pretty girl that they'll forget what the real story is?'

'Jenny's pretty dazzling,' Dev said.

She smiled at him in surprise but he didn't smile back. He'd made 'dazzling' sound like a bad thing.

'You know as well as I do, Richard, that the story is whatever they decide to make it. You don't think the only reason they're there is to faithfully record your brilliant vision for the future of the country?'

'Well …'

'You know they have other agendas. And don't rule out friendly fire either. You know there will be people inside the Party only too happy to co-operate. A lot of the old guard aren't sold on the changes you're making. They'll be looking for ways to undermine you.'

'Well, let them look. There's nothing to find, is there, darling?' Richard turned to her with a confident smile.

Jenny loved him more than ever for his unquestioning faith in her. She tried to avoid Dev's eye. He had promised to say nothing to Richard about Mr Hodge, but she hated being complicit with him in keeping secrets from Richard. She felt like a sleazy collaborator.

'Besides,' Richard continued, 'we could do with a little glamour at Conference.'

'I've already planned what I'm going to wear when I go on the stage after your speech,' Jenny said excitedly.

'No!' Dev said firmly. 'You *will not* be going on-stage after his speech. I hate that presidential crap anyway. It's about time it was done away with.'

Jenny's face fell. That was the bit she had been most looking forward to.

'I don't see why she can't join me on-stage,' Richard said, looking at Jenny's crestfallen expression.

'Richard, you're trying to project an image of stability and continuity. Being up there with a different girl on your arm every year isn't the best way to achieve that. The images of last year are still too fresh in everyone's minds.'

Including mine, Jenny thought. The press had made much last year of Julia's adoring glances at her husband, fresh from his triumph in the leadership election. They had looked every inch the golden couple. Jenny had been hoping to supplant that image in the public imagination this year.

'Hmm, you're probably right,' Richard said, agreeing with Dev. 'But you can still be in the audience in the hall,' he told Jenny.

Dev sighed. 'Well, if you insist on bringing her, we'll just have to do what we can to minimise the attention.'

'Such as?'

'Well, apart from staying in the background as much as possible, it would be useful if we could do something about the way she looks.'

'The way I *look*?'

'The way she *looks*?' Jenny and Richard screeched at the same time.

'She'll stick out like a sore thumb if she goes to Conference like that.'

'What's wrong with the way I look?'

'Nothing,' Richard said, stroking a hand up and down her arm. 'You're gorgeous.'

'There's nothing wrong with the way you look per se,' Dev said.

'You're just very … different from the kind of women who are usually at party conferences.'

'Thank God for that!' Richard said.

'I just think you could try looking a bit less … glamorous.'

'What do you suggest?' Jenny asked.

'Well, there's your hair for a start. It's very bright,' he said. 'You could tone it down a bit. Then there's your clothes—'

'My clothes!' Jenny hooted at the idea of Dev giving her style advice. 'Who died and made you Gok Wan?'

'What's wrong with her clothes?' Richard asked Dev. 'I think Jenny dresses really well.'

'They're just a bit too … eccentric and quirky.'

Jenny sighed. 'I suppose I could dye my hair a different colour,' she said, chewing her lip thoughtfully. 'Might be nice for a change. I've always kind of fancied being a redhead. What do you think?' she asked Richard.

'I like your hair the way it is,' he said. 'Don't change it for me.'

'I was thinking more along the lines of … nondescript,' Dev said.

'"Nondescript" – wow! That sounds really attractive! But I'm not sure Clairol do "nondescript".'

'Same with your clothes. You always look like you're wearing … outfits.'

'*Outfits?*' Of course she wore outfits – did he expect her to go around naked?

'Yes, outfits – like a girl in a magazine or something, all thought out and co-ordinated. Maybe you could try to look as if you just put on some clothes,' he suggested.

'Okay, so you want me to look more thrown together? A don't-give-a-shit kind of look?'

'Yes, exactly!' Dev was pleased. 'As if you have your mind on higher things. And more conventional.'

God, hadn't he realised she was being sarcastic? He wanted to give her a reverse makeover – he'd have her looking like the 'before' candidate in no time if he had his way.

'For God's sake, don't listen to him,' Richard said, getting up and clearing the starter plates away. 'And you,' he said sternly to Dev, 'leave Jenny alone. She's her own person. She doesn't have to change anything for me.'

Phew! Thank God Richard had stood up for her. She really didn't fancy the idea of going around with nondescript hair and lucky-dip clothes, though if Richard wanted her to, she'd do it.

'We should discuss what Jenny's role will be,' Richard said when he had served up the main course of roast lamb with redcurrant sauce and roast vegetables.

'Her role? She doesn't—' Dev began.

'Oh, before you start,' Jenny interrupted, holding up a hand to stop him, 'don't worry, I know it's not all about handing out trophies and opening village fêtes.'

A smile twitched at the corners of Dev's mouth. 'Well, I'm glad you're so … clued up.'

'So, what do you think her role should be?' Richard asked.

'She doesn't have one. I mean, it's not as if you're married. Once Conference is over, she can just fade into the background again.'

'But what about when I'm – what about after the election?'

Jenny smiled to herself. Richard was very superstitious about assuming he would be prime minister after the election, even though it was practically a foregone conclusion in the rest of the country.

'Well, you can cross that bridge when you come to it,' Dev said. 'No need to worry about it at the moment. Let's just get through Conference first.'

He thinks I'm a blip, Jenny thought, dismayed by Dev's casually dismissive tone. He doesn't think he'll have to deal with me after the election because I'm just a passing fancy and I'll be out of the picture by then.

'Yes, there'll be plenty of time after the election,' she said, looking pointedly at Dev. 'I'm not going anywhere.'

'Except Brighton,' Dev said, pursing his lips.

'Except Brighton.'

Dev sighed in frustration at the determined set of Jenny's jaw. He knew she thought he was being mean, that he didn't want her there because he had something against her. But he wanted to keep her out of the public eye for her own sake as much as Richard's – perhaps even more so. She didn't understand what she was getting into. If they allowed the media interest in her to spiral out of control now, there would be no way of shaking it off if she and Richard were to split up. You couldn't turn it on and off at whim, and she would be hung out to dry, with none of the support that was available to her now as Richard's partner. He had seen it happen, and he didn't want it to happen to her. Still, he couldn't very well explain his reasoning to Jenny and Richard – not when they were so intent on convincing themselves that they were in love with each other.

Chapter 9

The next day, Dev called in on Felix's birthday party as promised. England was experiencing an Indian summer and everyone was in the garden when he arrived, enjoying the beautiful late-September day. Dev came through the living room and sat on the steps leading down into the garden, waving to Richard, who was holding up one end of a piñata while Felix and his friends lined up to whack it. Julia was standing with a couple of mothers, drinking wine and chatting while they watched the games. It had been a long time since he had seen her and he realised he had missed her.

As if she had felt his eyes on her, she looked round at him. She excused herself to the people she was with and came over to join him. 'Hello, Dev,' she said, sitting beside him on the steps. 'Can I get you a drink?'

'No, thanks, I'm driving.'

She nodded, leaning her arms on her knees. 'How have you been? We've hardly seen you since Sally …'

'No, I've been … out of circulation for a while.' He looked directly ahead rather than at her, his fists clenched.

'How are your parents?'

'They're not too bad. Good days and bad, you know.'

'It takes time.' She smiled gently.

He nodded. 'How are you? How's the book coming along?

'Slowly, but it's getting there.' Julia was a writer of historical biography. Her first book had been published the previous year to critical acclaim and she was currently working on another.

'I suppose Richard and I splitting up is another reason I haven't seen you. But please don't let it be awkward. You're my friend too, Dev. Don't be a stranger.'

'I won't – although I won't have a lot of time for socialising for a while.' He laughed quietly.

'You look tired,' she said, studying his face. 'Don't let him push you too hard.'

'Richard thinks it's the other way around.' Dev laughed. 'He reckons I bully him.'

'Hah! I can't see anyone doing that,' she said. 'Oh, I know you can be an out-and-out thug when you want to be, but Richard's very passive-aggressive.'

'Really? You think so?'

'Believe me – I know of what I speak.'

'I do believe you.' He looked at her, thinking what an asset she would have been to Richard in an election campaign. She knew him so well, and she was so intelligent and pragmatic. For the umpteenth time he wondered what Richard could have been thinking to let her slip away from him – now of all times. Julia was the perfect politician's wife – sleek, classic, understated perfection from the top of her shining auburn bob to the soles of her pedicured feet. Next to her, Jenny would look like a street urchin.

'You'd have made my job a lot easier if you'd stayed together.' He had said it aloud without thinking and his smile faded as he saw the surprise on her face. 'Sorry,' he said.

They were silent for a moment. Julia took a sip of her wine. 'Did you know?' she said finally, looking straight ahead. She spoke very quietly, but her voice sounded tight and strained.

'Sorry?'

'Did you know?' She turned to him. 'About this girl?'

He was surprised by the bitterness in her voice. He looked down the garden, but everyone was preoccupied with the party. No one would hear their conversation over the squeals of the children. 'Not until he told me the other day.'

She smiled faintly. 'Well, at least I wasn't the last to know – I suppose that's something. He's made me enough of a bloody cliché as it is.'

'He probably didn't want to say anything if it wasn't necessary,' he said. 'I mean, they haven't been together very long, have they? I'm sure he just wanted to wait and see if it was going to turn into something serious before he told you.'

'Told me?' she hissed. 'He didn't *tell* me, Dev. I found out.'

That explained her bitterness. Someone else had told her, maybe even gloated about it, and she felt humiliated.

'I'm sorry. That must have been tough.'

'Yes, you could say that,' she said, an edge to her voice. She took a big gulp of her wine, looking out over the garden in silence. 'Would you have told me?' she asked eventually, still staring straight ahead. 'If you'd known earlier?'

Dev sighed. God, he wished Felix would come over to collect his present or something. He really didn't want to be having this conversation. 'No, probably not,' he admitted. 'It's not really my place, is it?'

Julia gave a low, bitter laugh. 'Men,' she whispered to herself, taking another gulp of wine. 'So my replacement's giving you trouble, is she?' she said in a stronger voice, turning to him. 'Well, good. Serves you right.' She smiled at him, taking the sting out of her words.

'Not really, it's just ... well ... you would have been an easier sell.'

That was understating the case: Julia would have been a positive asset, no selling necessary.

'Oh, come on, Dev – give me something. What's wrong with her?'

It was uncharacteristic of her to be so bitter and resentful. She obviously wanted him to dish the dirt, but that made him feel protective of Jenny. What could he say? The diplomatic thing – the thing Julia probably wanted to hear – was 'She's nothing compared to you' or 'I don't know what he sees in her'. But it wasn't true: he could see how easy it would be to fall for Jenny. 'There's nothing wrong with her,' he said. 'She's lovely.' He didn't want to rub her nose in it, but he couldn't criticise Jenny just to make Julia feel better. Jenny had done nothing wrong – she didn't deserve that.

Julia was looking at his face searchingly. 'Oh, God,' she groaned, 'not you too.'

'Me too – what?'

'Never mind.' She shook her head. 'So, how is she making your life difficult?'

'Let's just say she's not the asset you would have been,' he said carefully. 'She's very different from you—'

'Different in what way?' she pounced.

Dev stirred restlessly, darting a panicked look at Richard, but the piñata was still putting up a good fight. He wasn't going to be rescued any time soon. 'In lots of ways,' he began awkwardly. 'She's very young, for one thing—'

Julia's head snapped up. 'How young?'

Bloody hell! Hadn't Richard told her anything about Jenny apart from the fact of her existence? He'd give him a right bollocking when he came out from behind that bloody piñata.

'Twenty-four,' he said to Julia.

'Jesus!' she whispered, taking a sip of her wine. 'Figures, I suppose. Good old Richard.' She raised her glass to him in a mock salute. 'No cliché unturned. It's a wonder he didn't take up with someone from the office.'

'There's the fact that it's so soon too,' Dev continued, glad he had thought of something neutral to say that didn't involve talking Jenny down. 'So soon after your official separation, I mean. I know it was over between you long before that, but as far as the public and everyone else is concerned—'

'*What?*' Julia's gasp interrupted him. 'He told you that?'

Oh, bugger – he obviously wasn't supposed to know. Julia was horrified, and he felt like a shit for embarrassing her. She was an intensely private person and clearly didn't want anyone to know the truth about their marriage – even him. But surely she understood that Richard would have told him everything. 'I'm sorry. Richard told me you didn't want anyone to know, but I suppose he thought I was an exception.'

'He told you it was "over between us" when exactly?' She had become very still.

'He didn't go into details – just that it was a while before the leadership election.'

'Before – Jesus!' she whispered, gulping hard. 'And did he tell you why we stayed together for so long after that?' she asked, a strange note in her voice.

'You were keeping up the pretence for the sake of his career until you felt the time was right. Look, I'm sorry if I wasn't supposed to know, but obviously I'm not going to tell anyone else, and you did a great job keeping it hidden. I was absolutely gobsmacked when he told me. There's no way anyone would ever have suspected the truth.'

'The truth?' Julia laughed. 'I wonder if he'd know the truth if it jumped up and bit him.'

Just then the piñata crumbled and the pack of squealing children surged forward as toys and sweets fell in a shower to the ground.

Julia turned back to Dev. 'Do you really think he needs *you*? Don't you think he's plausible enough?'

He frowned, not sure what she meant.

'He had an *affair*, Dev. He cheated on me, and I found out about it and threw him out. Our marriage is over because I ended it, and *she* – that girl – is the reason.'

Dev felt winded, struggling to take this in. Richard had lied to him – and so had Jenny. He was surprised by how disappointed he felt to discover she wasn't who he'd thought she was. She had seemed so sweet and artless. How had he got her so wrong? He was usually better at reading people, and he knew the type well – all candy-floss fluff on the surface and hard as nails inside. He came across girls like that often enough in his line of work. He didn't dislike them. He even had a grudging admiration for their hard-headed pursuit of whatever they wanted in life. But somehow he didn't like thinking of Jenny as one of them.

He felt foolish now for imagining she was out of her depth and needed protecting. Maybe he had just seen what he wanted to see because he liked her. Thinking about it now, she wasn't even a particularly good liar. He remembered when he'd asked her if she'd been with Richard before his separation and she had checked what Richard had told him before answering – making sure they'd got their stories straight, he now realised.

His thoughts were interrupted by Felix running up to him. Almost simultaneously there was a commotion at the bottom of the garden as a fight broke out over piñata booty and two of the children began wailing. Julia jumped up and, with an apologetic glance at Dev, raced off to sort it out.

'Happy birthday, Felix,' Dev said, taking a present from his pocket and handing it to his grinning godson.

'Thanks!' Felix ripped the paper off to reveal a PlayStation game.

'Oh, cool! Thanks!' He thundered off again to show it to Richard.

Dev was grateful for the space to digest what Julia had just told him. Her attitude made total sense now, and he shared her anger. He looked over at Richard, herding children towards the trestle tables where food was laid out. He couldn't believe he had lied to him so blatantly. It wasn't just the lack of trust – surely Richard realised he needed to be in his complete confidence in order to do his job properly?

'Dev, come and have some food,' Richard called.

He was itching to pull Richard into a room and give him a good kicking, but it would have to wait. There was no time for a private conversation in the midst of the sausage rolls and singing 'Happy Birthday' to Felix.

When he was leaving, Julia walked out to his car with him, leaving Richard still occupied in entertaining the children. 'Will she be going to Conference – my replacement?' she asked as they reached the gate.

Dev sighed. 'Yes, against all my advice.'

Julia smiled at him sympathetically. 'I must admit I'll miss it,' she said. 'I know that probably sounds daft – it's such a nightmare in some ways.'

'You'll *be* missed. I can't see Jenny enjoying it much.' He noticed her wince at his mention of Jenny's name. 'He must be mad,' he said angrily, looking back to the house, 'risking losing all this for – for *her*.'

'I got the impression you were a fan?'

'Hardly! She's nothing compared to you. I don't know what he sees in her.'

He must be mad, risking losing all this. Dev's words echoed in Julia's head as she drifted in and out of the house, collecting detritus from the garden, slowly and methodically restoring order to the house after the party. The evening was still pleasantly mild. The children were in bed, Richard had left, and she was glad to be alone.

He must be mad. It was the standard response – the response she was bracing herself for if the truth about Richard's affair ever came out. It was one of the reasons she was so willing to go along with him in covering it up – because she didn't want to have to deal with that response. She knew what other women would say: how could he take such a risk? How could he think he'd get away with it when his life was under such public scrutiny? How could he be so reckless? How had he managed to keep it secret for so long? Men would wonder about the last one too, perhaps with grudging admiration.

But it wasn't the audacity of it that surprised Julia, or the ingenuity. She knew Richard to be a risk-taker; she knew he was clever and resourceful. She wasn't surprised that he would take the chance or that he would be able to keep it secret. She had no illusions about what he was. There was no point in taking up with an alpha male and acting outraged when he started thumping his chest. What surprised her was that she hadn't been able to outwit him somehow – that anticipating this hadn't enabled her to prevent it; that knowing his nature hadn't equipped her to thwart him.

It wasn't as if the thought had never occurred to her. She realized, now that it had happened, that the idea had always been in the back of her mind. She thought of it every time she interviewed a new nanny or met a member of Richard's staff. She assessed their attractiveness, wondering if they would appeal to him, gauging whether they were his 'type'. She wondered whether they were married or had boyfriends, and if so, whether they would risk losing whatever they had for a fling with Richard. She knew how attractive he was – how handsome and charismatic and dynamic. It wasn't just her: the most objective observer would have to admit he was all those things.

Looking back, it was as if she had been preparing for this moment all her married life. Naïvely, she had thought that being prepared would somehow protect her – that by being alert to the signals and aware of the possibility, she could prevent Richard straying. She had thought her own insight would enable her to avoid the banal, mundane betrayals other women had to endure.

But then it had happened, and all her preparation had meant nothing. It had come at her out of left field, hitting her with a devastating sideswipe from the blind spot she hadn't thought she had. And she was left thunderstruck, like countless women before her, dumbly asking herself how it could have happened, why she hadn't seen it coming. She really hated counting herself among those women. She despised the idea of herself as a victim, an unknowing fool. Forewarned is forearmed, people said, and she had believed it, put her faith in it. She had been prepared, like the good Girl Guide she had once been. And it hadn't made one iota of difference. Forewarned is nothing, she thought.

I don't know what he sees in her. She smiled wryly to herself as she loaded a tray with the last few tumblers and party streamers from the trestle table. She really wished he hadn't said that, but she knew she had asked for it – literally. Earlier she had wanted him to say it, when she had asked about … that girl. She had almost willed him to trot out the comforting platitudes, but she had thought she saw a softening in his face that had stopped him – admiration when he spoke about the girl; perhaps even fondness. And then the moment had passed and she was glad he hadn't fallen into the trap she had set – not because she liked his loyalty to the girl but because it meant she herself wasn't an object of pity to him. She didn't want his pity or his solidarity.

That was one of the very worst things about her current state, she found. She really couldn't bear the pity. The sympathetic looks, the prurient compassion she felt from others now made her want to claw her skin off. She wanted to shout at them to fuck off – and she never swore. She wanted to tell them that she had thrown Richard out, not

117

the other way around, and that if they wanted to feel sorry for someone, it should be him.

If only she'd known that Richard had lied to Dev too, she might have gone along with his story, if only to deflect the pity. Instead she had unwittingly told Dev the truth – and he had responded by sticking another pin into her, along with the others that were holding her down until she was nothing more than a specimen: a Wronged Woman, a generic type, devoid of any individuality or distinguishing features. They could put her on display in the Natural History Museum.

I don't know what he sees in her. The funny thing was, she *did* know what he saw in her – well, she could make an educated guess. She knew most women of her acquaintance would be at a loss to understand what Richard could possibly see in someone like Jenny – young, frivolous, probably ill-educated: 'A *nanny*, for God's sake,' she could hear them saying. Okay, they would probably allow that she was very pretty and very young – no surprises why he'd be attracted to her, they would sneer. But they wouldn't see the deeper attraction, the real allure of someone like that for Richard, the pull that went beyond sex.

Pretty and young was only half the story. Julia knew that it was the very things that separated them most that would have the greatest appeal for Richard – the things that other people saw as obstacles. From the few details she had been able to glean about Jenny, from what Richard had said and her own discreet enquiries, she knew that the girl came from a totally different world from Richard's, a world almost wholly unknown to him, and that made her as exotic and mysterious to him as any veiled concubine in the Orient. Her rootless childhood and peripatetic lifestyle would be irresistible to him, and he would gobble up her stories of disadvantage and abandonment with the lasciviousness some men reserved for tales of unbridled eroticism.

She couldn't decide if it made it better or worse to know that Jenny's otherness would appeal to him most – to understand that it was a way she had never appealed to him and never could, and therefore that there was no point in competing. She considered it for a moment – and decided it was no consolation at all.

Chapter 10

Dev spent a restless night, his mind racing as he went over and over what Julia had told him. The more he thought about it, the more furious he became, and by dawn he was too wound up to get any more sleep. By six o'clock he was up and dressed, pacing restlessly around the living room as he rehearsed what he would say to Richard, itching for the opportunity to confront him. An hour later, he decided he couldn't wait any longer. He grabbed his car keys and headed over to Richard's flat.

'Dev!' Jenny sounded surprised as she opened the door, wearing one of Richard's shirts, which reached almost to her knees.

'Morning, Jenny,' he said, pushing past her into the living room. 'Sorry if I got you up.'

'Oh, no, we were … up already.'

Oh, great – they'd probably been doing it just before he arrived. For some reason that just added fuel to his fury.

'Would you like some coffee or something? I've finally mastered the machine.'

'No, thanks.'

'Um … why don't you sit down?'

He appeared to be making her nervous. Good. 'I won't be staying long. I just came to tell your boyfriend to get stuffed. Where is he?'

'You just missed him.'

'He's already gone? Shit!'

'Yeah, he was going to some assembly thing at the children's school. Are you sure you wouldn't like some coffee – or tea? You look a bit wound up.'

He stared at her, fiddling with things on the dining table, making herself at home in Richard's flat, and something inside him snapped. 'Doesn't it ever bother you?' he asked.

'Doesn't what bother me?' she asked, looking up at him.

'That you're taking him away from his family – from his kids.'

She flinched as if he'd hit her. Good.

'Of course I think it's sad, but it's hardly my fault his marriage broke down. '

'I suppose you can tell yourself that if it helps you sleep at night.'

'What's that supposed to mean?'

'I'm not saying Richard isn't to blame too, but you have to take some responsibility.'

'You make me sound like a home-wrecker, and I'm not. I'd never do that.'

'Jenny,' he said, almost pityingly, 'I know you lied to me, so you can stop pretending.'

'Lied to you about what? I don't know what you're talking about.'

'I asked you if your relationship with Richard started while he was still with Julia, remember?'

'And I said no, because it didn't. Okay, they were still living together, but their marriage was over before I even met Richard. I don't know if he told you, but—'

'Oh, yeah, he told me all the same lies you did. But you can quit the innocent act. I know your affair caused the break-up of his marriage.'

'Our … our … what?' Her voice was barely audible. Obviously she didn't like being confronted with the truth.

'Your affair. Julia found out about it and kicked him out.'

Jenny sank into a chair. 'Who told you that?' she asked faintly.

'Julia did.'

'She … *found out*? She …'

Either she was genuinely shocked at this or she was one hell of an actress. Maybe Richard had lied to her too.

'What did Richard tell you? That he'd left Julia for you?' he asked mockingly. 'Jenny, they never leave their wives. Come on, you know that, don't you?'

Dev watched the play of emotions on her face as his words hit home – her sudden pallor, the slight trembling of her lower lip – with malicious triumph. It gave him a twisted sense of satisfaction that he had got to her. It seemed she had really believed that Richard had chosen her over Julia. 'Did you really think he'd left his wife for you?' he taunted her. 'That he'd abandoned his children for you?'

Jenny bit her lip. She turned away, hiding her face from him. When she looked up again, her eyes were hard. 'Well, shit happens,' she said. 'Richard and I fell in love. We didn't mean to hurt anyone, but we can't help how we feel.'

'How touching,' Dev snarled. 'Just don't kid yourself that he'd still be with you if Julia hadn't kicked him out.'

With that, he stormed out of the flat.

As soon as he was gone, Jenny gave in to the shaking and tears she had managed to control while he was there. She couldn't give him the satisfaction of knowing that Richard had lied to her, and she had believed every word. She had been such a fool. *Of course* Richard had been lying to her. It seemed so obvious now. All that sneaking around, the hiding, the secrecy – it hadn't been because of his career.

It had been because he was cheating on his wife with her and he didn't want to get caught. How could she not have seen it? Or had she believed him because she wanted so badly for it to be true?

The truth was Richard had never chosen her. He had gambled and lost, and she was the booby prize. He wouldn't be with her now if Julia hadn't thrown him out. She would still be his … mistress. She shuddered, feeling sick now as the reality of their relationship dawned on her. It was all so sordid and ugly. She was a home-wrecker, just like Dev had accused her. She had taken Richard away from his wife and children, and she hated that. But more than that, she hated the fact that he hadn't left them by choice. He had never loved her enough. Maybe he had never really loved her at all.

'Dev, you wanted to see me?' Richard strode into Dev's office.

'Yeah. I called in at the flat this morning but you'd already left.'

'Problem?' Richard asked, frowning as he took in Dev's expression.

'Yes, I have a problem. Richard, you're going to make it impossible for me to do my job effectively if you're not honest with me. I thought you understood that.'

'What are you talking about? What do you think I've lied to you about?'

'I *know* you've lied to me about you and Jenny. I know you were together before you split up with Julia.'

Richard sighed. 'Look, okay,' he said, 'maybe I was a bit economical with the truth. I just thought the fewer people who knew, the better. It's true Jenny and I started seeing each other before Julia and I officially separated, but you know that our marriage was over long before that, so—'

'Uh-uh,' Dev shook his head, 'try again.'

'What?' Richard looked at him sharply.

'I know it all. You two had an affair, and Julia threw you out.'

'Oh.' Richard sank into a chair. 'How did you find out?'

'Julia told me.'

'Hang on – you were at the flat. You didn't say anything about this to Jenny, did you?'

'Yes, I did. She'd lied to me about it as well. I mean, I'd expect it of her, but I thought you at least would—'

'Shit, Dev! Have you any idea of the damage you could have done? Jenny was probably very upset and angry. What if she decided to go tearing off to the papers with her story?'

'Why would she do that? I mean, if she hasn't done it by now—'

'I just wish you'd spoken to me first instead of blurting it out to her like that.'

'What do you mean – blurting it out?'

Richard sighed. 'Jenny wasn't lying to you. She just didn't know the exact truth.'

'Are you telling me she didn't know your marriage wasn't over when you met her?'

'No. I told her the same thing I told you – that Julia and I were staying together for the sake of my career, until the time was right.'

'Jesus!' Dev thought of Jenny's cold, defiant look this morning when she'd said, 'Shit happens.' He realised now that it had been bravado and instantly regretted the way he had spoken to her. He winced as he thought of the things he had said, that Richard wouldn't have been with her if Julia hadn't kicked him out – which might be true, but he wished he hadn't been so brutal. Still, he couldn't help feeling glad that she wasn't really as callous as she had tried to appear.

'How … how did she take it?' Richard sounded nervous. 'How did she seem?'

Dev thought of her face, the pallor, the trembling lip. He should have known she wasn't faking it. 'She was shocked,' he said dully, disgusted with himself now for being so nasty to her. It was Richard he had been angry with anyway – but she was the only one there so she had borne the brunt of his anger. 'I'd say she was very upset.'

'Christ, Dev! You could have really screwed things up.' Richard said.

'*I* could have screwed things up? Don't try to blame this on me. This is all *your* fault for not being straight with me in the first place – or with her.'

'Look, I'm sorry I lied to you, but it's what people do when they're having affairs.'

'Is that really the best you can come up with?'

'I don't have to come up with *anything* – not for you. This is between me and Jenny – and Julia. You're doing a bloody good job, Dev, and I'm really grateful, but I don't have to answer to you about my personal life.'

'You bloody do when putting a spin on your personal life is part of my job!'

Richard sighed. 'You're right,' he said, throwing up his hands in surrender. 'But just be a bit more bloody careful in future, would you?'

Look who's talking, Dev thought. 'You know, sometimes I wonder if I'm doing the right thing, helping to unleash you on the country.'

'No, you don't,' Richard said with a smug smile.

That was true. He genuinely believed Richard would be able to do real good in government. It was the only reason he had taken this bloody job. Despite his wealthy and privileged background, Richard had a well-developed social conscience and it was his genuine desire to help those less fortunate than himself that had led him into politics. They had met in college when they were both volunteering for a homeless charity. He had been impressed by Richard's willingness and capability, and his total lack of squeamishness when faced with some pretty grim situations. He was always ready to muck in cheerfully. Of course, some of that youthful fervour had been knocked out of him along the way, but Dev knew he was still driven by the same basic desire to change things for the better.

'No, I don't,' he conceded. 'That's the only reason I'm still here. But any more lies and I'm gone.'

'Understood. Now,' Richard smiled, 'have you seen the story about the health minister and the lap dancer that's in this morning's papers?'

'*Seen* it?' Dev said scathingly. 'Who do you think wrote it?'

'Oh! Right. Good job. You see, this is why you can't leave me, Dev.'

Jenny had spent the whole day in Richard's apartment, too floored by Dev's revelations to stir herself – not even to get dressed. She sat on the sofa, staring into space as she went over and over it in her mind, trying to figure out what it meant. Did it change anything? Did it change *everything*? In a way nothing was fundamentally different from how it had been this morning. But in another way everything was different. This morning she had believed that Richard loved her – that he wanted to be with her more than anyone else. Now she had no idea if that was true or if her happiness was based on a lie.

She still hadn't reached any conclusions when Richard finally came through the door.

'Jenny? What are you doing, sitting here in the dark?' He flicked a switch and the room was filled with light. She hadn't even noticed it getting dark.

He came over to the couch. 'Sorry I'm so late,' he said, bending to kiss her. She didn't respond. 'I didn't think you'd still be here.' He leaned over to kiss her again, but she turned her face away.

He sighed, sitting down beside her.

Jenny took a deep breath. She was no good at confrontation, but she had to let him know how she felt. 'I know you lied to me – about you and Julia.'

'Dev told me he was here this morning.'

'He thought I knew. Not surprisingly,' she added bitterly. 'Most people do know when they're having an affair.'

'Darling, I'm sorry I lied to you,' he said, stroking her arm lightly. 'I just wanted you so much.'

'I *asked* you – I specifically asked you, time and time again, and you told me it was over between you and Julia.'

'It was just that I was so desperate to be with you,' he pleaded. 'I love you so much, Jenny.'

'So you lied to me,' she said, tears making her eyes smart. 'You made me a mistress.' She spat the word at him. 'You made me the person who broke up your family and took your kids' father away. I would never have been that if I'd known.'

'I know you wouldn't,' he soothed, wiping tears from her cheek. 'I know you're not like that. That's why I lied to you – I knew you wouldn't stay with me if I told you the truth. I was desperate. A man in love will do desperate things.'

'*Do* you love me?' she asked him in a small voice. 'Is that even true?'

'Of course it's true!'

'Dev said you're only with me because Julia kicked you out.' She sniffed.

'Jenny!' He reached for her and pulled her forcefully into his arms. 'That's not true. Dev doesn't know everything. I'm sorry I lied to you, but I do love you – and I want to be with you, no matter what.'

She searched his eyes, desperately wanting to believe him – and not liking herself much for wanting that.

'Please forgive me,' he said.

She buried her head in the crook of his neck. She knew she would forgive him. She believed that he really did love her, just not as much as she had thought. And she loved him – maybe not quite as much as before, but she did love him. However it had come about, he was hers now.

'It's Jeremy's party next week,' he said, pulling back to look into her face. 'Our coming out. If you still want to, that is?'

'Yeah.' She nodded. 'Of course I do.' She blinked back tears, struggling to dredge up a weak smile. She should be so happy. She had waited so long for this, dreamed of standing at Richard's side in public, and now it was spoiled. She wished she could go back to not knowing.

'Darling.' He nudged her, and she lifted her face to his. 'You won't tell anyone else, will you?'

'No, of course not.' She shook her head dazedly.

'I mean even your friends – just in case.'

'I wouldn't tell anybody.' It wasn't something she'd want people to know anyway. A thought occurred to her. 'Why has Julia never said anything? She must have been angry when she found out. Why has she kept quiet about your … our affair?'

'I don't know. I'm just bloody grateful that she did. I suppose she still cares about my career.'

'Yeah, maybe,' Jenny said, laying her head back on his shoulder. Or maybe she still cares about you.

Chapter 11

'Do we *have* to go to this party?' Jenny fiddled with her earrings in the mirror.

Richard came up behind her, taking her by the shoulders and looking at her reflection. 'I'm sorry, darling,' he said, dropping a kiss on her shoulder, 'but *I* have to go. I need to keep Jeremy sweet – and to put on a public display of getting on with him. Anyway, Dev's tipped off one of the papers and they're going to get a picture of us arriving together. After tonight we won't have to sneak around any more – and it will give you a chance to meet everyone too. I thought you'd be glad you can be a proper part of my life now.'

'I am.' She put a hand over his, smiling back at him. She really was looking forward to their relationship being out in the open, but the down-side was that she would have to go to things like this party at Jeremy's house. She only knew Jeremy from television, but she was in no great hurry to meet him in real life. Even Richard didn't get on with him, and Richard got on with everyone. She was nervous about the evening and wished she could have had a less intimidating introduction to Richard's world.

'Anyway,' he added, wrapping his arms around her and resting his chin on her shoulder, 'I thought you were the ultimate party girl.'

'Mmm, just not the ultimate Moderate Party girl,' Jenny told him.

Truth was, she had only gone out so much in order to find someone to stay in with. Now that she had, she didn't care if she never went to another party as long as she lived. She would happily hang up her dancing shoes for good and spend the rest of her evenings snuggled up with Richard on the sofa or wrapped around him in bed.

'Not your kind of party, I suppose.' Richard smiled sympathetically at her.

'I prefer more intimate ones,' she said, turning around and reaching up to kiss him.

Richard groaned softly, kissed her back, then reluctantly pulled away. 'If you really don't want to come, you don't have to,' he said. 'It'll probably be very boring for you. I'll make your excuses, if you like. We could go out another time, just the two of us.'

'No – I'll go if you're going. I just want to be with you. Anyway, I would like to meet everyone. But what if they don't like me?' she fretted, turning back to the mirror and wondering for the umpteenth time if the pearl earrings were okay or if they just made her look like she was trying to be something she wasn't – Julia, in a word. Pearls weren't really her, but she was trying to be less *her*, trying to seem more serious and grown-up.

'I wouldn't worry about it. I'm sure they'll all love you. Except Jeremy,' Richard laughed, 'but he doesn't like anyone.'

She threw him an anxious look.

'Don't worry,' he said soothingly. 'I'll be with you.'

An hour later, Jenny stood alone in Jeremy's grand living room, trying to space out her sips of wine without much success. She was sorry she hadn't taken Richard up on his offer when he had given her the opportunity to chicken out of coming. So much for staying with her. They had been met almost as soon as they arrived by a tall, angular blonde, whom Richard had introduced as Susie.

'Susie's my right-hand woman,' he told Jenny. 'She runs the office. In fact, she pretty much runs my life.'

Susie had barely glanced at Jenny as they shook hands and then, after introducing her to Jeremy and his wife, Celia, she had whipped Richard off and Jenny hadn't seen him since. Celia had looked at her as if she was something she'd stepped in. But Jeremy's face as he put a limp hand in hers really shocked her. His phoney smile faded as his eyes swept over her from her hair to her shoes, and he stared at her as if he almost hated her. As soon as Richard had disappeared, Jeremy left her without another word, but she still felt his eyes on her from time to time and looked round to find him glowering at her shoes or her hair.

Richard was circulating madly and she was left alone kicking her heels, ignored by everyone and desperately trying to look as if she didn't care. No doubt Julia could hold her own at parties like this and wouldn't need Richard to hold her hand. She took another big slug from her glass, draining it in one go and picking up another as a waitress passed with a tray. Sod it, she thought, this lot probably wouldn't notice if she passed out drunk under a table.

'Hello, Jenny.'

She spun around to find Dev smiling down at her.

'Oh, hi!' A wide grin spread across her face as relief suffused her. 'God, it's so nice to see you.'

'Really?' Dev's face registered surprise.

Her smile faded as she remembered the last time they'd met. She had momentarily forgotten he thought she was the lowest form of pond life.

'Jenny,' Dev said quietly so no one else would overhear, 'I'm sorry about the things I said the other day when I came to Richard's flat. I thought you knew—'

'It doesn't matter,' she interrupted with a toss of her head. Damn!

Why had Richard put him straight about that? She'd rather Dev think badly of her than feel sorry for her. 'You weren't to know.'

'Still, I was out of order. I was pissed off with Richard for not being straight with me. I didn't realise—'

'Shit happens. Forget it,' she said, desperate for him to drop the subject.

'You might want to go a bit easy on that,' he said as she knocked back half her wine in one go. 'You'll be on the floor in no time.'

'Dream on!'

Dev laughed.

'Sorry – I'm just trying to anaesthetise myself against this lot.'

'Are they giving you a hard time?'

'Not really. They're not giving me so much as the time of day.'

'Where's Richard?' He sounded censorious.

'Oh, he's busy,' she shrugged, 'schmoozing everyone, as only he can. He wouldn't want me clinging to him.'

'He's an idiot.'

'I wouldn't want that either,' Jenny said hastily.

Dev looked unconvinced.

'You don't have to stay with me,' she said. She didn't want him to think he had to nursemaid her. 'I'm sure you want to mingle. I'm fine on my own, honestly.'

'I'm perfectly happy where I am,' Dev told her.

Jenny beamed up at him and Dev's heart did a flip. How does she do that? he wondered. How can she make me feel like a bloody hero just for standing next to her at a party?

'Don't mind them,' he said, nodding in the general direction of the crowd. 'They just don't know how to behave around a pretty woman.'

'Put her down, Dev,' a deep female voice interrupted. A tall, big-boned woman with straight white hair and a face like a rosy-cheeked bulldog joined them.

'Hello, Pauline.' Dev grinned at her, bending to kiss her cheek. 'This is Jenny. Jenny, Pauline.'

'Hello, nice to meet you.' Pauline took Jenny's hand in both of hers, giving it a sturdy shake. 'I hope this chap isn't pestering you.'

'Oh, no, he's being very chivalrous, actually – keeping me company while Richard's off working the room.'

'Impossible!' Pauline huffed. 'Dev hasn't got a chivalrous bone in his body.'

'Fantastic *Newsnight* last night!' Dev said to her. 'You held the line brilliantly.'

'Well, someone has to put these people in their place.'

'I was almost starting to feel sorry for the minister. D'you suppose he's picked his ego up off the floor yet?'

'Oh, he'll live.'

'Pauline gave the home secretary a mauling on *Newsnight* last night,' he explained to Jenny. 'She was a bloody star!'

'Silly little man had it coming,' she said briskly. 'Does that mean I'm back in your good books? I've been in the doghouse,' she explained to Jenny. 'I was very naughty – went off-*piste* a bit on *Question Time* recently.'

'A bit!' Dev scoffed. 'She said she was in favour of bringing in castration for sex offenders.'

'Chemical castration,' Pauline said, as if in mitigation. 'I wasn't talking about chopping anything off. Though that would be good enough for the blighters, if you ask me.'

'Which unfortunately they did,' Dev said wryly. 'But you more than redeemed yourself last night.'

'Anyone else you'd like mauled, just line 'em up!'

'I'll bear that in mind.'

'But we mustn't talk shop all night,' Pauline said. 'We'll bore poor Jenny here to death. So, what do you do, Jenny?'

She was chatting happily to Pauline and Dev when Richard finally came in search of her. 'Hello,' he said. 'I see you found some friends. Having a good time?'

'Yes.' No thanks to you, Jenny thought, slightly miffed that she could have been standing around on her own for the last half-hour for all he knew – or cared, a little voice in her head nudged.

Seconds later she found herself wishing he hadn't bothered to check up on her at all, as Jeremy's wife Celia sidled up to bend his ear. 'Richard!' she brayed, smiling as much as her Botox would allow. Her eyes flickered over Jenny, and she nodded at Dev and Pauline.

'Celia!' Richard greeted her.

'I saw darling Julia the other day, did she tell you?' Celia said.

'Um, no, she didn't.'

'She's looking marvellous, I must say.'

Must you? Jenny thought, gritting her teeth, while Pauline and Dev studied their shoes.

'I so miss our cosy little dinners. Julia was always such a fabulous cook! D'you remember the time—'

'More wine, Jenny?' Pauline boomed, drowning what Celia was saying. 'You're on the red, aren't you?' She grabbed a bottle from a nearby table and topped up Jenny's glass. 'It's pretty filthy. I'd go easy on it, if I were you – that cheap stuff gives you the most frightful hangovers. Dev, how about you? Care to take your chances?'

Dev shook his head, one hand over his mouth to conceal his laughter. He could have kissed Pauline – and cheerfully decked Celia, woman or no woman.

Jenny smiled gratefully at Pauline, who winked at her almost imperceptibly.

'I haven't given up hope of seeing the two of you back together again,' Celia was saying to Richard now.

'Ah, well, um, I don't think … That's very kind of you, but—'

Jenny wished just once he'd forget about being a twenty-four-hour Party person and tell the stupid, ignorant cow to get stuffed. She wished he'd stand up for her. She glanced at Dev and saw that he at least was looking gratifyingly murderous. Somehow she didn't think he'd just stand there and take it on the chin, being smooth and diplomatic, if his girlfriend was being insulted.

They were called into dinner, and Jenny was seated between Dev and David, the young shadow minister for education, who introduced himself to her, clearly intent on being charming. Richard was at the far end of the table beside Celia, and Jeremy was at the other end.

'Have you met Lord Kenton?' David introduced the man opposite her.

'Call me Simon,' the man said. He had more layers of crinkly neck than a tortoise. Jenny reckoned he must be a hundred if he was a day.

'So what do you do, Jenny?' David asked, turning to her.

'I'm a nanny.'

'Ah!' Simon's eyes lit up. 'Are you very strict?'

'Oh, well, not *very*.'

'Oh, go on, I bet you're quite the disciplinarian.' Simon's eyes twinkled.

'Discipline is quite a speciality of Jenny's, as a matter of fact,' Dev said quietly.

'Really? Tell me, how do you keep the little blighters in line? Do you make them sit on the naughty step – like that Supernanny woman on the telly?'

'Jenny's more of a believer in giving them chores, aren't you, Jenny?' Dev turned to her.

'Good for you!' Simon said, his face reddening in his enthusiasm.

'You have to be firm, don't you? Show them who's boss. I'm a great believer in discipline myself – never did anyone a bit of harm. There's not enough of it nowadays. Supernanny's a splendid woman – splendid!' For a moment he just stared blankly into space, seemingly lost in admiration for her. 'So, what sort of punishments do you give your boys if they misbehave?'

'Well, first of all, they're sometimes girls,' Jenny said. She didn't want to get him too excited — he looked as if he might keel over from a heart attack at any minute.

'Of course, of course. But just say, for example, I was one of your charges and I'd been a naughty boy. What might my punishment be?'

His eyes gleamed and Jenny had to bite her lip to stop herself giggling. 'Well, I might, um, make you tidy your room ...'

'Or clean the bathroom,' Dev put in.

'Really?' Simon looked at her eagerly. 'I like the sound of that.'

'I bet you do,' Dev said under his breath so only Jenny could hear.

'Yes, that beats the naughty step into a cocked hat.'

God, poor Mr Hodge, Jenny thought, going around thinking he's a freak. He should meet Simon. 'Well, that would only be if you'd been *very* naughty.'

'And that punishment would usually be reserved for the older ones, wouldn't it?' Dev added.

'My nanny died a couple of years ago,' Simon told her, his jowls sagging at the memory. 'I still miss her. I used to visit her in the nursing home, and she was very firm with me right up to the end. I remember I went to see her when I'd just been made a Life Peer and she didn't even congratulate me – just gave me a bollocking for slouching in my chair.' He brightened up again, seemingly delighted with this. 'Nanny was a marvellous woman,' he said, his jowls wobbling expressively, '*marvellous!*'

'Oh, don't talk to me about nannies!' Celia cut in. 'We've had frightful trouble with nannies, haven't we, Jeremy?' she called to her husband at the other end of the table.

'Frightful!' Jeremy chimed obediently.

'Most of them can't even speak English properly – and if they do, they have the most appalling accents,' she added, glancing at Jenny. 'Not at all what one would want one's children to pick up. We've been through three already this year alone. The last one was a thief. She stole several good pieces from my wardrobe.'

'Big girl, obviously,' Dev mumbled under his breath. Celia was built like a Sherman tank.

'Big girl with no taste,' she whispered back, and they smiled at each other.

'We discovered she was selling them on eBay,' Celia continued.

'Oh, poor you!' David said. 'That must have been miserable for you.'

'Resourceful big girl with no taste,' Dev whispered to Jenny.

'You know what I'm talking about, Richard.' Celia turned to him. 'You had that dreadful Spanish girl who walked out and left you in the lurch when Julia was away, didn't you?'

'Well, yes, but she was very much the exception.' He smiled across the table at Jenny. 'I've found most nannies to be very reliable.'

'Hmm.' Celia pursed her lips. 'I think that sort of behaviour is quite typical, actually. These young girls are so flighty. And some of them seem to think that sleeping with the man of the house is part of their job description. We had a Polish girl once who wouldn't leave Jeremy alone – obviously thought she was on to a good thing.'

What on earth would give her that impression? Jenny thought. 'Stupid Polish girl,' she whispered to Dev.

'She was always flitting about half naked, finding excuses to come downstairs in her underwear when she knew he'd be alone.'

'Game stupid Polish girl,' Dev whispered.

'She was always pestering him, wasn't she, Jeremy?'

Jeremy had a faraway look in his eye, but roused himself at Celia's prompt. 'Oh, yes, terrible nuisance,' he said absently. 'Terrible. Mind you, she did have some rather stunning underwear,' he said dreamily, a little smile tugging at the corners of his mouth.

'Jeremy!' Celia said sharply.

'Oh, I just mean … um … one wonders how she could afford it. It was obviously very expensive stuff – all matching sets, you know … lace and silk … lots of ribbons … corsets and … what do you call those bras that push you up here?' He cupped his hands under his chest.

'Jeremy!' Celia barked.

'Balcony bra,' Simon answered readily. 'Cunning little contraption, that.'

'I bet *your* nanny never flitted around in her underwear,' Jenny said to Simon with a playful wink.

'What?' His smile faded as he looked at her in shock. Then his face contorted and he made a strange groaning noise in his throat.

Oh, fuck, what had she said? She was only trying to make small talk. Please let him not be having an orgasm. Or a heart attack. She wasn't sure which would be worse. 'Are you all right?'

'Fine,' he rasped. He took a gulp of wine and promptly choked.

'Pull yourself together, Simon, there's a good chap,' Pauline said in her no-nonsense voice, thumping him on the back as he coughed and spluttered.

'Sorry, I didn't mean to—' Christ, she had to be more careful. She could have killed him with a remark like that!

'It wasn't your fault, Jenny,' Pauline said. 'But I think we should move on to safer topics. Now,' she looked around the table, 'who saw today's polls?'

David was gaping wide-eyed at Simon as he slowly recovered from his coughing fit. Finally he turned to Jenny. 'Are you coming to Brighton next week?' he asked her.

'Yes, I am.'

'Great! That should liven things up a bit.'

Chapter 12

The Moderate Party Conference began on the first Sunday in October. Jenny stayed in Richard's flat the previous night and was up early that morning, too keyed up to sleep any longer. It was a bright, blustery day and wind rattled the windows, echoing the rattling of her nerves as she stood in front of the mirror in Richard's bedroom. She was surprised by how nervous she felt about today. After all, she and Richard had already appeared in public together and there had been a brief flurry of stories about them in the press. But she knew that the media scrutiny would be intense at Conference. With that in mind, she had spent the previous week agonising over what to wear and had blown the last of her savings on a new outfit for the occasion. She had deliberately steered away from her usual boho style. The dress was still her beloved vintage, but designer vintage, and even though she had bought it at a hugely reduced price on eBay, it had cost her a small fortune. But Liam and Ollie had been impressed when she had shown it off to them earlier in the week.

'Do you think this dress is okay?' she asked Richard, turning to face him as he emerged from his dressing room.

'It's fine,' he said, frowning as he fiddled with his cufflinks.

'Fine? Here, let me do that.' Jenny held out her hand and he dropped the cufflinks into it, presenting his wrists to her.

'I don't know much about women's clothes,' he said. 'Or men's, for that matter, Dev's always having a go at me about what I wear. He'll probably make us both change.'

'God, I hope not. I blew the last of my holiday pay on this. But you look perfect,' she said as she finished fastening his cufflinks. 'And you're the one who matters. This is *your* big day. I'm just the sideshow.'

He left her to finish getting ready, and as she applied her make-up, the doorbell rang. A moment later she heard Dev's voice in the living room. He was travelling to Brighton with them on the train. When she had tweaked her perfectly tousled hair one last time, she went to join them.

'Hello, Jenny.' Dev turned as she came into the room and she could feel his eyes raking over her. 'Is that what you're wearing?' he asked.

She spread her arms in a what-the-fuck-does-it-look-like gesture, her face falling.

'What did I tell you?' Richard smiled crookedly.

'Don't I look all right?' she faltered.

'You look amazing,' Dev said. 'That's the problem.'

'Um … sorry?'

'You look as if you've just stepped out of *Vogue*. Remember what I said about keeping it low key? Not drawing attention to yourself?'

'Well, no one will be looking at me anyway – they'll all be focused on Richard.'

'Not with you dressed like that, they won't. There's going to be a lot of media attention on you no matter what, but we need to do anything we can to downplay it. Have you anything else you could change into?'

She raked through her wardrobe in her mind, but there was nothing Dev would consider suitable. 'Not really,' she said.

'Maybe we could get Susie or Amanda to lend you something,' Dev said, but as soon as he said it, he realised the other women were all much bigger than Jenny. There was no way she could borrow clothes from any of them without looking like a six-year-old playing dress-up. Damn it! 'No, that's not going to work.' He sighed.

'Maybe I should just stay in the background,' Jenny said, trying to hide her disappointment.

Dev glanced at his watch. 'No, I've got a better idea,' he said. He pulled his mobile out of his pocket and stepped away from her to make a call.

She heard him talking to Susie, briskly quizzing her about boutiques nearby. God, I hope he doesn't want to turn me into a clone of her, she thought.

Snapping the phone shut, he came back to her. 'Right, we're going shopping,' he said, grabbing her hand. 'We've just about got time. Richard, you go ahead to the station. We'll get a cab and meet you there.'

'But I haven't got any money to buy more clothes!' Jenny protested.

'Don't worry about that,' Richard said. 'Just get whatever you need,' he said to Dev, 'and I'll pay you back.'

'Bring your case,' Dev said to Jenny. 'We'll go straight to the station from the shop.'

'There's a boutique very near here that Susie recommends,' Dev told her as he flagged down a cab outside the building. He bundled Jenny and her case into it as he gave instructions to the driver.

A few minutes later they pulled up outside a small, exclusive shop and got out, leaving the cab waiting at the kerb. There were only a few customers inside and they all looked around as Dev strode purposefully in, ushering Jenny ahead of him.

'Okay, you take that side, I'll take this,' he said, pointing to the rails. She had to make an effort not to giggle. He was acting as though they were on an SAS mission.

He began raking impatiently through a rail of skirts and a sales assistant approached him. 'Can I help you, sir?' Tall and impeccably groomed, she had long, glossy blonde hair and spoke with a cut-glass accent.

'Yes,' Dev said. 'We're looking for something for Jenny here. We're in a bit of a hurry.'

'May I ask what the occasion is?'

'The Moderate Party Conference.'

'Ah, I see.' The girl assessed Jenny. 'What size are you – an eight?'

'Yes.'

'Okay, let's see.' She flicked speedily through the rails, moving from one side of the shop to the next as she pulled out several items, clearly focused on what she was looking for. 'How about these?' she said, laying skirts, jackets and tops on a glass counter, arranging them into outfits.

'Try this,' Dev said to Jenny, pointing to a green bouclé suit that the assistant had put together with a cream jersey top.

She was shown to a large changing room and dressed hurriedly, aware of Dev sitting on the sofa just outside. She could hear his foot tapping impatiently on the wooden floor.

'How's that?' the assistant called from the other side of the curtain, sounding rather breathless. Dev's urgency was communicating itself to her.

Jenny surveyed herself in the mirror. 'Um ... it's great! Perfect.' It wasn't something she would ever have chosen to wear, but it fitted perfectly, and it wasn't bad in a bog-standard classic way.

'Show me,' Dev called to her.

Jenny pulled back the curtain and stepped out into the room. She stood in front of him for inspection and experienced a guilty little frisson of excitement as he scanned her up and down critically. She felt like Kim Basinger in *9½ Weeks* when Mickey Rourke takes her shopping and bosses her around in the store – except without the scary whip-testing bit. The thought of Dev testing out whips beside her brought on another little shiver of excitement.

Get a grip, she told herself crossly. This was the twenty-first century – you weren't supposed to think it was sexy to be bossed around by a man telling you what you should wear, and you certainly weren't meant to find the idea of him wielding a whip remotely appealing.

'What do you think?' she asked.

Dev rose to his feet. 'It'll do,' he said. 'We'll take it,' he told the assistant.

The girl held the curtain to the changing room, looking at Jenny expectantly.

'I'm going to wear it now,' Jenny explained.

'Very well,' the girl said. 'If you could just take it off for a moment, I'll remove the security tags and hand it back to you. I'll get you a bag for your own dress.'

Moments later, Jenny had the outfit back on, her dress in a bag, and was standing beside Dev at the till while the sales assistant handed him a receipt.

'Thanks for all your help,' he said to her. They were about to go when his eyes dropped to Jenny's feet and he frowned.

'Do you sell shoes?' he asked the assistant.

She peered at Jenny's feet and frowned too. The shoes she was wearing didn't go with her new outfit. 'No, I'm sorry, we don't.'

'Well, never mind.' Dev sighed. 'Thanks again.'

The girl stepped out from behind the counter to see them to the door, and Dev's eyes fell on her feet. 'Could we buy your shoes?' he asked.

Her eyebrows shot up. '*These?*' She indicated her feet.

'Yes.' He grinned. 'I know it's an odd request, but we're desperate.'

Jenny looked at the girl's feet. She was wearing neutral cream pumps that would go with pretty much anything. But there was a problem. She tugged at Dev's sleeve. 'They'd be too big,' she whispered to him.

'What size do you take?' he asked the assistant.

'Five.'

'I'm only a four,' Jenny said.

'There's not that much of a difference,' he said dismissively, turning back to the assistant. 'Name your price,' he told her, smiling disarmingly.

Boy, he could really turn it on when he wanted to, Jenny thought. The assistant was smiling back at him, obviously charmed.

'Look, I'll throw them in for nothing,' she said, pulling the shoes off and handing them to Jenny.

'Thank you so much, you've saved our lives.' Dev grinned at her.

'Just make sure your chap wins the next election!' she called after them as they bustled out of the shop.

'I'll do my best!' Dev called back.

They just made it to the station in time, joining Richard and several other Party members in the private carriage allocated to them. Richard was engaged with Dev and others from the office for the whole train journey, but Jenny didn't mind. She was so happy to be a real part of his life instead of his dirty little secret that she was perfectly content to sit across the aisle from them, flicking through glossy magazines and listening to Richard being intelligent and serious as they rattled towards Brighton.

Her moment in the sun came when Richard took her hand in

front of everyone and they walked into the conference centre together, cameras following them every step of the way. She had watched Richard and Julia doing this last year, and it was like being in a movie she had already seen, as if she had somehow magically jumped into the screen. As Dev had predicted, there was a great deal of interest in her, and all the photographers wanted pictures of her and Richard together. They made their way through the throng of media and into their hotel. The lobby was a sea of grey and black suits, and they moved swiftly through it to the lifts.

'Oh, there's David,' Jenny said, 'and Pauline.' She waved at them as they walked through the lobby. 'It's like a big holiday camp, isn't it?'

'Not really,' Dev said as they stepped into the lift.

It was like a very high-security holiday camp, she thought as they got out. The entire floor had been sealed off and Party stewards patrolled the corridors. She recognised several people milling around, and Susie immediately materialised at Richard's side.

'Hello, Jenny.' She nodded cursorily to her before turning her attention to Richard, talking low and fast in his ear as they walked.

They were ushered to a suite with a policeman standing outside it, while Dev went to his own room.

'Wow!' Jenny gasped as she followed Richard into a spacious sitting room. 'This place is amazing!' It was the most luxurious hotel room she had ever been in, more a ritzy apartment, really. Two squashy sofas and a couple of armchairs were grouped around a low coffee table, and she threw herself onto one of the sofas. As soon as their luggage had been delivered and they were alone, she explored the rest of the suite. The bedroom was as sumptuously decorated as the sitting room. There were chocolates on the pillows of the enormous king-sized bed and a flower in the centre of the coun-terpane. Jenny stuffed one of the chocolates into her mouth and jumped off the bed again to take an inventory of the minibar and check out the wardrobe space. She found two pairs of slippers wrapped in cellophane, kicked off her shoes and unwrapped a pair, slipped them on and padded into the bathroom. It was all shiny marble, with two thick towelling robes hanging on the back of the door and a basket of Molton Brown toiletries on the washbasin.

'This is fantastic!' she squealed, running back into the sitting room, where she was surprised to see Richard had been joined by Dev and Susie. They were standing by the window, deep in conversation. Susie was holding a big diary and they were going through Richard's schedule, while a minion was busy hooking up a laptop. They looked startled as she hurtled in.

'So – what are you guys doing?' she asked, flopping into one of the armchairs.

'Just planning how to take over the country,' Dev said.

'We haven't tried on our slippers yet,' Susie smirked, glancing at Jenny's feet.

'Oh, well, plenty of time.' Jenny noticed a room-service menu on the coffee table in front of her and picked it up. 'Oh, I love room service. Why don't I order us all some food? I'm starving!'

'I'm fine, but you get whatever you want,' Richard said absently, barely glancing at her before going back to his diary with Susie.

'Dev, Susie, how about you?' She perused the menu. 'They've got cream tea. God, I love cream teas. Or sandwiches ...'

'Do you think you could read that without moving your lips?' Susie asked.

'Oh, sorry! I just thought ...'

'Thanks, Jenny,' Dev said, 'but I don't think anyone's hungry. We'll grab something later.'

'Maybe we should go to Martin's room,' Susie said in an undertone, throwing a significant look in Jenny's direction.

'No need for that.' Richard matched her hushed tone. He motioned to them to wait a moment, then crossed the room to Jenny. 'Darling, order anything you want from room service, but could you possibly have it in the bedroom? We're going to be working in here for a while.'

'Yes, of course. No problem.'

'Sorry – I'll make it up to you. I'm afraid this isn't going to be much fun for you.'

'No, it's fine. You warned me what it was going to be like. I wanted to come. I don't mind, honest.'

'Thanks.' He smiled at her.

'You should eat, though. You can't take over the country on an empty stomach.'

'We will, don't worry.' He turned back to Dev and Susie, not even noticing as she retreated.

'Those slippers look adorable on you, Jenny,' Susie said to her back as she left the room.

Back in the bedroom, she sat on the bed and bounced up and down a few times to cheer herself up. That Susie was a right cow. Jenny had only been trying to make herself useful, and she'd treated her like she was being a pest – and Richard wasn't a whole lot better. She couldn't help wondering if he'd have treated Julia like that. Maybe he wished she was here with him now …

Not wanting to brood about Julia, she busied herself unpacking her bags. When she had finished, she picked up the remote and flicked through the channels on the TV. There was nothing on – it was too early. She gazed listlessly at the room-service menu again, but she had lost her appetite. It wasn't much fun on your own. She sighed. It was such a waste of this lovely room. She and Richard should be having sex in it. There was bugger-all chance of that now.

Maybe she should go down to the lounge. At least there would be people there. She might run into Pauline or David, though they would probably be too busy to hang out with her. Or she could go for a walk along the seafront. It was cold, but bright and sunny. She got up and went to the window, breathing in the sharp tang of sea air, wishing Liam and Ollie were here. She'd been to Brighton before and it was a town where you could have a lot of fun if you were with the right people.

Well, there was always the tub. She could stay here, laze around and enjoy the room. Later she could have a long luxurious bath and use all the posh toiletries. She picked up the hotel brochure and idly flicked through it. There was a spa and a beautician, and she read through the list of treatments on offer. She could have a seaweed wrap or a facial. But first she'd go and explore the rest of the hotel and maybe have a wander along the front. After she had reapplied her lipstick, she pulled on her jacket, picked up her bag and went out.

Richard, Dev and Susie had been joined by Martin, the deputy leader, and they were all sitting around the coffee table now, deep in conversation. No one seemed to notice her as she went to the door.

'Where are you going?'

She jumped at Dev's voice, her hand on the door handle. 'Just out for a walk.' The conversation had suddenly stopped and they were all staring at her now.

'I don't think that's a good idea,' Dev said, glancing at Richard.

Richard got up as if from a signal and came over to her. 'Dev's right. You really shouldn't go out on your own while you're here.'

'But I wasn't going far – just for a walk around the town, and to explore the hotel.'

'The whole place is crawling with reporters, Jenny.'

'So they might take a picture. So what? I look okay, don't I?'

'You look gorgeous, but that's not the point – they'll be all over you the minute you set foot out there.'

'If I promise not to talk to strangers, can I go out?'

Richard shook his head. 'It's really not a good idea for you to go down there on your own. Wait until there's someone to go with you, okay?'

She sagged, deflated. So she was to be a prisoner in this room, only able to go outside if she had a minder with her. And when were any of them likely to be free to take her out? But she didn't want to be a burden, so she gave Richard a bright smile. 'Fine,' she said. 'No problem.'

'Thanks. I'm sorry this is such a bore for you,' he said before turning back to the others.

Back in the room, she flicked on the TV again and resigned herself to watching talk shows and flicking through magazines until lunch. She wondered what Julia had done at these conferences – of course, she would probably have had plenty of friends here to hang out with. After watching an American talk show where a line-up of boys waited to hear which of them had fathered the child of a stroppy teenager with yellow frizzy hair, she phoned Liam for something to do.

'Hi, babes, what are you up to? Having fun?'

'Hardly. I'm under house arrest.'

'What?'

'I'm under strict orders to stay in my room unless accompanied by a responsible adult, not to talk to strangers, yadda, yadda.'

'Bollocks to that! Come home.'

She sighed longingly. Liam would probably be making one of his great hangover Sunday-roast dinners. They could go to the pub later. 'I want to do this right, though,' she said, more to herself than to him.

'It's not like you to accept being grounded, Jenny. That doesn't sound like the girl I know and love. Have you forgotten everything you learned at school?'

'Are you suggesting I sneak out?'

'Hang on, let me get this straight. You've been told to stay in your room and it hasn't even *occurred* to you to make a break for it? God, you've been hanging out with those stick-up-their-arses bloody grown-ups for too long.'

'Are you accusing me of having a stick up my arse?'

'Remember who you are, Jenny. That's all I'm saying.'

Liam was right she thought, when they had hung up. She shouldn't be taking this lying down. At least sneaking out would be fun. She went to the door and listened to the voices in the other room. She was in luck – after she had been listening for a few minutes, Susie announced that it was time for Richard to go and do an interview, and she heard everyone else getting up to leave. As their voices faded, she opened the door gingerly, feeling like a guilty schoolgirl. The sitting room was empty, and she darted across it quickly and went out into the corridor. She smiled confidently at the security people as she headed in the direction of the lift, but at the last minute she veered to the exit for the stairs. She knew she would be in no danger of bumping into anyone there. She skipped quickly down the flights, feeling giddy with the thrill of her escape, and then she was out in the lobby – freedom! That was easy, she thought, pulling her mobile from her bag and dialling Liam's number.

'Liam, I'm out! I'm out!' She laughed.

'That's my girl. I'm proud of you, babes.'

'I—' She stopped suddenly. People were converging around her and cameras were flashing in her face.

'Jenny.' She felt a hand on her shoulder and turned to find Susie smiling at her tightly. Without a word, Susie turned her around and steered her back in the direction of the lifts. 'I thought you were going to stay in the room,' she said when they were alone.

'I was, I just ...' Grrr, she hated having to explain herself to this stuck-up cow. 'I just needed to get out for a bit. I was going stir-crazy cooped up like that.' Maybe there was a normal human being in there somewhere she could appeal to.

'God, you were only in the lobby a minute and already the press were starting to descend on you. Have you any idea how damaging it could be to Richard if you said the wrong thing? Obviously you know nothing about politics, but I'd have thought basic common sense …'

Nope, no human being there, Jenny thought disconsolately as Susie continued to berate her. When they got to their floor, she shepherded Jenny down the corridor to a room that had been designated as an office, the beds removed and replaced with tables, chairs and sofas.

'Look who I found in the lobby,' she announced, pushing Jenny ahead of her into the room, her hand still clamped on her shoulder, as if she had just made a spectacular citizen's arrest. Great, Jenny thought, they were all there to witness her humiliation – David, Jeremy, Pauline, Dev, Richard and a petite blonde Jenny didn't recognise. She gave a sheepish little wave.

'Sorry,' she said. 'I'll be good, I swear. I'll go back to my room and I won't make a break for it again.'

Dev sighed. 'If you want to go out, Jenny, I'm sure we can find someone to accompany you,' he said reasonably. He looked at his watch. 'Amanda, maybe you could go for lunch with Jenny,' he said to the petite blonde. 'We don't really need you right now.'

Jenny saw Amanda stiffen at this suggestion, her face a mask of outrage and indignation. Don't worry, Jenny thought. I don't fancy you for a minder either.

'No, that's not necessary, really – thanks anyway, Amanda,' she said, smiling at her as if she had been the one to suggest they go to lunch together. 'I'll just stay here and get room service – live the dream!'

Pauline got up then and came over to her. 'Why don't you come down to my room and meet Alan, my husband? He's here for the day and as bored out of his mind as you probably are,' she said. 'I'm sure he'd love to have someone to go for lunch with – if you'd like to, that is?' she asked.

'Oh, yes, that'd be lovely.' Jenny nodded gratefully. 'If he really wouldn't mind.' They left the room and she felt tears pricking her eyes as they walked down the corridor. 'Thanks, Pauline. I'm sorry to be such a nuisance.'

'Don't be silly,' Pauline said, patting Jenny's hand. 'Don't let Amanda and Susie get to you, and Alan really will be glad of the company.'

'Alan,' she said when they entered her room. 'I've found a lunch companion for you. This is Jenny. Jenny, this is my husband, Alan.'

Jenny resisted the urge to laugh when she saw Alan, who was a slightly taller, more masculine version of Pauline. They could almost have been twins. Maybe it was true that people grew more like each other the longer they were together.

'Jenny.' Alan sprang up and came over to shake her hand. 'I'm delighted to meet you.' He sounded as if he really meant it. 'Now, let's get you some lunch, young lady,' he said as Pauline left the room.

Jenny felt a lot brighter when she got back to the suite after lunch with Alan. The sitting room was empty, but papers and mugs of coffee were scattered all over the place, along with plates of half-eaten sandwiches. Evidently they had got room service without her. Still, she had had a lot more fun with Alan than she would have had here, and at least she had got out. They had shared a bottle of wine and she was mildly tiddly too, which helped her mood. She didn't mind having to spend the rest of the afternoon in the room now, and there were a couple of receptions tonight that Richard would be taking her to. She kicked off her shoes and went over to close the door between the bedroom and the sitting room when she heard Susie and Amanda's voices as they came into the sitting room.

'We must call for someone to come and clean up in here,' Susie said.

'Ugh, yes, it's a mess,' Amanda answered. 'Richard can't stand working in chaos.'

'At least we managed to get rid of Conference Barbie,' Susie said.

Jenny froze on the spot, her hand on the doorknob.

Amanda guffawed in response. 'The cheek of Dev trying to foist her on me!' she said indignantly. 'I mean, what does he think I am? Thank God Pauline stepped in and got her out of our hair.'

'God, what an airhead!' Susie exclaimed. 'She's carrying on like she's on a school trip or something. You should have seen her earlier – "Oh, my God, this room is amazing, can we get room service, let's get cream tea."' She spoke in a high-pitched breathless rush in a cruel imitation of Jenny.

'Shhh.' Amanda giggled. 'Richard will be back in a minute.'

'I don't know what he was thinking, bringing her here,' Susie continued.

'You can tell Dev doesn't want her around,' Amanda said.

'No, he tried really hard to persuade Richard not to bring her, but to no avail. She obviously has her claws in deep.'

'What on earth does Richard *see* in her?'

'God knows! I never got on great with Julia, but she doesn't deserve to be replaced by *that*. What on earth was Richard *thinking*?'

'It's more a question of what he was thinking *with*,' Amanda said, and they both laughed.

They fell silent suddenly as the door opened again.

'Dev!' Susie breathed, sounding relieved. 'I was just filling Amanda in about Jenny. I can see why you didn't want her to come – total nightmare!'

'Shut up, Susie,' Dev said.

'Really, though, what a twit – I mean, you'd think she'd never been in a hotel before.'

'She's just young,' Dev said.

'Yeah, right – it's like Richard's brought his five-year-old kid. Though a five-year-old would probably be less—' Susie broke off abruptly as the door opened again and Jenny heard someone stride into the room. Before she knew what was happening, the bedroom door was pushed open, almost hitting her. She jumped out of the way with a yelp.

'Jenny!' Richard said. 'Sorry, I didn't realise you were there. I thought you were still out.'

She looked past him to the sitting room, where Dev, Susie and Amanda had evidently realised she must have heard what they'd said – they looked shocked, and guilty. She felt her cheeks burning – which was ridiculous. They should be the ones feeling embarrassed, the way they'd been talking about her.

'Oh, hi, Jenny,' Susie said in a small voice. She and Amanda smirked at each other.

Dev shot them a stern look.

'I think I left my BlackBerry in here,' Richard was saying to her. 'Have you seen it?'

'No, I haven't.'

'Have you been having fun?' he asked absently as he searched the room.

'Oh, yes, I had a lovely time with Alan, Pauline's husband.'

'Good, good.' He smiled at her vaguely. She realised he wasn't even listening as he drifted out, leaving her alone again.

In the evening, she got to go to a couple of receptions, which was marginally more exciting than sitting in the bedroom watching

Oprah. Richard made a little speech at each one and worked the room, being charming to everyone. But she felt like a child at a grown-ups' party. All anyone wanted to talk about was politics – they were all keyed up about the conference, and it was hard work keeping up, trying to match their enthusiasm. She was glad when it was time to go back to the room – though she was disappointed to discover that Richard wouldn't be going to bed with her. As soon as they got back, she went into the bedroom to kick off her shoes. When she returned to the sitting room, Susie, Amanda and Dev were all huddled together with Richard on the sofa.

'We're going to be working for a bit longer,' Richard told her, not looking up from his laptop.

'Oh, okay,' she said. 'Goodnight, then.' She retreated into the bedroom and closed the door.

Several hours later she jolted awake, her heart pounding, and looked at the digital display on the clock by the bed. It was four a.m. – not that she really needed the clock to tell her that. It was always the same time when she woke feeling like this. Her hands shook as she threw back the duvet, her heart racing. She turned on the bedside light and went over to the window. Pulling back the curtains, she saw her reflection in the glass and mentally ran through the familiar signs: dilated pupils – check; tight, pinched look – check; wild, frightened expression – check. She put a hand to her forehead and felt the clammy sweat. She had to get out of here – *now*. She knew she'd die if she didn't get out of the building immediately.

Don't be ridiculous, she told herself, trying to stem the mounting panic. You're fine. She tried to force herself to breathe deeply, to concentrate on sucking air into her lungs, but she only managed one breath, exhaling shakily almost on a sob. She wiped her sweaty hands on her pyjama bottoms. Suddenly she became aware of the total silence in the room, and it occurred to her for the first time that Richard wasn't in bed. They must still be out there working. She pulled on the hotel robe – she knew better now than to think their room was private – and opened the door to the sitting room. Finding it empty, she left the room and padded down the corridor to the office, pushing the door open tentatively.

Richard, Dev, Susie and Amanda were sitting on two sofas facing each other with a table between them. Richard and Dev were both tapping away on laptops, and Susie and Amanda were bent over a document on the coffee table, conferring with each other in low voices. The room was strewn with coffee cups, beer glasses and room-service trays, and reams of paper lay everywhere. When she appeared at the door they fell silent and four grey, tired faces looked up at her. She cringed from the concern in Dev's face.

'Jenny?' Richard was gazing at her questioningly.

She felt herself blush under their scrutiny. She could practically feel Susie and Amanda rolling their eyes. 'I – you're still working?' she said faintly.

'Yes,' Richard sat back with a heavy sigh.

'Will you be coming to bed soon?' she asked, hating to have this conversation with the others listening.

'I doubt it.' Richard rubbed the back of his neck. 'I'm probably going to be here all night.'

'Oh. Right.'

'Can't you sleep?' he asked, getting up and coming over to her.

She shook her head. He stood in front of her in the doorway, blocking her from the others, but she didn't want them to hear. She pulled him out into the corridor.

'How's the speech going?' she whispered, knowing she sounded as agitated as she felt.

'It's getting there. Are you okay?'

She shook her head.

'Are you having one of your anxiety attacks?'

'Yeah,' she said. 'I need to get out.' She ran a hand through her hair restlessly.

'Out? Jenny, it's four in the morning.' He glanced at his watch. 'You can't go out.' She knew he was trying to be patient, but she could see the irritation in his face. 'It's not even safe.'

'I don't feel safe in here.' Her voice shook.

'Come on,' he said, stroking her arm soothingly, 'you're perfectly safe. Nothing's happening – you know that.'

'You could come with me. Some fresh air might do you good.'

'Darling, I can't. I have to get this speech right – have you any idea how important it is?'

Of course she knew how important it was. He'd talked about little else for weeks. His keynote speech was the highlight of the conference. Excerpts from it would be broadcast in every news bulletin, his words reprinted and analysed in every broadsheet. It was a defining moment for him not just as leader of the Party, but as potential leader of the country. He not only had to impress the voting public, but also silence his critics among the Moderates and unite the Party behind him. She knew some of the diehards weren't convinced about the direction in which he wanted to take them. The speech had been through multiple drafts already and would no doubt go through several more right up until it closed the conference on Wednesday.

'Yes, of course,' she said, her voice sounding breathy despite her best efforts to control it. 'I know. I just … Sorry.' She shook her head, curling her lips in an attempt at a smile. 'I'll be fine. You get back to your speech.'

'Just try to relax. Would you like something from room service? Something to help you sleep?'

'No, I'm fine, really.' She blinked to dispel the tears that were welling. She felt like a child playing up at bedtime. Just try to relax, he'd said – like it was that easy. But she knew it wasn't fair to feel hurt by his lack of understanding. How could she expect him to comprehend something so irrational and idiotic? Richard didn't have a neurotic bone in his body.

Inside the office, Dev, Susie and Amanda heard Jenny's high, anxious whisper and Richard's deep soothing tones. Dev saw Susie and Amanda roll their eyes at each other and he felt a sudden urge to slap them. He had seen Jenny's face and there was something horribly familiar about her drawn, tight features, the sheen of sweat on her skin, the darting, panicked eyes. It was the same helpless, inexplicable terror he had seen so often on Sally's face when she was confronted with a plate of food. He wondered what had made Jenny look like that.

Richard came back into the room, closing the door softly behind him.

'Everything okay?' Susie asked, gazing up at him with every appearance of genuine concern.

'Yes, fine. She's just having trouble sleeping.'

'Poor thing,' Amanda simpered.

'Look, it's after four,' Richard said, consulting his watch again. 'You lot should get some sleep.'

'I wouldn't say no,' Susie said, standing and stretching. 'I'm getting to the point where I'm not much use anyway.'

'Me too,' Amanda said, joining her. They said goodnight and left.

'How about you?' Dev asked Richard when they had gone. 'Are you going to bed?'

'No, I'm on a bit of a roll here,' he said. 'Don't want to lose it. But you go – I need to work on this draft on my own for a while.'

'Right. If you're sure?' Dev said, switching off his laptop.

'Yes, positive.'

'Okay,' Dev said. 'You should try and get a few hours' sleep yourself, though.'

'I will,' Richard said, not looking up from his speech. 'Later. Goodnight.'

Walking back to his room, Dev stopped at the door of Richard's suite. He wondered if Jenny had gone back to sleep. It didn't seem likely, given the state she seemed to be in. He hesitated for a moment before opening the door and peeping in. The sitting room was empty. He crossed to the bedroom door and tapped on it gently.

'Jenny?' he called softly, in case she was asleep. 'Are you okay?' He waited a few moments, listening at the door, but there was no answer, so he crept out and went back to his room.

Chapter 13

The next morning, Jenny woke up alone and wondered if Richard had come to bed at all. She was surprised she had gone back to sleep. Last night that hadn't seemed possible. In the light of day, it was hard to remember how overwhelming the sensation of panic was, and she felt silly for making such a fuss – but that was always the way, until the next time. While it was happening it was all too real and she had no control over it. She had suffered from panic attacks for almost as long as she could remember. They happened with less frequency as the years passed, but they were still completely random and she had no way of knowing when the next would strike. She just wished it hadn't happened here. She cringed at the thought of Amanda and Susie seeing her like that – and Dev. She hated showing weakness in front of people who might use it against her to their advantage. That was why she had pretended to be asleep when Dev came knocking on the door last night after she had gone back to bed. He didn't need to see any more of her basket-case side than he already had.

There was no sign of Richard in the suite as she left to go down for breakfast. As she walked along the corridor to the lift, she noticed a breakfast tray outside one of the rooms and automatically bent down to scoop up a couple of croissants as she passed. She stuck one in her jacket pocket and the other in her mouth. As she approached the lifts, she heard Susie and Amanda's shrill voices.

'Ooh, look, there's a lift!' Susie squealed. 'I love lifts! Can we go in it, can we?'

Amanda giggled. 'We've got carpet in our room!' she shrieked. 'Oh my God, it's amazing! Have you got carpet, Susie?'

'Yes, but I haven't tried it on yet.'

They both laughed uproariously.

'Give it a rest, you two,' Dev's voice broke in.

As she turned the corner to the lift, they fell silent. She finished chewing her mouthful of croissant and swallowed. 'Hi!' she beamed at them, determined not to let them get to her.

'Good morning, Jenny.' Susie smiled at her. 'You look very pretty today.' She might have been talking to a five-year-old.

'Thanks.'

'Morning, Jenny. Did you sleep all right?' Dev asked her.

'Fine.'

'I hope we weren't making too much noise,' Susie said. 'We all tend to get a bit carried away.'

'Oh, no, I didn't hear a thing. There were ear plugs in the complementary basket of stuff, so I used them.' Wish I had them in now, she thought.

'Oh, clever you!'

The lift finally arrived and they all got in. Dev pressed the button for the lobby.

'We're going to one,' Susie said, pressing the button for the first floor. 'We're getting our hair done.'

'Having breakfast on the run?' Amanda asked as Jenny took another bite of her croissant.

'Oh, did you get room service?' Susie asked. 'Another wish fulfilled.'

'Oh, no,' Jenny said, licking buttery crumbs off her fingers. 'I nicked this off a tray outside one of the rooms.'

Dev frowned at her. 'You stole someone's breakfast? Why?'

'Just a reflex. Never pass up free grub.'

Susie's perfectly sculpted eyebrows shot up. 'But Jenny,' she said, 'you could have all the croissants you want from room service. You don't have to steal food.'

'Where are you off to now?' Amanda asked her, eyes narrowed suspiciously.

'I'm going down for breakfast. And before you clamp me in irons,' she said, turning to Dev, 'I'm meeting Alan.'

'I know,' he said calmly.

'Oh. Right.' Of course he'd be keeping tabs on her. 'I suppose you put him up to it?' She had really enjoyed lunch with Pauline's husband yesterday and thought they'd got on well. She was disappointed to realise his invitation to join him for breakfast was just a favour to Dev. Poor bloke had obviously been lumbered with keeping her out of mischief for the morning.

'No, of course not – he just told me about it, that's all. I think he's really looking forward to it – he was saying how much he enjoyed lunch yesterday.'

'Oh, good.' She smiled.

When the lift stopped at the first floor, Susie and Amanda got out.

'Don't mind them,' Dev said as the doors closed, without turning to her. 'They're a right pair of wagons.'

Jenny laughed in surprise and he turned to her then, smiling.

'Why don't you come to breakfast with Alan and me? It's a buffet! I hear they've got every kind of fruit you can think of,' she said. 'And there's an omelette station!'

'Sounds great, and I hate to pass on an omelette station, but I've got to meet Richard in the conference centre. He's doing press interviews all morning.'

'Oh, okay. Would you like a croissant, then? I've got another.' She took it out of her pocket and waved it at him.

'Are they good?'

'Delicious! Stolen ones taste better, you know.'

'I'll take your word for it. I wouldn't look good meeting the press with croissant crumbs all over my suit.' They had reached the ground floor and the lift doors opened.

'Enjoy the buffet,' Dev called as he strode off.

Jenny's second day at Conference was no better than the first – if anything, it was worse. She enjoyed breakfast with Alan, but he was going home and she wouldn't have him to hang out with any more. Richard was spending almost every waking hour (and there were almost twenty-four waking hours in his day at the moment) holed up with Dev, Amanda, Susie, Martin, Jeremy and the rest of the 'team'. There was a gaggle of people around him constantly, and when he wasn't with them, he was doing TV interviews, talking to the press and attending debates. He was the hero of the hour and everyone wanted a piece of him. Unfortunately, there were no pieces of him left for her.

She was bored to yells, but she daren't admit it and give Dev the satisfaction of saying 'I told you so'. So she pinned a smile to her face and tried to project perfect contentment. Few of the spouses had stuck around, and those who had weren't inclined to be friendly. She was so bored by the second day that she went to watch David making his big speech on education. She thought she might learn something and be able to join in the conversation more at tonight's receptions, but she fell asleep to the soporific drone of his voice in the overheated hall.

She was surprised when, late in the afternoon, as she was polishing her nails for the umpteenth time, Dev came back to the room and suggested going out for a walk.

'Seriously, Dev, you don't have to keep me amused and take me out for walks like a bloody dog,' she told him. 'I know how busy you are.'

'Well, as it happens, I have some free time, and I'm going out for a walk because I'm getting cabin fever. I just thought you might like to come with me, that's all. But suit yourself.' He headed for the door.

'No, wait!' Jenny jumped up. 'I'm coming.'

Dev halted, grinning at her. 'Thought you might.'

She ran into the bedroom and grabbed her jacket, not even hesitating at the thought of going out with Dev. She was so desperate to get out, she would have agreed to go for a walk with the devil himself.

It was a bright, sunny day but there was a biting wind from the sea, and Jenny's light suede jacket was far too thin to offer much protection. Dev took her arm and she leaned into his body against the sharp wind, the salt air stinging her eyes and nose. She shivered.

'Don't you have a warmer coat with you?' Dev asked.

'No, this is all I brought. Anyway, I don't actually own a proper coat.'

'You don't own a coat?' Dev sounded incredulous.

She shook her head, teeth clenched together against the cold.

'Do you want to go back?'

'No, it's so nice to get out.'

'Well, have this,' he said, taking off his coat and putting it on her shoulders.

'I can't!' she protested. 'You'll freeze.'

'I'm fine,' he said. 'Put it on or I'm taking you back to the hotel right now.'

Jenny obeyed, feeling guilty as she pulled it around her. Her hands were lost inside the sleeves and the coat reached to her toes, but she had to admit it was heaven.

'Better?' He smiled down at her.

'Much, thanks. I don't think it's a great look for me, though. Better hope no one takes my photo now.'

'You look cute.' He laughed. 'So, how did you enjoy David's speech?'

'Oh, it was terrific!'

'Really?' He looked at her sceptically.

'Yes, he was brilliant – I had a ball! It was *so* interesting.'

Dev's mouth twitched. 'The secret to lying is to keep it within the bounds of possibility.'

'What makes you think I'm lying?' she said indignantly.

'I've heard David speak.'

'Well, I thought what he said was fascinating.'

Dev looked like he was struggling not to smile. 'What was he on about?'

Ha! He thought he was going to catch her out, but she knew the answer to that one. 'It was about education.'

'Yes – and?' He looked at her expectantly.

'Schools and all that,' she elaborated. 'Teachers. Exams. Universities.'

'Yes, I know what education is, thanks. But what exactly did he have to say about it?'

'Oh, it was all about how rubbish the education system is now and how fantastic it's going to be when the Moderates get in.'

'And what exactly are they planning to do about it to change things?'

'You should know!' she told him reprovingly.

'I do. I just want to hear it from you. I'd be interested to know how David gets his message across to the … man in the street.'

'Right. Well, the Moderates have got all these ideas for … policies, you know, that they're going to, um … implement.' Whoa, that sounded good. Lucky she was so great at bluffing.

'They're going to implement policies?' Dev's voice was full of suppressed laughter. 'That sounds pretty radical. Any idea what these policies entail?'

She racked her brain for some electioneering slogans. 'Um … putting the "great" back in Great Britain. Getting the country back on its feet. Returning to the values of, um … olden times.' She was on a roll now. 'Creating a modern Britain. Boldly going where—' Oh, no, that one was *Star Trek*. Better quit while she was ahead. 'All that sort of stuff. It's going to be brilliant!'

'Right.' Dev laughed. 'It sounds like David made a big impression.' He made no attempt to hide the fact that he was laughing at her now.

Jenny frowned at him, then laughed with him. 'Okay, I fell asleep,' she admitted.

'Oh dear, poor David.'

'Well, I didn't get much sleep last night,' she said defensively.

'No. I suppose we can't entirely blame David's oratorical skills for making you doze off.'

'You won't tell him, though, will you?'

'No, of course not – he'd be crushed.'

'I bet that's what he did say anyway – more or less.'

'Probably.' They had reached a bend in the road where a café over-looked the sea. 'How about a cup of coffee or something?' Dev suggested. 'It'd warm you up.'

'Oh, yes, please.'

It was a relief to be inside the warm fug of the café. Jenny cupped her hands around an enormous mug of hot chocolate with marsh-mallows floating in it. 'Mmm. This is delicious – do you want a taste?'

'No, thanks.' Dev glanced at his watch.

'Do you have to get back?' Jenny asked, suddenly feeling guilty that she was probably keeping him from his work but realising she didn't want him to go. It was so nice to have someone to talk to.

'No, I'm OK for time.'

She relaxed again.

'So how are you finding Conference in general?' he asked.

She shrugged. 'It's all right,' she said, not wanting to admit how miserable she was. 'I don't think that lot like me very much, though.'

'They don't dislike you. It's not personal.'

'It's just that they want Julia back,' she said.

'Julia was a great asset to the Party,' he said simply.

She looked him square in the eye. 'And you think I'm a liability, don't you?' She tried to appear tough and nonchalant, but she steeled herself for a brutal answer.

'I think you have the potential to do Richard a lot of damage politically.'

'I'd never do anything to hurt him,' she protested.

'You may not mean to, but unfortunately that won't stop you doing it. And it's not just about the politics. I don't think you're good for him.'

'Tell me what you really think,' she said with a hurt laugh.

'Julia was really good for him at these things. She kept him calm, ran interference to make sure he had some peace. She's very diplomatic, but tough with it. She kept people at bay and made sure the atmosphere around him was calm, so he was able to focus completely on the job. She even helped with his speeches sometimes – she had some bloody good ideas.'

'And I'm just a distraction, I suppose? A flaky, attention-seeking, high-maintenance drama queen – that's what you think, isn't it?'

'No, it's not. But I don't think you appreciate the pressure that

Richard's under. The demands on his energy and concentration are unbelievable. This job is so full-on – and it's only going to get worse.'

'And you don't reckon I can give him the support he needs – that I can do what Julia did?'

'No, I don't.'

Jenny buried her face in her hot chocolate, taking comfort from the thick, sweet drink. She didn't want Dev to see that he'd upset her.

'Look,' he sighed, 'I don't have any problem with you. If it's any consolation, I don't think Richard is good for you either.'

Jenny's eyebrows shot up. 'But how can you – you don't even know me!'

He evaded her eyes. 'It's just an impression. I don't think he can give you what you need.'

'Twenty-four-hour attention?' she said bitterly.

'I didn't say that.'

'I can change.'

'Why should you?'

'Maybe I want to – for him. Because I love him.'

'Wouldn't you rather be with someone who loves you the way you are?'

'Richard *does* love me the way I am.'

'Then why are you so eager to change for him?'

'Because … the way I am isn't what he needs right now. You said it yourself.'

'You go about things the wrong way round,' he mumbled, not looking at her. They were silent for a while. 'What happened last night?' Dev asked finally.

'Sorry?'

'You didn't sleep.'

'I just have trouble sleeping in strange surroundings sometimes.' Huh – after years of lugging her stuff in plastic bags from one foster home to another, she could pretty much sleep on a knife's edge. But she didn't need him to discover her neurosis on top of everything else. He had more than enough ammunition already.

'Was that all?' he asked. 'You seemed … upset.'

'No,' she said firmly. 'I was just tired.'

He looked at her for a moment. 'You know, you can go home anytime you want – honourable discharge.'

'Still trying to get rid of me?' She scowled. She might have known he'd just taken her out to have another go at giving her the boot.

He smiled. 'Look, I'm offering you a get-out-of-jail-free card,' he said. 'I won't even say I told you so.'

She spooned up the dregs of her hot chocolate. She had to admit she was tempted. What was the point in sticking around? She never saw Richard and she was a prisoner in her room most of the time. Dev had vetoed her joining Richard on-stage after his speech on Wednesday, which was the main reason she had wanted to come in the first place – and Richard had agreed with him on that point.

He was smiling at her, watching her face. 'What do you think? We could arrange a car for you. Just say the word.'

Jenny looked up from her mug, a slow smile creeping across her face. Sod it – she was only cutting off her nose to spite her face by staying. 'You really won't say I told you so?'

'I really won't.'

'Hmm.' She tapped her fingers on the table, considering. 'Of course, it would mean missing Jeremy's big speech on the economy tomorrow.' She was trying hard not to smile.

'It would,' he said seriously. 'It's up to you. I know it must be a tussle.'

She grinned. 'How soon can you get the car round?'

Chapter 14

Jenny was packed and ready to go. Richard had been almost insult-ingly unperturbed about her decision and had made no attempt to persuade her to stay, which almost made her want to change her mind. But she knew rationally that it was because he wouldn't have any time to spend with her, so it made no difference to him.

Dev was standing by the window with Richard when she came back into the sitting room.

'All ready?' Richard asked.

Dev smiled at her too, obviously pleased that she was doing the right thing for once. She was glad. She needed Dev on her side, and it would be good if they could be friends. Dev's mobile rang and he pulled it out of his pocket, checking the caller ID before answering.

'Matt – what's up?' His face fell and a frown creased his forehead. Whatever the person at the other end was saying, it clearly wasn't anything he wanted to hear. Suddenly he threw a glance at her, his eyes cold and angry. She felt the hairs on the back of her neck stand up and a terrible feeling of dread washed over her. Surely the call couldn't have anything to do with *her*. No, she was being paranoid – he was just angry about whatever news he was getting and had hap-pened to look in her direction … hadn't he?

'Hang on a sec,' he said into the phone. 'Sorry,' he said to

Richard. 'I have to take this.' He threw Jenny another flinty glance before striding out of the room, the phone pressed to his ear. 'Yeah, go on,' he was saying as he went out the door.

'Do you suppose they've finally found out that you and Jeremy can't stand each other?' She smiled playfully at Richard, trying to dispel the nervous tension.

'Hmm? Oh, yeah.' Richard smiled distractedly. He seemed to have been unnerved by Dev's behaviour too. He sat down in one of the chairs and Jenny perched on the arm.

They both jumped when the door opened and Dev strode back in. 'Right, we've got a problem,' he said to Richard, throwing his mobile onto the table.

'What is it?' Richard looked alarmed.

'*Her*,' Dev said, eyeballing Jenny. '*She*'s the fucking problem.'

'Jenny?'

'You know I didn't want her here, I said she shouldn't come. And now she's become the story, just like I said she would.'

'What's she done?' Richard asked, seeming somewhat relieved. His attitude made Jenny relax a bit too. He obviously didn't think it could be anything too serious. Maybe she had made some fashion faux pas. Or perhaps someone had spotted her nicking that croissant yesterday. It would be a bit embarrassing, but hardly the end of the world.

'Why don't you ask *her*? Though much good it'll do you,' Dev said bitterly.

'Jenny?' Richard turned to her.

'I don't know what he's talking about,' she said, trying to keep her voice steady. The way Dev was looking at her was making her shake. This wasn't about a stolen croissant.

Dev finally took his eyes off her and turned to Richard. 'That was Matt from the *Record*. He's a mate, so he gave me a heads-up.

They've been offered pictures of Jenny.'

'Pictures?'

'It appears she's done some topless modelling in the past that she neglected to mention.'

'What? I have *not*!'

Dev ignored her. 'They're still in negotiations,' he said to Richard, 'so at least we've got a bit of time.'

'But ... there must be some mistake,' Richard said faintly. 'They're probably fake.'

Dev shook his head emphatically. 'No, they're genuine all right. Matt will have checked it out thoroughly.'

'Oh, Christ!' Richard put his head into his hands. 'What do we do?' He looked up helplessly at Dev. 'Can we get them not to publish?'

Dev shook his head. 'No chance of that. It's too good.'

They were speaking about her as if she wasn't in the room, and loath though she was to draw their attention back to her, Jenny had to say something. This was all some terrible mistake – it *had* to be. 'It can't be me,' she said.

Dev's head shot up, eyes glacial. 'How many times did I ask you about stuff like this? And you assured me there was nothing.'

'There isn't,' she insisted. 'I've never done topless modelling.'

Dev sighed. 'Well, maybe it's not a professional job. It could just be some personal snaps.'

'Don't you know where they came from?' Richard asked.

'Matt wouldn't tell me that. He has to keep his cards close to his chest. He can't risk anyone else getting onto the story.'

Richard groaned. 'Have you any idea who it could be, Jenny?' he asked her, clearly struggling to remain calm.

'No.' She shook her head miserably, fighting back tears.

'One of your ex-boyfriends, maybe?' Dev suggested. 'One of the stalkers?'

Oh, Christ, some of them probably *did* have dodgy pictures of her. But she couldn't believe any of them would actually sell them to a newspaper. Then again, if Paul could kidnap a guinea pig, maybe he wouldn't balk at this. Or there was that time … *oh, shit*!

'Ah, the penny drops!' Dev said, watching her face.

'Jenny?'

'Well, I did pose for this magazine once … but I don't know how they could have found those pictures. It was just a once-off. I'd forgotten about it.'

'Shit!' Richard swore.

'I told you if there was anything they'd find it,' Dev said.

'It's not like it was my job. I just—'

'Oh, don't tell me,' Dev mocked, 'you only did it to pay for an operation for your sick granny, I suppose?'

Jenny narrowed her eyes. God, he could be a bastard when he wanted to be! 'No, I don't have a granny. I just needed the money to pay the rent. The landlord was a total sleazebag and he kept trying to make a move on me. He had a key and he used to let himself in when I was—' Dev was looking very angry, so she stopped. He probably thought she was just trying to make excuses. 'I needed to pay the rent so I could get away from him. A guy I knew at the time was starting up a magazine and he offered to clear my rent if I posed for it.'

'Why didn't you just do a runner?' Dev asked.

'That would be like stealing!'

'So you got your kit off instead – very noble.'

Jenny crossed her arms over her chest. 'It was just a tiny little magazine,' she said defensively, on the verge of tears. 'It folded after about a month. I didn't think anyone I knew would ever see the pictures.'

'How explicit are they?' Richard asked.

'Um … they're just topless.' She blushed, her eyes trained on the floor.

'Maybe this could have been avoided if you'd been honest with me in the first place,' Dev fumed. 'I specifically asked you—'

'Look,' Richard interrupted in a calming tone, 'what's done is done. We just have to decide how we're going to deal with it. What are our options?'

'Well, like I said, there's no way we can get them to pull it. So you're just going to have to brazen it out.'

Richard sighed heavily, and for a moment they were all silent.

'Or,' Dev said slowly, 'you could distance yourself from it.'

'How do we do that?' Richard looked at him hopefully.

'I'm talking about *you*, Richard. *You* could still distance yourself from it.'

Jenny's eyes flew to Dev. God, he was ruthless.

'What do you mean?' Richard asked.

Dev gave Jenny a long look. 'Nothing,' he said finally, shaking his head. 'Forget it.'

'By "it" he means me,' Jenny said to Richard, her voice shaking. 'He means you could distance yourself from *me*.'

'Dev?'

'You asked for all your options.'

'You can't be serious,' Richard said.

'Can't I? How serious are *you* about becoming prime minister? Richard, have you any idea of the damage this could do to you?'

Jenny looked at Richard, slumped in his chair, wringing his hands, and was overwhelmed by guilt. This was his big moment and she was going to ruin it for him. She had so wanted to be good for him. 'I'm sorry,' she said softly, touching his shoulder. She took a deep breath, steeling herself to say the only thing she could think of to make it better. 'Look, if you want to … to dump me, I understand. I'll disappear and never bother you again. There'll be no story then – I'd just be someone you went on a couple of dates with.'

'Of course I don't want that, Jenny,' he said. 'But maybe it's just as well that you're going back to London now.'

'Yes,' Dev agreed, 'the sooner, the better. And when you get back there, don't talk to the press. If anyone offers you money for a story—'

'Of course I wouldn't!' she said, horrified. 'I'd never do anything to hurt Richard.'

'That might actually mean something if we could believe one word that came out of your mouth,' Dev said wearily.

'Dev!' Richard chided. 'Give her a break. She made a mistake.'

'I wouldn't do anything to harm his career,' she protested.

'Unfortunately, it's a bit late for that,' Dev said. 'Because you already have.'

He was interrupted by the buzz of his BlackBerry. He frowned down at the message. 'I'm due to do some press briefings,' he said to Richard, shoving it back in his pocket. 'We'll talk about this again later. With a bit of luck we'll manage to get through Conference before the story breaks.'

'Okay, see you later.'

'See you,' he said as he headed for the door. 'Bye, Jenny.' He glanced at her one last time and left.

'Sorry about Dev,' Richard said when he was gone. 'He has a bit of a temper, but his bark is worse than his bite.'

Jenny sincerely hoped she would never have the chance to put that to the test. His bark was quite enough to be going on with.

'He's been under a lot of strain lately, and he feels very passionately about what we're trying to do. He's put a lot into it.'

'I know,' she said, wrapping her arms around him. 'And so have you. I'm so sorry.'

He shook her off tetchily. 'God, Jenny, how could you have been so stupid?' he said.

Jenny jerked away from him as if he had hit her. Clearly he had been keeping his anger with her in check while Dev was there, but now he was letting it out. She was grateful he had shown some solidarity, but she was shocked at how angry and frustrated he actually was with her.

'I – it was ages ago, I never thought—'

'I can understand that, but God, how could you not have told Dev? When he *asked* you.'

'I didn't think of it,' she whispered miserably, her eyes swimming with tears.

He sighed. 'I know,' he said, stroking her arm. 'Don't worry about it, we'll sort something out.' She put an arm around him, resting her head on his shoulder, and this time he didn't shake her off. 'I'm sorry,' he said. 'I've just been thinking about myself, haven't I, and not of how rotten this must be for you? It's my fault. You wouldn't have to go through this if it weren't for me.'

'Me? Go through what?'

'Having those … pictures of yourself printed in a newspaper.'

'Oh!' She hadn't thought about herself until now. She really wished he hadn't brought it to her attention.

'Anyway, you get back to London and try to forget about it for now. Dev doesn't seem to think this is going to break until after Conference. Maybe it won't be such a big story after all.'

But he didn't sound hopeful, and neither was she. On the drive back to London, instead of the freedom and exhilaration she had anticipated, she felt as if a black cloud was hanging over her head, ready to pour havoc on her.

When Dev got back to the room after the press briefing, he found Richard alone, hunched over his laptop. 'Has Jenny gone?' he asked.

'Yes,' Richard said, leaning back on the sofa.

'Damn. I was hoping to catch her before she left.'

'Why? So you could lay into her some more?'

'I wanted to apologise. I shouldn't have been so hard on her.'

'No, you shouldn't. She was very upset.'

'I just lost it. I'm sorry.'

Richard leaned forward, resting his arms on his knees and clasping his hands, his eyes trained on the floor. 'Dev, you don't really think I should ... distance myself from this, do you?'

'No.'

Richard looked up. 'But you said—'

'It shouldn't matter to you what I think anyway.'

'Of course it matters. What's the point in having advisers if you don't consider their advice?'

'I'm not here to advise you on your love life.'

'Well, as you've pointed out to me before, I can't really separate the private from the public any more. So ... do you think I should ... distance myself?'

God, was he looking for *permission*? 'Look, I was just thinking out loud. Of course I didn't mean you should dump Jenny.'

'Right.' Richard nodded. 'Good.'

Dev sighed. That was, in fact, exactly what he had meant. He knew how ruthless it seemed, but he honestly thought Richard and Jenny were fooling themselves, and since it would eventually happen anyway, it would be better for everyone if they split up now and got it over with. He didn't believe for a minute that Richard was really in love with Jenny. He was simply making do with what he could salvage from the wreckage of his marriage. Jenny was what he was left with, so he was knuckling down to the task of being in love with her with the grim determination of a hurricane victim determined to construct something from a pile of rubble. Not only that, he was trying to convince himself and everyone else that the makeshift structure he had managed to knock together was his dream home.

Dev thought the threat of the impending scandal might be just the catalyst Richard needed to see his tumbledown shack for what it was. If he was going to end up leaving Jenny anyway, why not do it now? Why risk damaging his career for something that wasn't going to last? It was on the tip of his tongue to put all this to Richard, but then he remembered the look on Jenny's face when he had mentioned it before, and he couldn't go through with it. She deserved so much better, but as long as she thought Richard was what she wanted, he couldn't be the one to take him away from her.

Chapter 15

'I wonder if you're the first person ever to get sent down from a Moderate Party conference,' Ollie said the following day, grinning at Jenny as he jumped onto the sofa beside her.

'Sent down? What do you mean? I wasn't sent anywhere.'

'It means expelled,' Liam said, coming into the room. He plonked a bowl of popcorn on the coffee table and joined them on the sofa.

'I wasn't sent down or expelled, or whatever you want to call it,' Jenny said, grabbing the bowl and shoving a fistful of popcorn into her mouth. 'I just decided to come home.'

'Yeah, right,' Ollie drawled. 'I bet that henchman of Richard's had a hand in it, didn't he?'

'I don't know who you mean,' Jenny said primly.

'I mean that big handsome bugger who was interrogating you in the kitchen the other day,' Ollie said, leaning across her to the popcorn.

'Shhh, it's starting,' Jenny said, turning the sound up with the remote control. Sky News was doing an in-depth interview with Richard from the conference.

'I can't believe you've got me watching this,' Ollie groaned as the programme began.

Richard looked so handsome, and unbelievably sharp when she knew how little sleep he would have had last night and the strain he was under, thanks to her. She was a little annoyed, though, to see that the interviewer was a young, attractive female journalist – and even more annoyed at the way the foxy cow's eyes sparkled as she fired questions at him, clearly trying to dazzle him with her intelligence and good looks. And of course Richard responded as he always did to female attention, flirting right back.

'I wouldn't kick her out of bed,' Liam commented.

'And he's totally flirting with her. Your boyfriend is nothing but a tart,' Ollie said to Jenny.

'He is not,' Jenny protested half-heartedly, trying to convince herself. 'He's like that with everyone.'

'Like I said – a tart.'

'He's a politician – he wants everyone to like him.'

The interview went on for an hour with ad breaks. Jenny hardly listened to what was being said as they discussed taxation, the economy, the possibility of an election, concentrating instead on Richard's face and the sound of his voice. It was nice being able to see him on TV, but it made her wish she could be with him right now. She didn't like to think of him there without her, surrounded by women in smart suits with even smarter political opinions, and Dev whispering in his ear that he should dump her. Maybe she shouldn't have been so quick to run.

Liam was snoring by the first ad break.

'Give him a break,' Ollie said to Jenny. 'He had a late night – and it's not exactly *Judge Judy*, is it?'

The flirting cranked up a notch in the final segment of the interview, when the journalist turned to lighter topics. In a more informal tone, she tried to pump Richard for information about his private life, carefully framing her questions in a spurious political context. Richard remained smiling and diplomatic while giving little away.

'You've always championed the family,' the girl said, 'some people have felt perhaps to the detriment of other, more marginalised groups in society, such as single parents and gay couples. Now that you're separated and a single father, will we be seeing a shift in focus from you on family issues?'

Richard assumed his tough-but-firm expression. 'Look, I'm a human being – I make mistakes, the same as everyone else. I tried hard to make my marriage work – my wife and I both did – but in the end, like a lot of couples in the country, we didn't make it and we decided separating was the best course of action for everyone involved. I have every sympathy for single parents – I always had. I believe they're entitled to every support, and that won't change. But I still believe in marriage as an institution, and that the family is the cornerstone of our society, the most important foundation for young people growing up in Britain today. I've said that I'm committed to supporting families in every possible way, and I stand by that commitment one hundred per cent.'

Julia wiped her hands on a piece of kitchen towel. She had finished stuffing and rolling the chicken ballotines for tonight's dinner party and was ready to move on to the next thing, but she was standing at the kitchen island, mesmerised, her eyes glued to the television, waiting for the ad break – she couldn't tear her eyes away for long enough to wash her hands and put the chicken in the fridge.

'I'm committed to supporting families in every possible way, and I stand by that commitment one hundred per cent.'

Liar, Julia thought, wrapping the chicken in clingfilm. Pity you couldn't have stood by your commitment to *this* family. Why was she watching him anyway? It was only going to infuriate her. But she couldn't help herself – she was still interested in Richard. No, it was more than that, she told herself with customary rigour. She was still absolutely fascinated by him. Of course they had got a female journalist to do the interview, and of course he was blatantly flirting with her, turning on the charm as only he could.

'This is ridiculous,' she chided herself, but still she couldn't take her eyes off him for a second. How could she find him so spellbinding after more than ten years together?

Finally the ad break came and she was released from her paralysis. She rinsed her hands under the tap and put the plate of chicken in the fridge, taking out a tub of cream at the same time. She quickly assembled the rest of the ingredients for the iced pear parfait before the interview resumed.

She watched Richard's tanned, handsome face as she whisked the cream, hardly listening to his words as she tried to unravel exactly what she felt for him. There was anger, of course – plenty of that. And bitterness. But there was something else too. This fascination with him … it wasn't love, was it? It couldn't be love – not now, not after what he had done. She wasn't the sort of woman who needed a man so desperately that she would accept any terms, endure any humiliation, ignore every betrayal. She had more self-respect than that. She had always been secretly proud of her black-and-white attitude to certain things, her moral certitude – marriage was one of those things. In her view, you were either married or you weren't, and being married meant keeping your vows, being faithful. Once those vows were broken, you were no longer married – it was as simple as that. Only at this moment, it didn't seem so simple any more.

As she turned off the whisk, the journalist was challenging Richard about his relationship with Jeremy, suggesting they weren't as united as they pretended to be. It was an open secret that they detested one another, but neither ever admitted it in public.

'Look,' Richard began, smiling charmingly, 'Jeremy and I—'

Julia smiled wryly to herself as she caught herself automatically noting that that was the third 'look' from Richard. She always used to tell him he sounded too defensive when he began replies like that, and she had counted the number of 'looks' in his interviews to tell him afterwards. She wondered if anyone was doing that for him now.

She put a pan of water on the hob, then assembled the rest of the ingredients in a bowl while she waited for it to simmer. She was glad she had decided to have this dinner party tonight. She enjoyed entertaining, and she hadn't done much of it since Richard had left. There had seemed no point. It struck her as sad that she had forgotten you didn't need a point beyond having a good time. That was the result of spending too many years in a world where everything she did was a means to an end – and the end to every means was Richard's career. Her life had revolved around him and his career for so long that she had forgotten the simple pleasure of cooking for friends. When the idea of this dinner party had occurred to her, she had suddenly realised that she need never again share a meal with people who bored her or whom she disliked, and the revelation had given her an almost giddy sense of freedom. She could invite only people whose company she enjoyed, with no thought to politics or diplomacy, and the rest of them could go hang. She could have *fun*. She wouldn't have to be on her best behaviour, being charming to bores and keeping quiet when someone expressed an opinion that made her blood boil. She could let her hair down. She could get drunk and talk about *Big Brother* or *The X Factor* if she wanted. Not that she would have anything to say about *Big Brother* or *The X Factor*, but she relished the idea that she could if she wanted to. And she wouldn't have to have Jeremy at her table ever again – that was one part of her life that that bloody girl was more than welcome to.

The timing was perfect too. Everyone would have been watching the interview and following the conference, and Richard would naturally come up in conversation. She could talk freely about him without her friends thinking she was freakishly obsessed.

When the water was simmering, she placed the bowl over it and began whisking. Richard would have liked this dessert, she thought. She missed his appreciation of her cooking. They had shared a love of good food. While she had put her talents as a cook at the service of his career, she knew he had always thoroughly enjoyed her food for its own sake. Part of her almost wished he could be there tonight – just as himself, as one of her friends, without any of the baggage.

'And you've started dating again recently?' the journalist was asking now, wrapping up on a light-hearted, personal note.

She watched as Richard answered, wondering at how fluently he lied, watching his face intently for any hint of the truth – but there was none. He really was amazing.

'Liar, liar, liar,' she said aloud. Not for the first time she wondered why she didn't tear it all down – why she didn't take revenge by exposing him for the lying cheat he was. God knows, she was angry enough. Was it just that she didn't have the guts? Or could she not bear to tear down something she had invested so much time and energy in helping to build? Deep down, she suspected it was neither of those things. She simply couldn't bring herself to do it to him. It was this … fascination. Yes, that was it, she thought wryly, with a self-deprecating laugh – people did very strange things in the name of fascination.

Chapter 16

Richard returned to London in a blaze of glory. His conference speech had been a huge success, and the Moderate Party's approval rating soared to a new high. The story about Jenny seemed to have gone quiet, and as the days passed, she began to hope that maybe the photos wouldn't be published after all. Perhaps having missed their opportunity to undermine Richard during the conference, they had decided it wasn't such big news. Then, just as Jenny was beginning to relax, they were told that the photos would be published the next day, Sunday.

When Jenny woke that morning in Richard's flat, she was vaguely aware that something was wrong, but it took her a moment to remember what it was. When she did, her first instinct was to hide in bed for the rest of the day – or maybe the rest of her life. But she immediately felt guilty for contemplating that. The bed was empty, which meant Richard was already up. She had brought this down on his head, and he was up, facing it head-on as he did everything else. The least she could do was face it with him.

She pulled a cardigan on over her pyjamas and went into the living room. She froze when she saw Dev sitting at the dining table. A thick pile of Sunday papers lay on it, and one was spread open in front of him. She considered creeping back to the bedroom before he saw her. So much for facing up to things, she scolded herself, forcing herself to continue.

'Morning,' she said breezily.

'Good morning.' Dev looked up at her.

'Where's Richard?'

'He's gone out for a run.'

'Oh.' She glanced at the paper in front of him, beads of sweat breaking out on her forehead but she was relieved to see that it was one of the broadsheets.

He took one of the papers from the pile and pushed it across the table to her. 'Could you take a look at that?' he said. 'Tell me if it's familiar.'

Instinctively she pulled her cardigan tighter around herself.

'Please look at the photo, Jenny.'

She picked up the paper reluctantly, quickly finding the page with her photo.

'Is it the one you told us about?'

She glanced at it briefly. 'Yes,' she said faintly. 'Of course it's the same one. I told you I only did it the one time.' He knew damn well it was the same one – he was just rubbing her nose in it, trying to humiliate her.

'But you also told me you'd never done it at all.'

She flinched at the truth of that.

'I just want to be sure this is all there is.'

'It is.'

'Good.' His eyes dropped to the article he was reading.

Jenny wiped away a tear. He wasn't looking at it now, but she knew he would have looked at it earlier. She hated the thought of everyone seeing her like that – him, Pauline … Julia. Not to mention the strangers who would be ogling her this morning. 'Um … do you want some tea?'

Dev looked up and his eyes widened when he saw she was crying. 'Jenny,' he said gently, 'don't worry too much about it. It's no more than you see on the average beach.'

'I suppose not.' She sniffed. 'I'm sorry – for causing all this trouble.' She waved at the paper. 'I know you wish Richard would just dump me.'

'What?' Dev asked sharply. 'Why do you say that?'

'Well,' she shrugged, 'it would make your job a hell of a lot easier.'

Just then, Richard breezed in, slightly breathless and flushed from his run, bringing a blast of cold air with him from outside. 'I hope you're not giving Jenny a hard time over the picture,' he said to Dev. He went up to Jenny and put an arm around her. 'I'm so sorry, darling,' he said, kissing her forehead.

'*I'm* sorry,' she said, turning gratefully into his arms.

'Honestly, it's ridiculous,' he stormed, to no one in particular. 'I can't believe they're making such a big deal out of this.'

'Can't you?' Dev looked askance at him.

'No, I can't,' Richard said defiantly.

'You're running for election, Richard. You're fair game.'

'Maybe I am, but Jenny isn't. She's not asking anyone to elect her. It's so unfair, dragging her into this.'

'Oh, don't be so naïve. You're running on a family values platform, for fuck's sake!'

'And what would *I* know about that?' Jenny mumbled.

Richard glared at Dev.

'It's nothing to do with you or your background, Jenny. I just meant that when Richard's spouting about family values all the time, naturally his personal life is going to be open to scrutiny and people will just be dying for a reason to take a pot shot at him.'

'But—' Richard began.

Dev held up a hand to stop him. 'I'm not saying it's right, I'm saying that's how it is. We just have to deal with it. So why don't we all sit down and discuss how we're going to handle it?'

Richard nodded and they all sat down at the table.

'There'll be no crying for a start,' Dev said firmly to Jenny. 'You will *not* be defensive about this, okay? You've done nothing wrong, remember. Just shrug it off as a bit of harmless fun. That's the best way to turn it into a non-story fast.'

'Okay.'

'Richard, the same goes for you. The line you should take is you don't have a problem with it, and it's none of anybody else's business.'

'Well, that'll be easy. That's exactly how I feel.'

'Right. In any case, it'll go away soon. There are lots of much more interesting stories out there,' Dev said with a gleam in his eye.

'Dev,' Richard said warily, 'you wouldn't …'

'Don't worry, I don't believe in shitting on your own doorstep. I'm not going to start briefing against Jeremy – tempting though it is.'

Richard sighed with relief and got up. 'Well, I'm going to hit the shower.'

'Okay, I'll leave you to it. Any plans for today?'

'I'm taking the boys to the Chelsea match this afternoon,' Richard told him.

'Oh!' Dev's eyes strayed uncertainly to Jenny. 'Jenny's not going with you?'

'Football's really not my thing,' she said to Dev. It could have been her thing, though – if she'd been invited, she would have been excited to go with them.

'It's rotten timing, I know,' Richard said, glancing at Jenny apologetically. 'I hate leaving you alone today, but I promised the boys …'

'No, it's fine.' She flashed him a bright smile. She wished Dev would stop staring. She could feel his eyes boring into her. 'Don't be silly. And I won't be alone.' She wondered if he would always keep part of his life separate from her. Maybe Dev had been right when he'd said Richard couldn't give her what she needed. She wished she could get that out of her head, but it always seemed to be there now, niggling away at her. She didn't need twenty-four-hour attention, but she needed *some* ... maybe more than he would ever be able to give her.

'Okay, then. Talk to you later, Dev,' Richard said.

'Have fun at the match. And say hi to Julia for me,' Dev called to him as he left.

Julia. Once Dev had gone, Jenny pulled the paper towards her, forcing herself to open it at the page with her picture. Shit, shit, shit! Why did Richard have to see Julia today of all days?

Richard paced restlessly around the kitchen of the house in Hampstead while he waited for the kids to gather their stuff together. He could hear them thundering around upstairs. Julia stood at the table, calmly chopping mountains of vegetables, while he paced and fidgeted. She had decided to take advantage of the children's absence this afternoon to do some bulk cooking. He wandered over to the corkboard and read the school notices and invitations to children's birthday parties that were pinned to it. He scanned the calendar, with its reminders of doctor's visits and school holidays.

'Oh, it's Geoffrey's fortieth on Friday,' he said, spotting it on the calendar. 'I'd forgotten about that. Did we get him a present?'

Julia looked up at him. 'And by *we*, of course you mean me. Yes, *I* got him a present.'

'Good.'

'And *I*'ll give it to him when *I* go to the party.'

'Oh, come on!' Richard laughed. 'I assumed we'd go together.'

'Why would you assume that? Richard, we're not a couple any more.'

'No, but I don't see why we can't turn up to a party together just because—'

'Don't you? Well, for one thing, I'm a single woman now.'

'Yes. And?'

'And what if I want to … you know …'

'What?' Richard laughed. 'Pull someone?'

'Well … why not?'

'Oh, come on – Geoffrey's crowd?' he scoffed.

'Well, you never know who else might be there, apart from the usual suspects. I've heard that cousin of his is coming – you know, the rather glamorous one who does the travel shows on TV.'

'Oh, God, he's an awful tosser!'

'You've met him, have you?'

'No,' Richard admitted. 'But I've seen him on TV. He's a prat!'

'Well, anyway, there might be someone I want to chat up. And I'm not going to have much luck if my ex-husband is hovering in the background, am I?'

'So are you saying you don't want me to go to this party at all?'

'Yes, that's exactly what I'm saying. It's you or me, and I've decided that for Geoffrey's party it's me. I'd appreciate it if you'd stay away.'

'But – but Geoffrey is one of our oldest friends,' Richard spluttered, looking petulant.

'*We* don't have friends, Richard. *I* have friends and *you* have friends. *We* don't exist any more. When are you going to realise that?'

'But I've known Geoffrey for ever. How's it going to look if I don't turn up for his birthday?'

'How's it going to look if you turn up with *that girl*?'

'She has a name, you know.'

'Oh, bully for her! How do you think I'd feel with you parading her in front of everyone we know? And it's not just me – it would be embarrassing for everyone.'

'Of course I wouldn't bring Jenny. I thought we'd go together, just the two of us.'

'Really? What – play the happy couple for a night? Pretend nothing's happened and everything's the same as it used to be?'

'No, but I thought we could be civil, put on a united front. We don't have to be at loggerheads, do we?'

'No, of course not. But there's a big difference between being civil and playing husband and wife.'

'I'm not talking about playing husband and wife. But it would be a perfect opportunity to show everyone that we're still friends.'

'And what would that achieve – other than cramping my style when I'm trying to get off with someone?'

'Well, it would quash any rumours about our separation being acrimonious—'

'Yes, yes,' Julia interrupted, 'I can see why *you*'d want to show everyone how wonderfully civilised you are and how marvellously you're handling the situation. I have no doubt it would be great for your approval rating. What I don't see is what's in it for *me*.'

'Well,' Richard frowned, looking confused, 'same thing, isn't it? I know how much my career means to you, and—'

Julia gave a harsh laugh. 'That's it, is it? That's what you think I should live for now? Some kind of vicarious job satisfaction?'

'Well, it's hardly vicarious. We both know that you've invested almost as much in my career as I have. You wouldn't want to do anything to jeopardise all our hard work, now that we're inches away from the prize – I know you wouldn't. You've put too much into it. We both have. We've always been a team on this, haven't we?'

'We *used* to be a team. But I'm not on Team Richard now. I got transferred out, remember?'

'So that's it? You're going to bale on me when the endgame is in sight?'

'I think you need to remind yourself who baled on whom,' Julia said stiffly, eyeballing him. He was the first to look away.

'Look,' she said, 'this is our reality now. We're separated. I'm not your wife any more. I won't be buying your gifts, I won't be going to parties with you, and I won't be nursing your career.'

'Right.' Richard watched her as she bent her head to her chopping board once more. 'I suppose a shag's out of the question then?' he drawled, smiling at her.

She didn't look up as she split a pepper open with a juicy crunch. But he thought he saw the corners of her mouth twitch.

Chapter 17

Jenny woke in Richard's flat to the soft murmur of voices downstairs. It was only seven a.m. according to the clock beside the bed. But she was getting used to almost never having Richard to herself. She had thought that once their relationship was public she would see a lot more of him, but it was scarcely better than when they had been sneaking around. Election fever was in the air – everyone seemed to agree that the current government was on its knees, and it was only a matter of time before it would buckle. When Richard wasn't going abroad for meetings with world leaders, he was travelling the country, being all things to all men, women and children. She saw more of him on television than she did in real life. Even when he was home, like now, she had to share him with Susie and Geoff and Jeremy and Amanda – and, most of all, Dev. He was a constant presence. It was Dev who was downstairs with Richard now, she could tell – she was as attuned to his voice as she was to Richard's. She might as well have been dating both of them. It was probably only a matter of time before they'd be having three-ways together. Mmm, how would that go … She let her mind drift pleasantly for a while before getting out of bed and pulling on a dressing gown.

Still, she appreciated the way Dev had managed to minimise the impact of the topless photo. She had laughed it off, as instructed, with a cheeky smile and a nonchalant shrug at her youthful indiscretion. It had been, as Dev had predicted, the most effective way of defusing the story – combined with the carefully positioned positive snippets about her that had been fed to the press to counterbalance it. Now, after several weeks, the photo was all but forgotten and she had been reinvented as a sort of twenty-first century Mary Poppins with attitude. She suspected Dev was becoming rather too fond of peddling the care-child-made-good angle. But it did wonders for Richard's street cred, and she was chuffed that she could be useful to his career. It was certainly a lot better than constantly being seen as a liability.

Padding into the kitchen, she found Dev sitting at the table having toast and coffee while he badgered Richard about his clothes. 'You're not wearing that tie!' he was saying.

'Why? What's wrong with it?' Richard fingered the knot uncertainly.

'There's nothing wrong with it.' Jenny stood on tiptoe to straighten it where he had messed it up. 'I think it's lovely.'

'Did you buy it for him?' Dev asked her with a wry smile.

'Yes. How did you guess?'

'Oh, I don't know – call it instinct.'

'At least it's not drab and boring. I think it's very appropriate.' Richard was visiting an inner-city project for youths leaving the care system this morning. 'It's nice and bright and colourful. It'll cheer the kids up.'

Dev eyed the tie again. 'Maybe you're right. It'll be a talking point anyway. Try and get someone to ask you about it,' he said to Richard, 'and tell them your girlfriend bought it for you. Women think that stuff is cute.'

'Really?'

'Really.' Dev rolled his eyes. 'You wouldn't believe the amount of guff we have to listen to from focus groups about your lovely hair and how cute you are with your kids.'

Jenny had sat down at the table and was shaking cereal into a bowl. Dev turned his attention to her, his eyes raking over her pyjamas and her dishevelled hair. 'You'd better get your arse in gear,' he said, taking a gulp of coffee.

'Me?' She looked up at him. 'What do you mean?'

'Well, you're not coming like that.'

'You want me to come?'

'You want Jenny to come?' Richard asked at the same time. He sounded just as surprised as she was.

'Yes, of course. You're not working, are you?'

'No. That photo hasn't exactly done wonders for my job prospects. I have an interview tomorrow, though, that I'm hopeful about.'

'Well, you'd better get cracking, then,' he said, glancing impatiently at his watch.

'Why?' Richard asked. 'I thought you wanted Jenny to stay out of the limelight as much as possible.'

'Didn't I tell you? Our focus groups show that she's really good for your image – especially with women. They love seeing you with her – makes you seem more human, apparently.'

Jenny beamed happily, delighted to be seen as a force for good.

But Richard looked put out. 'They think I need help seeming human?' he asked querulously.

'Of course you do, posh boy.' Dev grinned, taking a huge bite of toast. 'So – lucky we've got Jenny.'

'But I can't believe you think I need Jenny to—'

'Jesus, you don't really believe all that "man of the people" stuff we've cooked up for you, do you?' Dev mocked.

'Well, I …' Richard looked really put out.

'All that twaddle about you being an ordinary working father of two …'

'Well, I *am* a father of two. And I *work*.'

'And that shtick with you going around the supermarket, doing the family shop,' Dev continued, laughing.

'But I *was* going around the supermarket, doing the family shop,' Richard protested.

'But it was all set up, remember? How many other dads did you see in therc with a film crew in tow?'

'Just because there was a film crew doesn't mean it wasn't real.'

'Oh, don't mind him,' Jenny said soothingly. 'I think you look cute when you go around pretending to be a normal person.'

'Pretending to be a normal person!' Richard spluttered.

'I loved that programme where you went to the supermarket and made the kids dinner. You were almost like a real dad.'

'Yes, you were very lifelike,' Dev drawled.

'Almost! I *am* a real dad!'

'What about the bit where you went to that council estate in Liverpool and had tea with the housewives?' Dev laughed.

'Oh, that was so sweet!' Jenny said. 'It was almost like you were one of them – like you had the same problems and shared their concerns.'

'But I *do* share their concerns.'

'Yes, of course you do,' Jenny reassured him.

'The best was when you tried to get "down with the kids" on that sink estate in Birmingham. You even—' Dev could hardly speak for laughing now, 'you even wore a – a hoodie!' He collapsed in fits.

'I already owned that hoodie,' Richard said, clearly hurt. 'It's very comfortable.'

'Very sensible,' Jenny said.

'Sensible!' Dev hooted. 'Jesus, you were lucky they didn't kill you.'

'Oh, leave him alone,' Jenny said, noting that Richard was a bit upset. 'It's just that you're such a star,' she said to him. 'Having a fuck-up like me around makes you seem more human. I'll just go and get dressed.'

'She really has done wonders for your image,' Dev said seriously when Jenny had left the room. 'Your approval rating among the working classes has gone way up, and a lot of that seems to be down to her. Her troubled childhood is a real winner, apparently, especially with women. See if you can get her to talk it up more. The triumph-against-the-odds angle goes down a bomb with tabloid readers.'

'Jesus! I'm not going to exploit Jenny's rotten childhood for a few votes.'

'We might be talking more than a few here, Richard. People are seeing you in a different light because of her. People can relate to her in a way they can't relate to you. Look at where we're going today – she knows where these people are coming from, she can talk to them on their own level.'

'I'm still not going to exploit her past to improve my image.'

'I'm not asking you to exploit Jenny's past. That would be unbelievably crass.'

'Oh, good. Sorry, I thought—'

'No, you don't want to look as if you're using her to make yourself look good. You need to get Jenny to do it herself.'

Richard looked at him, aghast. 'And *I'm* the one who needs help to appear human!'

In the bedroom, Jenny was raking through the wardrobe, determined to find exactly the right thing to wear. She really wanted to please Dev. And Richard, of course – that went without saying. But she was just so pleased that, for once, Dev wasn't treating her like a waste of space. This was her big chance to prove to him that she wasn't a total fuck-up, that she could be good for Richard, and she was determined to get it right. Fortunately, quite a lot of her clothes had migrated to Richard's flat, but the choice was still limited and it was proving harder than she'd expected. The bed was already covered with clothes she had considered and discarded. She wanted to look young and fashionable but at the same time demure and ladylike. Her eyes lit up as they fell on a fifties wiggle dress in a deep red. It looked like something Doris Day might have worn, and you didn't get much more demure and ladylike than her. Plus it was vintage, and Richard was always going on about wanting to go back to old-fashioned values, so it was exactly the right look. She did up the buttons, pushed her hair on top of her head and pouted at herself in the mirror. Perfect.

'Oh!' Dev's eyes widened as she rejoined them in the living room. 'Is that what you're wearing?'

'Well, yeah,' she faltered. 'What's wrong with it?'

'Nothing, it's just—'

'You look gorgeous,' Richard said, taking her hand. 'Let's go — Susie's outside in the car.'

'Well, it'll certainly cheer up our troubled teens,' Dev said, almost to himself, as they went out of the door. 'There'll be more wood than in the Forest of Dean.'

'Susie, did you bring that *Homemaker* stuff?' Dev asked as they got into the car. Susie was in the front seat beside Phil, Richard's driver, and Jenny sat in the back between Richard and Dev.

'Here it is.' Susie handed him back a thick folder.

'*Homemaker* magazine want to do a piece on you,' Dev told Jenny, opening the folder. 'They run a "woman behind the man" series, and they want to do you as part of that. Do you know the magazine?'

'No.' Jenny shook her head.

'It's very cosy,' he said, taking a copy from the folder and flipping through it. 'Knitting patterns, recipes, home décor – very WI. The editor's a friend, so it'll be very positive. They'll probably ask you searing questions about Richard's favourite dinner. Do you think you'd be okay to do it?'

'I'm sure I could handle that.'

'Good. Here are a few back issues to give you a feel for the magazine.' He handed Jenny a bundle from the folder. 'Familiarise yourself with it. Try to work into the interview that you're an avid reader – find something specific you can mention that you like about it. It'll endear you to their readers.'

'Okay.' She flipped through a few pages of one of the magazines. 'Knitting's quite cool now,' she said. 'I could say I like the knitting patterns.'

'Can you knit?'

'No.'

'Would you wear something like that?' He pointed to the chunky blue cardigan opposite the knitting instructions.

'Christ, no! What do you take me for? I wouldn't be seen dead in it.'

'That's what I thought.' Dev smiled.

'But I could be knitting it for my granny.' She quite fancied the idea of herself as a knitter, clacking away busily with her needles, producing cosy woollens for her friends and family. She could make Richard a scarf ...

'You don't have a granny,' Dev pointed out.

'Well, if I'm pretending to knit, I might as well go the whole hog and have a granny too.'

'It'd be safer to keep it as close to the truth as possible. Say you like the problem page or the true-life stories or something.'

'Oh, all right.'

'They'll probably ask you for a recipe too, so have one ready.'

'A recipe? Okay. Maybe you could give me one?' she said to Richard.

'No, you don't want to do one of his poncy *Masterchef* things,' Dev said. 'Keep it simple, homey.'

'Okay.'

'Nothing too foreign, focus on good British produce …'

'Right.' Jenny nodded.

'Also try to stick to seasonal ingredients – mention air miles, how you can minimise your carbon footprint by shopping seasonally, supporting local farmers' markets …'

'Farmers' markets, okay.'

'Nothing too expensive either. Let them see you know the price of things – we're all on a budget, the economy slowing down …'

'Jesus, Dev!' Richard remonstrated. 'That's an awful lot for the poor girl to try and work into a bun recipe.'

'Well, just do your best,' Dev said to Jenny. 'And it doesn't have to be buns. It'd probably be best to stick to baking, though – it's old-fashioned, reassuring, wholesome.'

'Baking, right.' Jenny was trying not to laugh. This conversation was taking on a surreal quality.

'Or preserves,' Susie chipped in from the front seat. 'They have the same cosy, domestic vibe.'

'Right – great idea. Thanks, Susie.' Jenny smiled sweetly. What the fuck were preserves? She racked her brain for a recipe, but the only thing she knew how to make were Rice Krispie cakes and she didn't think they counted as baking. 'Do you have any recipes I could use?' she asked Dev.

'Sorry?'

'Could you suggest a recipe? You know – one that ticks all the boxes?' She glanced at Richard and saw his mouth twitching.

'Um … no, not offhand. Susie?' Dev leaned forward. 'Do you know any suitable recipes?'

'Well, there's your basic Victoria sponge.'

'Victoria sponge – very patriotic!' Dev said.

'Okay what's that – four, four, two, or is it four, two, two?'

Why was she babbling mathematical equations, Jenny wondered. It didn't sound much like a recipe. But Dev had pulled a piece of paper and a pen from his pocket and was scribbling Susie's numbers on it.

'God, I can't remember,' Susie said. 'My chalet-girl days are long gone. There's pound cake – that's easy to remember because it's a pound of everything. Pound of flour, pound of butter—'

'Pound of butter?' Dev paused in taking down the recipe. 'That can't be right, can it?'

'Pound of sugar ...' Susie continued.

'Jesus! It's a heart-attack on a plate.'

'It is quite rich,' Susie said. 'It's American.'

'Oh, that's no good then.' Dev drew a line through the ingredients he'd jotted down. 'We'll get the office on to it,' he said to Jenny. 'Susie, ask them to find a recipe. And make sure it's not too lardy, so Jenny comes across as being aware of health issues, the need to cut down on saturated fats ...'

She was feeling a little overwhelmed. This magazine interview was starting to sound a lot more complicated than she'd originally envisaged. It seemed she was going to have to work a whole Moderate Party manifesto into her cake recipe.

'And don't be afraid to talk about your difficult childhood,' Dev said, casting a quick glance at Richard. 'Don't go into all the gory details, but focus on the positives – how you overcame all the obstacles to work as a nanny. Talk about how much you like looking after children. But try not to mention Richard's children if you can help it.'

'Maybe I should take some notes,' Jenny said. It was starting to sound like a real minefield.

'No need for that,' Dev said briskly. 'Don't worry, they won't ask

you any awkward questions, and we'll have approval before it's published anyway. Just be yourself and you'll be fine.'

'Be myself ... right.' Jenny smiled wryly.

They were all subdued as they left the centre where they had spent the
morning – all except Jenny.

'That was really good.' She smiled happily as they pulled away.
'I'm so glad I came.'

'You didn't find it too ... depressing?' Richard asked her.

'Depressing? No, not at all. I had fun.'

'I hope those boys weren't giving you too much hassle,' he said.
'They were coming on a bit strong.'

'They were really sweet. I had a laugh with them.'

'Sweet' wasn't the first word that would have sprung to Dev's
mind for the brash youths who had cornered Jenny, openly ogling her
and flirting crudely. She had looked so tiny and defenceless surrounded by the hulking adolescents that he had been tempted to grab
her hand and run with her to the safety of the car. But she hadn't
seemed threatened by their size or their raging hormones, and had
given as good as she got, flirting right back and clearly enjoying
herself.

But he could see the visit had got Richard down – he was staring
glumly out the window. He had made a short speech and spent some
time chatting to the workers who provided support and halfway
houses for children leaving the care system. They had talked about
the dangers that faced them as they tried to make their own way in
the world. Many got into trouble with the law, developed addiction
problems and ended up living on the streets. The statistics were
bleak, but the work they were doing was admirable and inspiring,
and it was heartening to see how they were helping the kids to move
towards becoming capable, independent adults.

However, the kids' stories of their experiences in care were uniformly grim and heartbreaking. Most of them had spent their short lives being shunted from one foster home to another and between foster care and residential homes, rarely allowed to settle in one place for long. One girl had had twenty-seven different placements and had moved school with each one, the constant disruption making it impossible to settle or form friendships. There were stories of foster homes where they had been treated as second-class citizens, fed separately from the natural children, if there were any, and in one case even made to use different cutlery. Several spoke of their longing for a pet, which they were never allowed to have. Many had sensed they were 'not good enough' and that they didn't belong anywhere.

Richard had listened to them intently and was visibly moved by what they had to say. They were obviously pleased about his visit and appreciated the interest he showed in them. They acted cool, but Dev could tell they were impressed. Jenny had been an even bigger hit – and not just with the boys. The girls had looked at her with something akin to awe as they quizzed her about her clothes and her job, and giggled over Richard's good looks.

As he had watched Jenny talking to them, nodding in agreement with many of the things they said, it had hit Dev that she was just like them. He had peddled her rotten childhood without really thinking about what it meant. Now he marvelled at how she had risen above it all and avoided becoming one of the statistics. How had she remained so untouched by it, so unbroken? He looked at her now, trying to cheer Richard up as she babbled away to him about the kids, and had to swallow a lump in his throat. He felt an almost overwhelming urge to pull her onto his lap and wrap her in his arms. He wanted to buy her ice cream and take her to Disneyland and get her guinea pig back from that fucker who had taken it. If he had felt protective of her earlier when she was surrounded by those swaggering boys, it was nothing to how he felt now. Because he suddenly had a horrible feeling that the person she really needed protection from was Richard, and he was powerless to do anything about it.

Chapter 18

'I've got a new job!' Jenny squealed a couple of days later as she spun into Richard's office. He stood as she entered and she threw her arms around him, standing on tiptoe to kiss him.

'That's great, darling,' he said, but his smile was tight and his voice sounded strained.

'Congratulations!' a voice came from behind her and she spun around, noticing Dev for the first time, sitting in a chair in front of Richard's desk.

'Thanks.' She grinned, flopping into the chair beside him and wriggling out of her jacket. 'Sorry, I didn't see you there.' She had probably embarrassed Richard by throwing herself at him in front of Dev – that would explain his lukewarm response to her news.

'Anyway, the little girl is called Hannah, she's five years old, and *so* cute! I love her already. Lily, the mother, is a teacher and – you're not going to like this – very left-wing, but she's really lovely and she's not going to hold it against me that I'm going out with you. And she's very liberal, so she doesn't mind at all about the photos. I start next week, which is brilliant because it means I'll be able to save up for Christmas and buy proper presents and—' She stopped abruptly as she realised she was babbling and both men were watching her in stony-faced silence.

'So,' she said, glancing nervously between them, 'you wanted to see me?'

'Yeah,' Richard said hesitantly. They both looked at her warily, saying nothing.

'Well? Spit it out – the suspense is killing me.'

Dev took a deep breath. 'More pictures have surfaced.'

'Oh! Pictures of me? N-naked pictures?'

'Yes. Unfortunately this does tend to happen after there's been one story on you. Other people see the opportunity to make a quick buck and they jump on the bandwagon.' At least Dev didn't seem as angry with her as he had the first time – he must be getting used to her fuck-up ways.

She sighed heavily. 'Well, that's bad, I suppose, but it's nothing they haven't seen before, is it?'

'Well, these do appear to be more ... explicit.'

'Oh. Shit,' she said softly.

'However, that's not the worst part.'

She gulped. 'It's not?'

'No.' Dev sighed. 'It's not just the photos. There's a story too.'

'A story? What kind of story?' It was the first time Richard had spoken. Clearly Dev hadn't filled him in yet on this bit.

In answer, Dev turned to Jenny. 'Does the name Gerry Donnelly mean anything to you?'

Jenny felt her stomach hit the floor. Oh, God. She hadn't thought about Gerry in a very long time. She didn't want to think about him now. But he couldn't ... surely he wouldn't ...

Dev was watching her reaction closely. 'I'll take that as a yes.'

'Who is he, Jenny?' Richard asked.

'He's ... an ex-boyfriend.' Her voice came out thin and reedy. She hated this. She couldn't even look at Richard.

'So, what's the story?' Richard asked, his voice full of dread.

'Apparently this Gerry Donnelly was a married man whom Jenny had an affair with. The story's come from his daughter – seemingly there's no love lost. She got her hands on these photos and has decided to get her revenge on her father – and on Jenny, who she claims destroyed her parents' marriage and broke up her family.'

'That's preposterous!' Richard said. 'This girl is lying, she must be.'

Jenny looked at him in silence. She loved him for believing in her. And she hated herself for having to let him down yet again.

'Jenny?' Dev prompted her.

'What do you want me to say?'

'I was kind of hoping you'd deny it,' Dev said. It was clear from his tone that he no longer had any hope of that.

'It was a long time ago,' she said quietly, hanging her head.

'So it's true?' Richard asked.

'It's true that we had an affair,' she mumbled. 'I don't know about breaking up his marriage, though. *I* was the one who got kicked out – at least at the time.'

Dev looked at her sharply. 'What do you mean, you got kicked out?'

'His wife found out about us and went ballistic. She threw me out.'

'You were living with them?' Dev asked.

'Oh, Christ,' Richard said, 'were you the daughter's nanny?'

'No, I—'

'Hardly,' Dev interrupted. 'Apparently this daughter of his is only a couple of years older than Jenny.'

'You never told me about this,' Richard said dully.

She could see he was struggling to come to terms with it. She couldn't bear the disappointment on his face. 'Well, it's not the sort of thing you boast about. Besides, we never did that thing where you trawl through each other's past.'

'Maybe you should have,' Dev said.

Jenny ignored him. 'Look,' she said to Richard, 'I know I must seem like an awful hypocrite, always saying I wouldn't have been with you if I'd known you were still with Julia. But that's really how I feel. With Gerry, I knew it was wrong, but I was young. I made a mistake. I'd never be with a married man again – not knowingly, I mean.'

'How young were you?' he asked her.

'I was … young.' She shifted awkwardly in her seat. 'He was my first, um … my first proper boyfriend,' she said, blushing. They shouldn't be having this conversation in front of Dev.

'Your first lover, you mean?'

'Um … yes.'

'And he was old enough to be your father?'

'Yeah,' she said faintly, 'he was. I've always been into older men.' She smiled, trying to lighten the atmosphere. Richard didn't smile back.

She was aware of Dev becoming very still beside her, looking at her intently. 'Why were you living with them?' he asked. 'You weren't their nanny. If this guy was old enough to be your father—'

'What does it matter? It happened, and I'm sorry it did, but I've never done anything like that again. I'm not some kind of serial home-wrecker.'

'Jenny, I know you're not a home-wrecker,' Dev said gently. 'How old were you when this happened?'

'I was … fifteen,' she mumbled, looking down at her hands. She glanced up at Richard from under her eyelashes, trying to read his expression. Was he shocked? Disgusted? She couldn't tell. 'Okay, I was having under-age sex,' she said defiantly to Dev, 'so sue me. I also drank when I was under age. I'm hardly the first teenager to jump the gun a bit. Everyone does shit like that when they're young.'

'Why were you living with the family?' Dev asked again, but she had a feeling he had already guessed the answer.

'I, um … I was fostered by them … for a while.'

'So who was this Gerry?' Richard asked.

She looked at him sadly. He still didn't get it.

'He was her foster father,' Dev said to him. 'Wasn't he, Jenny?'

She nodded dumbly. It was easy to read the expression on *his* face – fury, disgust, loathing, contempt: it was all there, clear as day.

'Jesus!' Richard whispered.

'We fell in love,' she said pleadingly, willing Richard to meet her eyes. 'Look, I know it was wrong, but—'

'Wrong!' Dev roared. 'Jesus, that doesn't even *begin* to cover it! You were under age, and he was your foster father, for fuck's sake!'

She had been wrong to think he wasn't as angry with her as the last time. She had never seen him this angry before. He was incandescent with rage and she found him terrifying in this mood. 'But it's not as bad as you make it sound. It's not as if he was my stepfather or anything,' she said shakily. 'I mean, it's not like I was having an affair with my real mother's husband.'

'Jenny,' Dev put a hand on her shoulder and turned her to face him, 'you weren't having an affair. That's not an *affair*, it's rape!'

She flinched at the word, stunned into silence. She saw now that he wasn't angry with her at all – he was angry with Gerry. 'Well, technically, I suppose—'

'Technically, legally, morally, any bloody way you want to look at it, it's rape.'

'No, it wasn't – I wasn't … it wasn't like that. It was just as much my fault as his.'

'Is that what he made you think?'

'He didn't *make* me think anything. I wasn't a child. I was fifteen, and I was mature for my age – precocious, even. Everyone said so. I knew what I was doing.'

'You were a child in the eyes of the law – a child in his protection.'

'Well, in reality I was a horny teenager. I wanted it to happen just as much as he did – maybe more so. He didn't force me to do anything.'

'Please don't sit there and make excuses for him,' Dev said. 'I can't listen to that.'

'I'm not! But I'm not going to try to make excuses for myself by saying he took advantage of me, because he didn't. *I* did something bad. *I* was in the wrong, end of story.' Damn him, why couldn't he just accept that she had been sexually precocious and leave it at that? She didn't want his excuses for her behaviour. She'd rather he shouted at her and called her a slut and a liar and a marriage-wrecker – anything rather than treating her like a victim.

Richard still hadn't said anything. He was watching the two of them, evidently bewildered and panicked by what was unfolding in front of him. 'What happened when it all came out?' he asked finally. 'Wasn't he arrested?'

'Oh, it didn't come out. I'm not sure what his wife told the social workers about me. I just know I was moved on immediately after she found out about it.'

'God, what kind of woman was she?' Dev fumed. 'And how were the pair of them ever allowed to foster children? Her reaction to all this was to throw *you* out on the streets?'

'Well, not on the streets. I got a new family by the following week. I never saw or heard from Gerry again. I didn't know his marriage had broken up until now.'

Richard leaned back in his chair, sighing heavily. 'Dev's right,' he said. 'None of this is your fault, Jenny.'

She opened her mouth to protest, but Dev interrupted her. 'Anyway, don't worry, this is all going to go away now and you won't have to hear another word about it.'

'It is?' Richard asked. 'You mean you can get them to pull it?'

'Of course. Jesus, Richard, the *Record* may not be the last bastion of ethics, but no one's going to publish photos of what's basically child pornography.'

'Oh, right.' Richard's features smoothed. 'Well, that's a relief, isn't it?'

'Yeah,' she said shakily, 'great.' She was glad that there weren't going to be any more naked pictures of her in the paper, but she wasn't at all happy about the reason they were being pulled. 'So,' she said with a bright smile, 'lucky I was under age, then, isn't it?'

Dev shot her an odd look. 'I suppose that's one way of looking at it.'

'Well, if it had happened a few months later, it'd be all over the papers. So you see, sometimes being precocious pays off.'

Jenny hadn't thought about Gerry for a very long time, and she resented being forced to think about him now, shying away from the memories that flashed through her mind as she made her way home.

The Donnellys had been her third foster placement. They were a comfortably off middle-class couple with two children of their own – a girl two years older than Jenny and a boy two years younger. Gerry was an architect and Niamh was a stay-at-home mum. Jenny had always wondered what had made them decide to foster. It certainly didn't seem to come from an excess of maternal feeling on Niamh's part. It wasn't that she had been cruel, just cold, distant and uninterested.

So when Gerry had started to show an interest in her, Jenny had responded with puppy-like eagerness. He was a handsome man, cultured and educated, and she had been flattered by his attentions. She saw now how easy she had been to manipulate. Gerry had made her feel special. He had praised her, telling her she was beautiful and clever and interesting. And that was all it had taken. She hadn't really thought about the age gap between them except in so far as it stroked her ego to be noticed by an older man. Besides, Gerry had said she was more mature than other girls her age, and she certainly felt that way when she was with him.

Their affair had begun when he started getting her to help out in his office during the school holidays. He had his own business so they were often alone. The first time she'd had sex was on the black leather sofa in his office. At the time, she had found their illicit liaison very exciting and romantic. It had made her feel grown up, powerful and sophisticated. Gerry bought her little presents and told her he loved her. They had even managed to go away for a weekend together. It had been going on for about six months when his wife had discovered them on that same black leather sofa and it had come to an abrupt end.

Now she could see how sordid and exploitative their relationship had really been. Dev was right about that. She had been naïve and eager to please, longing to love and be loved, and Gerry had taken advantage of that. She saw now how wrong he had been. She wasn't entirely blameless, but he was the grown-up and should have known better.

She remembered when he had taken those photos of her. It was the weekend they had gone away, to a small seaside town in Galway. He had recently taken up photography as a hobby. She had posed naked for him, writhing about on the bed in sheets that still smelled of sex, the sun pouring in through the open window, the salty sea air playing across her skin, while Gerry moved around the room, murmuring instructions as he clicked.

She shuddered, pulling her jacket tighter around her. She was so grateful those photos wouldn't be published. She felt guilty now for getting angry with Dev. She knew he was concerned about her and just being kind. Maybe she should call him and apologise, she thought, pulling her mobile from her bag. She hit the speed dial for Richard's office, but then changed her mind. Dev might think it was weird if she called him. Best not. On the other hand, she felt bad about the way she'd behaved towards him. She flipped the phone open again, but lost her nerve. No, she couldn't call him. It would definitely seem weird. She dropped the phone back into her bag.

'So you didn't know about any of that?' Dev was saying to Richard.

'No.' Richard shook his head slowly, still clearly a bit stunned. 'Jenny's … full of surprises.' He looked down at his fingers drawing patterns on the wood of his desk.

'Right. Well, nothing you can't handle, I'm sure,' Dev said, getting to his feet.

'God, I don't know. Can I?' Richard mused. 'You know, she's a lot more complicated than she seems on the surface.'

Oh, God, Dev groaned inwardly. Richard was about to go into confessional mode. He had to get out quick. 'Course you can,' he said, glancing at his watch. 'Well, I'd better get back to work. You're not paying me to stand around talking about your girlfriend.'

'You remember you said maybe she wasn't right for me?'

Don't you dare. 'Yeah, I was talking crap,' Dev said, backing towards the door. 'I didn't really know her then. She's perfect for you.'

'You really think—'

'Absolutely, she's a great girl – the best thing that ever happened to you!' He grabbed the door handle and bolted out of the room before Richard could say any more.

Back in his office, Dev sank into his chair and put his head in his hands, allowing himself a moment to wallow. This was shaping up to be one of the crappiest days ever. First he'd had to hear that awful story about Jenny, and now he'd had to listen to Richard testing the waters for dumping her. How could he? He had no idea how lucky he was.

Richard was right about one thing, though. Jenny was a lot more complicated than she appeared – a lot more complicated and infinitely more fascinating. The more he got to know her, the more Dev was captivated by her. He recalled the first time they had met, at Tim and Fiona's wedding. He had been attracted to her then because she was fun and flirtatious, and bloody gorgeous to boot. But now he saw she was so much more than the bubbly, carefree girl everyone saw when they looked at her. The more he discovered about what her life had been, the more he realised what an extraordinary person she was. She was innocent and experienced, brave and vulnerable, tough, naïve, amazingly strong and incredibly beautiful, and when she was around he felt more alive than he had in ages. Put simply, he was crazy about her. It was just his luck that the person to make him feel that way was Richard's girlfriend.

What really killed him was that Richard didn't even realise what he had. He didn't see what a truly amazing person she was, and he didn't want to know. He wanted her to stay the bright, uncomplicated girl he had signed up for, and he seemed increasingly scared off the further he got below the surface. Dev had seen how nervous he'd been when he heard about Jenny's affair. He had definitely looked like a man searching for an exit.

Still, he wasn't happy about the way he himself had handled things with Jenny. He had been too rough with her. He shouldn't have shouted at her and he should never have used that word – *rape*. It had really upset her – understandably so. But he had been so angry, and it had just come out in the heat of the moment. Maybe he should call her and apologise …

He looked at the phone and noticed for the first time that the voicemail light was flashing. He pressed the button to listen to his messages.

'Hi, Dev, it's Jenny. I, um ... I just wanted to say sorry for being an ungrateful cow earlier. And thanks for – for making it all go away. Okay, bye,' she said quickly and rang off.

He smiled, soothed by her soft, lilting voice and relieved that he hadn't screwed up too badly. At least she recognised he was on her side, even if he hadn't expressed it very well. He hit the button to replay the message.

Chapter 19

'Rough night last night?' Jenny asked Liam as he crawled into the kitchen dressed as a gladiator.

'Ugh, if I don't get a proper chef's job soon, I'm going to end up getting shagged to death,' he said, pulling out a chair and easing himself gingerly into it. 'Those fucking hens are insatiable.'

'Shagged to death – what a way to go!' Ollie smiled dreamily.

'Don't worry, I think we're on a roll,' Jenny said, pouring him a cup of tea. 'I mean, Ollie's working and I'm starting my new job tomorrow – you'll be next, I'm sure.'

'And I got a call-back for that movie I auditioned for,' Ollie said, 'so make the most of me now. I may be too famous to talk to you soon.'

'You did? Oh, that's brilliant! So we've got even more to celebrate,' Jenny said, raising her china cup to him in a toast.

She loved the snug feeling of being inside on dark winter mornings like this. Thick November rain lashed against the windows and it was dark as night outside, but she had made tea in her flowery china teapot, there was a plate of croissants she had crisped up in the oven and her little dysfunctional family was gathered around the table for breakfast; all felt right with her world.

'Have a croissant,' she said, pushing the plate towards Liam.

'There's chocolate or plain – and we've got jam.' She took one, the chocolate still warm and oozing as she bit into it. 'So, Ollie, what should I pack for a country weekend?'

'What sort of country weekend?' he asked through a mouthful of croissant.

'You know, one of those Big-House country weekends that your lot go on.'

'My lot?'

'You know – nobs, toffs.'

'Are you going away with Richard?' he asked, licking jam and crumbs off his fingers.

'Mmm. Next weekend we're going to stay with this Lord Kenton character in his country house. He's a bigwig in the Moderate Party.'

'You mean Simon Kenton?'

'Oh, you've heard of him?'

'Of course. He's pretty famous – mainly for being a randy old bugger. He's had loads of mistresses. You'd better watch yourself with him.'

'Ugh, he's ancient!' Jenny said, wrinkling her nose. 'I met him at Jeremy's. So, what do you think I should bring?'

'A hot water bottle,' Liam said. 'Those nobs are stingy as fuck with the heat. No offence.' He nodded to Ollie.

'None taken,' he said. 'He's right, you should bring all your warmest clothes – it's always freezing in those big old houses.'

'Okay, what else?'

'Well, that depends. What sort of weekend is it going to be?'

'I told you – a weekend in the country.'

'Yes, but what are you going to be doing? What activities?'

'You think we'll be doing *activities*? We're not toddlers!'

'Oh, there are bound to be activities, Jen.' Ollie grinned evilly. 'Hunting possibly – not fox hunting, of course, though I wouldn't put it past that old bastard, but drag hunting, fishing ... spot of shooting, maybe, if you're lucky.'

'Shooting! You're joking!' Jenny's vision of a country-house weekend had consisted mainly of sitting in front of a huge blazing fire eating toasted crumpets.

'Nope. There'll be lots of nice long walks in the fresh air. You'll definitely need your wellies,' he said, gazing at the window, which was still being pelted by rain.

'Oh, great, I can bring my hot pink ones that I got for Glastonbury last year.'

'A waxed jacket would be handy, riding boots, riding hat ...'

'I don't have any of that stuff.'

'You'll need a warm jacket for going shooting, with big pockets that you can stuff all the birds you kill into.'

'Sounds like a flak jacket would be more useful than a waxed one,' Jenny said.

'How about one of those belts for holding bullets, like Rambo wears?' Liam suggested.

'Plus-fours, of course, are a must,' Ollie continued, 'as is a deer-stalker hat.'

'Oh, shut up, you're winding me up!' She tore off a lump of croissant and threw it across the table at Ollie as he succumbed to laughter.

'Seriously, though, you should bring your wellies – and wrap up warm.'

She and Richard drove down to Lord Kenton's country pile the following Friday evening. Jenny gasped as they turned off the road into a long, winding drive towards a huge old house with a lake in front of it.

'It's fucking Brideshead!' she said as they crunched to a halt on the gravel and got out.

Richard took her hand and led her to the house. They stepped into a vast draughty hall, smelling of mildew and dog, and lined with gilt-framed paintings – dark, gloomy pictures of horses and dogs, hunting scenes and a couple of old-fashioned portraits of chubby, pasty-faced gentry. A glass case in the centre of the hall displayed a couple of stuffed pheasant that had seen better days. An ancient threadbare rug ran the length of the hall and the paint on the walls was blistered and peeling. Jenny wondered if Simon Kenton had fallen on hard times or was just stingy.

'Ah, Richard, there you are.' Simon appeared from a room off the hall, flanked by two very tall, lean dogs.

Jenny instinctively recoiled as they bounded up to her. One buried his nose in her crotch, while the other leaped up at her, almost knocking her over. At full stretch it was almost taller than she was. She grabbed Richard's sleeve in panic and hid behind him.

'Oh, don't worry, m'dear, they won't hurt you. Down!' he shouted, shooing them away from her and back towards the door from which he had come. 'Hello, Jenny, nice to see you again,' he said, shaking her hand. 'Well, come in, come in. I'll have your things brought up to your room. How was your journey down? Not too much of a bugger, I hope.'

He ushered them into a huge, ornately decorated living room. The furniture looked expensive and old, but very faded and shabby. It was almost as cold in here as it was in the hall, despite a roaring log fire blazing in the huge fireplace. Maybe that was because Dev was standing in front of it, blocking the heat. David was sitting on one of the sofas between a very attractive young girl and a sour-faced older woman.

'Your man is already here,' Simon said to Richard, waving a hand at Dev.

'Hello, Dev,' Jenny greeted him. 'I didn't know you were going to be here.' Though she might have guessed. Anywhere Richard went, Dev was sure to follow.

'You know David,' Simon was saying to her. 'And this is his girl, er—'

'Emma.' David jumped up, introducing the girl beside him.

'And this is my wife, Margaret,' Simon indicated the other woman on the sofa. Her eyes raked over Jenny and she nodded almost imperceptibly, a tight smile on her face.

'You weren't at Jeremy's party,' Jenny said, shaking her hand.

'I never go up to London.' Margaret made it sound as if 'going up to London' was something only very vulgar people did.

'Well, I'll have you shown to your room and you can get freshened up,' Simon said to Richard. 'I take it your man will be joining us for dinner?'

'Most unusual,' Margaret murmured huffily, glancing towards Dev.

'My ...' Richard followed Simon's eyes to Dev, who rolled his eyes. 'Oh, he's not – you know Dev, Simon. You've met him before. He's our director of communications.'

'Right, right. I knew he did something for you. I wasn't sure what.'

'I wish you'd told me he'd be with us for dinner – and on his own,' Margaret said in an undertone to her husband. 'If I'd known, I'd have invited another lady. I can't stand an unbalanced dining table.'

Their bedroom was an enormous high-ceilinged room, dominated by a decrepit four-poster bed complete with canopy. It was the temperature of a walk-in freezer.

'Does Simon think Dev is your servant or something?' Jenny giggled as they unpacked their cases.

'He knows damn well who Dev is. He's just being a bugger.'

'Why did he invite him if he's just going to be mean to him?'

'He didn't invite him – at least, not until I asked him to.'

'Why did you do that?'

'I'm hoping we can get some work done so the weekend isn't a complete waste of time.'

Jenny tutted. 'You're such a workaholic. It's never a waste of time spending a weekend with your friends.'

'They're not exactly my *friends*, Jenny.'

'Then why are we here?'

'Simon's been very good to me. He's very influential in the Party and he backed me in the leadership contest. Having his support made a huge difference.'

'So now you're his bitch?'

'Something like that,' Richard smiled, 'but I prefer *protégé*.'

'Is David his *protégé* too?'

'He wishes.' Richard laughed. 'David is grooming himself as the next leader of the Party.'

'*Really*? Cheeky bugger! You've only just got started. Is that why Simon doesn't like Dev – because he's not licking his arse all the time, like the rest of you?'

'You have such a lovely turn of phrase.' Richard laughed. 'That, among other things. He also doesn't like Dev because he's not ex-public school and he doesn't come from a solid Moderate background. Simon's an awful snob. And, of course, to add insult to injury he's upset Margaret by throwing her dining table out of whack.'

'Why didn't he bring anyone? Does he have a girlfriend?'

'Not at the moment.'

'I'm surprised. He's so good-looking, you'd think women would be throwing themselves at him.'

'Do you really think he's that good-looking?' Richard sounded peeved.

'Don't look like that! I'm not saying I fancy him or anything. But objectively, you know, he *is* very good-looking.'

'I suppose.' Richard shrugged.

'Has he broken up with someone recently?' Jenny had noticed the framed photo Dev kept on his desk and had wondered about the fragile girl with wispy dark hair.

'Not recently. He's just going through a dry patch at the moment.'

'Oh.'

'He's not impotent,' Richard added hastily.

'Right. That's ... good to know.' TMI, actually, but whatever.

'I mean, you know, just in case you were thinking that was why—'

'No, I wasn't. God, you men and your willies – you're unbelievable! Just because someone hasn't had a girlfriend for a while, you think people will automatically jump to the conclusion that they're impotent.'

'Well, we'd better get ready to go down and face the music.'

The dining room was bathed in lambent light, the flickering candles glinting off sparkling crystal and polished silver. They sat down to dinner with an even number, Margaret having called in last-minute reinforcements in the shape of her nearest neighbour, Liz.

'You're lucky,' Liz informed Dev as they took their seats. 'I was just about to sit down to supper when Margaret called. Another few minutes and you'd have been out of luck.'

'It's very much appreciated, Liz,' Margaret said. 'I'm sorry about the short notice, but you see the position I was in.' Her eyes drifted witheringly towards Dev.

'Oh, not at all, happy to help,' Liz said, smiling at Dev. 'My cottage pie will live to fight another day. It's no hardship to trade my solitary supper for one of your dinners, Margaret – and with a handsome companion thrown in.'

'I hope the dinner will make up for the inconvenience,' Margaret said as a young girl passed around the table, ladling soup from a tureen into their bowls.

'You live alone, then?' Dev asked Liz.

'Yes – divorced. Hubby ran off with one of the stable boys last year. Bit of a shocker, but there you are. You can't fight human nature, can you?'

'No, I suppose not.'

'Shouldn't have been such a shock, really, I suppose. His obsession with anal sex should have tipped me off from the start. But hindsight is a wonderful thing, isn't it?'

Dev nearly choked on his soup. 'Any children?'

'Yes, he did make it through the front door the odd time. We have two – a boy and a girl. Grown up now, of course, but they're what make it all worthwhile. Can't regret having known the old bugger when I got them out of it.'

While Dev chatted to Liz, the others discussed tomorrow's proposed hunt.

'Do you ride, Jenny?' Simon asked her.

'No.'

'Well, I'm sure we can organise a suitable mount for you.'

Jenny looked at him in alarm. 'Oh, no, please don't bother. I'd rather just stay here.'

'Nonsense! I'll get my man on to it. We'll put you on something really gentle to start you off.'

'Emma's a very skilled rider, aren't you, darling?' David smiled proudly at his girlfriend.

'Well, I ought to be. I've been horse-mad since I can remember. Mummy used to say my first word was "horse".' Her whinnying laugh made Jenny wonder if she'd actually merged with a horse at some stage.

'Julia was always an excellent rider,' Margaret said to Richard. 'She had one of the best seats I've ever seen.'

'Yes, she's ... very fond of riding,' Richard said. He glanced at Jenny, giving her a reassuring smile.

'Will you be joining the shoot on Sunday, Jenny?' David asked her.

'Of course she will,' Simon blustered. 'Ever handled a gun, my dear?'

'A gun? No!'

'Well, never mind. You seem like a smart gel – you'll pick it up in no time. I'll show you the ropes myself.'

'Oh, thanks very much, but really I'd rather just stay in. Is everyone going?'

'I'm not sure,' Margaret said. 'I may.'

'Jane will be coming,' Simon said to her.

'Oh, well, I'll sit it out in that case,' she said.

'Who's Jane?' Jenny asked.

'She's my husband's mistress,' Margaret said loudly, causing a hush to fall over the table.

'Oh,' Jenny said faintly, concentrating very hard on her soup.

'Excellent shot, Jane,' Simon boomed, 'and a damn fine horse-woman.'

'Well, she has so much experience in spreading her legs,' Margaret said. 'And if she didn't ride so much, she'd have no excuse for how she got so bandy.'

Jenny nearly bit the bowl off her spoon. Poor Margaret – no wonder she was so bitchy, with her husband flaunting his mistress in front of her like that. 'Maybe I could stay here with you and keep you company,' she said to her.

'Oh, please don't bother, my dear.' Margaret smiled acidly. 'I'm sure you and Jane will get on like a house on fire – you have so much in common.'

'I doubt it. I've never ridden a horse in my life – or shot a gun.'

'No, but you do sleep with other women's husbands, don't you? It'll give old Jane a boost, meeting a mistress who's actually managed to oust the wife – give the poor old thing hope.' With that she turned to David and calmly began asking after his parents, leaving Jenny gasping for breath. Between the cold and the tension, every muscle in her body ached, and her shoulders had relocated to somewhere around her ears. How was she going to endure a whole weekend with these awful people?

'Oh, Margaret,' Simon called to his wife, 'Jane will be staying to dinner tomorrow after our ride.'

'Excellent! I'll have the cook kill the fatted calf then, shall I?'

'Yes, do that,' Simon flung back at her. 'I wish someone would kill that fatted cow!' he growled to himself.

As appetisers were placed in front of them, Jenny found herself longing for the icy sanctuary of the bedroom.

'What are you doing?' Richard asked her later as Jenny stood by the bed pulling on a pair of leggings.

'I'm getting ready for bed. I'm going to put on everything I brought.' When she had donned two pairs of socks, jeans and two layers of jumpers, she got into the huge bed.

'Hurry up,' she said to Richard. 'I'm bloody freezing here!'

'I'll be there in a sec. Just let me get my coat on,' Richard said. She peeped out from the bedclothes to check if he was serious, but he was stripping down to his boxers.

Climbing into the bed, he pulled her into his arms for a long kiss. 'I think we're going to have to huddle together for warmth,' he said suggestively.

'How are you at dry-humping?' she asked, wrapping her arms around him as he nuzzled her neck.

He laughed. 'It's been a while, but I'm sure it'll come back to me.'

'Well, I sure as hell amn't taking anything off.'

'You know, the real trick to creating body heat is to get naked first.' Richard's hand slid under her two layers of jumpers, stroking her back.

'Really?' Jenny grinned at him. 'Who told you that – some lechy Boy Scout leader?'

'It's a well-known fact.' His hand was warm and persuasive against her bare skin.

'Hmm.' She shifted restlessly as a flush spread across her. 'Maybe I could afford to lose one layer,' she said, raising her arms to allow Richard to peel off her outer jumper. His head disappeared under the duvet and he pulled up her second top, trailing hot kisses across her stomach while his hand skimmed along the waistband of her jeans.

'You're warmer already,' he murmured against her stomach. 'You don't need all these clothes.' She groaned as his roving hand moved between her legs and she pushed into it, frustrated by the thickness of her clothes between them. 'You'll feel much better if you take them all off,' he said as he unzipped her jeans.

'I think you're right.' She giggled as she wriggled out of them, pulling the leggings off too. 'In fact,' she said, her hands going to the waistband of his boxers, 'I think you're overdressed yourself.'

At breakfast the next morning, David, Dev and Emma looked as pale and haggard as Jenny and Richard.

'I take it no one slept well?' Jenny asked as they helped themselves from silver salvers laid out on a sideboard.

'No, the chattering of our teeth kept us awake, I'm afraid,' David laughed. Emma joined in half-heartedly.

'I think my bed had been salvaged from the *Titanic*,' Dev said. 'I slept on the floor in the end – it was more comfortable.'

At least the food here was good, Jenny thought as she helped herself to bacon, scrambled eggs, sausages and mushrooms.

They were sitting at the long dining table eating in silence, too weary to speak, when Simon appeared, looking bright-eyed – well, as bright-eyed as someone so ancient could ever look. 'Did everyone sleep well?' he asked, rubbing his hands together.

'Great, thanks!' they chorused.

'Like a log!' David embellished.

'Morning, Jenny.' He zeroed in on her, his eyes glinting. 'Looking forward to your ride this morning?'

'Oh, well, I *was*,' she said regretfully. 'Pity we won't be able to go.'

'What? Why not?'

'Well, the weather.' She waved a hand towards the window and the rain beating against it steadily.

'Ha!' Simon hooted as if she had made a joke, and Emma and David joined in. 'A spot of rain isn't going to stop us, is it?'

'It isn't?' Jenny gulped.

'Of course not!'

'There's another problem, though. I haven't got a hat or anything.'

'Oh, don't worry. I'll get Margaret to make a few calls and we'll have you kitted out in no time.'

'Oh,' Jenny said weakly. 'Thanks.' She pushed away the rest of her breakfast, her stomach churning already at the thought of having to get on a horse.

'Ah, Richard,' Simon bent to talk in his ear, 'a couple of our grooms have come down with the dreaded lurgy, so we're a few men short. I wonder if your chap could help out.'

Richard looked at him in confusion, realisation only dawning when Simon glanced at Dev. 'Oh!'

'I'm sorry, I know it's an imposition, but we really are a bit stuck.'

'Dev's our communications director, Simon,' Richard said patiently. 'He's an expert in the media, strategic communications ...'

'Oh.' Simon frowned. 'No experience with horses?'

'No, I'm afraid not.' Richard suppressed a smile, while Dev rolled his eyes.

Simon left the room again, mumbling something about not being able to get the staff these days.

'We need to talk,' Dev said to Richard after breakfast, signalling the front door with his eyes. Jenny and Richard followed him as he strode out the door and around the side of the house. The rain had slowed to a light drizzle.

'I've had enough of this,' he said once they were well out of earshot. 'I'm going back to London.'

'We can't!' Richard protested.

'No, *you* can't. I can, and I'm going to. Jesus, I can't stand another minute in that house.'

'No, Dev, you can't just bugger off.'

'We're clearly not going to get any work done. You're going to be too busy riding around like Lord Muck taking pot shots at the wildlife.'

'I suppose you're right,' Richard muttered. 'What will you tell Simon?'

Dev grinned. 'You can tell him I'm leaving your service because I got a better offer, or I've run off with the scullery maid or something. You know how hard it is to get decent staff these days.'

Richard laughed. 'So, are you going straight away?'

'Soon as I've packed. Jenny, do you want to come with me?'

She was taken aback by the offer. But he had thrown her a lifeline. She felt terribly disloyal, but the thought of making her escape was irresistible. She wasn't sure which she was dreading more – having to get on a horse or having to sit through another meal with Simon and Margaret sniping at each other. And tonight, to add to the torture, the mistress would be added to the mix. 'Can I?' She turned eagerly to Richard.

'No!' Richard said petulantly, shooting Dev a cross look. 'You can't take Jenny.'

'You don't need her here. You can suck up to Simon very well on your own.'

'What about David's who's-got-the-best-girlfriend contest?'

'You've already won that, hands down. It wouldn't matter if Emma actually sprouted hoofs and a tail. Simon's mad about Jenny.'

'Well, all the more reason why she shouldn't go. Darling, you can't leave me here on my own,' he said to Jenny.

'But they're talking about putting me on a horse today. At least, I think that's what a mount is.' It suddenly occurred to her that it might be something much worse. 'They'll kill me.'

'Jenny's right. I think she should come with me. You can't let them put her on a horse.'

'Even if I don't fall off, I'll die of hypothermia. One way or another, I'll be dead before the weekend's out.'

'And do I have to remind you that they're planning to give her a gun tomorrow?'

Richard looked defeated. 'You're right,' he said. 'Save yourselves.'

'Really?' Jenny grinned. 'You don't mind if I go?'

'No. I should never have brought you here. They're an appalling bunch.'

'Oh, but what will be *my* excuse for leaving?' she asked.

'Invent some nanny emergency,' Dev said. 'Simon will love that. We'll tell him you had to get back to London to sort out some out-of-control children – just like Supernanny on the telly.'

Chapter 20

'Think of me when you're having fun back in London.' Richard kissed Jenny before she jumped into the car beside Dev.

'Oh dear, I feel bad now about leaving Richard here on his own,' she said, turning to wave at him as they pulled out of the driveway.

'I can bring you back if you like,' Dev said, slowing down slightly.

'No!' she yelped. He laughed.

As he cranked up the heat, she sank back in her seat, giddy with relief at escaping. 'Mmm, this is the first time I've been warm since we arrived,' she said.

The rain had started up again, and with the heat in the car and the rhythmic whirr of the windscreen wipers, Jenny soon found herself struggling to stay awake. 'Sorry, I didn't get much sleep last night.' She shook her head, trying to prop open her droopy eyelids.

'Why fight it?' Dev smiled across at her. 'We're going to be here for a while. Might as well make yourself comfortable. You can recline that seat if you want.' He leaned over and showed her how, and she snuggled back happily, giving in to the drowsiness that overwhelmed her.

By the time she woke up, it was dark and they were on the outskirts of London.

'Good sleep?'

'Mmm, yes.' She yawned and stretched. 'Your car is much more comfortable than the bed last night.'

'Are you hungry?' Dev asked. 'We missed lunch.'

She thought about it for a moment and realised she was. 'I'm starving!'

'Do you fancy going for a bite to eat when we get into London?'

'Oh! Um ...' He had taken her by surprise. She didn't want to hurt his feelings, but she wasn't sure she felt up to sitting across a restaurant table from Dev for an entire dinner, just the two of them. She was used to having Richard around to act as a buffer between them. 'I think I'll just get a takeaway and slob out on the sofa.'

'That sounds like a good idea.'

She looked across at him. He seemed tired and a bit fed up, and she felt guilty. After all, he had rescued her from a weekend in Hell, and maybe he wanted some company. 'Would you like to come?' she asked impulsively.

'Sure. Thanks.' He seemed a bit surprised at the offer. Damn – she could have got away with it. It occurred to her that he was probably just being polite asking her to dinner, hoping she would refuse so that he could have an evening to himself.

'I mean, only if you feel like it,' she added. 'If you don't have anything else to—'

'No, that'd be great. But it's my treat.' Jenny opened her mouth to protest, but he continued, 'I was going to take you to dinner anyway, so this'll be a cheap date.'

'It might not be – Ollie and Liam will probably be home and they might want in on it.' Especially if they knew he was paying, she thought.

'That's fine,' he said. 'They're welcome. When you say takeaway, though, I guess you mean Indian?' He looked at her hopefully.

'Of course I mean Indian. Is there any other kind?'

'A woman after my own heart.' He grinned at her.

True to form, Ollie and Liam jumped at the chance of a free dinner.

'Unless you want us to clear out,' Ollie whispered when they were alone in the kitchen while Dev was in the loo.

'What?'

'You know, if you want to be on your own with him.' He gestured in the direction of the hallway.

'No, of course not. Why would I want to be alone with Dev?'

'Well, I just thought – you ran away from Richard with him.'

'I didn't run away from Richard, I ran away from the country.'

'We thought maybe you were shagging *him* now,' Liam whispered.

'Of course I'm not shagging him. We left with Richard's blessing.'

'Come on, you can tell us,' Liam said. 'We won't judge you.'

'Oh, don't be daft, of course we'll judge you.' Ollie grinned. 'But we'll find in your favour. I mean, who could blame you?' he said admiringly.

'I am *not* shagging Dev,' Jenny hissed.

Unfortunately Dev chose just that moment to emerge from the loo. Jenny's eyes flew to his face as he appeared in the doorway, but she couldn't tell if he'd heard.

'Right,' he said, rubbing his hands together, 'have you decided what we're having?'

'Jenny, we did *warn* you about the country,' Ollie said sternly, ladling fragrant basmati rice into his bowl.

'But you insisted on going despite all our advice,' Liam added.

'I know, I know. But I've learned my lesson – never again.'

She, Dev and Ollie were squashed together on the sofa and Liam sat cross-legged on the floor while they helped themselves from the myriad dishes laid out on the coffee table in foil trays, filling the room with warm, spicy aromas. Jenny poured red wine into three glasses. She was disappointed Dev wasn't drinking since the wine was her only contribution to the meal.

'You could have a beer,' she suggested.

'Thanks, but I'd better stick to water. I'm a bit knackered and I still have to drive home.'

'This is great,' Ollie said, falling on the food as if he hadn't eaten for days – which he possibly hadn't.

'So what were you guys going to do for dinner before we came home?' she asked.

'It was a toss-up between a student party in Kentish Town and the launch of a new wine bar in Hampstead,' Ollie said. 'Slim pickings either way. So thanks,' he said, raising his glass to Dev in salute.

Jenny was shocked. Ollie never expressed gratitude to anyone for providing him with free grub. He took it as his due – a just reward for granting someone the pleasure of his company and the honour of gazing at his chiselled features.

'And thanks for bringing our girl home in one piece.' Liam raised his glass, joining in the toast. She was disconcerted to see he was actually *smiling* at Dev. Liam never warmed to people this quickly. What was up with the pair of them?

'At least the silly season will be upon us soon,' Ollie said. 'We'll be awash with free grub then.'

'I can't believe it's almost Christmas already,' Jenny remarked. The following day was the first of December. 'I suppose everyone's going home for it?' she asked a little shakily. She tried to appear blasé, but she was desperately hoping that someone would be staying in London.

Liam and Ollie both answered, 'Yes.'

'My ma would kill me if I didn't turn up for Christmas,' Liam said regretfully.

'Oh, come on, you love it!'

'How about you, Jenny?' Dev asked. 'What will you do?'

'Oh, I don't know. Maybe I'll push off to the Canaries or some-thing until it's all over.'

Dev pulled a face. 'Sounds a bit bleak.'

'Bleak? You're just jealous because I'll be basking in the sun in blissful solitude, while you'll all be freezing your nuts off, surrounded by warring relatives.'

'You're not a Christmas person, then?'

'No.' She hated Christmas, and felt the approach of the holiday season with an increasing sense of dread because for her it was a big countdown to nothing, a constant reminder that soon everyone would clear out of London and it would become like a ghost town. She felt so alone in those few days when everyone else seemed to have somewhere better to be, someone better to be with, and all her friends deserted her to rattle off on trains or planes to be with their families. Because Christmas was a time for families, as people were so fond of saying, and she had no family. It was a time for tradition, and she wasn't part of any traditions. Christmas wasn't for the likes of her.

'Won't you be with Richard?' Ollie asked.

'I don't know.' She shrugged. 'We haven't discussed it yet. I doubt it, though – not for Christmas Day, anyway.' She had put off asking him what his plans were because she was dreading the answer.

Liam looked furious. 'He has children,' she said to him defen-sively. 'Of course he'll have to be with them at Christmas.'

'And what about you?'

'I'll be fine,' she said. 'I'm a big girl.'

'Well, don't go to the Canaries, please,' he said. 'You were mis-erable there last year.'

Dev looked from Liam to Ollie. Jenny guessed he was wondering why neither of them invited her to spend Christmas with them. 'I'm not going home for Christmas,' he said.

'Oh. Are you staying in London?' Jenny asked politely, relieved the conversation had moved away from her.

'No, I'm going to New York.'

'Wow, Christmas in New York – that'll be lovely,' she said.

'Yeah. My folks are going away. We didn't want to do the traditional family Christmas this year ...' He trailed off, seemingly lost in thought for a moment. 'So I'm meeting up with some friends in New York. Why don't you come?'

There was a stunned silence and everyone looked at him as if he'd just suggested Jenny give him a lap-dance.

'What?' Jenny gasped.

'I mean, if you're not doing anything—'

'Oh, no, I couldn't ...' She began to refuse automatically.

'Why not?'

'Well, because it's Christmas – and it's your friends. I wouldn't want to intrude.' Isn't it bloody obvious why not? she thought crossly. He had done the polite thing and offered, and now he should do the polite thing and accept her refusal. It wasn't as if he meant it, after all. No one really wanted an outsider around at Christmas – if she had learned nothing else from the years of foster homes, she had learned that.

'I mean it,' he persisted. 'You'd enjoy it. Why don't you come?'

Because ... because she'd spent more than enough Christmases as the beggar at the feast – the poor foster kid at the edge of someone else's family but never really a part of it. God, that was worse – much worse – than rattling around London on her own, the idea of which was beginning to appeal compared to spending another Christmas as a charity case. It had been a huge relief when she was old enough to stay on her own over the holiday and no longer had to feign gratitude for the crumbs from other people's tables.

'It's not going to be a traditional family Christmas,' he said, as if reading her thoughts. 'Just a couple of friends and anyone they want to bring. There's plenty of room,' he added. 'My friend Mel's brother lives in New York and we'll be staying in his apartment.'

Jenny was tempted. It wouldn't be a family scenario, just a casual collection of friends – she wouldn't have to feel like an outsider. His invitation seemed genuine, and she was touched by his kindness and thoughtfulness. He was throwing her another lifeline. Could she – dare she – reach out and grab it?

'I don't know ...' She wavered.

'Have you ever been to New York?'

'No.'

'You'd love it. Come on,' Dev coaxed, 'just say yes. It's got to be better than moping around in the Canaries on your own.'

'You should go,' Liam said firmly, taking her by surprise.

But it was impossible ... wasn't it? She still didn't know what Richard's plans were. If he was able to spend time with her over the holidays, she wanted to be available. And besides, she didn't think she could afford to go to New York. She might be able to stretch to a cheapie in the Canaries, but a flight to New York would cost a lot more. 'Thanks, but I really don't think I can.'

'Well, the offer's open if you want to change your mind.'

They were both tired after the long journey, and Dev left soon after. Jenny walked down to the door with him. 'Thanks again for the rescue,' she said. 'And the Indian.'

'My pleasure.' Dev's eyes narrowed as he looked across the road. 'This is going to sound a bit daft, but there's a bloke over there and it looks like he's watching the house.'

Jenny peered into the shadows and saw a short figure with a familiar mass of unruly dark hair just before he ducked behind a tree.

'Oh! It's Colin.'

'Colin? Isn't he one of your stalker exes?'

'He's the one who started the support group I told you about. And you're not daft, he *is* watching the house.'

Dev frowned. 'Do you want me to have a word with him?'

'No, it's fine.' She brushed away his concern. 'He's harmless.'

Dev glanced across the street again uncertainly. 'Are you sure?'

'Yes, it's fine. Go on.' She raised a hand and waved at Colin, and he emerged sheepishly from behind the tree. 'I'll go and say hello to him.'

Dev went to his car but he didn't start the engine, and she was aware of his eyes on her as she crossed the road to Colin.

'Hi, Colin. What are you doing here?'

'Don't worry.' He smiled, holding up his hands in a gesture of sur-render. 'I haven't reverted to my old ways. I'm just doing a quick patrol – making sure no one's backsliding. Christmas can be a hard time for people.'

'I suppose so. Will you be going home to your folks?'

He grinned. 'Yeah, the usual.' He blew on his hands. 'You know what my mum's like about Christmas.'

'Yeah, I remember.' The Christmas she had spent with Colin had been one of the better ones. His mum had really taken to her and made her feel part of his big, boisterous family straight away, and his brothers and sisters had treated her like part of the furniture, as though she'd always been there. It almost made her wish they were still together. But his mother probably hated her now for breaking her lovely son's heart. Besides, it wasn't a good reason to be with someone – because you coveted their family. He was right: Christmas was a dangerous time for lonely people.

'How about you?' he asked. 'Doing anything special?'

'I don't know yet. I might go away.'

He nodded silently. She thought he looked a bit sad. 'Well, have a good one, whatever you do,' he said finally with a gentle smile.

'Yeah, you too. And don't stay out here too much longer – it's bloody freezing.'

As she walked back to the house, Dev started his car and pulled away.

Chapter 21

'Do you want to put the fairy on the top, sweetie?'

'Yes!' Hannah stretched her arms up to Jenny, who reached down and picked her up, lifting her over her head so that she could impale the fairy on the topmost branch of the Christmas tree.

'There.' She put Hannah down again and stood back to survey the tree.

'Pretty!' Hannah's eyes shone as she peered up at it.

'Isn't it beautiful?' Jenny agreed. The fairy was tilted drunkenly to the side and she stood on the little stepladder to adjust her to a more upright position. 'Your mummy will be so pleased when she comes home.'

It really was beautiful, she thought. This was the bit of Christmas she loved. She was as delighted with the sparkle and glitter as five-year-old Hannah was.

'I can't wait till Mummy sees it!' Hannah said.

As if on cue, there was the sound of a key in the lock and the front door opening. Hannah ran to the hall to greet her mother, squealing excitedly as she dragged her in to see the Christmas tree.

'Oh, my goodness!' Lily gasped. 'You two have been busy, haven't you?'

'Hannah did most of it,' Jenny said.

'You like it?' Hannah asked her mother.

'It's gorgeous. You've done a fantastic job, sweetheart,' she said and gave Hannah a kiss.

After a quick chat, Jenny left, with Lily still exclaiming in admiration over their handiwork. Outside, she stopped at the gate to see how the tree looked from the road, the lights glittering into the darkness from the big bay window. Hannah and Lily were still standing in front of it, Hannah pointing things out to her mother. She couldn't hear their voices, but she knew what Hannah would be saying – that she had put the fairy on top, that her favourite decoration was the fat, shiny Father Christmas with the glittery white beard. It had been fun this afternoon doing the tree with Hannah. She didn't know how Lily could bear to miss all that – how she could let someone else have those precious moments with her daughter and not be consumed by jealousy. If Jenny had a child …

She shivered, pulling her jacket tighter around herself as she turned to go. It seemed a lot of people had decided to put their trees up today. As she walked down the dark road to the Tube, Christmas trees that hadn't been there this morning sparkled from the windows of several houses. This was the part of Christmas she hated, she thought as she passed rows of warm, cosy living rooms and wondered about the life that went on inside. She knew she would love Christmas if she could be on the other side of one of those windows. She *should* love Christmas – the sparkle and glitter, the twinkling street lights, the brightly wrapped presents: it was exactly her kind of thing. She always felt that one day it would be her favourite time of year – a time when she would be inside one of those houses.

She felt oddly comforted, descending into the grimy warmth of the Tube station. It wasn't Christmas down here – this was probably the one place in London left untouched by the festive cheer. Down here, everyone was equal; no one belonged to anyone. For a while they were all just rootless, anonymous strangers in transit between the meaningful bits of their lives.

Each year she consoled herself with the thought that next Christmas would be different – next year she would have somewhere to go where she belonged and would be part of it all. But so far it hadn't happened, and with each passing year she felt an increasing sense of panic that it never would. Every year she found herself somewhere different, trying to figure out the choreography of some other family's rituals. But no matter how hard she tried, she always felt a little out of synch, and no matter how kind they were she couldn't help feeling she made everyone else a little uncomfortable.

Over the years, she had spent Christmas with the families of friends and boyfriends who had taken pity on her – a really happy one with Colin's family; a disastrous one with Ollie's. The year they were together, she had gone with Ollie to his parents' huge pile in the Wiltshire countryside. His mother had taken an instant dislike to her and hadn't bothered to conceal that she saw Jenny as trouble and a bad influence on her precious boy – as if Ollie needed leading astray! She made Jenny's life a misery for the whole two days she had managed to tough it out. His father, on the other hand, had taken rather too much of a shine to her and had stuck his tongue into her mouth under the mistletoe in front of the assembled family. Ollie had been as glad as she was to make his escape the day after Boxing Day – which had done nothing to endear his mother to Jenny, as he had originally planned to stay until New Year.

'I'm sorry Mummy was so bloody to you,' he had said as they rattled back to London in the old banger he had borrowed from his sister as a getaway car. They had spent the rest of the week holed up in their little nest, snuggled into each other, safe from Mummy, 'that randy old bugger Daddy' and the rest of the world.

But blood was thicker than water, and the next year – and every year since – Ollie had returned home like the dutiful prodigal son he was. She knew Liam felt guilty for being unable to invite her to spend Christmas with his family, but they both knew his mother wouldn't welcome her. Last year, Richard still hadn't publicly separated from Julia (or privately, she now realised), so she had decided to avoid it by escaping to the Canaries. She had walked on the beach and sat alone at outdoor cafés and told herself it was just another day. But she couldn't kid herself: on which other day would she be rattling around in the Canaries on her own? That was possibly the worst Christmas ever.

This year should have been different, she thought as the train rattled through the tunnel. She had found the person she wanted to be with, not just this year but every year. She should be looking forward to Christmas. But nothing had changed. For ages she had avoided bringing the subject up with Richard, wanting to cling as long as possible to the hope that they could spend it together. She fantasised about going away with him – or just staying at his flat in London, making up new traditions of their own. But she put off asking him about his plans because she had an awful feeling that they wouldn't include her.

She had finally plucked up the courage to broach the subject last weekend, and it was even worse than she had anticipated. 'What are you planning for Christmas this year?' she had asked tentatively, trying to sound casual. She didn't want to seem pushy. 'I thought we might ... do something.' She looked at him hopefully, but his expression was enough to crush her hopes.

'Jenny, I can't. I'll be with the boys.'

'Oh, yes, of course,' she said quickly. 'I knew you'd want to spend the day with them.'

'It's the first Christmas since Julia and I split up and we want to make everything as normal as possible for them. I mean, Christmas is for the kids, really, isn't it? It's a time for—'

'Families,' she finished. 'Yes, I know. I didn't mean – I wasn't expecting you to spend Christmas Day with me. But afterwards – Boxing Day and—'

'Oh, didn't I tell you?' he interrupted. He looked shifty and her heart sank. He knew damn well he hadn't told her whatever it was. 'Julia and I agreed that I'd stay with them for the holiday,' he continued.

'For ... the whole holiday?' she said faintly. She had thought that at least this year she would have just the day itself to get through on her own, possibly two days at the most.

'Look, it's only a week, and like I said, we have to think of the boys first and foremost.'

'And you're going to be staying ... there, with them? In the same house?' She felt dazed.

'Well, on the day after Boxing Day we're going to my parents in Devon. We do it every year. It's tradition.'

'Tradition, right.'

'Don't look like that,' he said, pained. 'It's not a big deal. I mean, it's not as if I'll be sleeping with Julia just because we're in the same house – any more than I was sleeping with her before I left. It won't be any different.'

No. It wouldn't be any different. That was exactly what she was afraid of. It would never be any bloody fucking *different*! She would always be the one to be overlooked and abandoned in favour of someone more important, more lovable, more loved. She swallowed hard against the bile rising in her throat.

'No, I understand,' she said, smiling sweetly at him. 'It's fine – I don't mind. It was just a thought.'

Richard smiled back at her, relief smoothing his features. 'You're amazing, do you know that?' he said, brushing her hair away from her face. 'What did I do to deserve you?' He kissed her lips. 'What will you do – for Christmas?' he asked, nuzzling her neck.

'I don't know. I'll think of something. It's just another day – no big deal.'

'You should go home with Ollie or Liam.'

'Yeah, maybe.' That was his solution – fob her off on someone else to salve his conscience.

He held her face in his hands, looking into her eyes. 'Promise me you won't go haring off to the Canaries,' he said. 'You had a miserable time there last year.'

What difference did it make to him where she went, she thought, as long as she was out of sight and out of mind?

'I mean it,' he said. 'I hate to think of you being on your own.'

'Don't worry about me.' She smiled cheerfully. 'I'll have fun – I always do.'

'You do, don't you?' He kissed her. 'I love you,' he murmured against her mouth.

'I know you do,' she whispered. But not enough. Never enough.

'Jenny, come in here,' Liam called from the kitchen when she got home. 'We have something to give you.'

She went to the kitchen to find Ollie and Liam sitting at the table, a present wrapped in shiny Christmas foil on the table between them. As she sat down, Ollie slid it across to her.

'Is this my Christmas present?' She picked up the small flat parcel but didn't open it. 'It's too early – we haven't even got the tree up yet, and I haven't got yours ready either.' She was confused. They usually exchanged presents just before everyone went their separate ways for the holiday.

'We have to give it to you early,' Liam explained. 'When you open it, you'll see why.'

'Oh, okay,' she said, intrigued as she slid it open. Inside was a plain white envelope. She opened it and gasped when she saw it was full of fifty-pound notes. 'Oh, my God, what—' Her fingers flicked through them – there was five hundred pounds in all. She looked at them in shock.

'It's for New York,' Liam said. 'That's why we had to give it to you now, so you can book a flight.'

Ever since she had told them Richard wouldn't be around over the holiday, they had been trying to persuade her to take Dev up on his offer. 'Thanks, but I can't accept this. It's way too much,' she said, pushing the envelope away from her. They usually gave each other token presents that cost less than twenty pounds. 'You can't afford it.'

'It's from both of us,' Ollie said.

'Even so—'

'And a few other people chipped in too,' Liam said.

'Other people? Who?'

'Colin and some of his lot. They had a whip-round at the support group.'

'What?' she gasped. 'You asked my exes to chip in for my Christmas present?'

'They were happy to do it,' Liam told her. 'And it's not like they don't owe you for all the years of stalking.'

'Besides, some of them still send you presents to try to win you back,' Ollie pointed out. 'At least this way you can have something you want.'

'But how did you even get in touch with them?'

'It wasn't hard,' Liam said. 'Colin's outside the house all the time these days. He's like a fucking missionary, trying to round up sinners.'

Her fingers strayed towards the envelope. Could she really have this?

'So, do you like what we got you?' Ollie asked.

She picked the envelope up again, hugging it to her chest. 'Thank you.' She grinned at them. 'I love it!'

***

'I can't believe you're seriously thinking of going to New York with Dev for Christmas,' Richard said later that night when she told him.

Excited at the prospect of going to America, she had raced over to his flat to tell him about the guys' present. But she hadn't expected this reaction. 'Why? What else am I going to do? You don't want to spend it with me.'

'You know it's not that I don't want to, Jenny.'

'Anyway, I don't see what the problem is. You're going to be spending it with Julia, and I haven't made a fuss about that.'

'I'm not going to spend Christmas with Julia,' he said reasonably, as though he were explaining something to a small child. 'I'm going to spend it with my children and their mother. It's not the same thing.'

'Well, I'm not going to spend Christmas with Dev. I'm going to spend it with a group of people instead of being on my own. I thought you'd be glad – you said you didn't want me to be alone.'

'But I didn't think you'd go haring off to New York with Dev. You're not even friends.'

'Well, maybe we are now. You should be glad we're getting along.'

'I am,' he said, but he didn't sound happy.

'It was really nice of him to invite me.' She didn't want to sound accusing, but it was more than Richard had done.

'It was, but do you think he really meant it? He probably didn't think you'd accept.'

She was shocked and hurt that he would say something so mean to her. She would probably have thought he was right if Dev hadn't repeated the invitation to her several times, urging her to go with him. 'He meant it,' she said with confidence. 'And the guys gave me this money specifically so that I could go.' She looked at him pleadingly, willing him to be happy for her. She had been so keyed up about

247

the idea, but now she felt deflated. He was making her feel guilty, as if she was betraying him. 'You wouldn't mind if I was going away with Ollie or Liam.'

'That's different.'

'Why?' She searched his face.

'It just is,' he said impatiently.

'No, tell me, why is it different?' she insisted, her anger rising. 'Because you think I haven't shagged them? I have.'

'What, you—'

'Yes, both of them. The person I haven't shagged – the person I will *never* shag – is Dev. Now can I go to New York with him?'

He was looking at her as if he hardly knew her, as if he was seeing her for the first time. 'I'm not stopping you,' he said finally.

She flinched at his tone and his expression, appalled by the damage she'd done. How could he think that? Of course he was stopping her. Damn it, she shouldn't have lost her temper. How could she have lost control like that? She had to make it better. She took a deep breath, steeling herself. 'I won't go if you really don't want me to,' she said, trying to look as if she didn't care too much either way. But she meant it – she would do anything to make him go on loving her. If he said he didn't want her to go, she wouldn't. She just prayed he wouldn't say it.

Chapter 22

Julia hugged her coat to herself as she hurried up the path to her house, a taxi sitting at the gate.

'Did you have a nice time?' Lisa, the babysitter, stood up as she came into the living room.

'It was all right. Any problems?'

'No, they were both good as gold.'

'Good. The taxi's outside, so I won't keep you.' When she had paid the girl and waved her off, Julia returned to the living room and removed her coat, flopping onto the sofa. She was so relieved to be home. After a few minutes she got up and went to the kitchen. She took a bottle of white wine from the fridge and poured herself a glass. Then, instead of returning to the living room, she went to her study and switched on the computer. She sat at the desk, sipping her wine, while she waited for it to boot up. She would just check her emails before going to bed – and maybe have a quick look on Facebook. She was too restless and wound up to go upstairs straight away. Sitting at the computer, she felt guilty that she hadn't got any writing done today. She really should use this energy to try to catch up, but her head was too fuzzy – and it was just going to get fuzzier, she thought, sipping the wine. She really didn't need any more, but she felt like it.

She had found the party tonight a bit depressing, and she was cross that an evening out among friends, which should have been enjoyable and cheering, had left her feeling angry and disheartened. It wasn't just being without a partner, though she knew that was part of it – having nowhere to put all the sexy feelings brought on by the dressing up, the knowledge that she looked good, the wine, the beautiful food. When she was with Richard, sex would have been the natural end to an evening like that.

But it wasn't just that she was going to bed alone that bothered her. It was how the other women at the party had behaved towards her. There had been nothing subtle about the way Sophie had come trotting up while she was chatting to Nigel, barging into the conversation before pulling him away. As if she'd be remotely interested in Nigel in *that* way! She had felt quite offended by the implication and was tempted to shout at Sophie, 'Oh, calm down, for God's sake, I'm not going to shag him!' But she had been too taken aback to react at all.

And Sophie hadn't been the only one. As the evening went on, she was aware of other women's eyes on her while she spoke to their husbands. Now that she was single, she was seen as a threat – a predatory woman on the hunt for a new man and not scrupulous about where she found him. And these were people who supposedly *knew* her. It would be quite funny if it wasn't so bloody insulting.

It wasn't as if she had changed in any fundamental way. True, she had been flirting a bit with Geoffrey before Sarah had intervened and 'rescued' him from her clutches. But that was all it had been: harmless, innocent flirting. She had always flirted with the men at parties before – with these very same men, in fact – and no one had taken it seriously. But now that she was single – and apparently, in their eyes, desperate – she wasn't to be trusted. It was so bloody infuriating it made her want to throw things. It was so unfair – some little tart had made off with her husband and *she* got labelled as a dangerous woman.

When she had checked her emails she clicked on Facebook and typed in her password. Maybe she could have a rant about the party to someone and let off steam. There were only two friends on line, however, both of whom had been at the party, so she couldn't bitch about it to them. She decided she would send a private message to her friend Sheila. Single and in her late forties, Sheila would know exactly where she was coming from, having herself been at the receiving end of hostility from smug marrieds. Then again, in Sheila's case, their anxiety might have been warranted – she was a bona fide (and self-confessed) man-eater. Julia opened a message window and began typing furiously, hitting the keyboard hard, her anger reignited as she went back over the events of the evening.

She felt better after she had had a good vent, and was just about to log off from the site when she noticed a pop-up ad in the corner for a dating agency. She was vaguely aware of having seen it before, but only noticed it properly now. Out of idle curiosity, she clicked on the icon to take a free tour of the site and view some members. It would be interesting to get an idea of what was out there, now that she was a single woman. She filled in a form that allowed her to register for free and looked through a few profiles, becoming increasingly depressed by the illiteracy of most, peppered with bad spelling, appalling grammar and nonsensical LOLs. And why did people use text-speak when they were on a computer?

She narrowed the parameters of her search, specifying age (over thirty) and including reading and opera in her interests to weed out the Neanderthals. Even with the criteria thus tightened, there were a surprising number of matches, and she began looking through them, idly at first, but with increasing interest as, to her surprise, she found several who sounded promising – intelligent, good-looking, with a sense of humour and similar interests to hers. She bookmarked a few. Then she began to create a profile for herself, just for fun, trying to hit the right balance between sounding interesting enough to get some responses and not giving the wrong impression about what she really was – which she suspected was a boring old fart. It was surprisingly difficult to word it to her satisfaction.

Oh, screw it, she thought, taking a huge swig of wine. It didn't matter what she put – she could be whoever the hell she wanted to be. After all, it wasn't as if she intended to meet up with any of these people in real life. God forbid! She could be a horny housewife looking for afternoon fun, or an uneducated immigrant on the hunt for a sugar daddy. She was a writer, for God's sake – she should use her imagination! So, a little bit pissed and a whole lot pissed off, she threw caution to the wind and, while sticking to the truth about her personal details, used words like 'adventurous' and 'open-minded' to describe herself. When she had finished, she switched off the computer and went to bed, feeling a little better.

The next morning, as she checked her email, Julia was surprised to see several notifications that she had received messages on the dating website. She had almost forgotten about it, apart from a brief flashback at breakfast, which made her smile to herself, after which she had put it out of her mind. She had no intention of doing any more about it, but now her curiosity was piqued and she couldn't stop herself going back to the site to see what kind of responses she had attracted to her profile. As she had suspected, her slightly racy description of herself had brought out a fair share of opportunists who made no bones about the fact that they were looking for no-strings sex. Several were even upfront in telling her they were married, she noted with distaste.

One after another, she deleted messages offering her 'afternoon delight' while LOLing at nothing like lunatics. There were a couple from women, and even though she had given her real age, a few from guys as young as twenty-three. Then she came to one that actually sounded quite normal. His picture was nice, she thought, studying his face – he was quite attractive, looked healthy and well dressed. As she read his profile, her interest grew. He made no reference to her 'adventurous' character, instead concentrating on the fact that, like her, he was a creative person and shared her love of opera and literature as well as her appreciation of fine wine and good food. A civil servant, he had recently taken up painting in his spare time, and was becoming increasingly passionate about it. Julia's hands hovered over the keyboard uncertainly. Should she? No, this was crazy. But then, she told herself, even if she did contact him, she didn't have to take it any further. She was still completely anonymous, hidden behind her username. She could disappear into the ether any time she felt like it. On a whim, she sent him a message.

'Why don't you come in and I'll show you what I'm working on at the moment?'

'Well, maybe just for a minute,' Julia said politely, glancing at her watch.

Her civil servant had turned out to be a middle-aged Customs officer who had droned on all evening about his methods for spotting smugglers, tapping his nose knowingly as he outlined the various tricks they used. She told herself it was her own fault as he related yet another story of a lowlife who had failed to get past him. After all, he *was* a civil servant. It wasn't his fault that she had seen the words 'civil servant' and immediately imagined a Whitehall mandarin in the upper echelons of government administration. It served her right for being such a snob. Well, she had paid for it on their date.

He was a nice enough man, but boring as all hell, and despite the apparent match in their online profiles, they had absolutely nothing in common. He liked to spend his evenings watching TV. He was an avid fan of soaps and had become quite exercised on the subject of the latest sacking from *The Apprentice* – she hadn't had the first idea what he was talking about. She couldn't wait for the date to be over – going to bed alone had rarely been so appealing. But first she had promised to go and see his paintings. That was her fault too – in a desperate attempt to salvage an evening she should have known was beyond redemption, she had expressed a keen interest in his hobby and tried to steer the conversation towards that in the hope of finding some common ground.

'Well, you're obviously very good at your job,' she had said as he launched into another tale of derring-do in the Customs hall, 'but I want to hear about your painting. What medium do you work in?'

But he was remarkably reticent on the subject, and despite quizzing him about his style and influences, his inspiration, working practices and subjects, all she managed to coax out of him was that he found painting 'relaxing' after a long day on the job – which had brought him neatly back to the job in question.

She had followed him to his home in her car, blessing the fact that common sense had dictated she should drive herself and not drink when she was going to meet a stranger. At least she had peace for the journey, and she could leave whenever she wanted to. As she parked behind him outside his house, she was tempted to leave there and then – to pull away with a screech of tyres and leave him standing dumbfounded on the pavement. Instead, she turned off the engine and got out reluctantly, following him inside.

'I do all my painting in the kitchen,' he told her, leading the way down a narrow hallway. 'It's got the best light. These are some of my earlier efforts.' He waved an arm at the pictures that lined the walls of the hallway, and Julia glanced at them as she passed. From the fleeting glimpse she got, they appeared competently executed, but hardly inspiring. They were all curiously old-fashioned subjects – Victorian street scenes, country cottages, fields with horses and dogs. He seemed to draw his inspiration from chocolate boxes.

He flicked a switch, illuminating a large, tidy room, and Julia saw a small canvas propped against a vase on the table. 'This is the latest.' He indicated the painting with a proud smile. 'I just finished it last night – well, it needs the odd touch-up here and there.'

Julia came to the front and stifled a gasp. 'Oh, gosh ... yes, I see ... It's, um ...' She peered closer at the canvas. Was it really what she thought it was? Surely not! She looked again. It was a landscape with a coach and horses. The paint was thin in places and she was sure she could see the number '3' poking through on one of the horses' heads. 'Is that ... is that a number on the horse's head?'

'Yes, that's right – it needs another coat in places. Number three,' he pointed to the horse, 'that's brown. There was a lot of brown in this one.' He pointed to tree trunks and the dark earth beneath the horses' hoofs. 'I put the paint on too thickly in the beginning. I almost didn't have enough brown left at the end, so it's a bit thin in places.'

'Oh, right. So it's painting by numbers. When you said you'd taken up painting, I thought ...' She trailed off, not at all sure how to finish that sentence.

'You thought I made them up out of my own head?' he laughed good-naturedly at the notion. 'No, no – I've no talent for that sort of thing. But they're nice paintings, aren't they? And at least they're proper pictures – you can tell what they are, not like some of this modern rubbish.'

'Right.' Julia smiled stiffly. Oh, God, she had to get out of here before he started sounding off about modern art. 'Yes, well, they're lovely. And it's such a nice relaxing hobby, as you say.' She glanced at her watch. 'Goodness, is that the time? Well, it's been a lovely evening,' she said brightly, the rictus smile still in place, 'but I really must be going. I've got an early start in the morning.'

'Are you sure you won't have a cup of coffee?'

Oh, Christ, was that a suggestive twinkle in his eye? 'No, thank you, I really do have to go.' She started to make a bolt for the door before she had even finished speaking.

'We must do this again some time,' he said, following her.

'Yes, we must. I'm going to be out of the country for a while, but—'

'Well, you know where I am – virtually speaking.' He tapped his nose conspiratorially.

'Right, yes. Well, goodnight. Good luck with the painting!' she called, and darted out into the night.

Chapter 23

On Christmas Eve the airport was thronged with people going home
– or away — for the holidays. Jenny had experienced it last year when
she had fled to the Canaries, but today was completely different.
Today she enjoyed the bustle and chaos, the air of excitement and
anticipation, because today she was part of it. This time she had
brightly wrapped presents in her suitcase and someone waiting for
her at the other end of the journey. She hadn't been able to get on the
same flight as Dev, who had flown out a few hours earlier, but he was
going to wait for her at JFK and they could get a taxi into Manhattan
together.

'Love you lots,' she said, standing on tiptoe to kiss Richard as he
left her at the gate.

'Me too.' He gave her a lingering kiss. 'And don't open your
present before Christmas morning.' He smiled, pulling away.

'I won't – promise! The same goes for you,' she said, poking him
playfully in the chest.

'Well, have a great time,' he said and kissed her on the forehead
one last time before she joined the queue to go through security.

Dev stood waiting for Jenny in the arrivals hall at JFK. She had said
there was no need for him to hang around the airport waiting for her,

and he knew she was perfectly capable of getting a taxi into Manhattan on her own. But he wanted to wait for her. It was her first time in New York and he knew it would be more fun for her if she had someone to share it with. It would be more fun for him too. He wanted to be there when she got her first glimpse of the New York skyline. He was looking forward to seeing her reaction and hearing her first impressions of the city, already anticipating her excitement. Most of all, he wanted to see the wraparound smile that always lifted his heart. He needed it after being alone on a seven-hour journey with too much time to brood. He had got into a bit of a maudlin mood on the plane, and when he wasn't sleeping, his thoughts had constantly strayed to last Christmas and how different things had been then. He had begun to think that taking a break wasn't such a good idea. At least when he was working he had no time to dwell on dark thoughts.

Then the doors opened and she was there, her face lighting up as she spotted him. Seeing her, he felt something shift inside him. It was as if there was a string at the top of his head, pulling his body up straight, lifting his mouth at the corners, making him feel almost weightless. She ran over to him and his gloom melted away.

'Hi, Jenny.' He bent to kiss her cheek. 'Good flight?'

'Oh, it was brilliant!' she said, taking his arm as he led her out of the terminal.

God, if she was that pleased about a flight, how was she going to react to New York?

'I had my own TV screen and I could watch whatever I wanted. They had *Friends*! And there was a lovely man beside me who bought me lots of drinks and kept going on about some sky-high club or something he wanted me to join ...'

'Sky-high club?' Dev gulped. 'Are you sure it wasn't the mile-high club?'

'Oh, yes, that was it. Have you heard of it?'

'Um ... yes. You didn't ... I mean ...'

'Oh, don't worry, I didn't go for it. I thought it sounded a bit dodgy, to be honest – one of those pyramid-selling things maybe. He had a real hard-on to get me to join it.'

'I bet,' Dev said drily.

The cold seized them as soon as they emerged from the building, their bodies hunching against it automatically. Dev frowned as he took in Jenny's clothes. She was inadequately dressed, as usual. Despite his warnings that it would be freezing, she was only wearing a short denim jacket – and snow was forecast for tomorrow. Thankfully they were soon in a cab and speeding towards Manhattan.

'So who else is going to be there?' she asked.

'Mel – she's one of my oldest friends. We went to school together. It's her brother's apartment, but he's gone to his in-laws for the holidays. And Ian – he's a friend from college. He's living in Boston at the moment. He's here on sabbatical, teaching at Harvard. He's bringing his girlfriend, who I've never met. And me and you – that's it.'

He looked out the window as they sped along the freeway, feeling the usual buzz of excitement at being back. He loved New York and it had been a while. The last time he had been here was a couple of years ago with Sally. The photo he kept on his desk was from that trip. She was standing on Bow Bridge in Central Park, a wisp of dark hair blowing across her face as she smiled into the camera. She looked happy. But he knew she hadn't been happy that day – not really. She was making an effort for his sake, not wanting to disappoint him. It was always an effort for her. It broke his heart. She had tried to respond to his enthusiasm as he had dragged her around the city, showing her all his favourite places and snapping endless pictures of her as if it was his last chance – and it hadn't been far off.

His thoughts were interrupted by Jenny's shriek of delight when she caught her first glimpse of the Manhattan skyline.

'Oh, my God, I can't believe I'm in New York!' she squealed, grinning at Dev before she turned back to gaze out the window, taking in everything as they made their way into the heart of Manhattan. The city was at its movie-set best, the trees that lined the streets bedecked with thousands of fairy lights, and Jenny was like a child, gasping over it all and keeping up a running commentary. It was *Breakfast at Tiffany's*, *Miracle on 34th Street*, then *Home Alone 2: Lost in New York*!

'Sorry, I'm babbling,' she said, turning back to him.

'I like your babbling.' He was grateful for the distraction. 'Don't stop on my account.' He was glad she was here. She would throw light into the shadows that hung over the city for him now. She would make it all new and exciting again. He was feeling much lighter by the time they pulled up outside the apartment building on Central Park West.

Jenny was in love with New York already. It was just like in the movies – the yellow taxis, the skyscrapers, the sidewalk Santas, the trees strung with thousands of fairy lights. The apartment building even had a doorman. She could barely contain her excitement as they took the lift to the twentieth floor, itching to get out on the streets.

The door to the apartment was opened by a tall girl with long hair the colour of a shiny conker. 'Hi!' She beamed at them both and pulled Dev into an enthusiastic embrace. 'It's so good to see you,' she said. 'And you must be Jenny.' To Jenny's surprise, she swept her into a hug too. 'I'm Mel. It's really nice to meet you.' She had the same soft Northern accent as Dev. 'Well, come in.' She beckoned them into a spacious hall with polished wooden floors.

'Why don't you dump your stuff here for now?'

Jenny had been wondering how five people would squeeze into

one apartment, but she realised she needn't have worried as Mel led them into a vast living space that was more football pitch than living room. You could have fit a herd of cattle into it with room to spare.

'Oh, wow!' She rushed over to the windows that ran the length of one wall, overlooking Central Park.

'This is some place!' Dev said to Mel, joining Jenny at the window.

'I know.' Mel grinned smugly. 'Aren't we lucky?'

'Mark's obviously doing well for himself.'

'Yeah. My brother's a film producer,' she explained to Jenny. 'I'll just put the kettle on and I'll show you around. I bet you could do with a cup of tea.'

The apartment was stunning. Besides the cavernous living space, there was a separate kitchen/diner, four bathrooms and four bedrooms. The floors were wooden throughout and it was decorated simply but elegantly in a classic style. Jenny was thrilled with her bedroom, which had a view of the park.

When she had finished showing them around, Mel made tea and they sat on one of several cream sofas that were dotted around the living room.

'Is Ian here yet?' Dev asked.

'They arrived last night, but they've gone out shopping.'

'What's his girlfriend like?'

'Aw, she's a pet. I think he might have met his match.'

'Really? Ian?' Dev looked sceptical.

'You'll see. She doesn't put up with any of his bullshit. She's not his usual type.'

'Not the cow-eyed, slavishly adoring, please-let-me-lick-your-boots-Ian type then?'

'No, definitely not.' Mel grinned.

'So, how are you? When did you get here?'

'I'm good. I got into New York a couple of days ago, so I saw Mark and Claire before they left.'

'Have you been away?' Jenny asked her.

'Yeah, I took a year out to go travelling.'

'Where have you been?'

'Oh, all over – Australia, China, India … I was in South America just before I came to New York.'

'Wow, that sounds great!' Jenny said.

'Yeah, it was. But it's back to reality and London once Christmas is over.'

'So, what are the plans for the next few days?' Dev asked her.

'Well, today I thought we might just take a wander around, look at the shop windows on Fifth Avenue, go to see the tree at Rockefeller Plaza, then have an early dinner at a diner. You guys are probably tired after your flight.'

'You *thought* we *might*.' Dev chuckled. 'Good job trying to sound casual.'

'What?' she asked innocently.

'You might be able to fool Jenny because she doesn't know you like I do. But don't try to pretend to me that you haven't got the whole thing mapped out like a military operation – you probably have colour co-ordinated spreadsheets and everything.'

'Oh, that's so not true!' Mel protested, laughing. 'They're not colour co-ordinated,' she added under her breath.

'I knew it!' Dev smiled at her affectionately. 'So what's on for tomorrow?'

'Tomorrow – presents first thing, of course, then breakfast, ice skating in Central Park, maybe go for a walk to take in the windows of some further afield shops, like Barneys and Macy's, go for a drink somewhere, and then Chinese for dinner. How does that sound?'

'Sounds good to me,' Dev said, looking at Jenny questioningly.

'It sounds brilliant!' she said to Mel. 'I can't believe we can actually do stuff on Christmas Day!' This was clearly where she should have been coming for Christmas all along.

'It's great – not like England, where everything shuts down. Well, you two go and get settled in, and when you're ready we'll hit the streets.'

'How are you finding working for Richard Allam?' Jenny heard a strange voice say as she made her way back to the living room, having showered and changed. 'Last I heard you were trying to prise off some little tart who'd got her claws into him.'

'Eh, that'd be me!' Jenny smiled cheerfully, announcing her presence.

Four heads spun in her direction, registering varying degrees of confusion, embarrassment and guilt. Dev and Mel had been joined by a couple who she supposed must be Ian and his girlfriend. Dev looked ready to throttle Ian.

'I've got the claws to prove it,' she said playfully, holding up her nails, painted dark red with silver snowflakes for Christmas.

'Oh!' A dark blush had stained Ian's cheeks. 'You mean you're—'

'Jenny,' she said, holding her hand out to him with a smile to show she wasn't offended.

'Hi, I'm Ian,' he said, taking it. He looked embarrassed but amused at the same time. 'God, sorry about that, I didn't realise—'

'It's fine.' Jenny shrugged. 'I've been called worse.'

'You're such an ass, Ian!' the tall blonde beside him said, giving him a hearty punch on the shoulder. 'Hi, I'm Carol. Pleased to meet you.' She shook Jenny's hand. With pale blonde hair, creamy skin and perfect, dazzling teeth, she had the face of a cheerleader – wholesome, corn-fed, all-American.

Ian was grinning at Jenny now, his eyes appreciative. 'Well, I see why you were so keen to prise her away from Richard, you old sly boots,' he said, winking suggestively at Dev, who looked even more pissed off.

'Oh, we're not ... I mean, I'm still ...'

'Jenny and I are just friends,' Dev said.

Carol rolled her eyes. 'Way to dig yourself a bigger hole, ass-wipe!' she said, bestowing another hefty thump on Ian's chest.

'Oof! Ladies and gentlemen, my girlfriend, the heavyweight champion of Cleveland!' Ian laughed, clutching his chest.

'Okay, let's go,' Mel said. 'Jenny, haven't you anything warmer than that to wear?' she asked, eyeing Jenny's thin jacket with concern. 'You'll freeze.'

Jenny shook her head. 'This is all I've got.'

'Maybe I should—' Dev began.

'There! Dev'll keep you warm, Jenny,' Ian interrupted, earning himself a dig in the side from his pugilistic girlfriend.

'I'm sure there's something of Claire's you could borrow,' Mel said, heading for the master bedroom.

Jenny was swimming in the red fleece jacket Mel had found but she was extremely grateful for it as they wandered along the crowded streets. She had never felt cold like this in her life. They lingered at the shops along Fifth Avenue, moving slowly from window to window, taking in the spectacular animated displays. Then they walked on to the Rockefeller Center, where trumpeting angels lined the path leading down to the plaza and the most glittering, colourful Christmas tree Jenny had ever seen. As they stood above the ice rink, watching the skaters glide and swirl in front of the tree, Jenny decided she was glad Richard had deserted her for Christmas. If he hadn't, she wouldn't have been standing here now, and she really couldn't think of anywhere she'd rather be. She realised she wasn't even wishing he was here – this moment couldn't have been any more perfect.

'I'm so glad I came,' she said, turning to Dev, her eyes filling with happy tears.

'I'm really glad you came too,' he said, smiling at her.

The way he was looking at her, she felt he really meant it – and somehow a perfect moment got even better.

'So, how did you two meet?' Dev asked Ian and Carol later as they sat over dinner in a diner.

'Oh, that is *such* a cute story.' Carol smiled affectionately at Ian as she stole fries from his plate.

'We met at a party,' Ian said to Dev.

'Yeah, I fucked him in a closet. I totally thought he was someone else.'

'You'll have to forgive Carol, she's a bit shy.' Ian laughed.

'Oh, that *is* a cute story,' Mel put in. 'One to tell your grandkids.'

'Well, at least you're not one of his students,' Dev said to Carol. 'That's how Ian usually gets girls – preying on susceptible students, playing the windswept, brooding poet and dazzling them with his knowledge of John Donne.'

'Oh, I know,' Carol hooted. 'He tried that one on me. He was all, like, look at me, quoting poetry in an English accent, how romantic am I? I'm like, yeah, you *are* English, get over it, dick-for-brains. It doesn't make you fucking Shakespeare. It was only when I got him in that closet with his pants down that I saw his true potential.'

'Like I said, she had a very sheltered upbringing. She's practically Amish.'

'Zip it, douche-bag,' she said, elbowing him in the ribs affectionately.

'It didn't take,' he croaked, clutching his ribs.

'So, you're from Cleveland, Carol?' Mel asked.

'Yes, but I'm living in Boston now. I usually go home for Christmas, but my folks have gone on a cruise this year. How about you guys?'

'My parents have gone away as well,' Dev said. 'They're staying with friends in France.'

'I've been travelling for the year, so I decided to spend Christmas here and take advantage of my brother's free apartment,' Mel told her.

'How about you, Jenny?'

'Oh, I don't have any family,' she said. 'I was fostered.'

'That sucks! Don't you ever visit with any of your foster families over the holidays?'

'I'm not really on good terms with any of them,' Jenny said, avoiding Dev's eye.

'So how come you're not spending Christmas with the amazing Mr Allam?' Ian asked. Dev frowned at him and he took the precaution of moving a little away from Carol.

'He has kids,' Jenny said. 'He's with them.'

'That kinda blows,' Carol said.

'Well, I'm very glad you're here with us, Jenny,' Mel said, raising her glass in a salute.

'So am I.' Jenny smiled at her. Christmas Eve had never been so much fun, and she was looking forward to tomorrow with real enthusiasm instead of the usual dread.

Chapter 24

Jenny couldn't remember ever being as excited about Christmas as she was when she woke up the next morning. She got out of bed and opened her curtains, hugging herself with delight at the view. It was very early and she didn't think anyone else was up, so she decided to open Richard's gift in the privacy of her room. She took it from the bedside locker and hopped back into bed, taking her time carefully unwrapping the tiny package, spinning out the anticipation. Inside was a box bearing the name of an exclusive Knightsbridge jeweller. She opened it to find a pair of diamond stud earrings cushioned in velvet – at least, she supposed they were diamonds. They could just as easily have been glass for all she knew, but she didn't think this shop (or Richard for that matter) would deal in glass. No, they were definitely diamond earrings, and she definitely felt ... disappointed.

Her initial reaction came as a shock and she brushed it aside, not even wanting to acknowledge it, and got on with the serious business of enjoying her present. They really were lovely, she thought as she removed one from the box and looked at it more closely. She didn't wear diamonds, of course. It wasn't just that she couldn't afford them – they simply didn't hold any particular appeal for her and she had never hankered after them. But Richard wasn't to know that. Most women loved diamonds. And there was no reason why she couldn't start wearing them now. Maybe they were an acquired taste, like wine or anal sex.

She took them out of the box and went to the dressing table to put them on, looking at her reflection in the mirror. Turning her head from side to side, she tucked her hair behind her ears to get a better view. Pity they were studs – she much preferred dangly earrings. But it would be good to have some studs for a change, and they were really classy. The only problem was, she didn't have anything they would go with – she didn't wear the kind of clothes that went with diamonds. But she could always buy something new – it would be a good excuse to get a new dress. Wasn't she a bit young for diamonds, though?

Try as she might to whip up the appropriate feelings of delight and excitement, they just wouldn't come. God, she must be an awful spoiled ungrateful brat to be disappointed when her boyfriend gave her diamonds. It was what women dreamed of, wasn't it? Diamonds are a girl's best friend and all that. But that was just it – it was so *standard*. It was as if Richard had never met her – as if she was some random woman he had drawn in a very high-end Secret Santa.

Later, when they were all up, they opened presents by the tree. Mel had organised a sort of Secret Santa and they had all been instructed to buy four presents for less than twenty-five pounds. Jenny got a box of chocolates from Dean & DeLuca, a book of poems (from Ian, presumably), a black-and-white print of the Manhattan skyline and a pair of furry handcuffs (she suspected Carol was behind those). When she had opened everything, Dev picked up a huge present from under the tree and handed it to her.

'This is for you too,' he said.

Jenny was astonished. 'For me?' she squeaked. She assumed Richard had given it to Dev to put under the tree as a surprise for her.

But then she read the tag, and saw that it was from Dev. Oh, no! He'd made a point of telling her there was no need to buy any presents apart from the Secret Santa ones, and she had taken him at his word and not got him anything.

'Well, aren't you going to open it?' he asked when she continued to stare dumbly at the box in her hands.

'Oh, yes.' She set to, fleecing the paper off and opening the large box inside. She pushed aside layers of tissue paper and lifted out the most gorgeous coat she had ever seen. It was deep red with a raised pattern in a wonderfully soft, squashy fabric. The style was perfect – cinched in at the waist, with a full skirt – and it was just so ... so *her*.

'You don't like it,' Dev said. It was a statement rather than a question and she realised he had misinterpreted her silence.

'Oh, no – it's *gorgeous*!' she said, her eyes flying up to him. 'I adore it! Thank you.' She jumped up and kissed him on the cheek.

'You're welcome. I'm glad you like it.'

'But I feel awful – I didn't get you anything. You said—'

'I know. I didn't want you to worry about getting me anything. Please don't feel bad. I just got you this because it was going to be really cold here and I knew you didn't have a coat.'

She grabbed it, scattering gift wrap and tissue paper, and put it on. It was a perfect fit. 'How does it look?'

'Beautiful,' Dev said.

'Awesome!' Carol breathed.

'Oh, Jenny, that's gorgeous,' Mel said. 'It really suits you. Did *you* buy it?' she asked Dev, disbelievingly. 'I mean, as in actually pick it out?'

'Yes, I did. I'm not completely useless, you know.'

'I'm impressed! Look out, Trinny and Susannah.'

'Look out Richard,' Ian muttered, giving Dev a strange look and earning himself a discreet whack from Carol.

'It's not very Moderate, though, is it?' Jenny said to Dev.

'I'm off duty,' he told her, 'and so are you.'

'Oh, I love it so much.' She hugged herself. 'I have to go and see.' She ran into her bedroom and looked at her reflection in the mirror, stroking the soft material on her arms. It was so beautiful – and so exactly what she would have chosen. She thought it was the nicest Christmas present she'd ever had. Oh, except for Richard's earrings, of course, she reminded herself, her eyes drifting to the box abandoned on the dressing table. Feeling guilty, she opened it and put them on.

'That should keep us going until dinnertime,' Mel said to Jenny later, when they were alone in the kitchen, clearing up after a long, leisurely brunch.

'It'll keep me going all week!' Jenny said. 'I'm stuffed.'

'Don't worry, you'll work up an appetite skating.'

There had been bagels with cream cheese and smoked salmon, scrambled eggs, crispy bacon, grilled tomatoes and stacks of pancakes made by Carol, smothered in maple syrup – all accompanied by copious amounts of champagne and coffee.

'How does Dev seem to you?' Mel asked her as they loaded the dishwasher.

'Fine.' Jenny shrugged. 'Same as ever.'

'Oh, okay.' Mel looked unconvinced.

'Why? Do you think something's up with him?'

'He looks very tired. I'm just a bit worried about him.'

'Well, he has been working very hard. It's pretty stressful being at Richard's beck and call.'

'Yeah, I suppose. It's just – it must be hard on him, you know ... I mean, Christmas and everything, and not being with his family. He must be really missing Sally.'

Jenny's stomach gave a little lurch. 'Who's Sally?'

'Hasn't he told you about her?' Mel looked at her curiously. 'I thought he might have talked to you ...' She trailed off, snapping the door of the dishwasher shut.

Just answer the question, Jenny thought. Who the hell is Sally? Her thoughts flew to the photograph on Dev's desk. Was that Sally? And why was he missing her? She realised her heart was pounding, but she didn't want to appear too eager for information.

'Sally was his sister,' Mel said finally, turning to her. 'She was my best friend too. She died earlier this year – not long after Christmas, in fact.'

'Oh, my God!' Jenny's mouth was dry. 'What happened to her?'

'She had a massive heart attack.'

'She must have been very young to have a heart-attack.'

'She was,' Mel said, tears glinting in her eyes. 'But it wasn't that, really. I mean, that was what killed her in the end, but she'd been killing herself slowly for years,' she said, her voice breaking. 'She was anorexic.'

'God, that's awful. I'm so sorry,' she said and patted Mel's arm.

'Thanks.' Mel smiled sadly at her, wiping tears from the corners of her eyes.

'Poor Dev.'

'They were very close – Sally and Dev.' Mel sniffed. 'He did everything to try and get help for her. He was always persuading her to go into clinics, paying for therapy, finding new treatment programmes to try. He'd have her go and live with him for months so he could keep an eye on her. He was at his wit's end. But there was nothing he could do – nothing any of us could do. He always thought he'd save her in the end, and he still can't quite believe that she's dead. Neither can I.' Her voice broke and her eyes welled up again.

'Is that why they didn't have Christmas together this year – him and his parents?'

'Yeah. None of them could handle having the usual family Christmas with Sally missing.'

Jenny was stunned. Dev had never given her any inkling that he was grieving for a beloved sister. But Richard must know. She was surprised he'd never mentioned it.

'I'm not sure if he's ever really talked to anyone properly about it,' Mel said. 'You know Dev – he just gets on with things.'

'Yeah.' But that was the trouble – she didn't know Dev, not really.

It was a bright, sunny day, the sky clear blue, the air sharp. After brunch they strolled through Central Park and went to the Wollman Rink.

'Have you ever been ice skating before, Jenny?' Mel asked her as they laced up their boots.

'I've gone a few times with kids I've minded,' she said, 'so I'm better at mopping up tears and drinking hot chocolate than the actual skating part. I fall over more than anything else.'

True to form, she landed on her arse almost as soon as she hit the ice, much to the amusement of some local teenagers, who performed a syncopated dance routine as they whizzed around the rink. She looked up to find Dev standing over her, holding out his hand. She grabbed it, but as he pulled her to her feet, she lost her balance again and wobbled backwards, falling onto the ice and taking Dev with her. 'Oof!' she exclaimed as he landed half on top of her.

Neither of them moved for a moment, both winded and breathing heavily, the white clouds of their breath mingling in the air between them.

'Sorry!' Jenny giggled as Dev lifted his weight off her, resting on the ice beside her.

'Are you okay?' he asked.

'Yeah, I'm fine. You?'

'Never better.' He grinned, sitting up. 'Okay, let's try this again.' He stood and pulled her up again. This time he didn't let go of her hand, instead towing her along with him as he skated. After a while Mel whizzed up to them and took Jenny's other hand and the three zipped across the ice, Jenny squealing with pleasure at the sensation of skating. They showed her how to move her feet and lean over the skates to keep her balance, and after a while they let her go and she skated off on her own. It was great fun once she got into a rhythm, though she still had a few falls. Dev helped her up each time, pulling her into the solid warmth of his chest to steady her before he released her again.

Dev, Mel and Ian were all competent skaters, but Carol had clearly taken lessons and she spun and wove around an awed Ian, even performing a couple of jumps, while he watched in silent adoration.

'Your friend's in love,' Jenny told Mel as they skated alongside each other.

'What?' She sounded surprised, then followed Jenny's gaze. 'Oh, Ian – yeah, I think you're right.'

As Jenny skated off, Mel looked at Dev, whose eyes were on Jenny as she moved across the ice. I don't think Ian's the only one, she thought.

Fortified against the cold by their exertions on the rink, they walked some more, strolling past Macy's and Barneys to look at their window displays, enjoying the quiet of streets that yesterday had been manic. Then, when the cold began to bite through to their bones again, they retreated to the warm mahogany cocoon of the King Cole bar in the St Regis Hotel.

As they chatted and laughed over cocktails, Jenny kept glancing at Dev and thinking about what Mel had told her. He seemed happy today – and yesterday when he'd said he was glad she'd come, he'd looked as if he really meant it. He had certainly seemed genuinely pleased to see her when he'd picked her up at the airport. She didn't know why it should make a difference to him whether she was here or not, but she was glad if it did. It had been so kind and thoughtful of him to invite her, especially now that she knew what he was going through. She didn't like to think of him being sad. As she watched, he turned to Mel, bending towards her to talk low in her ear. They'd make a cute couple, she thought. They looked good together. Mel was lovely, and they were obviously really close. Dev was probably lonely, and he deserved to be with someone nice. But for some reason she didn't really like the idea of him and Mel together.

'How's Julia?' Ian was asking Dev now. 'Have you seen her at all recently?'

Dev shot a glance at Jenny and she turned quickly to Carol, pretending she hadn't heard. But Carol clearly had. 'Who's Julia?' she asked Jenny.

'She's Richard's ex-wife,' Jenny said, smiling calmly, not wanting to get Ian into trouble. She got the impression that if he hadn't been on the other side of the table he'd have come in for some sound pummelling.

Carol rolled her eyes. 'Sorry about Ian,' she said. 'He's such a dick.'

'Oh, it's fine,' Jenny said.

'He has one major redeeming feature – I'm talking *major* here.' Carol smiled. 'But only I get the benefit of that, so there's no reason why *you* should have to put up with his ass-hat ways.'

Jenny laughed. As she tucked a stray lock of hair behind her ear, she heard Carol gasp beside her. 'I love your earrings! Are they diamonds?'

'Oh, thanks.' Jenny had forgotten she'd had them on. She probably shouldn't have gone ice skating in diamond earrings. 'And yes, they are – I think. I got them from Richard for Christmas.'

'Aww. You must be missing him a lot.'

'Yeah,' Jenny said faintly, because she knew it was the right answer. But the funny thing was, she wasn't missing him at all. She was having way too much fun. She never had this much fun with him. Did she ever have any fun with him? She must, she thought. And if she didn't, it was because he was so busy at the moment with the election and everything. Anyway, they had fun in bed. Pity he wasn't here – they could have tried out her new handcuffs ...

'Jenny? What do you think?' Mel was looking at her expectantly.

'Oh, sorry – I was miles away.'

'We were just saying maybe we'd hit the shops in the morning – you, me and Carol? The guys are planning to go downtown, looking at gadgets.'

'That'd be great. Actually, there's something I want to look for anyway.' She glanced at Dev.

'What's that?'

'Oh, um, I don't know yet. I just need to buy a present for someone.'

They went back to the apartment to change before heading out to dinner at a local Chinese restaurant. Mel was right – the combination of exercise and the biting cold had given Jenny quite an appetite, further fuelled by the wonderful smells that were emanating from the dishes that covered the table: fat, succulent prawns sizzling with garlic and chilli; Peking duck; orange beef; pork with ginger ...

'Gosh, do you think we ordered enough?' Mel laughed.

'There may have been one dish on the menu that we missed out on,' Dev said.

'Well, it *is* Christmas. Since we're not doing anything else traditional, the least we can do is eat ourselves silly.'

'Christmas is just the best, isn't it?' Carol said to Jenny as she put a spoonful of rice on her plate.

'Yep, sure is.'

'I thought you weren't a Christmas person,' Dev said, smiling at her.

'Well, I've been converted. I don't know about all the other ones, but *this* Christmas is definitely the best.'

'That was lovely, wasn't it?' Julia silenced the TV with the remote as the closing credits rolled on *Tosca*.

'Yes,' Richard said. 'It was a stunning production.'

It had been so relaxing watching it with Julia, knowing that she was enjoying it as much as he was. He knew if he had been with Jenny she would have perched quite happily on his lap and watched it with him. But she would have done it to please him, and the knowledge that she wasn't enjoying it for her own sake would have taken the edge off his pleasure.

The children were in bed and they sat side by side on the sofa, a log fire cracking and sparking merrily in the grate.

'I got some of that cheese you like,' Julia said, getting up. 'You know – the one with cumin seeds in it. Shall I get us some?'

'Oh, yes, please.' Richard grinned. 'Might as well be hung for a sheep as a lamb.'

As Julia left the room, he sank back into the sofa with a contented sigh. It had been a really good day. The Christmas lunch, of course, had been wonderful – the goose cooked to perfection, and all Julia's little trademark touches, the apple sauce spiked with cloves and cinnamon, the potato stuffing, those wonderful crunchy roast potatoes. The crab and apple tian he had made for starters wasn't half bad either. And it had been fun getting together this morning with old friends and neighbours. Julia had hosted their morning champagne reception as usual, and it was as if nothing had changed. There was no awkwardness, no standoffishness towards him, which he had dreaded.

It was just like old times. And the best part, of course, was the boys –
seeing the excitement and wonder on their faces when they came
downstairs, tousle-haired and sleepy-eyed, to see what Father
Christmas had brought them.

'Here we go.' Julia came back into the room bearing a tray with
cheese and crackers, a bottle of port and a couple of glasses.

Richard stood to take it from her, placing it on the coffee table in
front of them as she settled back into the sofa beside him. He poured
them both a glass of port, handed Julia hers and held his up in a
toast. 'Here's to a really great day,' he said.

'It was good, wasn't it?' She clinked her glass against his. 'James's
face when he saw that bike!' She smiled fondly.

'Yeah, his eyes nearly popped out of his head.'

'I'm glad we were able to do it like this,' she said thoughtfully as
Richard cut himself a big hunk of cheese. 'So civilised. I'm really glad
you're here – it's very important for them.'

'Well, of course – they're my children,' he said, surprised. 'Where
else would I be?'

'I don't know.' Julia spread the soft cheese on a cracker.
'Somewhere else?'

'I'm their father, Julia,' he reminded her. 'I'll always be here for
them.'

'Good.' Finishing her cracker, she took a gulp of port and placed
her glass back on the coffee table. 'Richard, there's something I
wanted to talk to you about.'

'Go on.'

'Something I want to tell you,' Julia continued, smoothing her
hands over her skirt.

Richard nodded to her to go ahead as he took a bite of cheese and
cracker.

'Rupert Underwood has asked me out and ... well, I'm starting dating again – that's all,' she continued, relieved that it was out in the open. 'I don't even know why I'm telling you this, only— Richard, are you all right?' She slapped him on the back, as he seemed to be choking. 'You have to chew, you know,' she said as he spluttered, taking a huge gulp of port, which only made things worse. Tears poured from his eyes as he gasped for breath. She waited for the coughing to subside. 'Are you all right now?'

He nodded.

'Gosh, you gave me a bit of a scare. You'll have to be more careful. My Heimlich manoeuvre's a bit rusty. I can't guarantee I'll be able to save you if you keep wolfing things down like that. Are you sure you're okay now?'

'Fine,' Richard croaked, wiping tears from his face with the back of his hand.

'Well, as I was saying, I don't know why I'm even telling you this. I mean, it's not as though I need your permission, is it? Only I suppose I felt it would be a bit strange for you to hear it from someone else – you know, on the dreaded grapevine.'

She had tussled with herself about this. Really there was no reason in the world why she should tell Richard she was planning to start dating again. It was none of his business. They were separated, and he was the one who had moved on, found someone else. She didn't know why she felt the urge to give him fair warning – it wasn't as if he had ever done it for her. Was it that she hoped to hurt him with the information? She examined her motives, checking for spite, but she honestly didn't think that was it. She knew she owed him no such courtesy, but her better nature had prevailed. 'So,' she said, 'that's all I wanted to say. Just a little warning shot across the bows, so you won't be on the back foot if you hear it from Geoffrey or someone. I just thought I should tell you.'

'Right.' Richard seemed dazed. 'Thanks – I suppose.'

He was shocked, she could tell. He looked ... crestfallen.

'Well, what did you think was going to happen?' she said reasonably, not bothering to pretend she couldn't see how he felt.

'I don't know.' He smiled at her ruefully.

'You didn't think I was going to become a nun, did you?'

Of course he should have known that Julia wouldn't be without a man for long. She was a very attractive woman. She was intelligent, good company – and she had a very high sex drive. It would surprise a lot of people to know that, he thought. It had surprised him, when he first knew her. She could come across as a bit prim and prissy to those who didn't know her. He had always liked the fact that she didn't flaunt her sexuality. It gave him a good feeling to know that part of her was just for him – 'for your eyes only'.

Only it wasn't for his eyes only now. She was going to go out on dates with another man. She was going to let another man kiss her and touch her. Another man would undress her and take her to bed and discover a whole other side to her that they'd never suspected. Rupert Underwood. Rupert bloody Underwood! He was a decent enough bloke. Good-looking ... fit. He could see him now, running his hands up Julia's long, stockinged legs, finding the incredibly soft flesh at the tops of her thighs. He imagined him undoing the little pearl buttons of her cardigan, peeling off her clothes to reveal some sensational underwear. Julia was a believer in serious underwear. He could imagine Rupert's delighted smirk as he unhooked her bra and took her gorgeous full breasts in his hands ...

'Richard, are you all right? You've gone a bit green. Maybe you should go easy on the cheese.'

'I'm fine,' he said and took a slug of port. 'So – Rupert Underwood! Do you fancy him?'

'I don't know … I suppose I'll find out. But if I don't, there are plenty more fish in the sea, aren't there? Actually, I went out a couple of weeks ago with a very nice man.'

'Oh?'

'Yes – a civil servant.'

'Really? What department is he in?'

'Oh, you wouldn't know him,' she said dismissively. 'He's a civil servant by day, but he paints.'

'Huh! Don't they all?' Richard said churlishly.

'Well, no, they don't, actually. *You* don't paint.'

'I'm not a civil servant either. Did he show you his etchings?'

'He did show me some of his work, as a matter of fact. It was very … interesting. Really not at all what I was expecting.'

'Sounds great.'

'Yes, he was,' she said, sipping her port and trying to look wistful. 'I may see him again.'

'Great!' Richard's smile was more like a grimace, she noted with satisfaction.

'I think it will be fun, in a way, dating again.'

Richard smiled weakly at her. He wondered how long it had been for her. But presumably if she was informing him that she was just starting to date again now, there hadn't been anyone else since he'd left. Almost nine months – it was a long time for someone who enjoyed sex as much as she did. She would probably go up in flames if he touched her now. Even if she wanted to, he doubted she'd be able to resist him if he made a move. It wouldn't take much – he would only have to lean over and kiss her, cup a breast, tease a nipple, slide a warm hand under her skirt … and they knew each other so well, it would be amazing – all the better for having been a while.

But it wouldn't be fair to her. She was trying to move on – she was making an effort and he should leave her to it. Besides, he had Jenny to consider now. He couldn't do that to her. He got up with a determined effort. 'I'm going to hit the sack,' he said, picking up the tray. 'Goodnight – and thank you for a lovely day.'

'Night. Thank you too.'

Chapter 25

The following two days were a whirl of activity and Jenny collapsed into bed on their last night in New York, her mind replaying a kaleidoscope of images: the five of them standing on Brooklyn Bridge, their breath white clouds in the air as they laughed and posed for photographs against the backdrop of the Manhattan skyline; watching kids skateboarding in Central Park, spinning in the air and returning to earth with a clatter of wheels; huddling with Dev on the deck of the Staten Island Ferry for her first glimpse of the Statue of Liberty, which she had found strangely moving; eating epic diner breakfasts while Carol and Ian sparred fondly; buying hot dogs spiked with mustard and onions from handcarts on the street and eating them, hot and delicious, in the cold air; the flashing neon of Times Square; the spectacular views from the River Cafe where they had eaten tonight; a blur of tree-lined streets and sparkling fountains, of yellow cabs and tall buildings gleaming in the winter sun. She fell asleep to the now-familiar lullaby of honking horns and screaming sirens.

She woke at four a.m. in a familiar state of panic, her heart already pounding wildly, beads of sweat breaking out on her forehead before she was even fully conscious. Unfortunately, the fact that it was familiar did nothing to lessen the overwhelming terror that gripped her. The fact that she didn't at first remember where she was only added to her free-floating anxiety. She sat up in bed and turned on the light, looking around the room and orienting herself – she was in New York with Dev and his friends. Shit! Why did this have to happen here?

Throwing back the covers, she got out of bed and looked at herself in the mirror over the dressing table. Her pupils were huge. She made a conscious effort to slow down her breathing, but it was no use. All she wanted was to get outside, and no matter how irrational she told herself it was, she couldn't shake the feeling that something terrible was going to happen if she didn't go out immediately.

She went to the window and drew back the heavy curtains. Traffic still flowed past Central Park and she watched it for a while, trying to reassure herself that life was going on as normal, that nothing was going to happen to her, that it was safe to get back into bed and go to sleep. But she knew from experience that there was no chance of sleeping – she was feeling far too jittery. She opened the door of her bedroom and crept out into the living room, hoping that if she at least extended her pacing area it might help. Without turning on the light, she went to the window and looked down at the scene below. She had been standing there for a few minutes when she heard the soft click of a door opening down the hall.

'Jenny!'

She spun around at the sound of Dev's husky voice. She hadn't heard him approach, but he was standing close to her, clad only in boxers, and she was momentarily distracted by the sight of his bare chest.

'You couldn't sleep either?' he said.

She shook her head silently, knowing her voice would be shaky if she spoke.

'Bloody jet lag!' He sighed wearily, ruffling his hair. 'Fancy some tea?' he asked, turning towards the kitchen.

He had his back to her now so she had to dredge up the breath to speak. 'No – no, thanks.' Her voice betrayed her, as she had known it would.

Dev came back. 'You okay?'

She gave him a wobbly smile before turning away, looking out of the window.

'Are you sure?'

She turned to find him standing right in front of her, frowning down at her. She evaded his eyes. She knew how she looked. She had seen it often enough – her features drawn, her skin stretched taut, her mouth a tight, pale line, the sickly sheen of sweat on her forehead. 'I'm fine,' she mumbled.

'You don't look fine. Are you ill?' She felt his hand on her chin, tilting her face up so that she was forced to look at him.

'No, I'm—'

'You're upset. What's happened?'

'No, nothing. I'm—' Her eyes were welling up, and she blinked rapidly to dispel the tears. She felt so foolish. How could she explain to him that she was in a blind panic about ... absolutely nothing? He couldn't possibly understand.

'What's wrong?' he persisted.

'Nothing, really,' she said, squirming under his intense gaze. She sighed in defeat. 'It's just a panic attack,' she admitted reluctantly. As if he didn't think she was flaky enough already!

'A panic attack?'

'It's silly.' She shrugged.

'It's not silly.'

When she looked up at him she was surprised there was none of the impatience or derision she had expected to see in his face. She knew Richard tried to be patient with her when she freaked out on him, but he never quite managed to hide the irritation in his eyes or to keep the bracing tone from his voice. He never actually said 'Pull yourself together,' but she could tell that was what he was thinking. She had expected Dev's reaction to be the same.

'Does this happen often?'

'Not so often. Sometimes.'

'It happened in Brighton,' he said, and she nodded, remembering he had seen her like this before.

'What do you usually do for it? Do you have anything to take?'

What she usually did, if he was home, was crawl into Liam's bed. He never minded what time she woke him up – though she had got him into hot water on a couple of occasions with girlfriends who thought their worst suspicions about Jenny had been confirmed when they caught Liam in bed with her. Sometimes he would light a joint and they would smoke it together in the dark, and she would eventually fall asleep again snuggled up to him. However, she didn't think Dev would approve of these 'remedies'.

'It'll pass. You just have to sit it out, really.'

'Does it always happen at night?'

She nodded. 'Always at the same time. I wake up in a panic, usually around four in the morning. I just feel I have to get out of the house – that something terrible is going to happen if I don't.'

'Do you want to go outside now?'

She nodded, stroking her arms agitatedly.

'Right. Well, let's go then.'

'But it's four in the morning,' she protested, dismayed that he was taking her seriously instead of just telling her she was being ridiculous.

'There's no law against it. And this is supposed to be the city that never sleeps, remember?'

'It'll be freezing,' she said, gazing wistfully out of the window.

'You've got a coat.'

'But it's the middle of the night in New York. I'm actually much safer in here, even if I don't feel it,' she said, repeating what Richard had said to her in Brighton, trying to be rational.

'Jenny, it's the Upper West Side of Manhattan. Come on, let's see if this place lives up to its insomniac reputation.'

'You don't have to – it'll pass,' she protested half-heartedly, really hoping he wouldn't take her up on it. She was starting to feel better already, just at the thought of getting out.

'I'm not sleeping anyway. Come on – get dressed,' he said, already heading back to his bedroom.

Jenny blinked back tears of gratitude as she raced to her room to put on some clothes. She couldn't believe he was being so kind and understanding. She had to hide her neurosis as much as possible from Richard, knowing he just didn't get it, but she had just fallen to pieces in front of Dev, and he had been so calmly accepting, as if a panic attack was no different from migraine or toothache – no less real and just as beyond her control. He hadn't treated her like a freak or tried to talk her round – and had been so matter-of-fact about going outside with her. Richard would never have indulged her like that.

The streets were quiet, but they certainly weren't the only ones not sleeping. There were a surprising number of people still walking the pavements despite the early hour, and several bars and restaurants were open for business. Dev took her arm and they leaned into each other against the biting cold. They walked in silence, and Dev matched his pace to hers, seeming to understand that she didn't want to talk. They strolled towards Midtown, and by the time they reached the Rockefeller Center, Jenny realised that her breathing had returned to normal and her heart was no longer fluttering. She could feel that colour had returned to her cheeks and her features had relaxed, her skin no longer taut and stretched over her face. She had forgotten her panic and started to feel normal again without even realising it.

As they started back towards the apartment they came across a diner that was open.

'Mmm.' Jenny breathed in the delicious smell of coffee that was wafting out.

'Do you want to go in?' Dev asked.

She nodded. She could do with something sweet right now to complete the cure. Sugar was better than Valium, in her experience, for soothing frazzled nerves.

The heat wrapped around them like a blanket as they stepped through the door, and Jenny felt her muscles relax – they had tensed against the cold. She removed her coat and slid into the booth opposite Dev.

'Feeling better?' he asked when they had ordered hot chocolate and Danishes.

'Yes. I'm fine.'

The waiter brought their order and she sipped her hot chocolate, feeling the sugar soothe and calm her. She was suddenly overtaken by a feeling of overwhelming contentment in the moment. She was so happy to feel warm and calm again, and to be sitting with Dev, eating Danish pastries, drinking hot chocolate and feeling cared for and … safe. He had made her feel safe. 'You're very kind,' she said, shocked to feel tears stinging her eyes.

'No, I'm not.' He laughed disparagingly.

'You are, though,' she said.

'Well, don't tell anyone. I have a reputation to uphold.'

'Sorry,' she said, wiping her eyes hastily with the back of her hand. 'I'm a mess.'

'You're lovely.'

She looked up and found herself staring right into his eyes. He was gazing at her in a way that made her breath catch, and she turned her head away in confusion.

'It's almost dawn,' she said, glancing out the window. A familiar weariness was seeping through her body – a deliciously languid, soporific sensation, like slowly coming down from a drug. It was always like this after an attack – no doubt all that nervous energy was exhausting. She yawned.

'Tired?' Dev asked.

'Mmm.' She knew she would sleep now. She looked across at Dev. Disturbingly, she found herself fantasising about curling up on his lap and falling asleep snuggled up to his chest with his arms wrapped around her. He seemed so warm and solid.

She wondered what would have happened if she hadn't been with Richard when she'd met him at that wedding. They'd been flirting and he was very attractive. When he'd asked her out, she would have said yes. They might still have been together now. It would certainly have been a lot less complicated than life with Richard. She could have been here with him as his girlfriend. They could have gone home and got into bed together, and she could have slept with his arms around her. She wondered what it would be like to be with him in that way.

'You're very quiet.'

'Just thinking.' God, she was being ridiculous, she chided herself. She didn't see Dev like that at all. She was just feeling a bit down in the aftermath of her panic attack, and a bit lonely, and she wanted the comfort of being held in strong arms. 'I wish Liam was here.' She hadn't realised she'd said it out loud until Dev's head shot up. He seemed a little annoyed, but he said nothing, just sighed and looked down again.

Shit! She hadn't meant to say that out loud. It was rude and ungrateful, when he was the one who *was* here, and he was being so kind to her. She felt she'd hurt his feelings. 'I'm sorry, I didn't mean—'

'It's fine.'

'Thanks for coming out with me.'

'No problem. Shall we go?'

Jenny felt awkward on the walk back to the apartment. Dev was being as kind and solicitous as ever, but even though she told herself she was being daft – after all, why would he care? – she couldn't shake the feeling that she had hurt him.

Bloody Liam, Dev thought angrily as he stomped along. It wasn't fair – Liam wasn't here, and he *was*, and still Liam was the one she wanted, the bloody conquering hero! And then another thought struck him: she hadn't said she wished Richard was here.

He slowed his pace, aware that Jenny was struggling to keep up. He was being ridiculous, acting like some moody, lovesick teenager. He had no right to feel possessive about Jenny. Why shouldn't she want her friend here, someone she had known half her life? That was bound to be more comforting than a virtual stranger – which was what he was to her, he told himself sternly. He felt her darting anxious glances at him and he smiled down at her, putting an arm lightly across her shoulders. The last thing he wanted to do was make her anxious, and he was relieved when he felt her relax against him.

'Better try and get some sleep,' he said when they got back to the apartment. 'We're going home tomorrow – it'll be a long day.'

'Yes,' she said. 'Sorry for getting you up.'

'I was awake anyway, remember?'

'Well, goodnight – or I should say good morning?' she said, glancing at the window. 'I guess we're going home *today*.'

Chapter 26

Dev scrolled through the photos in his camera, stopping as he came to one of Jenny standing on Bow Bridge, the low winter sun sparkling on the water behind her. She was in almost exactly the same spot where Sally was standing in that photograph he kept on his desk. But though the composition of the two photos was almost identical, their subjects were worlds apart. Where Sally looked distant and sad, Jenny was beaming into the camera with a smile that seemed to go right through to the core of her being. Her happiness was almost palpable.

On the flight home she had told him it was the best Christmas she had ever had, which made him feel glad and sorry all at once. He hated to think of the lousy ones she must have endured in the past, but it felt good to make someone else happy, especially when all his attempts to do that for Sally had failed so dismally.

He smiled to himself as he scrolled through the images, but he felt a little guilty for having enjoyed himself so much. If he was honest, it was the first truly happy Christmas he had had in some time, but he shied away from that thought because it felt like such a betrayal – of Sally, of his parents.

The truth was, the last couple of Christmases they had spent together had been leaden affairs, which they had tried and failed to lighten with false cheer and surface gaiety, the effort leaving them weary and defeated. They had worked out a complicated, intricately choreographed dance of denial and pretence, which they had all followed meticulously, so careful not to shatter the illusion that none of them believed in. He and his parents tried to mask their tension and anxiety as they watched Sally struggle to eat and their disappointment when she only managed a single slice of turkey breast and half a carrot. She, for her part, tried to stifle her panic at having consumed even that much and her agony at being the cause of their unhappiness. No one was fooled and he sometimes wondered why they didn't just acknowledge the truth and admit how they felt. But the truth was unbearable, so they smiled and pulled crackers and pretended their hearts weren't breaking.

The trip to New York had been a true holiday – not just from work, home and routine, but from himself, from grief and sadness and guilt. He felt better for it – carefree, lighter, younger. It had been good to see Mel again. He had missed her while she was travelling, and he was glad she would be moving back to London soon and they could see more of each other. It had been fun to see Ian again too, and Carol was lovely. She was just what Ian needed to keep him the right side of obnoxious – he could be a cocky shit, given half a chance. But most of all he had loved having Jenny there. Making her happy, watching her eyes light up with wonder and excitement was the best feeling in the world and he couldn't get enough of it – which was why she was sleeping upstairs in his spare room at this very moment. He wanted to extend the holiday a little longer. He didn't want to give her back. So, as they had driven home in the early morning, both tired after the overnight flight, he had suggested she stay at his place and come to Jeremy's birthday party with him tonight rather than both of them returning to empty homes. He was dreading Jeremy's party and annoyed that he was back from New

York in time for it, but Richard had asked him to put in an appearance since he couldn't be there himself – all part of the keeping-Jeremy-sweet plan. And if Jenny was with him it might even be fun.

'Hello.' Jenny came into the room, smiling, looking unbelievably sexy in the T-shirt he'd given her to sleep in. 'What time is it?'

He glanced at his watch. 'Two o'clock. You slept well.'

She jumped onto the sofa beside him, curling her legs under her. 'Did you – sleep?'

'A bit – not long.'

'Ooh, photos – let's see.' She leaned close to him to look at the photos on his camera as he scrolled through them, her chin resting lightly on his shoulder. He felt her soft hair tickling his cheek, her breath warm on his neck as she laughed at a picture of Ian and Carol clowning around on Brooklyn Bridge. 'Carol's lovely, isn't she?' she said.

When he turned to answer her, her face was so close they were almost touching and he was overcome with a painful hollow feeling, like hunger pangs – only what he hungered for was her. He wanted to run his fingers through her hair, to take her little heart-shaped face in his hands and kiss her beautiful mouth, to slide his hands under his T-shirt and find her small, pert breasts. He wanted to make her feel good – to push her down on the sofa, cover her body with his, and make her whimper and moan with pleasure.

'What?'

Shit! He was ogling her like an idiot. He cleared his throat. 'Are you hungry?' he asked.

She seemed to consider it for a moment. 'Yes,' she said finally, lifting her head off his shoulder and stretching. 'I'm starving!'

'Well, why don't you go and get dressed and I'll make us some breakfast? Or lunch. Whatever.'

***

There were delicious smells of bacon and coffee as Jenny made her way back to the kitchen, showered and dressed. Dev was standing at the cooker with his back to her, so she took the opportunity to put the gift-wrapped box she was holding behind her back on the table.

'I decided to go for breakfast,' he said to her over his shoulder. 'I hope that's okay?'

'Mmm, perfect. It smells great,' she said, going to stand beside him. 'And breakfast is my favourite meal of the day.'

'Great! What kind of eggs would you like?'

'Umm – scrambled? Do you know how to make them?'

He laughed. 'Yeah, I think I can manage that.'

'Do you want me to do anything?'

'No, thanks – it's almost ready.'

She pushed away from the oven and wandered around the kitchen while she was waiting. She liked Dev's house. It was very obviously a man's house, but still a lot more homely than Richard's place.

'Wow, you've got a lot of cookbooks,' she said, her eyes running along the bookshelves over the worktop.

'They're Sally's,' Dev said quietly, turning to follow her gaze.

'Oh.'

'My sister,' he explained. 'She used to live with me. She—'

'I know. Mel told me about her. I'm really sorry.'

'Thanks.' He turned back to the cooker. 'It's quite common for anorexics to be obsessed with cooking,' he explained. 'Cooking for other people, of course.'

'Do *you* like cooking?' she asked, sensing from the hunch of his shoulders that he didn't want to talk about Sally any more.

She knew she was right when she saw his shoulders relax. 'I quite like it, yeah. I'm no Richard, but I wouldn't starve, left to my own devices.'

'Unlike me,' Jenny said.

'Oh, I don't know. I thought those fruit scones you made for *Homemaker* were pretty impressive.'

She laughed. He knew damn well she had simply passed along a recipe the office had come up with for her.

'Okay, it's ready. Could you just grab the toast and coffee?'

Dev carried two plates to the table, stopping dead when he saw the gift-wrapped parcel. 'What's that?' he asked, putting the plates on either side of the table.

'It's for you,' Jenny said, sitting down. 'It's just ... it's just a token. It's nothing, really.' She felt awkward now. She wished she could have just shoved it at him and run away.

Dev sat opposite her, still not touching the gift. 'Jenny, I told you – you didn't have to—'

'It's not because you gave me a present. It's just to say thank you for New York. I had *such* a lovely time. I just wanted to ...' She trailed off.

Dev picked up the parcel and tore off the paper. He was holding it in his lap, so she couldn't see it from where she sat, but she heard when he opened the box and removed the tissue paper. Then he just sat there, looking bewildered, blinking down at the box.

'It's a snow globe,' Jenny blurted finally. God, she knew it was a crap present to give a bloke. She'd racked her brains for something that wasn't too personal without being too impersonal or too boring. It had seemed like a good idea at the time.

'I know what it is,' he said, lifting it out of the box with both hands and placing it on the table. 'Thank you.'

'It's a bit of a daft present, I suppose. If you think it's too girly—'
'No, I don't.'

'Well, if you don't like it, you don't have to use it or anything ...' She was talking total drivel now. You didn't *use* a snow globe.

'Jenny,' he said firmly, eyeballing her, 'I love it.'

'Do you really?' She beamed.

'Really. I'll use it all the time. In fact, I'm going to use it right now.' He picked it up, shook it and placed it back on the table. They both watched as the snowflakes fell on the tiny skaters and skyscrapers of Manhattan.

'So, what time do we have to be at Jeremy's party?' Jenny asked later as they sat over a second pot of coffee.

'Not until half eight, nine. I can drive you home to change, if you like.'

'No need, thanks. I can wear the dress I bought in New York. I'm still not sure it's such a good idea, though, me going to this party.'

'It's a great idea. Richard wanted me to go to sort of represent him. It'll be even better if you go too.'

'I'm not so sure. Jeremy really doesn't like me.'

'Jeremy doesn't like anyone.'

'That's what Richard says. But he seems to *really* dislike me – more than most.'

'There's something you don't know about Jeremy,' he said. 'There's a reason why he might dislike you – resent you, even. I think he might be jealous of you.'

'*Jealous?* Why on earth would he be jealous of me?'

Dev just shrugged and said nothing.

'Oh, my God!' Jenny gasped. 'Is he in love with Richard? Is he gay?'

'What? No – nothing like that!'

'I bet that's it and you're just not telling me. You know, I've seen him looking at my shoes or my clothes really admiringly sometimes – not like men usually look, like he fancies me or anything, more like he fancies what I'm wearing.'

'Honestly, he's not gay. Jeremy just ... notices things like that.'

'But you're not going to tell me what it is?'

'Nope.'

'I'm going to go on thinking he's gay, you know, if you won't tell me.'

'Feel free.'

She sighed. 'You tell me he has a good reason to dislike me but you won't tell me what it is? That's not fair!'

'I didn't say that. I said he might have a reason. I didn't say it was a good one.'

Jenny gave a little growl of frustration. 'Anyway, there's another problem with me going to his birthday party. I haven't got him anything.'

'That's okay – you can sign the card on my present.'

'What are you giving him?'

'Bottle of whiskey.'

Jenny made a face.

'What? It's a very nice bottle of whiskey – a single malt. He likes whiskey.'

'Bit boring, isn't it?'

'Well, Jeremy's a bit boring, so it's perfect for him.'

'That's a lovely sentiment. Are you going to put that on the card? "I saw this and thought of you, you boring old fart"?'

Dev laughed. 'Well, do you have a better idea? What would you have got him?'

'I don't know. What does he like doing?'

'Sums.'

'Seriously, though, he must have some hobbies.'

'Seriously, counting money. Oh, and drinking whiskey, of course – single malts.'

'Doesn't he do any sports?'

'There was a rumour going around for a while that he'd played a game of golf, but I never believed it.'

'That does sound a bit far-fetched.'

'So – what do you think? Do you want to put your name to the bottle of whiskey?'

'Yes. It's a fantastic idea – inspired, really!'

'So, how old is he?' Jenny asked as they walked up the path to Jeremy's house.

'You don't ask a – I mean, I don't know,' Dev said, ringing the bell.

The front door swung open and Celia stood there, shock registering on her face before she rearranged her features into a tight smile.

'Dev, lovely to see you.' She pursed her lips close to his cheek in the ghost of a kiss without actually touching him. 'And you've brought Jenny!' She threw Dev a panicked look and then bestowed one of her plastic smiles on Jenny, crinkling her eyes as though she was squinting in the sun. But she seemed almost frightened.

'Dev asked me to come—'

'That's all right, isn't it, Celia?' Dev put in. 'Jenny was at a bit of a loose end, what with Richard away, so ...'

'Yes, of course, of course,' she gushed, seeming to recollect herself. 'Gosh, sorry, I'm being terribly rude, keeping you standing out here. Do come in.' She ushered them through to the living room, where a crowd of people were standing around with drinks.

'Hi, Jenny,' David greeted her as Dev was borne off to the other side of the room by someone she didn't recognise. 'Good to see you again. I didn't know you were coming.' He seemed surprised that she was there, but she supposed it was no secret that she and Jeremy weren't exactly the best of friends – or perhaps he was surprised she had come without Richard.

'Oh, I was home alone, feeling a bit sorry for myself, and Dev took pity on me and brought me along. So, where's Emma?'

'I didn't bring her. It's strictly inner circle today.' He grinned.

'Oh! I hope Celia doesn't mind, then, that Dev brought me. I wasn't exactly invited.'

'Well, Dev wouldn't have brought you if you weren't *in the know*, would he?'

'In the know? About what?'

'About, you know,' David faltered, his smile slipping, 'about Jeremy's, um ... hobby.'

'Oh, that! So it's true?' She couldn't understand why Jeremy was so secretive about the fact that he enjoyed the occasional round of golf. It wasn't *that* shameful, was it? She'd have thought it was quite an acceptable pastime for an MP.

David relaxed. 'Oh, yes, absolutely. You'll see – he's upstairs getting togged out right now.'

'Oh, he's going to ... wear the clothes ... tonight?' Well, that explained it. Jeremy was obviously ashamed – quite rightly – of his love of golfing attire. He must be quite obsessed with it if he was going to wear a golfing outfit for his birthday party. She'd just have to try not to look too appalled when he appeared in a pair of banana-coloured trousers and one of those hideous diamond-patterned jumpers.

'Jenny, dear,' Celia interrupted, 'let me get you a drink. What would you like?'

'I'll have white wine, please.' Jenny smiled at her. This was great! She'd made it into some sort of inner circle. Maybe now they were all going to be friends.

'Here you are,' Celia said, moments later, handing her a glass.

'Thank you. And I hope you don't mind me coming, Celia. I mean, it's very nice of you to have me, but—'

'Oh, not at all, dear ... not at all.' Celia seemed a bit distracted, constantly glancing nervously in the direction of the door.

Party nerves, Jenny thought. 'It's a lovely party,' she said reassuringly, looking around the room. 'So, where's the birthday boy?'

'Oh!' The question seemed to startle Celia, whose hand flew to her throat in a protective gesture. 'He'll be down shortly. He's just ... he's getting changed. I wonder, did Richard ever tell you – or perhaps Dev would have – about Jeremy's little, um ...'

'About the golf,' Jenny supplied, smiling in what she hoped was an accepting, non-judgemental way. 'Yes, I know all about it.'

'Golf?' Celia seemed confused, but was distracted by the arrival of Pauline.

'Hi, Pauline.' Jenny smiled at her as Celia drifted off.

'Oh, hello, Jenny.' She seemed as surprised as everyone else to find her at this party.

'I came with Dev,' she explained. 'Where's Alan?'

'He didn't come.' Pauline gulped half a glass of wine in one go. 'He can't stand seeing Jeremy in his get-ups. Finds it too embarrassing.'

'I suppose it can be a bit cringe-making.' Still, Jeremy must be taking Pringle sweaters to a whole new level if Alan couldn't even bear to look at him in one of his outfits.

'Yes, well, one has to try to be tolerant, doesn't one?' Pauline said staunchly. She took two more huge gulps of wine, as if bracing herself for something. 'Support all lifestyles and all that.'

'Yes, absolutely! After all, golfers are people too—'

'Dev!' Their attention was drawn by a high-pitched shriek and their eyes flew to Celia, who was pulling frantically at Dev's sleeve, interrupting his conversation. 'Jeremy will be down soon. He's just getting *dressed*!'

Dev turned to her, brow furrowed in confusion. 'Yes, I know.'

'No, you don't understand! He's getting *dressed*,' Celia hissed, stressing the word as if it had a hidden meaning.

Dev's expression changed, and his eyes darted to Jenny. Then he strode across the room and grabbed her arm. 'Jenny, we should go. Something's come up.'

'What? But the party hasn't even got started yet.'

'Well, I think it's better if we leave before it does.'

'But we haven't even seen Jeremy—'

'Hello, everyone!' a familiar voice boomed and Jenny looked over to see ... Jeremy ... sort of. She felt her eyes widen in shock and her jaw drop. She blinked hard, but the vision in the doorway didn't change. It was half Jeremy, half a spectacularly ugly woman with shoulder-length auburn hair and a five o'clock shadow. He was wearing a pink wrap dress, his massive feet wedged into a pair of Manolo slingbacks that Jenny recognised, having coveted them herself. Suddenly yellow trousers and loud sweaters didn't seem like such a bad thing.

'Oh!' she gasped before she could stop herself. She couldn't take her eyes off him as he smiled expansively around at his guests. Fortunately all eyes – except Dev's, which were still on her — had turned in his direction, so she had a chance to compose her features.

'So, you've seen Jeremy now.' He sighed, dropping her arm.

Jeremy was moving through the room now, greeting everyone with a charming smile. Jenny thought she had never seen him so relaxed. 'Was that what you were going to warn me about?' she hissed to Dev as she watched the birthday boy steadily make his way in their direction. 'That Jeremy's a – a—'

'A transvestite, yes,' Dev hissed back. 'Shhh, don't laugh – here he comes.'

'Hello, Dev,' Jeremy purred silkily. 'And Jenny – what a lovely surprise to see you here.'

Up close, Jenny could see that his make-up was trowelled on, caking over the dark stubble of his chin. 'Jeremy, hello! Happy birthday!'

'Thank you. Another one bites the dust,' he added wistfully. He was behaving very differently, as if he was actually pretending to be a woman. 'I hope it didn't come as too much of a shock to see me in my glad rags,' he simpered.

'Oh, no! You look … amazing!' Jenny stuttered.

'Thank you, you're very kind,' he said, patting his hair.

God, he really thinks he's hot, she thought in amazement.

'I do like to make an effort. I can't quite achieve your standards, I'm afraid, but—'

'Well, no, of course not—'

'I brought Jenny,' Dev interrupted. 'I didn't know you were going to be … um, pushing the boat out.'

'Well, it *is* my birthday!' Jeremy giggled coyly, his eyes twinkling. 'I mean, if you can't relax at a private party among friends in your own home, when can you, eh?'

'Never!' Jenny smiled brightly.

'Never would have been a better option,' Dev said bluntly, knocking back the remainder of his glass of wine before stalking off.

'Oh dear, I think Dev finds my alter ego a bit intimidating,' Jeremy said confidentially to Jenny, watching him go.

'Oh, he's just a bit … conventional.'

'Well, now that the cat's out of the bag, so to speak, we can have a proper chat. There are some things I've been dying to ask you for ages. First of all, where did you get those wonderful shoes?'

She was stuck talking fashion with Jeremy for an age. She found him at once compelling and repulsive in this guise. He was more relaxed, more charming and a lot friendlier than she had ever known him to be before, but behind the wannabe suburban siren, Jeremy still lurked. His smile was warmer and more genuine, but the lizardy eyes hadn't changed, and they still chilled her to the bone. Talking to him now, she felt like a cobra's prey – seduced by his charm, but all the while knowing he was waiting to annihilate her.

When he finally moved on, she made a bolt for the kitchen to get her breath back. After a few moments, Dev followed her in.

'And you said Jeremy was boring,' she whispered, laughing.

'Sorry about that,' he said in a hushed voice, jerking his head in the direction of the living room. 'I should have warned you, but I didn't think—'

'It's okay. God, it was hard to keep a straight face, though.'

'I know. He's not terribly convincing, is he? All the same, you didn't have to agree with him when he said he couldn't match up to your standards. That wasn't very diplomatic.'

'Well, it's pretty obvious, isn't it? Surely even he must realise that!'

'Still, you didn't have to put the boot in. He's obviously gone to a lot of trouble.'

'Oh, my God, is this why you thought he might be jealous of me?' she asked, aghast. 'Because I make a better girl than he does?'

'Yes.'

Jenny laughed. 'But I *am* a girl!'

'I just think you're the sort of woman he'd like to be.'

'What sort of woman is that?'

'You know, very glamorous, petite, very … feminine.'

Jenny giggled. 'Maybe he should try to be the sort of woman Celia is – it'd be less of a stretch. She's borderline at best.'

'I agree it'd be more achievable, but he doesn't want to be like Celia, he wants to be like you.'

'Well, that's got to be the weirdest compliment I've ever received.'

'They say imitation is the sincerest form of flattery.'

'So, you think I should invite him over for girls' nights – have pillow fights and plait each other's hair?'

Dev shrugged. 'I just think you could humour him a bit. Give him some make-up tips or something – talk to him about lipstick.'

'I just wish you'd said all this earlier. If I'd known what his real hobby was, I could have thought of a much better present.'

'What's that?'

'The complete works of Trinny and Susannah. That boy needs some serious help.'

'What's all this I hear about you taking Jenny to Jeremy's birthday party?' Richard asked Dev. It was their first full day back at work after Christmas. 'What were you thinking?'

'Well, I didn't know he was going to be channelling Joan Collins that day, did I?'

'Ooh, unfair to Joan.' Richard winced. 'How bad was it?'

'Actually, he was looking particularly lovely in what Jenny tells me was a copy of a Diane von Something dress.'

'She seems to have taken it in her stride anyway.'

'Actually, she may have done you some good with Jeremy. She gave him some style advice. Apparently he's been dressing all wrong for his body type.'

'Easy mistake to make, I suppose.'

'Yeah, I gather there's not a lot out there for the gal with a prick. So, did you have a good Christmas?'

'Yes, lovely. It was great spending time with the kids.' And Julia. It had been great being with Julia. 'I don't need to ask if you had a good time. I've heard about nothing else from Jenny.' His tone was almost accusing.

'She really enjoyed New York,' Dev said blandly.

'She loved that coat you gave her. Where do you get off giving my girlfriend such romantic presents?'

'Romantic? It was a coat!'

Richard couldn't explain it, and it sounded silly when he put it into words like that, but he thought there was something very personal and romantic about Dev's gift. He reckoned Dev knew it too – he was just being disingenuous.

'It was cold, we were going to New York, and I knew she didn't have a coat,' Dev said.

'She didn't?'

'No.'

'You could have given her an anorak.'

'I could, but it wouldn't have kept her very warm.'

'Why not?'

'Can you see Jenny wearing an anorak?'

'No,' Richard admitted, smiling. 'She'd freeze first.'

'Exactly.'

'Well, I think she likes that coat more than the diamond earrings I gave her,' Richard said peevishly.

'Diamond earrings! Not over-burdened with imagination, are you?' Dev scoffed.

'Oh, come on, all women love diamonds.'

'Who told you that? Susie? I suppose she picked them out too.'

'Well, what do I know about women's jewellery?'

About as much as you know about women, Dev thought, but he said nothing. Diamonds were all wrong for Jenny. He couldn't believe Richard hadn't seen that. He didn't deserve her. He obviously had no idea who she was.

Chapter 27

After a gruelling January, with some of the heaviest snows England had seen in decades, and the government continuing to lurch from one crisis to the next, February brought milder weather and the promise of change. At the end of the month the prime minister made a long-awaited visit to the Queen, Parliament was dissolved and an election called for April. The Moderates, so long waiting in the wings, burst on-stage with the eagerness of understudies who had been perfecting their roles over the course of a very long run, waiting for their moment to shine. At last their time had come, and they were primed and ready to take the country by storm.

The day of their campaign launch was bright and sunny. Crocuses and daffodils poked through the earth in London's green spaces, heralding spring, and there was a feeling of change in the air and the promise of new beginnings as Jenny and Richard drove to the campaign headquarters. Jenny was very proud that Dev considered her a real asset to Richard now and wanted her to be prominent during the campaign. She wished she could shake the impression that Richard didn't feel the same way. Although he deferred to Dev in almost everything concerning his public image, they had argued over whether she should come today. Richard had simply said he didn't see the need for her to take the time off work — she wasn't central to the campaign.

Besides, he said, he didn't want to appear 'showbizzy' and detract from the politics by putting any of the focus on his personal life. Dev had argued forcefully for Jenny's 'humanising' influence, and Richard had caved in, albeit reluctantly. But the feeling that he didn't really want her with him today was only adding to her nervousness.

'Do I look okay?' she asked him, fidgeting nervously with her skirt.

He glanced at her briefly. 'You look great,' he said, his mind clearly somewhere else.

Jenny sighed and continued to fidget. She knew he was keyed up, excited about finally getting started. She couldn't blame him for being distracted and aloof. But it wasn't just today. He had been distant a lot lately – ever since coming back after Christmas, in fact. At first she had put it down to missing his children after spending so much time with them. It was only natural he'd be a bit down about being apart from them again. But there was a niggling voice in her head that said maybe it wasn't just his children he was missing. Perhaps being with his family over Christmas had reminded him of what he had lost and he regretted the way things had turned out – having ended up with her. After all, he had never chosen her over Julia in the first place. When she questioned him about what was wrong, he said it was nothing, which didn't reassure her in the least.

She couldn't help feeling she was competing with Julia. She wanted to show him that she could be every bit as good for his career as her – better, in fact. She wanted him to see that she could be the perfect prime minister's wife. She had the common touch that he and Julia lacked. She could win the hearts of the public and capture the imagination of the media in a way that Julia never could.

⁂

The new year had brought changes in Jenny's home life too. Ollie had decided to try to make a go of it in Hollywood and had moved to LA at the end of January.

'And what about Jenny and me?' Liam had said huffily when he announced his intentions. 'Have you thought about us at all in this little plan of yours?'

'What's it got to do with you and Jenny? You don't want to come and try your luck in Hollywood, do you?'

'No, and neither should you. You'll go there and be a waiter and everyone will ignore you, and you'll come home in six months' time with your tail between your legs. You don't have to go to Hollywood for that. You can be a waiter here.'

'I'm not going there to be a waiter. My agent has meetings set up already.'

'Well, I think you're being very selfish,' Liam said.

'Selfish?'

'You're just going to move out, lock, stock and barrel, and leave us in the lurch? You're not going to pay rent any more?'

'Well ... since I won't be living here any more, I thought ... um, no.'

'You know what this means, don't you? We're going to have to get someone else in to share the flat.'

'Oh, no, are we?' Jenny groaned. She hadn't thought about that before.

'We barely make the rent as it is, with the three of us,' Liam pointed out.

'Well, I'm sorry for putting my career ahead of your living arrangements,' Ollie said.

'So you bloody should be.'

'Oh, Liam, darling,' Ollie said in his best Celia Johnson tones, 'if only I'd known how you felt about me before, I would never have thought of leaving you.'

'Shut up.'

'It won't be so bad,' Jenny said, not wanting to make Ollie feel guilty. 'I mean, we're hardly here as it is.'

'*You* don't care because you know you're going to be living it up at Number Ten soon,' Liam said.

'True. But it might be fun, getting someone new in,' she said, warming to the idea. 'We can advertise, and then we can interview loads of candidates and give them a hard time. You can glare at them and intimidate them,' she said to Liam, 'and I'll ask them loads of questions to see if they're our sort of people.'

'What kind of questions?'

'Um ... do you like cats, for instance.'

'We don't have any cats.'

'No, but ... I don't think I'd particularly want to live with someone who didn't like them. What else? Three-ways, yes or no? What's your position on recreational drugs? Can you make a margarita? Toilet roll over or under? Ooh, I'd better make a questionnaire.' She got up and rummaged around until she found a notebook and pen, then sat down again.

'A questionnaire is all very well,' Liam said, 'but we don't want to end up with just anybody. We have to be specific about what we want from the start.'

'Like what?'

'Well, sex for starters.'

'You think we should ask them to have sex with us?' Jenny giggled. 'I guess that would sort the men from the boys,' she said, tapping her pen thoughtfully on the page.

'No.' Liam smiled. 'I just mean do we want a guy or a girl?'

'Guy,' Jenny said decisively.

'Girl,' Liam said simultaneously.

'If we get a girl, you'll just end up shagging her and then she'll leave.'

'If we get a guy, *you*'ll end up shagging *him* and we'll never get rid of him.'

'No, I won't! I'm in a relationship. I've never cheated on anyone.'

'Well, that'll be even worse. He'll fall in love with you and mope around the place because you won't shag him.'

'We could get an ugly girl,' Jenny suggested.

'You could get a lesbian,' Ollie put in.

'I don't think a lesbian would feel very comfortable here,' Liam said, his eyes sweeping the room, indicating Jenny's girly décor.

'A hermaphrodite would be ideal.'

'How about a hermaphrodite lesbian?'

'I know just the person!' Ollie said suddenly, his eyes lighting up.

'You know a hermaphrodite lesbian?'

'Well, no. But a person of indeterminate sexuality. I think he might actually be asexual.'

'A sexual what?' Jenny asked.

'*Asexual*. It means he's not interested in having sex with anyone – boy, girl, gay, straight, nothing.'

'Wow!' Jenny breathed. 'Does that really exist?'

'Well, I've never seen him show any interest in either sex. He's very quiet, keeps himself to himself, and I happen to know he's looking for a place. His name's Blue.'

'Blue?'

'Well, that's not his name, but it's what he's called. At least, I don't think that's his name. But he's from Brazil, so I suppose it could be. Or maybe it's just because he's got blue hair.'

'A blue-haired Brazilian of no known sexuality – he sounds perfect,' Liam said.

'Does he like cats?' Jenny asked.

'I don't know. You can ask him when he comes over for his interrogation.'

'We don't need to go through all that checklist bollocks now, do we?' Liam asked. 'Not now that we're getting someone one of us knows.'

'I still want to do the questionnaire,' Jenny said. 'Not as a test, but as a getting-to-know-you kind of thing. Though I do want to know the answer to the toilet roll question. Over would be a deal-breaker.'

She didn't know if Ollie had coached him beforehand, but Blue had passed the toilet roll test with flying colours and moved in the following week. He barely spoke, but he had a gentle, sweet demeanour that endeared him to Jenny instantly, and even Liam warmed to him. She had been very grateful for his quiet presence last week, glad it was Blue rather than Ollie or Liam who had been with her when a bombshell had been dropped in her lap disguised as an innocuous-looking email.

She had been curled up on the sofa with her laptop, idly clearing out emails from an old address she no longer used while watching TV with Blue, deleting the endless ads for Viagra and offers to add three inches to her penis. She fully expected the email from 'Maria5678' with the heading 'You don't know me' to be from a sexy Russian claiming to be her perfect mate, but decided to check just in case. She was shocked when she opened it and it began 'Dear Jenny, You don't know me, but my name used to be Maria Hannigan ...' She only realised her gasp had been audible when Blue's head shot up and he looked at her questioningly.

'What's wrong?' he asked eventually when she didn't answer his silent query.

'Nothing,' she said, her voice barely audible as she scanned the rest of the email quickly. 'It's just this email. It – it's from my mother!'

Blue gave her a sympathetic smile and turned back to the TV, seemingly taking that as reason enough for her reaction. She was glad he didn't realise how momentous it was that her mother had got in touch. She needed time to digest this, to decide how she felt about it and what she wanted to do before everyone else came in with their opinions. She had read the email over and over since then until she could almost recite it by heart. But she still wasn't sure exactly how she felt about it.

As they neared the campaign headquarters, Richard took her hand and gave her a reassuring smile and she felt herself relax, only realising then how tense she had been. She squeezed his hand, smiling back at him. She was being silly, worrying over nothing. Of course he wanted her with him today. Everything was going to be fine. Things were changing, but it was all for the best. She missed Ollie and the way things used to be, but as Liam had said, she would probably be moving out herself soon anyway. She expected Richard would want to make their relationship more permanent once he was elected. It wouldn't seem right to be having sleepovers at Number Ten. They could start putting down roots and have a family. Ollie would strike gold in Hollywood and become world famous; she and her mother would get to know each other and start building bridges; Richard would be elected; and she would be the best prime minister's wife the country had ever seen.

Dev was waiting for them as they pulled up, opening Jenny's door for her.

'How do I look?' she asked him as she stepped out of the car.

'Perfect,' he said.

'*Too* perfect?' she asked warily.

'No. Just … perfect.'

'Really?' She checked her reflection in the car window. 'I've changed a bit from the girl you met at that wedding, haven't I?'

There was something almost sad in his expression. 'I liked the girl I met at the wedding. Remember?'

'Oh … yes.' She had a lump in her throat. It must be nerves, she thought as she went to join Richard.

Chapter 28

The following Saturday morning Jenny lay in bed with Richard, the bright winter sun streaming through the windows.

'Try to relax,' he said, his hand stroking her hip. The softness of his hair brushed against her skin as he trailed kisses along her stomach.

'Look who's talking.' She laughed.

They had barely slept a wink all week. Richard was too wound up about the campaign and the stress of constant media scrutiny, while she had been a nervous wreck about today ever since she had got that email, veering nauseatingly between excitement and panic for the rest of the week. She tried to let go and just enjoy finally having some time with Richard, but her mind was whirring, going over what she should wear, what she would say …

'I know what'll relax you.' She felt his mouth widen in a grin against her stomach and then his lips trailed lower, his head moving between her legs. She felt his tongue and tried to focus on the sensation, but she couldn't get into it. She knew it was going to take her for ever this morning, and she couldn't relax and take her time. She looked at the clock on the far wall. It was almost noon. She wanted to get up and start getting ready.

He looked up at her. 'Dev will be here soon,' he reminded her before bending to kiss her again.

'So I'd better get on with it, is that what you're saying?' Jenny laughed. 'Oh, my God, that is *such* a turn-on, knowing I have a window for this. That *really* makes me feel relaxed.'

He lifted his head and rested it on her stomach, grinning at her sheepishly. 'Sorry.'

She pulled a pillow from behind her head and whacked him with it playfully. 'Look, let's just forget it, okay?' she said, smiling. 'It's not going to happen anytime soon, and we haven't got all day.'

'Okay.' He grabbed the pillow and tossed it aside, rolled off her and stood up. 'I'm going to take a shower.'

Later, Jenny stood in front of the mirror, her fingers shaking as she pulled up the zip of her dress. Damn! She was almost sick with nerves. She had to calm down. After all, what was the worst that could happen? She tried out a smile in the mirror, attempting to quell the butterflies in her stomach.

'Hi,' she said, smiling idiotically at her reflection. 'Hi, I'm Jenny. Hello, are you …? Nutcase,' she whispered to herself. She stood up on her toes and turned around, surveying herself from every angle. Perfect, she thought.

Three outfits later, she went into the living room. Dev and Richard were standing in the kitchen, drinking coffee, discussing polls and dissecting newspaper stories and TV interviews, as they always were these days.

'Hello, Jenny.' Dev smiled at her.

'Hi, Dev,' she said, joining them in the kitchen. 'How do I look?' She did a twirl in front of him.

'Gorgeous!'

'Seriously, if you were seeing me now for the first time, what would you think?'

Dev's eyes lingered on her. She knew she had asked him to look, but she was starting to blush under the intensity of his gaze. 'I'd think you were stunning,' he said. 'So what's the occasion?'

'It's a big day for Jenny,' Richard said.

'I'm going to—' She gulped, hardly able to say the words. 'I'm going to meet my mother.'

'Your *mother*?' Dev looked at her sharply. His shock was evident. 'I thought you'd given up on finding her.'

'I had. But she found me!'

Dev's eyes darted to Richard. 'When did this happen?'

'Just this week,' Jenny said. 'I got an email from her. I couldn't believe it!'

'Right.' Dev was looking at her warily, and Richard seemed to be taking his cue from him. The smile had gone from his face and he was clearly rattled.

'You don't think this is something to do with me?' he asked Dev.

'Well, the timing's a bit of a coincidence, isn't it? Do you know how she found you, Jenny?'

'On Bebo.'

'But you shut down your Bebo account.'

'She'd found me before I shut it down and she kept my email address. Apparently I added her as a friend. I didn't even realise.'

'And she didn't choose to contact you until now?'

God, why did he have to find a way to rain on her parade? She was feeling nervous enough about today without him putting more doubts and worries into her head. 'She couldn't get up the nerve until now.'

'And now she's got the *nerve*,' he said angrily. 'She's got nerve, all right.'

'What are you saying? Do you think she's some kind of spy or terrorist or something?'

'Of course not. I just think you and Richard need to be cautious about new people coming into your life now,' he said reasonably. 'You don't know who you can trust. There will be people who want to be around Richard because of who he is.'

'So you think she just wants to use me to get close to Richard because he's going to be the prime minister? You don't think it could possibly be that she wants to meet *me*?'

'I'm just saying you need to be aware, that's all.'

'I can take care of myself,' she said coldly. 'I always have.'

Richard gave her a brief kiss. 'I hope it goes really well. See you tomorrow.'

'Tomorrow?' Dev frowned. 'You're not coming to Manchester tonight?'

'No, I decided not to. I'm staying at my place.' Richard and Dev were attending a big gala dinner in Manchester hosted by some businessman who was a major supporter of the Party. She had told Richard she didn't fancy it, but secretly she hoped that lunch with her mother would segue into dinner, and she didn't want to have to put a limit on their time together.

'Well, if you change your mind, you know where we are,' Richard said.

She left the kitchen, taking her coat from a hook in the hallway and pulling it on – her gorgeous red coat. She stroked the sleeves lovingly. It always made her feel better, wearing it.

Dev came over to her and stood against the door. 'I'm sorry. I didn't mean to upset you.'

'It's okay,' she said in a small voice.

'So, does she live in London?'

'I'm not sure, actually,' she said, animated again and forgetting their earlier spat. 'She didn't say where she lives.'

'What do you know about her?'

'Hardly anything. She said very little in her email. I guess I'll find out all about her today.'

'You know, Jenny, maybe you shouldn't—'

'What?' she snapped. Was he going to tell her she shouldn't go?

'Just … maybe you shouldn't get your hopes up too much,' he said gently. 'These things don't always work out as you hope they will.'

'Oh, I know that! Don't worry, I'm not expecting it to be some fairytale reunion. Anyway, look on the bright side – sometimes things do work out.'

'Of course. I just don't want you to be disappointed.'

She gave him a hard look. 'You never know, Dev, she might actually like me. Some people do, you know,' she said, yanking the door open.

'Jenny, I didn't mean—' he called after her, but she was gone, slamming the door.

'Damn!' Dev moved to the window, watching Jenny tripping happily down the road, swinging her bag. She looked like a little girl, he thought – so open, so guileless, wearing her heart right out there on her sleeve where anyone could tear it to shreds and trample on it. He wished she didn't remind him so much of a wide-eyed child in a fairytale, innocently skipping through the woods to her doom. *What big eyes you've got, Grandmama.* He just prayed that that bloody woman who had the gall to call herself her mother had grown a heart in the intervening years and wouldn't crush her. But he didn't believe people changed – not fundamentally. And he didn't hold out much hope for anyone who could walk out on the six-year-old version of the beautiful girl who was rushing down the road, bursting with excitement because she was going to meet her mother.

***

Jenny sat in a corner of the hotel lobby watching the door avidly, scanning everyone entering. She couldn't believe this was really happening. She had dreamed about this moment so often, it didn't seem possible that it was actually coming true. She wouldn't admit it to Dev, but growing up she had often fantasised about joyous fairytale reunions with her mother – a beautiful, rich woman who wafted into whatever foster home Jenny was living in and whisked her off to a life of love and luxury while the other kids looked on in envious awe. Sometimes it turned out she was actually a princess. Invariably her mother had been separated from her by some evil force or cruel twist of fate and had spent years searching tirelessly for her. When she found her, she clung to her and sobbed with happiness, swearing they would never be parted again.

But they were just childish dreams. In reality, she had never felt any true desire to find her mother. When she had come up against a brick wall in her half-hearted attempts to trace her, she had been quite happy to leave it there. She dreaded risking more rejection by approaching someone who quite likely didn't want to be found.

However, her mother finding *her* was another matter, and ever since she had received that first email she had been allowing her imagination to run riot, dreaming again of a beautiful woman who would fill her life with love and happiness. Her fantasies were a little more realistic now and her mother wasn't always rich – although sometimes she was, and she would take Jenny to lunch at Le Gavroche or the Ivy, the sort of places she had only ever been with Richard. Sometimes she was quirky and fun, and they would go to wonderful exotic places, hidden parts of London that only a very few people knew about. She imagined picnics in the park and afternoon tea in elegant hotels, sitting on plush velvet sofas, eating colourful cupcakes and drinking from bone china cups. She wondered if she had any half-brothers or sisters, any aunts and uncles who would be glad to be reunited with her.

She continued to scrutinise the faces of people coming through the revolving doors, searching for familiar features. She had no photograph, but her mother had given her a description, and she was looking for a petite woman in her late forties with short blonde hair wearing a green coat. She jumped as she saw a flash of green out of the corner of her eye, relaxing again as a woman with long dark hair entered the lobby. She returned to her daydreams and continued to monitor the traffic through the door, so focused on it that she didn't hear when someone approached her from the side.

'Excuse me,' a woman's voice said, 'are you Jenny?'

Chapter 29

Jenny ran down the street as if someone was chasing her. She didn't want anyone to see her. She wanted to make herself small, invisible even, to disappear off the face of the earth. She automatically headed for the nearest Tube station, but when she got there, she went right past it. She didn't want to go home. She couldn't bear the thought of anyone looking at her with sympathy. There probably wouldn't be anyone there – Liam had got a job in a top hotel and was working eighteen-hour shifts these days, and Blue was such an innocuous presence he hardly counted as a person at all, even if he was around. Still, she didn't want to risk it. She didn't think she could cope even with him right now. She slowed down eventually, as if she was out of range of whatever was hunting her, and continued to wander the streets aimlessly, unaware of where her feet were taking her. She just wanted to get lost in the crowds and not be seen.

After she had been waiting for her mother for almost an hour, she had started to get anxious, imagining transport problems and fretting over whether she might be at the wrong hotel. She checked her phone for messages every few minutes, but there was nothing. She started to wonder if she could have got the dates mixed up. Then she had heard the voice beside her.

'Excuse me, are you Jenny?'

She had looked up to see the receptionist standing beside her, a piece of paper in her hand.

'Yes?'

'You were meant to be meeting a woman called Maria here?'

Jenny nodded.

'Well, she just called. She said she's sorry, but she won't be able to make it.' The girl smiled apologetically.

Jenny looked at her, waiting for more. 'What did she say?'

'That's all,' the girl said, looking at the note in her hand. 'Just that she's not able to come and she sends her apologies.'

'Oh. Thank you,' she said in a daze. She stayed where she was for a while, still watching the door, thinking there must have been some mistake. Why hadn't she said what had prevented her from coming? Why hadn't she rung Jenny's mobile? She had given her the number in case there were any complications. And then it dawned on her. She had no contact number for her mother. She hadn't said where she lived. She hadn't even told her her surname – just that it had once been Hannigan, but not what it was now. Right from the start she had wanted to be able to disappear if she changed her mind. As if once wasn't enough to pull that stunt.

God, she should have seen this coming. What the hell had she been thinking? She should have known better. Her mother wasn't the warm, loving woman of her dreams. That woman had never existed, except in her head. This was a woman who could walk out on a six-year-old child. What the fuck had she expected from someone like her? Why would she even want to know her anyway? It was probably for the best that she hadn't turned up. Jenny was better off without her.

Anyway, it was certainly nothing to be upset about, she told herself. Nothing had changed. She hadn't had a mother yesterday and she had been perfectly happy, so there was no reason to be unhappy about it today. What did she need a mother for at her age? She could buy her own cupcakes, arrange her own picnics in the park. She had people in her life who loved her. She had Richard. The thought of Richard filled her with an overwhelming longing to see him. She needed to feel his arms around her and know that he loved her. Suddenly she knew where she was going. With a renewed sense of purpose, she started walking in the direction of the nearest Tube station.

She got a taxi from the station in Manchester to the hotel where Richard was staying. She should be able to make it in time for the pre-dinner reception. She hadn't told him she was coming, deciding to surprise him. She couldn't wait to see his face when he spotted her. When she arrived at the hotel, she got a key to his room and went up. It only dawned on her then that she hadn't brought anything with her. But it didn't matter. She wasn't exactly dressed for a formal dinner, but she had dressed up to meet her mother, so she looked respectable enough. And she knew Richard wouldn't mind, not when he heard what had happened. Maybe he would even cry off dinner and they could spend the evening curled up in bed together.

She dumped her coat and went back downstairs, quickly finding the room where the reception was being held. It was already in full swing, a cacophony of chatter and laughter assaulting her ears as she entered. She scanned the room, moving slowly around the edges of the throng, but she couldn't see him anywhere. Then her eyes lit on a familiar face.

'Jenny!' Susie shrieked, her eyebrows shooting up.

'Hi, Susie. Where's Richard?' God, why did her voice sound so breathless and shaky?

'He's not here,' she said, her expression softening.

'Not here? But—'

'There was an emergency at home. He's gone back to London.'

'At – at home?' Jenny looked at her blankly.

'Little Felix,' Susie explained. 'He was rushed to hospital – suspected meningitis.'

'Oh! Oh, my God!'

'Is everything all right, Jenny?' Susie was looking at her with what appeared to be genuine concern.

'Oh, yes, fine.' She tried to sound calm – or at least normal. 'I just wanted to see Richard. I didn't realise …' Just then she felt eyes on her and turned to find Dev looking right at her.

'Well, I'll be off. Thanks, Susie. Bye.'

'Jenny—'

She saw Dev break away from whoever he was talking to. He was starting to make his way across the room towards her. She ran from the room and towards the lifts, once more moving as if she was being chased – except this time she suspected she really was, and she didn't want Dev to catch up. He was the last person she wanted to see right now.

Dev watched Jenny shoot out of the door before he could reach her.

'What was Jenny doing here?' he asked Susie.

'She was looking for Richard. She seemed in a bit of a state.'

He had noticed the wild panic in her eyes from across the room, the tightly drawn features that seemed about to collapse at any second. She was obviously upset and it wasn't hard to guess why. He suspected the meeting with her mother had not gone well.

'When I told her he wasn't here, I thought she was going to lose it,' Susie said, a note of censure creeping into her voice. 'She's going to have to get used to not having him at her beck and call.'

'Here, Susie, hold this,' he said, handing her his glass of champagne.

'Dev! Where are you going?' she hissed at his retreating back.

He rushed from the room just in time to see Jenny disappearing into a lift, the doors closing in front of her. He raced over and jabbed the call button, and the second lift came almost immediately. When he got out on the third floor, he made straight for Richard's room. She was opening the door as he reached her. 'Jenny!'

She spun around, that hunted look still in her eyes.

'What is it? What's the matter?'

'Nothing,' she said stiffly. 'I'm fine.' She stepped into the room and made to close the door, but he put his hand on it, stopping her.

'Jenny – what happened?'

'Nothing.' She shook her head, releasing her hold on the door.

'I can see it's not nothing,' he said. She was as white as a ghost, her lower lip trembling.

'Just leave me alone, Dev,' she pleaded.

'No,' he said, stepping into the room and closing the door behind him. 'You've been left alone long enough.'

She had her back to him now, but he could see how tightly her fists were clenched. 'What happened with your mother?' he asked.

'She – she didn't come.'

'Jesus!'

'It doesn't matter. I'm better off without her,' she said turning to face him. 'Which is just perfect, since she doesn't want to know me. Everyone's a winner,' she said, with a smile that was painful to witness.

'Jenny—'

'Well, you did warn me. You were right. I shouldn't have thought … so if you've come here to gloat, just get on with it.'

'What?' He felt as if she'd hit him. 'Is that what you think?'

'No!' she gasped, a hand flying to her mouth. 'No, I don't! Oh, God, I don't know why I said that. I didn't mean it. I'm sorry, I'm sorry.' Tears welled in her eyes and she blinked hard.

'Hey, it's okay.' He reached out and touched her shoulder, but she flinched away.

'She just—' She drew a ragged breath, fighting to keep control. 'She just left me sitting there! How could she just leave me sitting there waiting for her like an idiot?' Her voice was rising hysterically. 'But what did I expect? I mean, what the fuck was I thinking? She walked out on me when I was *six*! How—' She heaved in a breath that came out as a screech of pain. 'How could she *do* that?' Her face crumpled, and she sobbed like a heartbroken child, huge tears splashing from her eyes. 'How could she do that?' She looked at him pleadingly.

He didn't know if she was referring to her mother walking out on her when she was a child or not showing up today. Either way, he didn't have an answer. 'I don't know,' he said, pulling her into his arms. His hand went to the back of her neck, pressing her head to his snowy white dress shirt, but she resisted.

'Your shirt.' She pulled away. 'I'll ruin your shirt.'

'It doesn't matter.'

'Still …' She continued to hold herself away from him.

'Oh, sod my shirt!' He ripped off his tie and opened the buttons of his shirt, then pressed Jenny's head to his bare chest and rested his chin on top of her head. She didn't resist this time and she wrapped her arms around him, burrowing into him. He was appalled to find the touch of her hot, wet face against his bare skin so arousing. He shifted uncomfortably as she sobbed, her little body jerking and shaking against his. He held her tightly, stroking her back soothingly as she cried.

Finally her tears subsided. 'Jenny?' He caressed the side of her face until she looked up. 'Better?'

She nodded, blinking. He leaned down and pressed a soft kiss to her forehead, stroking her hair soothingly. Then his eyes dropped to her mouth and his lips followed. He pressed a quick, comforting kiss to her wet, trembling mouth, tasting the salt of her tears. But no sooner had he pulled away than his lips returned to hers as though drawn by a magnet and he kissed her again and again – soft, slow, seductive kisses. He knew he should stop. Soon she would pull away. She would tell him to stop, and he would. Her hands came up to rest on his shoulders, but instead of pushing him away, she pulled him closer, winding her arms around his neck and burying her fingers in his hair. He groaned softly as she ran her tongue along his bottom lip and he opened his mouth against hers, kissing her deeper because right now it felt too bloody good, too perfect ever to stop. He would stop when she pushed him away.

Chapter 30

Jenny opened her eyes, blinking against the sunlight flooding the room. It took her a moment to remember where she was, and then it all came back in a rush – her mother; coming to Manchester; Dev coming up to her room; Dev kissing her. Dev ... shit!

'Good morning.' The voice came from behind her – husky, northern; the wrong voice. She felt a hand on the back of her neck, stroking her skin softly; the wrong hand.

She turned on her side to face him and he reached out and brushed a lock of hair away from her face, gazing into her eyes with an intensity that shocked her. Uh-oh! Dial it down, she thought. 'Oops,' she said, raising her eyebrows and smiling mischievously in an attempt to lighten the atmosphere.

He smiled back, but there was something intimate, proprietorial almost, in his smile that infuriated her. Crap! She knew that look.

He leaned across to kiss her and she pulled away, feeling a bit guilty when she saw the hurt that flashed across his face. But what did he expect? Surely he didn't want to have sex again. Admittedly, she had never been in this situation before. She wasn't in the habit of sleeping with people she shouldn't, and she had never been unfaithful to a boyfriend, so she was new to all this. All the same, she was pretty sure that when you had big-stupid-mistake sex with someone, you didn't wake up the next morning and do it all over again. No, you had the talk and then you got out of there as fast as you could with any remaining shred of dignity you could muster.

'Jenny—' He reached out to her and she sat bolt upright in the bed, holding the sheet to her. 'What's going on?' He sat up beside her.

'I think you'd better go,' she hissed, wriggling away from his hand as he pushed her hair back to see her face more clearly. 'What if someone catches you in here? What if Richard came back?'

'He's not going to come back here.'

'Still …'

'Relax,' he said, smiling at her indulgently.

Before she knew what he intended to do, he leaned in and kissed her. God, he was such a good kisser! She succumbed for a moment, just letting herself enjoy it. Maybe just one more time … No, she had to stop this. She pulled away, her hand pushing firmly against his chest. 'Stop! We can't.'

He pulled back. 'You're right.' He sighed. 'Sorry.'

'Look, last night was … lovely. But it was a mistake,' she said firmly. 'We both know that.'

'Do we?' He frowned at her in confusion.

'It just happened, and it shouldn't have, but—'

'Jenny, that isn't something that *happens* to you. It's something you *do*. Something *we did*.'

God, he wasn't going to let her off the hook. 'Okay, it was something we did. Something we shouldn't have done.'

His expression softened. 'Look, we didn't plan for this to happen, but I can't say I'm sorry it has.'

'Well, I can!' She saw him flinch at her words. 'Look,' she said, more gently, 'last night I was upset and you were … very kind to me, and I'm grateful—'

'Kind? Grateful?' he snarled.

'But it was a mistake, so let's just forget it ever happened.'

'Forget it? I don't want to forget it.'

'Well, I do! Look, one thing led to another and we had sex, that's all – get over it. It doesn't have to change anything.'

'It changes everything.'

'Just because we ended up having sex in the heat of the moment doesn't mean—'

'You think that's all it was – just the heat of the moment? Jenny, I didn't make love to you last night because I got carried away, because I can't control myself. I made love to you because I love you. I'm *in love* with you.'

'Oh, don't be ridiculous!' she snapped irritably. 'You don't love me. What are you – twelve?'

'Twelve? What's that – the last time you gave a fuck about anybody?' Dev stormed, throwing back the sheets and sitting up on the edge of the bed.

'No,' she said to his back. 'That's when you think you're in love with everyone you snog.'

'We did a bit more than snog,' he said, grabbing his clothes from the floor. Standing up, he started to dress hurriedly.

'So what did you think? One shag and hey presto, we're a couple? Jesus! Grow up! It was just sex – it doesn't have to mean anything.'

'No.' Dev pulled up the zip of his trousers. 'You can say whatever you like about your part in it, but you can't tell me how I feel or what it meant to me. I may not have intended it to happen, but I didn't do anything last night that I haven't wanted to do for a very long time.'

'Yeah, you wanted to screw me and you got your wish. Congratulations! You don't *love* me. You fancy me, that's all.'

He shook his head emphatically. 'I love you – God help me!'

'Well, I love Richard.'

'No, you don't,' he said matter-of-factly.

'*What?*' she gasped. 'How *dare* you? How can you say that to me?'

'Because it's the truth,' he said, buttoning his shirt.

'What do you think – that I'm one of those people who want to be close to him because of who he is? That I'm with him for what I can get out of it?' She couldn't believe he was saying this to her.

'No. You think you love him, but you don't. You want *him* to love *you*. It's not the same thing.'

She looked at him in stunned silence. She just wanted him to go. He was slipping his feet into his shoes.

'I love you,' he said aggressively. 'So get over that!' Grabbing his tie and shoving it in his pocket, he stalked out of the room, slamming the door behind him.

When he was gone, Jenny stared at the door numbly, paralysed by shock.

Bloody hell! She punched the pillows furiously. What was it with her and men? Everywhere you looked there were women banging on about men who never called, men who disappeared after sleeping with you once or twice – feckless, unreliable, commitment-phobic men. Why the fuck couldn't she *once* meet a man like that? Were they just an urban myth? Why couldn't she shake off a single guy she'd ever slept with? Why couldn't she just have a one-night stand like a normal person, instead of every casual shag leading to declarations of undying love? She thought she could at least have relied on Dev to see last night for what it was – a big stupid mistake that should never have happened, and that certainly should never happen again.

She could have handled it better, though, she thought as her temper started to wear off. She shouldn't have got so angry and said such horrible things. She didn't even mean them. She had just freaked out when she saw that look on his face and she couldn't seem to help herself. She had lashed out at Dev, but it was herself she was angry with. Because if she was honest, she had wanted the same thing as he had. She had wanted to stay in this bed with him and make love again, and she had wanted it to be the beginning of something. But she didn't *want* to want that. She didn't want to be that person who threw away what she had the minute something new came along. She wanted to be dependable and trustworthy and faithful. Richard loved her. He didn't deserve to be treated like that and she wouldn't do it to him.

'Ugh!' She groaned in frustration, throwing herself back against the pillows. Dev's smell lingered there, conjuring memories of last night that set her body tingling. She had often wondered what it would be like to be with him. Well, now she knew. It was bloody fantastic. He had been so warm and tender, so passionate and … loving.

She buried her face in the pillow, breathing in his scent, remembering the feel of his lips, warm and firm against hers as he had kissed her on and on. He was right: it wasn't something that had happened to them. It was something they had done – something *she* had done; something she had made happen. She knew she had clung to him whenever he seemed about to pull away, not wanting him to stop. She had known what she was doing when she took his hand and dug her nail into his palm as they moved to the bed, desperate not to break the spell, to keep them both in the trance of desire that had overtaken them. It had been her doing. He would have stopped. He *had* stopped.

'We can't,' he had breathed, pulling a little away from her.

She had whimpered and pulled him closer, her body arching up to his, telling him what she wanted, and he had soothed her and said, 'Shhh,' and then he had put his fingers inside her and made her come again and again. But it still wasn't enough. She wanted more.

'We can't, sweetheart,' he had whispered, smiling ruefully. 'No condoms.'

So she had rummaged in her bag and found one, and then it was all her doing when he entered her with a groan and she felt him warm and real inside her, his weight on top of her, pushing her into the bed.

He had told her he loved her and she had refused to believe him. But she had felt loved when he touched her, when he kissed her, when he entwined his fingers with hers and looked into her eyes as he moved inside her. It had felt like love when her body rose to meet his and she had clung to him as if he was the only solid thing in the world. She didn't think she had ever felt so loved – and that thought scared the hell out of her.

Fuck! Dev slammed the door of his room. *Fuck, fuck, fuck!* Impatiently, he stripped off last night's evening clothes and headed for the shower. He stood under the spray, trying to clear the jumble in his head. He didn't know who he was angrier with – himself or Jenny.

What are you – twelve? Her words came back to haunt him. She was right: he wasn't a fucking teenager, he should be able to control himself. He should have been able to stop, no matter what she said ... despite her little hands pulling him into her ... despite her greedy mouth and her needy whimpering. Even when she had kissed him back and wound her arms around his neck, even when she arched her body, pushing it into his, he should have been able to stop. Even when she handed him that bloody condom, practically serving herself up to him on a plate – even then he should have stopped.

She had been upset and he shouldn't have taken advantage of that. It served him right that she thought it was nothing more than a stupid mistake. He only had himself to blame. And then, to top it all, he'd had to go and tell her he loved her! He had practically bludgeoned her with it, as if he could bully her into loving him back, as if it was her fault that she didn't feel the same way. She had every right to be angry with him, forcing his feelings on her like that. After all, he knew she was with Richard. She had never given him any reason to think she was interested in him in that way. Except last night, of course ...

And then she calmly suggested he forget it. If only he could! It was emblazoned on his memory. She was so bloody gorgeous. He just wanted to go down the hall, climb back into bed with her and spend the day there. He wanted to spend the rest of his life making her happy. He would love her properly, like no one else had ever loved her. Instead, he would have to bring her back to Richard – bloody Richard, who was only with her by default and didn't love her half as much as Dev did.

He shouldn't have got angry and lashed out at her, acting like a spoiled brat because things hadn't gone his way. But he had woken up so happy this morning, so full of hope. He'd thought everything was going to be different from now on. He'd thought it was the start of something. They'd slept together and he'd thought it was going to change everything. Christ, maybe he *was* twelve after all.

Jenny was surprised when Dev knocked on her door and offered to drive her back to London, acting as if nothing had happened between them. He was very polite and solicitous, but the journey was tense, and she was glad that he spent most of it fielding calls on his phone.

She took the opportunity to ring Richard on the way, enquiring after Felix.

'He's fine,' he said, sounding tired. 'He gave us quite a scare, but he's absolutely fine. It's a virus. We can take him home tomorrow.'

'Great. That's such a relief.'

'Sorry I missed you. I hope the dinner wasn't too much of a bore.'

'No … not at all.'

'Well, at least Dev was there. I'm sure he looked after you.'

'Yes, he did. Absolutely!'

'Oh, how did the meeting with your mother go?' he asked, as if he had just remembered it.

'Not great. She stood me up,' she said with a light laugh. 'First time in my life I've been stood up and it's by a middle-aged woman!'

'Bloody cheek!' Richard said, mirroring her tone. 'Oh, well,' he said, more seriously, 'maybe it's for the best.'

'Yes, that's what I think. She could have turned out to be a right wagon – criticising my clothes, disapproving of my boyfriend …'

'She'd have loved me. I'm very good with mothers.'

'I bet you are.' Jenny laughed. 'Still, what if she was one of those mothers who steals her daughter's boyfriends?'

'You're definitely better off without that.'

'Plus now we don't have to worry about her being a secret agent trying to dig up dirt on you.'

When she hung up, she caught Dev looking at her strangely, but he said nothing.

'Are you hungry?' he asked after a while. 'Do you want to pull in somewhere and get something to eat?'

'No, I'm fine, thanks.' She was starving, having missed dinner last night and breakfast this morning, but she didn't want to prolong the journey with Dev any more than was absolutely necessary. The strain of it was giving her a tension headache.

When she got home there was an email from her mother in her inbox. She hesitated a moment before opening it, bracing herself.

Dear Jenny,

I'm sorry I wasn't able to meet you today. I really tried, and I was actually on my way, but in the end I just couldn't go through with it.

The truth is, I suffer from depression and I've been very low for the past few months. I think about you a lot when I'm down, so when I saw you in the papers, I thought it might help me to see you. I don't know if you ever tried to find me, but I've always feared you turning up at my door one day, and it's caused me a lot of anxiety over the years. So I thought if I contacted you, I could put those fears to rest, as well as seeing for myself that you're okay and happy.

However, almost as soon as I sent that email, I wished I could take it back. I have a family now, a husband and two daughters who know nothing about my previous life. They are the most important people in the world to me and I can't risk that. So I think it's for the best if we don't try to meet again. I'm sure you will understand.

Best wishes,
Maria

She read it twice to make sure it was as self-pitying as it first appeared. Then she clicked 'delete'.

Chapter 31

In the days that followed, the campaign became all-consuming, and Dev was grateful to be able to throw himself into his work to the exclusion of everything else. Richard began a punishing tour of the country and Dev mostly travelled with him, occasionally staying behind in London to oversee media operations. Either way, there was no time for brooding. Even better, it meant he hadn't seen Jenny since the morning they had driven back from Manchester.

Richard, too, barely saw her.

Dev was coming into the office earlier every day and going home later every night, too exhausted to think. This morning he had come in earlier than ever in an attempt to get some work done before Richard started bombarding him with demands. He was enjoying a rare moment of calm, reading through the early editions of the papers, when he was interrupted by Richard summoning him to his office.

He found him pacing around the room, looking rather agitated. 'Dev, come in. Close the door.'

Dev did as he asked and waited expectantly as Richard continued pacing for a moment before finally coming to a standstill in front of him, hands on his hips. 'We've got a problem,' he said. He looked shell-shocked.

'Okay.' Dev waited for more. It was obviously something serious. Richard wasn't easily rattled. 'Well, what is it?' he said finally when Richard remained silent.

'It's Julia.'

'*Julia?*' That was the last thing he had expected to hear. Had she decided to dish the dirt about Richard's affair with Jenny?

'Yes, Julia. Look, I'm just going to say this and I don't want you to go ballistic, okay?'

Dev gazed at him in exasperation. 'What about Julia?'

'She's pregnant,' Richard said, ashen-faced.

'Right. I see.' Dev frowned. 'But I don't see how that's our—' Realisation dawned even as he spoke. He looked at Richard in horror. 'Oh, God. Please tell me it's not yours.'

'It's mine,' Richard said shortly.

'Christ!' Dev pinched the bridge of his nose. 'Jesus, Richard!'

'I know, I know.'

'When did this happen?'

'At Christmas.'

'Christmas! Does Jenny know?'

'Jenny?' Richard appeared thrown by the question. 'No, of course she doesn't. But you seem to be missing the point. We have more important things to think about than Jenny.'

Dev fought the urge to hit him. 'Well, obviously she's going to find out,' he said coldly.

'I know, I know. Oh, God, what a mess.'

'I presume Julia is keeping the baby?'

'What?' he asked absently. 'Oh, yes.'

'God, Richard, how could you have let this happen?'

'Look, the point is, it has happened and we have to deal with it.'

Dev leaned against Richard's desk, his arms folded. 'So what are you going to do?'

'I don't know.' Richard sank into a chair and buried his head in his hands. Then he looked up, and Dev knew he was lying. He had already decided what he was going to do.

'You're going back to Julia, aren't you?'

'I don't know if she'll have me.' Richard's head drooped dejectedly.

'Well, seemingly she already has,' Dev said.

Richard shot him a warning look. 'I haven't had time to think about it yet. She's only just sprung it on me. It was a bit of a shock for her too, as you can imagine.'

'What does *she* want to do?'

'I don't know. I'm not sure she knows herself yet. She's a bit stunned. We're meeting this evening to discuss it.'

'But you want to get back together?'

'If she'll have me, yes. At the end of the day, we're a family.'

'Oh, very touching. That'll make a lovely soundbite,' Dev said. 'Is that the line you're planning to take on it?'

Richard heaved a sigh. 'I know it's not going to look good, but at least there's nothing political in it. It's just private life stuff. Besides, Julia and I are still married. It's not as if I was committing adultery. Okay, we'd separated, but we're not divorced yet. Maybe this baby is what we needed to bring us to our senses and get us to work on our marriage instead of throwing it away.'

'And where does that leave Jenny?'

Richard looked at him rather peevishly. 'You're very concerned about Jenny in all this.'

'Well, yes. You, on the other hand, don't seem very concerned about her at all.'

'Of course I'm concerned about her. But you said yourself that this thing with Jenny wouldn't last. You were dead set against her right from the start. You never thought she was someone I could be with in the long term.'

'That was before I knew her.'

'I thought you'd be jumping for joy if I went back to Julia.'

'Well, I'm not. How do you think this is going to look, for one thing? You've been parading Jenny around as your girlfriend, and then – bam – you go home for Christmas and get your ex-wife up the duff.'

'Not my ex-wife. Julia and I are still married.'

'So what does that make Jenny? Just a bit of fun? A bit of fluff on the side?'

Richard sighed helplessly. 'Look, I've been an idiot. I know this is going to be hard on Jenny, but I'm sure she'll understand. Julia and I have two children, and we're about to have another. We're a family.'

'Oh, don't worry,' Dev said bitterly, 'I'm sure Jenny will understand. If there's one thing that girl understands, it's being abandoned.'

Julia opened a bottle of red wine to let it breathe in readiness for Richard coming over. She was sure he'd welcome a drink in the circumstances. She could do with one herself, she thought, sniffing the bottle longingly. Pity the reason she needed one was the very reason she couldn't have one.

She was stunned at finding herself in this position. She had never imagined she would have another child. It wasn't that she was too old – she was only thirty-five – but she was firmly of the belief that motherhood was for the young, the younger the better, and she had thought her family was complete. When Richard had left, she had taken the opportunity to have a break from the Pill. And, of course, she had never intended to have sex with him when he was home at Christmas. She really hadn't ...

It had been so like old times, sitting companionably together on Christmas night, watching the opera, eating cheese and crackers, drinking port. It would have seemed the most natural thing in the world for them simply to go upstairs to bed together. It was so com-fortable – and yet not, because there was a frisson that hadn't been there before, a sexual undercurrent because they weren't as familiar with each other as they had once been. There was an element of the forbidden about it. They weren't supposed to want each other any more – and if they did, they certainly weren't meant to act on it. She had caught Richard looking at her sometimes during the evening – appreciative, even lustful glances. She'd really thought he was about to make a pass at her at one point. But then he had got up and announced he was going to bed, leaving her alone in the room, and she'd felt as if a bucket of water had been thrown over her. She sud-denly realised to her dismay that she had been counting on him to make a pass, expecting it ... longing for it.

Almost on autopilot, she had uncurled herself from the couch and gone into the kitchen, where Richard was rinsing glasses at the sink. He had turned and a look passed between them, and it was as if they had made a mutual decision. She still wasn't sure who made the first move, but suddenly there was kissing and licking and crashing of teeth, and then he was pushing her face-down over the table and she clung to the edges while he rammed into her again and again, his hand on her mouth so she wouldn't wake the children.

Even then, it hadn't occurred to her that she might get pregnant. It was one time – what were the chances? Besides, stupid, sponta-neous sex with an ex was one of those things that weren't supposed to count – like calories consumed standing up or in other people's houses. You weren't meant to get pregnant when your almost-ex-husband bent you over the kitchen table while the children slept upstairs.

Still, life was full of surprises ... and now Richard wanted to come back. Though he had been rattled by the news, she could tell he also saw it as an opportunity. She heard the tentative hope in his voice when they spoke on the phone. He wanted them to get back together and have a fresh start, and tonight he would use his considerable powers of persuasion to convince her that that was what she wanted too. But was it? Suddenly it was make-your-mind-up time, and she had to decide before he got here and started confusing her. God, she really could do with that drink.

Chapter 32

When she left work the following day, Jenny made her way to Richard's flat in Mayfair. She hadn't been spending much time there lately – not much point when Richard was never there – and she missed it. She longed for the campaign to be over and for everything to go back to the way it used to be – staying over at Richard's flat, with Dev calling around all the time. To her surprise, she found herself hankering after their little *ménage à trois*. She missed Dev. She hadn't seen him since Manchester and she got the feeling he was actively avoiding her.

Then again, she had hardly seen Richard either in the last couple of weeks. The campaign took up all his time and energy, and the few snatched moments they did have together, he was aloof and on edge. She tried not to get too paranoid about it and put it down to the enormous pressure he was under, but she couldn't help feeling that she was being sidelined somehow, edged out of his life.

And the reality was that things would never go back to the way they had been. When the election was over, Dev would no longer be working for Richard. They might hardly see each other, she thought with a pang. Richard would be prime minister and busier than ever. He would be living at Number Ten ... but would she? She used to think of it as a given, but now she wasn't so sure. She wasn't sure of anything any more, and as she made her way to Richard's flat, she felt nervy and full of foreboding. She had been on edge since he'd phoned this morning and asked if they could meet.

'We need to talk,' he had said ominously, refusing to elaborate when she asked what it was about, saying he didn't want to go into it on the phone.

His brisk tone had unnerved her – as though he was setting up a business meeting rather than a date with his girlfriend, especially when he asked if she could come to the flat between six and seven. He had a live TV appearance later tonight and was flying to Scotland tomorrow, so she knew she was only being allocated a small window of time with him. But she had to accept that that was the reality of his life now. She should probably be grateful he was squeezing her into his hectic schedule at all.

But instead of being happy that he was making time for her, she had been worrying all day about why he thought they needed to talk. Had his rivals dug up some past indiscretion of hers that would cause him embarrassment? Could he possibly have found out that she had slept with Dev in Manchester? Her stomach churned. She didn't think Dev would have told him, but what if someone else had seen – Susie perhaps?

You're being ridiculous, she told herself as she took the lift up to his flat. She was probably worrying over nothing. There could be plenty of perfectly innocuous reasons why he might want to have a serious talk with her. Maybe they wanted to involve her more in the campaign, and he had sounded so businesslike because it *was* a business meeting. Maybe Dev would be there and they would all discuss how she could help. Or maybe he wanted to talk to her about what would happen after the election. Perhaps he was going to invite her to move into Number Ten with him ... or ask her to marry him ...

Or maybe it was all just a pretext for a booty call, she thought, brightening. They hadn't seen each other properly in ages. He might just want a quickie before he went away tomorrow and had made up some reason he needed to talk to her because he didn't want to admit he was planning it down to the last detail. She could imagine Amanda pencilling it into his diary – '6.00 to 7.00, sex with Jenny'. He would probably jump on her the second she was inside the door. She smiled to herself, getting quite hot at the thought. Everything was going to be fine.

'Jenny, hi.' As soon as he opened the door, she knew everything was not going to be fine. He was tense and serious, and she didn't think he'd be pouncing on her any time soon.

She reached up to kiss him and he turned his head so that her lips landed on his cheek. He gave her a brief peck in return. 'Thanks for coming,' he said stiffly. He took her coat and waved her to the sofa, his behaviour so formal and polite she almost wanted to giggle.

'Have you eaten? Do you want anything?' he asked her.

'No, I'm fine, thanks.'

'Would you like a glass of wine?'

She noticed there was a bottle open on the coffee table. 'Am I going to need one?' She smiled nervously. He didn't answer or return her smile. Oh, God, he knows about Manchester, she thought. He knows and he's going to break up with me. 'No, thanks,' she said as he sat down beside her.

He turned to her, his expression anxious and uncertain. It was an agonisingly long time before he spoke. 'Jenny, there's something I have to tell you. There's no easy way to say this, so I'll just say it. Julia is pregnant.'

'Oh!' It took her a moment to realise why he was telling her this – another split second before she understood the significance of what he was saying. 'Oh! It's yours.' It was a statement, not a question.

'Yes.'

'Oh.' She couldn't think of anything else to say. What else was there to say? She looked down at her hands, tears blurring her vision. There was only one reason why he was telling her this, one reason for that look on his face. She suddenly wanted very badly to hit him. She wanted to knock that stupid expression off his face.

'I see.' She brushed away the tears. 'You're going back to her.' She felt her face collapsing, exploding, metamorphosing into something monstrous and bulbous and freaky, but she was powerless to stop it.

'Jenny!' He reached for her and she pulled away, wiping frantically at the tears that were gushing from her eyes.

'You're going back to her,' she repeated, her voice sounding ugly and alien to her.

'Yes. Jenny, I'm sorry, but—'

'How – how long— When did it happen?'

'At Christmas.' So he had cheated on her with his wife. It was almost funny. 'Julia and I – we still love each other—'

'*I* love you! You said you loved me.'

'I did. I still do, in a way. But what we had – well, we were never going to be for keeps, were we?' he said.

'I thought we were.'

'Julia and I have a family together.'

'*I* wanted to have a family with you.'

'You're so young, Jenny—'

'But you knew all this!' she wailed. 'You already had a family with Julia when you split up. It didn't stop you then. And you knew how young I was when you met me.'

'I know. I'm completely in the wrong here – I know that. I've been weak and selfish, and I've ended up hurting the people I care about the most. I'm sorry, Jenny – I never meant to hurt you, truly.'

Her heart went out to him because he looked so guilty and sad and ... *hurt*. She mustn't make a fuss – she didn't want to make it harder on him than it already was. She wanted him to remember her as someone sweet and loving and dignified – not hysterical and needy and angry. There would be no bitterness, no recriminations, no accusations. Maybe then he would realise that he loved her after all. Maybe he would change his mind and stay with her. He had to stay with her, she thought with mounting panic. It *had* to work with Richard because of what she had given up for him. Even though Richard was the one saying goodbye, all she could think about was losing Dev, and the realisation hit her with a force that almost took her breath away. She tried to stem the sobs that racked her body.

'Come here.' This time when he reached for her, she didn't pull away. He took her in his arms and soothed her while she cried into his shoulder.

'I'm sorry,' she whispered. 'It's just that I love you so much.'

'I know.' He brushed her hair back from her face. 'I don't deserve you.'

She smiled weakly at him, wiping tears from her face. 'No, you don't,' she said, punching his chin playfully. Light, light – keep it light. You're good fun. Don't be needy; don't cling. That's not attractive. No one loves that.

'Thank you,' he said, pressing a kiss to her forehead. 'You've made this easier on me than it should be.'

She swallowed hard against the bile rising in her throat. She didn't want this to be easy for him. It wasn't supposed to be easy. It was meant to be bloody unbearable, like it was for her. Why did she do that? Why couldn't she just tear him to pieces, claw at his flesh like she wanted to? Now she would be the one left with all the bad feeling – not just the hurt and the anger at him, but the anger at herself for letting him off the hook so easily, for not making him feel all the pain she could conjure up, not letting him see himself for the shit he was.

She thought about telling him she had slept with Dev, to get back at him, but decided against it. It would probably only make him feel better.

'So – a baby!' she said.

'Yes. It came as a bit of a shock, I can tell you – for both of us.'

For all of us, she thought – for *all* of us.

'Still, it brought me to my senses, I suppose. It made me realise what's important – what I really want.'

She nodded understandingly. Not me. I'm not important. I'm not what you really want. Acid was seeping through her body, eating her away. Soon there would be nothing left.

She got up, smoothing down her skirt. 'Well, I guess that's it. I should go.' There was nothing more to say. Besides, she got the feeling her time was up.

He stood, looking at her anxiously. 'If there's anything you need ...'

She nodded silently.

'Any time you want to come and pick up your stuff, just let me know.'

'Oh! Yes.'

He bent and kissed her, pulling her to him briefly before letting her go. 'I'm so sorry, Jenny. You're such an amazing girl. You deserve so much more.'

She didn't answer. She didn't think she could open her mouth without screaming. She just turned and walked out of the door.

When she got home, the flat was in darkness. She was glad no one was around. She was in no mood for company. She went straight to her bedroom and just stood in the middle of the floor. She wasn't even crying any more. There was nothing to do, because nothing she did would make the slightest difference. She could shoot her veins full of heroin, or lie in bed drinking all day and never go to work again, and it wouldn't make one iota of difference to her life. It wouldn't make her feel any better or any worse. Richard still wouldn't love her – he would still go back to Julia. It didn't make any sense. She had thrown away everything for him and now he didn't want her. It crucified her to think of what she had given up for him – and all for nothing.

She couldn't stop thinking about Dev – the way he had looked at her, the way he had touched her. So much love, hers for the taking – and she could have taken it, she could have *had* it. Instead she had pushed him away for Richard's sake, only for him to toss her aside like so much rubbish. She wished she could go back to that morning in Manchester knowing what she knew now. But it was too late.

Sleep – she should try to get some sleep. It wasn't late and she wasn't tired, but maybe sleep would make her feel better – and perhaps things would look better in the morning. People always said that, didn't they? Anyway, she'd had enough of consciousness for one day.

She knew sleep wouldn't come naturally, so she went into the kitchen, got a bottle of vodka from the freezer and poured herself a large measure, gulping it down. It felt good – sharp and real. She poured another glass and brought it into the bedroom, kicked off her shoes and lay back against the pillows while she drank, waiting for oblivion to descend. The vodka was good, but she still felt too wide awake, everything still in too-sharp focus. She needed more. When she had drained the glass, she went into the kitchen and got the bottle. On the way back to her room she made a detour to the bathroom, rooting in the medicine cabinet. She knew it contained a bottle of sleeping pills that Ollie had once been prescribed. He hadn't liked the way they made him feel and had only taken one or two, but he was always offering them around if anyone had trouble sleeping. She found them, glad to see there were still a few left.

Back in the bedroom, she poured another large glass of vodka and washed down a couple of the pills with a large slug. Then she shook another couple into her hand and swallowed them too. She knew she should stop – it could be dangerous – but she didn't have the will. She might as well take the rest – it would make no difference, either way. So she kept on taking them, pill after pill, until the bottle was empty.

Chapter 33

Dev found Richard in a whiny, fretful mood when he called later to accompany him to the television studios.

'God, I really don't feel up to this,' he muttered as Dev tried to prepare him for the interview. 'It's been a hell of a day.' He sagged on the sofa, shoulders slumped, a martyred expression on his face.

He was clearly looking for sympathy, but Dev had no patience with him in this self-indulgent mood. 'Well, it's going to get a hell of a lot worse if you don't pull this off. Come on, concentrate. And, by the way, the hangdog look won't go over well on TV.'

'Sorry.' Richard sighed dejectedly. He was silent for a moment. Then he said, 'Jenny was here earlier.'

'Oh. You told her about Julia,' Dev said dully.

'Yes.'

'How did she take it?'

'Surprisingly well, actually. Better than you,' Richard gave a dry laugh. 'She didn't give me such a hard time, either. She was upset, of course, but you know Jenny – she'll bounce back. She doesn't let anything get her down for long.'

Dev looked at him. He wondered if *he* knew Jenny.

'Oh, don't look at me like that!' Richard snapped. 'I do feel like the most unbelievable shit.'

'Not without reason.'

'Look, it wasn't easy for me either.'

Oh, poor you!

'I really care about Jenny. But if Julia hadn't found out about her and kicked me out, it would never have gone as far as it did. Julia's always been the one.'

'Well – now we know. How was Jenny when she left?'

'She was upset.' Richard shrugged. 'She cried a bit. But she was very sweet. She tried to make it easy on me.'

'She should have cut your balls off!'

'Thanks for the support. Luckily for me, Jenny's better than that.'

'She's better than you deserve.'

'I do know that,' Richard said.

Dev sighed. 'Did you tell her everything? Did you tell her Julia's pregnant?'

'Yes.'

'Does she know it's not common knowledge – that we don't want it to come out until after the election?'

Richard's eyes widened. 'No ... shit! It never occurred to me to go into that with her. Do you think she'll tell anyone?'

'I don't think she'll go to the papers or anything, but she could easily tell a friend. If she doesn't know we want it kept quiet ...'

'Bugger! You'll have to go and talk to her.'

'*Me?*'

'Well, I'm probably the last person she wants to see right now.'

No, that'd probably be me, Dev thought.

'Besides, I've got to do this TV thing and I'm going to Scotland in the morning.'

'You mean right now? You really think now would be a good time to have that talk with her? Five minutes after you've told her you're going back to your wife?'

'The sooner the better, don't you think? Before she says anything to anyone. You could go around now. I don't need you to hold my hand in the TV studio tonight.'

Dev was torn. He wanted to go and check on Jenny, make sure she was all right, and this would give him a legitimate excuse to do so. But the memory of the last time he had tried to comfort her held him back. He didn't want her to think he was being opportunistic, hoping for a repeat of that night. Neither did he want to appear concerned simply for Richard's career. He supposed he could console himself with the thought that Jenny could hardly think less of him than she already did – he had nothing to lose. It was a small consolation.

'Well, maybe now wouldn't be the best time,' Richard was saying. 'But you're going to have to talk to her at some point. I'll leave it up to you,' he said, standing and patting Dev's arm. 'Whatever you think.'

'Great. Thanks.'

'When you do see her, would you give her this?' He took a key from his pocket and handed it to Dev. 'It's the key to her flat. I forgot to give it to her earlier.'

Dev took it and put it in his pocket. 'I'll go now,' he said, determined to get over his qualms. Let Jenny think what she liked – it wasn't going to stop him doing what he thought was right.

There was no answer at Jenny's flat. The lights were on in the living room, so he persisted, leaning heavily on the bell, but there was still no answer. Damn! Either she was out, or she was in and refusing to answer the door. The second option filled him with dread. He thought of the state she had been in that night in Manchester. He hated to think she was in there now, all alone and similarly distraught. He leaned on the bell one last time, but there was still no response. Giving up, he was walking back to his car when he saw a figure emerge from the shadows across the road. A vaguely familiar boy crossed the road and approached him.

'Hello. Looking for Jenny?'

'Yes, how did you know?'

'I've seen you here with her before.' Dev remembered him then – Colin, Jenny's chief stalker, the one who ran the support group. 'Been locked out of Paradise, have you?' He smiled sympathetically, looking up pointedly at the light in Jenny's window.

'I don't think she's home,' Dev said curtly, turning to go to his car.

'Oh, she's home all right.'

'What?' Dev turned back.

'Sorry, mate.' Colin threw him a pitying look. 'She's home – she just doesn't want to see you.'

'How do you know?'

'I saw her – she came home about an hour ago.'

'Maybe she went out again.'

Colin shook his head. 'She didn't. Just accept it, mate,' he said gently. 'It's over.'

But Dev was already brushing past him and striding back to Jenny's front door. He pressed the bell again repeatedly. Shit! She was in there, probably crying her eyes out. Open the door, he begged her silently. Just open the fucking door.

Colin had trotted after him and was standing beside him. 'Look, we've all been there,' he said, putting a restraining hand on Dev's arm. 'I know it's hard, but you have to respect her decision.'

'Fuck off!' Dev snarled, shaking away Colin's hand and ringing the bell again.

'Come on, give it up,' Colin said persuasively. 'Why don't we go and have a cup of coffee and talk about it?'

Dev whipped around to him. 'I said fuck off!' he shouted. He turned back to the door, kicking it in impotent frustration. Damn!

Then he suddenly remembered – he had a key. Cursing himself for being such an idiot, he pulled it from his pocket and put it in the lock.

'Oh! You have a key! Why didn't you—'

He let himself in and slammed the door in Colin's face before he could finish his sentence.

He raced up the stairs and knocked on the door of her flat. He didn't expect an answer, but he didn't want to give her a fright by just barging in without warning. 'Jenny?' he called through the door. 'It's me, Dev.' He put his ear to the door, listening, but he couldn't hear anything.

He knocked again, harder this time. 'Jenny, please open the door.' Still no answer. He used the key then and let himself in.

The flat was eerily quiet. There was no one in the living room or kitchen. She must have gone out again after all, he thought – Colin had missed her. But he still went to check all the rooms. When he saw a light on in one of the bedrooms, he knocked on the door rapidly before pushing it open – and there she was, lying on the bed, fast asleep. She must have worn herself out crying – or drunk herself into a stupor, he thought, catching sight of the vodka bottle on the bedside table. She must have really knocked herself out to sleep through his persistent ringing of the doorbell. He approached the bed and looked down at her, shaking her shoulder gently.

'Jenny.' He shook her again, harder this time, but there was still no response. Fear gripped him and he wondered how much of the vodka she had drunk. Maybe he should try to rouse her – she could have alcohol poisoning. Then he caught sight of the pill bottle and his heart leaped into his mouth. He snatched it up and read the label.

'Jesus!' he breathed, the bottle falling from his hand to the floor.

'Jenny!' he shouted, shaking her vigorously now. She flopped back lifelessly from his hands. His heart hammering, he slapped her hard across the face, but still she didn't wake. With shaking fingers he grabbed the phone, dialled 999 and called for an ambulance. His voice sounded strange and hollow, his tongue so thick in his mouth he was afraid they wouldn't understand what he was saying.

Then he went back to the bed and sat her up. He slapped her face again as hard as he could bear to, and her eyes flickered open a fraction. She moaned softly, her head flopping to the side as her eyes closed again.

'No! Jenny, you've got to stay awake. Please, I need you to stay awake for me.'

She mumbled something incoherently, her speech slurred.

'There's an ambulance on the way. I just need you to stay awake until it gets here. It won't be long.' He prayed that it wouldn't.

Only when Dev was sitting outside in A and E did he think to contact Richard. It had all been such a blur from the moment the ambulance team had arrived. He hadn't thought about any of the wider implications until he had dialled Richard's private mobile and he had picked up. Then he realised he couldn't risk telling him what had happened on an insecure line. He just said Jenny had been rushed to hospital and asked him to come as quickly as he could. Then he sank into a chair, slumped forward on his knees and buried his head in his hands. Weariness overwhelmed him.

About half an hour later, a white-faced Richard rushed in. 'Dev, what's happened? Where's Jenny?' He looked panicked.

Dev stood to meet him. 'She's in there.' He nodded to a treatment room. 'They're working on her now.'

'What happened to her?'

Dev propelled him into a chair and sat down beside him. 'She took an overdose. When I went to her flat, I found her unconscious.'

'Jesus!' Richard was obviously struggling to take this in.

'She'd taken sleeping pills and drunk some vodka. But she's going to be fine.'

Richard nodded absently. He looked severely shaken. 'Thank God you went over there.'

'It was lucky you'd given me the key,' Dev's voice wobbled. It was lucky Colin had been there too – lucky he was such a nosy parker. There were so many variables he didn't want to think about it.

'Oh, God, Dev.' Richard put his head into his hands. When he looked up again, there was the gleam of tears in his eyes. 'She seemed fine! When I told her, she took it so well.'

'Appearances can be deceptive,' Dev said tightly.

'Do you really think she meant to ...'

'I don't know.'

They sat in silence for a long time.

'I think someone might have followed me here,' Richard finally said.

Dev gave him a sharp look. 'What do you mean by "someone"? Press?'

'Yeah. I think they followed me here from the TV studio.'

'Shit! Did you say anything to anyone about where you were going?'

'I just said that there was an emergency – nothing specific. I didn't even mention Jenny.'

'Well, we can put out a story that Jenny was rushed to hospital with food poisoning or a burst appendix or something – the most mundane emergency we can think of. The hospital staff will have to maintain patient confidentiality.' He spoke robotically. He didn't want to think about how to spin this right now. He didn't care. He just wanted Jenny to be all right.

'Christ, when I think what could have happened!' Richard raked a hand through his hair agitatedly.

'But it didn't. She's going to be fine. They don't think she took too many—' He broke off as he saw Richard's face and realised he had misunderstood. He wasn't thinking about what could have happened to Jenny. 'Don't worry, Richard. You'll be fine.'

Just then the door of the treatment room opened and a doctor came out to them. 'She's awake now,' he told them, 'though she's still very groggy. We'll be admitting her. Has her next of kin been notified?'

'She doesn't have any family,' Richard answered.

'Can we see her now?' Dev asked.

'Well, for a moment – perhaps just one of you?'

'You go,' Dev said to Richard. 'You're the one she'll want to see.'

'Right. Maybe you could get started on that thing we were discussing.'

'I'll take care of it,' Dev said. 'Don't I always?'

Richard opened the door and Dev glimpsed Jenny lying in the bed with tubes coming out of her arm. She looked so small and fragile.

'Darling,' Richard said, taking her hand, 'you gave us the most awful fright. Please don't ever—' The door swung closed and Dev heard no more.

He walked briskly down the corridor and out of the hospital, glancing around for waiting journalists. He strode to the edge of the kerb and flagged down a cab, apparently unobserved. He had left his car outside Jenny's flat, but he decided he would collect it in the morning. He felt dazed on the drive home, staring unseeingly out the window, his mind blank. It was only when he got out of the cab and was fishing money out of his pocket to pay the driver that he realised he was shaking. His hand trembled as he handed over the notes, and his legs felt weak as he walked to the door. His mobile beeped, but he ignored it. He couldn't deal with anyone yet, and he wasn't ready to answer questions about Jenny. His face felt as if it was cracking and the numbness inside him was about to melt. He fumbled with the key, his fingers wooden and clumsy. Once inside, he went to the living room, sat down on the sofa and started to cry.

Chapter 34

The next day Dev picked Jenny up from the hospital. When he arrived she was already sitting on her bed waiting, fully dressed – but not in the clothes she had been wearing last night when he found her. Instead she had on a cream dress with a red tulip print, her cardigan and flat pumps the exact colour of the flowers on the dress. She had a red scarf tied in her hair, and a lump came to Dev's throat as he saw that she even had red tulip earrings. God, what was wrong with him? Why did he find that so bloody touching?

'Dev!' She beamed up at him when he came in.

'Hello, Jenny. You look beautiful.'

'Ta-da!' She struck a pose. 'Do you like it? It's my getting-out-of-hospital outfit.'

Dev couldn't help smiling. 'Where did you get it?'

'I got Liam to bring me in my stuff this morning. All I had was the dress I was wearing last night, and that was a bit ... messed up,' she said, the smile slipping.

'I brought you these.' Feeling idiotic, Dev handed her a huge bunch of flowers.

'Oh, they're gorgeous!' She took them from him and buried her nose in the blooms. 'You shouldn't have. That's so sweet. Why would you go and do a thing like that?'

'Well, it's normal to bring flowers to people in hospital, isn't it?'

'Oh, they're for the cover story, I suppose. Very clever!'

'The cover story?'

'Yeah – Richard told me you're going to make something up or something, to keep him out of the shit. Sorry I landed you in it.'

'Richard told you about that? Already?'

She nodded. 'Last night. I was a bit out of it, but I spoke to him again this morning, so don't worry – I know my lines.'

'Right,' Dev said faintly. 'Good.' He couldn't believe Richard had bothered her with that when she was lying in hospital after taking an overdose. 'Okay,' he said briskly, 'let's get you out of here. Got all your stuff?'

'Yes.' She hopped off the bed and staggered a little. He reached out to steady her and she took his arm gratefully. 'Whoa, head rush.' She giggled.

She looked well, but close up he could see the sickly pallor of her skin.

'Thank you.' She picked up her bag. 'I was only here the one night, so this is all I have with me,' she said, swinging it onto her arm. 'I bet I look a right tart compared to the other patients with all their luggage.'

Dev linked her arm as they walked down the corridor and she leaned on him slightly.

'Now,' she said, 'I need to talk to you about something. Richard tells me you're thinking of giving me a burst appendix.'

'That's right.'

'Not very glamorous, is it? Couldn't I have something a bit more interesting?'

'What did you have in mind?'

'Hmm.' She frowned thoughtfully. 'What about a snake bite?' she suggested, with childlike glee. 'I could have been bitten by a cobra!

That'd be exciting, wouldn't it?'

'In central London?'

'Oh, yeah. I suppose that wouldn't work.' She looked disappointed.

'It could have escaped from the zoo, I suppose.'

'Now you're thinking.'

'Or you could have been bitten by a tarantula.'

'Ugh, no. I don't want to be bitten by a tarantula.'

'But you do want to be bitten by a snake?'

'You know what I mean. Ooh – I know! A poisoned umbrella!'

'What?'

'Yeah. I could have got in the way of an assassination attempt on a Russian spy.'

'Hmm, I can see how that might happen. It's rush hour, you get jostled in the crowd ...'

'Exactly. It could happen to anyone.'

'Probably happens every day.'

'So I can have umbrella poisoning?' She grinned up at him.

'No. You're getting a burst appendix.'

'You're no fun at all.'

'Shut up or I'll give you an ingrown toenail.'

'Thanks for picking me up,' she said, sitting in the car beside him. 'There was no need. I could have got a taxi.'

'Don't be daft.'

She looked across at him, noticing how pale and drawn he was. 'Dev,' she said in a small voice, 'I'm sorry. I know you were the one who found me, and I'm really sorry about that.'

'You're sorry I found you?'

'Oh, no! No, I wasn't trying to ... I didn't really want to off myself.'

'You didn't? Then why—'

'I don't know,' she said, tears stinging her eyes. But she tried to explain. If anyone deserved an explanation, it was him. 'It was like … you know when you just lash out at someone in the heat of the moment but you don't really mean to hurt them? It was like that.'

'Except you lashed out at yourself.'

'Yeah, something like that. I'm all I've got.' She laughed wryly. She looked down for a moment, blinking rapidly. 'Anyway, I'm sorry you had to find me like that,' she said. 'It must have been horrible for you.'

'I'm just glad I did find you.'

'So am I,' she said, suddenly throwing her arms around him and holding on tight. 'Thank you.'

'You're welcome,' he murmured against her hair, hugging her back.

'Okay,' she said, straightening back into her seat. 'Let's go home.'

'You can't go home, Jenny. There'll be press all over the place. You need to rest and recuperate. You need to get out of London for a while – lie low.'

'Oh! So where were you planning to take me, then?'

'I've got the weekend off and I'm going home to visit my parents. I thought you might like to come with me.'

'Oh, no, I couldn't do that. They don't even know me. I couldn't impose on them.'

'You won't be imposing. They love it when I bring friends home – especially my mum.' He smiled fondly. 'The more people to fuss over, the merrier, as far as she's concerned.'

'Dev, I'm not your problem any more. I'll just go home. I'll take my chances with the press. And don't worry, I won't say anything I shouldn't.'

'It's not about that. You need to rest, Jenny,' he said. 'I've been to your flat and it's surrounded by press staking it out. You won't get a minute's peace there – especially once the news breaks about you and Richard.'

'I could go to a hotel – some place where the press will never find me.'

'No, I'm not taking you to a hotel.'

'How come you've got the weekend off anyway? Shouldn't you be in Scotland with Richard?'

'No – Alan's taking over.' Alan was Dev's deputy.

God, poor Dev – she obviously *was* still his problem. She was seen as someone who could damage Richard and had to be managed, and he had been given the task of babysitting her. If it wasn't for her he'd be out on the campaign trail.

She suddenly realised that this was it – once Richard's reconciliation with Julia was announced, she would be completely out of the picture and there would be no reason for Dev to see her again. They would go back to their own very separate worlds. She found the thought strangely terrifying. She considered her options. She could go home now and start her new life without Richard ... without Dev. Or she could grab her last chance to spend time with Dev.

'Come on,' Dev pleaded. 'My mum will be disappointed if you don't come. She's already expecting you.'

'Okay, then. Let's go to your parents'.'

'Great!' He gunned the engine and pulled out into the traffic.

'Wait, though – I don't have any clothes. Can we go by my place?'

He looked at her a little warily. 'I actually have some stuff of yours in the boot – from Richard's flat.'

'Oh. Oh, great. That's handy. That was very ... efficient of him.'

It was one of those lovely spring days when the world feels as clean and fragrant as freshly laundered sheets. They were soon on the motorway, bowling out of London, and as the landscape turned green, Jenny felt herself relax. She rang Liam as they drove to let him know she wouldn't be home.

'I'm going to Yorkshire with Dev for the weekend, to stay with his parents,' she told him.

'Great. He seems like a good bloke – unlike that tosser he works for.'

'It's not like that,' she mumbled into the phone, aware that Dev could hear. 'He's just doing his job. I guess he drew the short straw and got lumbered with babysitting me. They think it's a good idea if I don't go home just yet – wait until the press interest in me dies down a bit.'

'Well, they're right about that. A few of them have been hanging around outside here. I had a bit of a punch-up with one of them last night. They caught me coming home with the boss's wife and tried to take a picture.'

'Oh, God.' Jenny groaned. Liam's boss was a very famous Michelin-starred chef. 'Sorry!'

'Don't worry about it, sweetheart. All he got for his trouble was a couple of broken fingers and some very bruised balls.'

Jenny laughed.

'Well, enjoy Yorkshire. Take care of yourself.'

'Jenny,' Dev said when she had hung up. 'I'm sorry, but I couldn't help overhearing. I didn't draw any short straw. I volunteered.'

'You did? Why?'

'Because I care about you.'

'Oh.'

'As a friend,' he added quickly.

'Really? So we're friends now?'

'Aren't we?' He smiled at her. 'I like to think so.'

'I'd like that too.' She took a deep breath, trying to get up the courage to say what she needed to say. 'Dev,' she said, 'I'm sorry I was so horrible to you that morning – you know, after we ... that morning in Manchester. I was just so wound up that day about seeing Mum – and then not seeing her. I said a lot of things I didn't mean.' She was struggling to find a way to tell him how she really felt.

'I said some pretty daft things myself that morning, as I recall. You were right, I was being ridiculous.'

'You mean ... when you said you were in love with me?'

'Yes. I'm sorry if I made you uncomfortable. I don't know what came over me. Let's just say I had a rush of blood to the head.'

'So you didn't mean it either?'

'Well, I meant it at the time, but I'm over it now. So you don't have to worry about me trying it on or anything – or joining your merry band of stalkers.'

'So you're over me now?' Her voice sounded hollow to her own ears.

'Yes.' He turned to her and smiled affectionately. 'I'm over you.'

'I must be losing my touch – first Richard and now you.'

'Never.' He cleared his throat, turning his eyes back to the road. 'Actually, I'm seeing someone else now.'

'Really? Where did you meet her?'

'Oh, it's someone I've known for ages. We've been friends for ever, but recently we discovered it was something more.'

'Sounds great!' She smiled at him, finding it took a huge effort. Her face felt frozen.

'Yeah, it is.'

They arrived in the dusk of early evening. Jenny had slept for a good deal of the journey, and woke up just as Dev was driving through a quaint little village.

'Almost there,' he said as he turned into a driveway just beyond the village. At the end of the long sweep of gravel, a large house was surrounded by fields, the glow of light from the windows warm and welcoming.

Dev helped Jenny out of the car and got their bags out of the boot. As they approached the door, it was opened by an attractive woman with a neat brown bob.

'Hi, Mum.' Dev bent to embrace her, giving her a kiss on the cheek.

'Oh, it's so lovely to see you, sweetheart.' She beamed as she threw her arms around her son.

'This is Jenny,' he said when he was released.

'Hello, Jenny.' Dev's mum smiled, taking her hand. 'You're very welcome. It's lovely to have you here.'

'Thank you. It's really nice of you to have me, Mrs Tennant.'

'Oh, call me Sue,' she said as she ushered them past her into the house. 'Now, supper will be ready soon, so come on and I'll show you to your room so you can get settled in.'

'Where's Dad?' Dev asked her.

'He's out on a call, but he should be back shortly.'

Sue led the way upstairs and Jenny followed her, with Dev behind, carrying their bags.

'You'll be in here, Jenny,' she said, stopping outside a door. 'I'll leave you to get settled – come down when you're ready. There's an en suite in your room and I've left you some towels. If there's anything else you need, just shout.'

'Thanks.'

Dev handed her the bag he had brought from Richard's. 'See you soon. If you need anything, I'm just next door,' he said, leaving her to it.

***

When she had showered and changed into jeans and a jumper, Jenny went downstairs and found everyone in the large rustic kitchen.

'Just in time, Jenny,' Sue said, straightening up from the oven. Dev was helping her place dishes on the table, and at the sink a tall grey-haired man was washing his hands. He turned as she came into the room and grabbed a towel to dry them quickly.

'Hello, I'm Daniel,' he said, coming towards her and shaking her hand. 'Pleased to meet you, Jenny.'

'Nice to meet you too.' He was very handsome – she could see where Dev got his good looks.

Dev pulled out a chair for her and she sat beside him at the large round table. Sue served her, piling her plate with delicious beef casserole, mashed potatoes and roasted vegetables. She relaxed as she ate, not talking much, but listening as the conversation flowed around her, enjoying the cosy domestic scene. Dev's father was a doctor and he entertained them with stories about his day, while Sue talked about her friends in the village.

'I met Mel's mum today,' she told Dev. 'She's delighted that Mel's home and done with traipsing around the world. Have you seen much of her since she got back?'

'A bit. I haven't had much time for socialising lately.'

'You work too hard.' Sue frowned at her son.

He gave her an indulgent smile. 'It won't be much longer – only until this election is over.'

'Well, it'll be nice for you having her back in London.'

'Mel's a great girl,' his father joined in enthusiastically.

'Jenny, I was thinking maybe you'd like to come shopping with me tomorrow?' Sue said to her. 'I'm trying to find something for a wedding next month, and so far it's been hopeless. It's always the way when you're looking for something, isn't it? Anyway, I thought it might help to get another opinion – and you have such a good eye for clothes.'

'Mum,' Dev chided.

'Only if you feel up to it, of course.'

'I'd love to,' Jenny told her.

'Oh, good. We can go to town tomorrow, then. Unless you had any plans, Dev?'

'The plan, Mum, was for Jenny to rest and recuperate – and to lie low, not to go haring around the shops after you.'

'Oh, don't mind him. I'd love to go with you. I'm not an invalid, you know,' she said to Dev.

'You *are* just out of hospital, Jenny.'

'We'll take it easy, I promise,' Sue said to her son.

The next day Jenny slept until almost lunchtime, the drug still in her system making her very droopy. She went shopping with Sue as promised in the afternoon, and she had fun helping her find an outfit for the wedding. She was worried at first that her presence might cause problems, but no one seemed to recognise her, or if they did, they discreetly pretended not to. Despite being supposedly on a weekend off, Dev spent most of the day on the phone to the office or Richard. She knew he had spoken to Richard several times throughout the day, but if Richard had asked after her, he never mentioned it.

She had lots of fresh air, delicious food, plenty of sleep and kind, solicitous people looking after her. She should have felt very rested and content – and she did, except for one thing. But that one thing seemed to cancel out all the rest, leaving her agitated and twitchy as she lay in bed that night. That one thing was Dev – the one thing she wanted above all else; the one thing she felt would heal her, make her whole; the one thing she now knew she could never have. It was driving her crazy knowing he was next door, one wall separating them.

If you need anything, I'm just next door. If only she could go in there and say, 'I need *you*.' She ached to crawl into his bed, to lie wrapped in his arms, to feel his weight on her, to be loved by him. If only she could go back to that morning in Manchester, knowing what she now knew. If only she hadn't been such a blind idiot. But she had had her chance with him and she had well and truly blown it. Their timing had been lousy.

Now he was over her and he was with someone else – someone he had known for a long time; a friendship that had turned into something more. From the dinner conversation this evening, she guessed it was Mel. She could tell in New York that they were close, though she hadn't seen anything to suggest they were interested in each other romantically. But clearly that had changed since her return to London.

She pressed her face into the pillow to muffle the sobs that threatened to escape from her throat. She couldn't believe she was crying again! What was the matter with her? She *never* cried. That night in Manchester was the first time she could remember really crying since she was a child. But now that she had started, she couldn't seem to stop.

'Do you really have to go today?' Sue asked the next morning as they were having breakfast. 'Couldn't you stay another couple of days?'

'Sorry, Mum. I've got to get back.'

'Well, I can see that *you* have to get back to London, Dev – I do realise that bloody man can't wipe his own nose. But do you have to go, Jenny? Couldn't you stay another few days?'

'Well, I don't know ...' She looked at Dev uncertainly.

'Only if you'd like to, of course,' his mother added.

'You should,' Dev encouraged her. 'Stay the week. It'll do you good. I could come and pick you up next weekend.'

She was tempted. She had phoned Lily, who had told her to take as much time as she needed to recover. She was still feeling very tired, and she did find it relaxing here. Besides, it would mean she'd have another opportunity to see Dev. 'If you're sure it's no bother?' she said to Sue.

'Quite the opposite,' Sue said. 'I'd love to have the company.'

'Then I'd love to stay.'

Dev left after lunch, and Jenny walked out to his car with him.

'Are you okay?' he said, studying her face.

'Yes, I'm fine.' She smiled – she didn't want him to go.

'Are you sure?' He stroked her cheek with the back of his hand.

'Yes.' She nodded breathlessly. His eyes darkened as he looked down at her and she held her breath, silently willing him to kiss her. Then he leaned down and pressed his lips to her cheek.

'See you on Sunday.' He got into the car and drove off.

Dev looked at Jenny in the rear-view mirror. She was standing in the driveway, waving at him. He hated leaving her and fought the urge to turn the car around and go back and get her. But he knew it would do her good: his mother would look after her and cosset her, and help her get better. She was looking healthier already, the colour back in her cheeks, some of the old spark returning to her eyes.

Still, he had heard her crying in her room last night and it tore at his heart. He had longed to go in to her and comfort her. But God knows where that would have led. Even just now in the drive, he had almost kissed her. This was pathetic, he thought, sighing. He was driving away but already he was looking forward to next Sunday when he would see her again.

**

The following days fell into an easy rhythm. Jenny slept a lot. She usually woke quite early in the morning, when the sun streamed into her bedroom, and shared breakfast with Sue on the little patio in the garden, Daniel having already gone to work for the day. The weather was mild and sunny, and she often fell asleep again there, lulled by the low hum of voices from Radio 4 while Sue pottered around in the kitchen. In the afternoons she would go on shopping trips with Sue in the village, and they would meet up with her friends in the tea shop, or they would drive to the nearest seaside town for a walk along the seafront. Other days she just lay in the hammock in the garden, reading and dozing. In the evening she would help Sue prepare dinner, and when Daniel came home they ate together, chatting, sometimes watching TV before bed.

Jenny had never felt so peaceful and relaxed in her whole life. It was all so easy and undemanding. She didn't have to make any decisions or try too hard to please anyone. She could just be. Though she was really looking forward to seeing Dev again (so much that it worried her if she thought about it), part of her was dreading him coming at the weekend to take her back to reality, out of this lovely warm cocoon.

Sue and Daniel were such easy company, and they both seemed to like having her there. She suspected Sue liked having someone to mother – and she was very good at it, quietly solicitous, but not over-bearingly so. They could chat together or sit in silence just as comfortably. When Sue began talking about Sally one day, Jenny was a little alarmed, not knowing what she should say. But she quickly realised she didn't have to say anything – Sue just needed someone to listen.

'She was an unhappy person,' Sue said with a sad smile. 'It was nothing to do with her circumstances or us, or anything that happened to her. There was nothing we could do about it, nothing that made her feel better or happier. It was just in her. That's an awful thing – you're so helpless. And you blame yourself, of course, at first. You keep thinking, What could we have done differently or better?

But the truth is, there was absolutely nothing we could have done that would have made any difference.' Sue's voice caught and her eyes welled up with tears.

'We couldn't save her … from herself,' she continued. 'Dev always thought he could save her if he just found the right doctor, got her into the right programme. Men think like that, don't they, in terms of solutions? Poor Dev … he tried everything. 'It doesn't stop you feeling the guilt, of course – knowing that there's nothing you could have done. But it does lessen it a bit, over time. I've met up with people whose children have committed suicide by more … straightforward methods, and they all feel the same way.'

Suicide! The word gave Jenny a jolt. She had never thought of Sally's death like that before. She felt immediately guilty. '*I'm not …* a sad person,' she said tentatively, wanting to reassure Sue, who had been so kind to her.

'Sorry?' Sue looked confused.

'I mean, I'm not naturally a sad person. It's not in me, like you were saying about Sally.'

'No – I can see you're not.' Sue was still bewildered.

Jenny sighed, looking down at her hands. 'I just mean you don't have to worry that I'm going to try it again or anything. I wasn't even trying really the first time, it just—'

'Try? Try what?'

Oh, God, she didn't know. Dev hadn't told her. Not hard to see why, in the circumstances – he wouldn't want to freak her out by telling her he was leaving a suicidal girl with her.

'I don't know what Dev told you,' she began, 'but I didn't really have a burst appendix like it said in the papers.' She took a deep breath and looked Sue in the eye. 'I took an overdose.' She watched nervously as Sue absorbed this information. 'I'm sorry, I thought you knew. I thought Dev … he should have told you.'

'Dev wouldn't consider it his place to tell me that – it's personal,' Sue said, sounding rather defensive of her son. 'But I'm glad *you* told me, Jenny. Thank you.'

'Well, you have a right to know when I'm staying in your house,' she said, still surprised Dev hadn't seen it that way. Perhaps Sue wouldn't have let her stay if she'd known. 'I just didn't want you to be worried that I'd try it again while I'm here. Turns out the best way to do that would have been to keep my mouth shut.' She laughed wryly. 'I didn't even mean it the first time,' she continued, feeling compelled to explain it to Sue as best she could. 'I have no intention of ever doing it again, but if you want me to leave, I understand.'

'Leave?' Sue sounded alarmed. 'Of course I don't want you to leave. I did suspect there was more to it than Dev told me. But I'm not worried. I'm sure Dev wouldn't have left you here if he'd thought there was any danger of you doing that.'

'Dev was the one who found me,' Jenny told her quietly.

'Really?' A strange look that Jenny couldn't decipher flickered across Sue's face at this. Jenny wondered what it meant. She seemed panicked almost. Was she worried that Dev had found another hopeless case to try to save? Was that why Dev wanted to be friends with her now – so he could try to rescue her?

Chapter 35

The following Sunday Dev went back to his parents' house to pick up Jenny and bring her back to London. He was leaning against the kitchen table, talking to his mother, when she walked in. He got a jolt when he saw her. She had dyed her hair a rich dark brown, and her face was devoid of make-up, making her skin appear almost translucent. She looked different, but still so bloody gorgeous.

'Dev!' Her face lit up when she saw him and she treated him to that wraparound smile.

'Hello.' He felt his own mouth spread in a wide, answering grin. 'How are you?'

'I'm great – really well.'

'You look good. I like the hair.'

'Do you?' Her fingers played with it. 'I thought it might help me be a bit more incognito when I go back to London.'

'Worth a try.' It wouldn't work, he thought. She was as stunning as ever and would still stand out in any crowd. He leaned away from the table. 'Are you ready to go?'

Her face fell a little, but she recovered quickly, smiling again when she said, 'Yes.'

'Oh, I thought you'd stay for lunch,' his mother said, not hiding her disappointment. 'Jenny and I made rhubarb tart.'

Dev glanced at his watch. 'You made rhubarb tart?' he asked Jenny.

'Well, I helped.'

'I suppose I could stay for lunch,' he said and was rewarded by Jenny's face lighting up once more. God, how could you ever refuse her anything when she had that weapon at her disposal? 'As long as we leave straight after.'

On the drive back to London, Jenny felt all the relaxation of the last week ebb away. She was as nervous as a kitten. When Dev reached across to her, she jumped, thinking for a moment he was going to touch her leg. Her heart was already pounding in anticipation. But he was just reaching into the side pocket of her door to get a map. Of course he wouldn't be putting a hand on her thigh, she told herself. She was being ridiculous! He would never touch her in that way again.

The closer they got to London, the more tense she felt. She was aware that this was the last bit. Once Dev dropped her off at home, she would probably never see him again. She wanted this car journey to go on for ever.

'Oh, look!' She pointed as they passed some large signs for a stately home. 'Have you ever been there?'

'No.'

'I've always wanted to see it.'

'Really? I didn't think that would be your sort of thing.'

'Can we go?'

'Now?'

'Oh, you probably haven't got time. I'm sorry – you'll need to get back to London.' She tried not to look disappointed.

'I really do need to get back. Sorry. Anyway, I think we've passed the entrance.'

With a huge effort of will, she refrained from asking him to stop at the theme park, the medieval castle, the village fête or the car-boot sale that were all signposted along their route. But when he pulled up outside her door, she couldn't contain herself any longer. 'It's the market today,' she said. 'Why don't we go?'

'To Camden Market?' He looked at his watch. 'It'll almost be closing.'

Her heart sank. She knew she was clutching at straws, trying to eke out this last bit of time with him. She didn't want to say goodbye. But he had probably wasted enough time with her already. She had to cut the cord some time. Now was as good a time as any.

'I suppose we could catch the tail end of it,' he said, and her heart leaped. Just then his mobile rang. He answered it, talking the whole time he took her bag from the boot and carried it upstairs for her. 'Sorry,' he said when he finally disconnected. 'I've got to go. But we can do the market another time, okay?'

'Sure, okay.' But she knew there would be no other time.

The following Sunday night Jenny was at home alone when the doorbell rang.

'Jenny?' a familiar voice crackled through the entry phone. 'Hi, it's Colin.'

'Oh.' She was shocked into silence. She hoped he wasn't back-sliding.

'Could I see you for a minute? I don't want to come in. Can you just come down to the door?'

'Okay.' She grabbed her keys and ran downstairs. When she opened the door, Colin was standing there, hands behind his back, a huge grin on his face, clearly very pleased with himself. 'Hi,' she said. She was a bit disconcerted by him turning up like this, but he looked so damn happy, as if he was about to burst out laughing. She couldn't help smiling back at him.

'Hello, Jenny. I just came to give you this.' He drew one arm from behind his back and held up an animal cage. Inside, a ball of white and brown fluff was snuffling around, its eyes shining brightly in the darkness.

'Oh, my God, Johnny Scrambod!' Tears sprang to her eyes as Colin handed the cage to her. 'I don't believe it!'

Colin still had that grin plastered to his face.

'Thank you so much. How did you—'

'We finally got Paul to see the error of his ways and become one of us.'

'Oh, that's great!'

'Yeah. So ... the circle is complete. My work is done.' Colin had always had a slight tendency to speak like someone from a *Star Wars* movie.

'Does this mean you'll be hanging up your binoculars?'

Colin laughed. 'Yeah. You'll be glad to hear you won't be seeing me out here again.'

'Well, it's been a while now since I've broken any hearts. I think I'm losing my touch.'

'Hardly.' He smiled. 'But it's true we haven't had any new recruits for a while. Well, apart from that Dev bloke, but he seems pretty sorted.'

'Dev?'

'Yeah, you know, tall, looks a bit cross most of the time? Don't tell me you've forgotten him already. Poor bloke!'

'No, I just ... he wasn't ...' Bastard! But she couldn't tell Colin that Dev had only joined the group to spy on them – it would be too humiliating for him. 'We weren't together long,' she said. 'It wasn't serious – for either of us.'

'Really? He seems like a top bloke. Actually, it was him who started the campaign to free Johnny Scrambod. I'll say this for you, Jenny,' he grinned, 'you always had great taste in men.'

'Thanks.'

'Anyway, our little group is starting to break up. Mac's getting married.'

'Mac? Oh, that's great!'

'Yeah, we're all going to the wedding.'

'Maybe you'll meet someone nice there.'

He smiled smugly. 'No need for that – I'm bringing a date. I think everyone is, actually.'

'Oh, Colin, that's great. I'm so pleased for you, really – for all of you.' He looked so happy – he couldn't stop smiling.

'Yeah, well … we're all moving on, I guess. I'm going to close down the website.'

'Great. That's brilliant. Well, thanks again for bringing Johnny Scrambod back. Take care,' she said.

'You too. Bye, Jenny.' He nodded and turned to go. He was halfway across the street when she put Johnny Scrambod down in the hall and ran after him.

'How do you do it?' she asked.

'What?'

'Move on – how do you do that?'

His eyes widened. 'Oh, has someone— Shit!' He winced sympathetically. 'I'm sorry.'

'Yeah, well – probably serves me right for all the hearts I've broken, right?'

'No,' he said. 'You did your best – we all knew that. You really tried.'

'Tried? What do you mean?'

'You tried to love us. It wasn't your fault that you … you just didn't.' He laughed softly to himself. 'Mac said sometimes you were trying so hard he could almost see steam coming out of your ears.'

'God,' she breathed. She felt winded. All those boys ... all those boys who had known her better than she knew herself. What was it Dev had said? *You go about things the wrong way around*. Had she really never loved any of them? She had tried – she had done her best, as Colin had said. She had found men who loved her and set about doing her damnedest to love them back. But when it didn't work, she'd simply moved on. It was easy, because as hard as she tried, she had never quite succeeded – not even with Richard.

'I *did* try, didn't I?' she whispered. 'I tried really hard.'

'Don't beat yourself up about it. It shouldn't be such hard work.'

'No. It's not hard work at all, is it? It's so easy. It just happens, when you're not even looking. I guess that's why they call it falling.'

'I guess so. Well, I'd best be off.'

'Bye, Colin, and thanks – for Johnny and ... for everything.' She gave him a kiss on the cheek. 'Give my best wishes to Mac.'

'Will do. Hey, maybe you should—' He broke off. 'No, bad idea. Well, bye, then. I do have a list of tips for moving on. I'll send them to you. Number one rule,' he pointed a finger at her, 'no stalking, okay?'

'No stalking – promise.'

Chapter 36

'Jenny! Jenny, did you see me? I scored a goal!' Hannah came thundering off the playing field and ran up to Jenny on her chubby little legs.

'I know! You were brilliant!' Jenny stroked her blonde hair, which was darkened and matted to her head with sweat. 'Are you hungry?' she asked as she put on Hannah's jacket, already knowing the answer. She was always hungry after football.

'Starving!'

She took her hand and they walked across the Heath to Hampstead village. It was a lovely Saturday morning and the Heath was full of people enjoying the sunshine. Lily had gone to a wedding, so Jenny was babysitting for the day.

'Jenny?' Hannah broke into her thoughts. 'I love you.' She beamed up at her.

'I love you too, Hannah.' She smiled down at the little girl, her heart giving a lurch.

'I love you second best,' Hannah chirped on.

'Wow, second best! I'm flattered!'

'Because Mummy's first best,' she explained.

'Of course she is,' Jenny said cheerfully, to show that she wasn't offended to be second. 'Mummies are always first best.'

'Is your mummy your first best?'

'No, you are.' She smiled down at Hannah, swinging her hand.

'But what about your mummy?'

'I … I don't have a mummy.'

'What about your daddy, then?'

'I don't have a daddy either.'

'Same as me.'

Jenny squeezed Hannah's little hand in hers. She wondered if it bothered her, not having a father. Lily was single, and she knew Hannah's father hadn't been involved from the beginning. It was all Hannah had ever known and she seemed to take it in her stride. But as they wandered along the high street, she wondered if the little girl ever felt the gap on days like this. It seemed like happy families day in Hampstead today. Everywhere you turned, good-looking young couples were pushing buggies, swinging toddlers between them, pausing to peer into estate agents' windows. It was like a living advertisement for family life.

And in the midst of it all, she and Hannah knew life wasn't like that.

She took Hannah to the Coffee Cup and sat opposite her, watching her eat raisin toast and give herself a hot chocolate moustache. She sank her teeth into her own raisin toast and looked around the buzzing little café. They were all in here too – the couples, the families, all the people who belonged to each other. And herself and Hannah, the impostors, who didn't belong to each other but looked as if they did.

It would be Jenny's birthday soon. Another year older with nothing to show for it – some experiences, yes, but nothing lasting. Richard – another dead end, back with his wife; her exes – all moving on; Dev … Her mind shrank away from thoughts of him, but she forced it back – Dev, who had someone else now. So there was no point in pining for him. That would get her precisely nowhere. No more wandering around Primrose Hill in her spare time hoping to bump into him. The world was never that small when you wanted it to be. Anyway, what would be the point? She could tell herself they were friends and it was okay to ask him to go for a casual drink. Maybe he'd even accept. But it wouldn't change the fact that he was with someone else now. He had moved on and so must she.

Hell, she'd never had any trouble moving on before. A whole gang of men out there could testify to that. Slash and burn – it was her forte. No, she'd indulged that moping crap long enough and it was time to snap out of it. She didn't want to find herself in ten years' time still looking after other people's children, hovering around the edges of other people's lives. She wanted a bit of what these people had for herself, she thought, looking around at the golden couples – and she wasn't going to get it sitting around feeling sorry for herself. She needed to find herself a new boyfriend. It was time to dust off her dancing shoes – starting tomorrow.

On second thought … She reached into her bag and took out her mobile – no time like the present. She typed a text to Liam:

Where's the party 2nite?

Starting … right … now, she thought, pressing send. A moment later her phone chimed and she read Liam's answering text:

She's back! Tony's place, KentishTown. C u l8r

The following Tuesday night, Julia stood in the kitchen of Richard's constituency house, looking out into the garden. The light was fading, but she could still see the men moving around out there, turning their suburban garden into a scene from a James Bond film. You couldn't tell from here, but they were all armed to the teeth.

Security around Richard had already increased exponentially and the results weren't even in yet. However, early exit polls indicated a landslide victory for the Moderates.

'Welcome to the goldfish bowl,' she mumbled to herself, but Dev, standing beside her, heard.

'This is what you wanted,' he said.

'You know what they say – be careful what you wish for.' She smiled ruefully, and was relieved when he smiled back. He was so defensive and angry about the way things had happened – still so protective of that girl. She could understand his feelings, but it was unfair of him to resent her for it. After all, she had only taken back what was rightfully hers. She knew he understood that on some level and didn't blame her for it. He just hated what had happened to the girl.

'I'm not complaining, really,' she said. 'It's just going to be a bit of an adjustment. And I do worry about how it will affect the kids.'

'They'll be fine.' He smiled down at her. 'You all will.'

'They loved this morning,' she said. They had all dressed up in new clothes and gone to the polling station together. Afterwards they had posed for family photographs at the behest of the assembled media. 'And they're going to have a ball tomorrow. Of course, that's assuming—'

Dev grinned. 'Come on, this is me. You don't have to pretend it's not a sure thing.'

'He's going to be really good, isn't he?' She gestured across the kitchen to Richard, who was surrounded by office and constituency people. 'That's the main thing.'

'He's going to be great.'

It had been a good day, Julia thought as Dev drifted away. She had enjoyed going off to the ballot as a family, the feeling that they were embarking on this great adventure together. It was like setting off on the most amazing trip. All day, people had wandered in and out of the house, and she had kept them all fed and happy. She had made two vast trays of lasagne yesterday, knowing an elastic feast would be required. The house was still full of people and Richard was constantly surrounded. The result was a foregone conclusion, but the atmosphere was oddly subdued, despite the undercurrent of triumph. Everyone was on a high about the expected result and keyed up about tomorrow, but they were too exhausted after the long slog of the campaign to feel much more than relief at the moment. Tomorrow they would be swept up and carried along by events, and they would relax and celebrate properly. For now, they were just happy to heave a huge collective sigh of relief that it was over and they had done all they could. Now it was out of their hands.

Dev was right – this was what she wanted. Nonetheless, she didn't think it unreasonable to mourn the passing of her old life just a little – or that mixed with the elation there was an element of trepidation. It was only natural to feel a little nostalgic for a life she had cherished – and to be a bit nervous about what the future would hold. There was the loss of privacy to contend with, and she knew that wasn't going to be easy – the lack of independence, the public scrutiny. Already their freedom was being curtailed, she thought, glancing out at the men in the garden.

Still, she knew there would be lots of compensations. Richard would have the opportunity to make a real difference, and she would have the satisfaction of being part of that. She would have a front-row seat while history was being made. And she knew there would be lots of fun and exciting aspects to the job too. They would be fine. She would cope – she always did. Adapt and survive.

Looking around the room, she sighed contentedly. The kitchen was full of friends and well-wishers, Party people and neighbours, the sound of excited chatter reverberating around the walls, the cheery heat of the Aga enveloping them all in its warm fug. She hoped she wasn't smug – she couldn't bear smugness – but she was content. Looking across the room, she caught Richard's eye and he smiled at her.

This was where she wanted to be. She had got her life back, and she could only feel glad about that. It wasn't just Richard but the whole package that came with him. She wasn't one of those women who had thought her life was over when her husband left. She was independent and resourceful. She could have had a life without Richard, and it would have been a good one – she had no interest in martyrdom. But this was the life she wanted – this life with him, with their children, surrounded by the friends and neighbours they had known for years; and beyond that to be involved in something bigger than themselves, to be among people who cared about things – big, important things. It was *her* life and she was glad to have it back. Everything was as it should be again.

As he watched the results coming in, Dev found his mind straying to Jenny. He wondered what it would have been like if she had been here today – if she was still with Richard. What would she have made of it all? And what kind of prime minister's partner would she have been? No doubt she would have taken it in her stride, as she did everything. She would have done her best to slip chameleon-like into Richard's world – adapt and survive. And she would have succeeded, mostly, blending in almost seamlessly with her surroundings, only the occasional flash of brilliant colour giving her away.

He wondered where she was tonight …

At four thirty a.m. Jenny was standing across the road from Dev's house. If Colin could see me now, she thought, he'd be so disappointed. She was breaking the number one rule for moving on. Then again, she wasn't stalking Dev so much as his house. She knew he wasn't in. He would probably be at the victory party by now, and most likely, he wouldn't be home all night. Surely standing outside an empty house didn't count as stalking.

It did count as psychotic, though. This was getting to be a bad habit, and she needed to get a grip. The first time she had come here was one night when she had had a panic attack. She had decided that since she wanted to be outside she might as well go somewhere rather than wandering the streets randomly. So she had ended up here, and she had found it strangely comforting to know that Dev was just a few feet away. After that she hadn't waited for a panic attack and had taken to coming here on her way home from parties. The first had been in nearby Chalk Farm, but since then she had made longer and longer detours to pass his house on the way home. She knew it was sad and crazy, but it had become a sort of ritual and she couldn't seem to stop herself.

As she watched, a taxi pulled up outside the house and her heart lurched as she watched Dev emerge from the back.

Oh, shit, she had to get out of here – and fast. He couldn't find her loitering outside his house like a nutter. Still, she couldn't quite tear herself away and stood watching as he paid the driver, the light breeze ruffling his dark hair. Just as she dragged her eyes away and turned on her heel to go, he looked up.

Shit, shit, shit! She walked quickly away, not sure if he had seen her but praying he hadn't. She would have broken into a run but it would only have drawn his attention to her.

'Jenny!' She heard him call from the other side of the street, and picked up her pace. 'Jenny, is that you?' His voice was closer now behind her. Bugger! He would easily catch up with her – one of his strides equalled about four of hers. There was nothing for it but to face the music. She stopped and turned to find him within a couple of feet of her.

'Oh, hi!' She smiled brightly, attempting a fancy-meeting-you-here expression.

'Hi,' he said, a little breathlessly. 'What are you doing here?'

'I might ask the same of you.'

He looked at her disbelievingly. 'I live here. That's my house.' He waved across the road.

'Oh, yes, of course – I knew that.'

'So – what *are* you doing here?'

Jenny quickly ran through her options in her head. 'Oh, I just happened to be in the neighbourhood.'

'Really?' He looked at his watch. 'It's a quarter to five. What on earth would you be doing in the neighbourhood at this time?'

'I'm … I'm on my way home from … a party.' Well, that was true anyway.

'Ah! Right.' He nodded. 'Well, that's a coincidence. For a minute there, I thought—'

'That I was stalking you? I'm not!'

'No, of course not.' He gave a short laugh. 'I just thought maybe …' He didn't finish the thought. 'Where was the party?'

'Oh, on that road over there.' She pointed to the one that crossed the end of his street. If she told him it had been in Chelsea, he'd know how crazy she was. 'I've been wandering around looking for a cab, actually.'

'You could have taken mine.' He glanced across the road, but the cab had driven away.

'Oh, well, never mind. I'll just, um, walk …'

'*Walk?* Don't be silly. Come inside and we can call one for you,' he said, nodding to his house.

'Oh, no, really, there's no need,' she said.

'Please, come in for a while and I'll call you a cab. We can have a chat. I haven't seen you in ages.' He looked at his watch. 'Or we can stay outside, if you like,' he said, and she wanted to cry that he remembered about her panic attacks. She felt tears pricking her eyes.

'Jenny,' Dev said, putting a hand on her arm, 'is everything all right?'

'Yes, of course,' she said. 'Everything's fine.' She was unable to meet his eyes.

'Are you having a panic-attack?'

She shook her head.

'Then what—'

'I lied,' she said desperately, finally looking up at him, her eyes wet with tears.

'What?'

'I lied. I *am* stalking you.'

'You are?' He looked astonished, and … amused. As well he might.

'I'm sorry. I know it's wrong. I'll get help, honest—'

'Hey, don't worry,' he said. 'I'm not going to call the police. Come on in and we can talk about it.'

She let him lead her across the road. 'We can sit out here,' he said, sinking onto the steps and pulling her down beside him. 'Is that okay?'

She nodded dumbly.

'So how long has this been going on – this stalking business?'

'Oh, not long, really. And I'll never do it again, I promise.'

'I won't have to get a restraining order?' He was smiling at her – he obviously found this very entertaining.

'No. I'm a reformed character. You'll never see me out here again, I swear. I'll go for therapy or I'll – I'll start my own support group, or I'll—'

'Jenny,' he interrupted, taking her hand. His thumb stroked over her fingers. 'I lied too.'

Her eyes flew to his. 'You *are* going to call the police?' Her eyes darted to the road – she was half expecting to hear the wail of sirens as they came to take her away.

He laughed. 'No, not about that. I lied when I said I was over you.'

For a long moment she held his gaze, almost afraid to breathe. Then, somewhere inside her, something started beating again. 'You did?'

'Yes.'

'So you're – you're *not* over me?'

'No. Not at all. I meant everything I said to you that morning in Manchester.'

'But what about your girlfriend – the one you're seeing?'

'There's no one. I made it up.'

'*Why?* Why would you do that?' She was torn between wanting to thump him and to throw her arms around him and never let go.

He sighed. 'Because I thought you needed a friend, and I wanted you to feel that I could be a friend to you – that you could come to me if you were upset or needed to talk, and I wouldn't try to … that there wouldn't be any funny stuff.' His fingers were playing with hers, tangling and caressing. She felt herself loosen with every brush of his fingers against hers. It was getting easier to breathe by the second.

'That you wouldn't pounce on me, you mean?'

'Yes. That I wouldn't pounce on you.'

'What if I want you to pounce on me?'

He grinned. 'Well, that would be a different matter.'

'You think you could arrange something?'

'I'm sure I could.'

Jenny gulped. 'Like, right now?'

'Just say the word.'

She leaned close to him. 'Pou—' His mouth swooped down on hers before she could get the rest of the word out. She buried her hands in his hair as he put his arms around her, pulling her into a kiss that she thought might last the rest of the night and all the next day.

'I love you,' she said when they came up for air.

'I love you too.' He kissed her mouth, her eyes, her forehead.

She laid her head on his shoulder, clasping his hand in hers, and they watched the sun come up, the sky streaked with pink. It was going to be a beautiful day.

Acknowledgements

They say you should write about what you know ... but they also say rules are made to be broken. So when a story set in the world of UK politics popped into my head, I decided to ignore that advice and write it anyway, despite knowing very little about that world. I am therefore enormously grateful to Richard Balfe for sharing his insider knowledge with me. His enthusiasm and generosity in responding to all my queries made researching the background for this book so easy and turned what could have been a headache into a real pleasure. Thank you, Richard, for your time and patience – and for a lovely evening at the Reform Club. Any lapses in authenticity are entirely my fault.

Thanks also to my good friend, Deirdre Kennedy, for answering my medical queries.

I am lucky to have a very supportive family who shared in the excitement of *The Disengagement Ring* and talked it up to anyone who would listen. Special thanks once again to Trish, Emer and my mum, the first readers of this book and my number one fans; my brothers, Fin and Brian; Will, the littlest publicist (and the cutest); Jordan, especially for the cool guinea pig name; my aunt Eithne, who knows all about the ups and downs of this writing life; and all the Cleary clan in Limerick.

A big shout-out and a very special thank you to writer, blogger extraordinaire and all-round inspiration Keris Stainton, who started the online writing group that transformed my writing life in so many ways – all of them good. And for making me join Twitter. You were right.

Thanks to all my lovely writer friends – especially Claire Allan, Fionnuala Kearney, Luisa Plaja, Trina Rea, Michele Zimmer-Brouder, Debs Riccio, Anstey Spraggan, Fionnuala McGoldrick and Emma Heatherington. Writing can be a lonely activity, so I'm lucky to have such good company to share the highs, the lows and the procrastination. It wouldn't be half as much fun without you guys.

Thanks to my agent Ger Nichol, for having more faith in me than I have in myself, and for thinking I can walk on water – because all writers need a bit of unconditional love; and to my editor, Ciara Doorley, for making me stay in the boat – because we all need the tough love too. Thanks to Ciara and everyone at Hachette Ireland for being so lovely to work with, and for all their hard work and commitment in turning the stories in my head into real three-dimensional books on shop shelves.

Finally to all the readers who got in touch to tell me how much they enjoyed *The Disengagement Ring* – thank you, it means a lot. And thanks to everyone who has bought this book – I hope you enjoy it.